# Acknowledgments

Without my husband Steve's love and support, I never would have gotten this book written. Honey Bear, I'm eternally grateful for your epic well of patience for my bizarre sleeping and writing schedule. I love you.

To my tribe, present members and those I've yet to meet: Thanks for the support, the laughs, and the friendship. If you'd like to join my tribe, sign up for my newsletter at KatieMorton.com so we can keep in touch.

If you contributed to my campaign to help me get the book edited and the cover designed, there are no words to express what your help means to me. It all goes much deeper than dollars, doesn't it? I'm so touched and honored that you would give something to support my dream. I owe you, big time. Don't hesitate to call in favors.

And last but never the least, to my daughter: I love you, just the way you are. Always have, always will.

# CHAPTER ONE

**M**y heart pounded in my ears as I strained to hear the voices on the other side of the door.

"You think Kelly Ryan is an alcoholic?"

"She told me she's always setting goals like sticking to one drink and she can't do it, so yes, I think she's an alcoholic."

"Oh wow. She told me on the way here she was only going to have one, but obviously that's not happening."

"Yeah, she's had a drink in her hand all night, and I'm betting it's not the same one."

I panicked, searching for somewhere to leave my half-empty glass of wine. I spotted a hallway table, and I winced as I left my glass there on the polished wood surface without a coaster. I zipped back to the door in time to hear, "Although we are at a cocktail party, and I don't think she's even drunk…"

*I want to leave, but I've been at this party for three hours and I've had three glasses of wine and I will seriously wet my pants if I don't get into this bathroom in ten seconds, this bathroom that contains my best friend, Toni, and my shrink—well, after tonight, my ex-shrink, Jill.*

The door opened and I was face to face with Jill, who had just informed Toni of her inflated opinion that I was an alcoholic. *I would spend time expressing my anger and indignation, except—for the love of God! Toilet! Now!* I pushed past their shocked faces into the powder room and slammed the door.

Once I was perched safely on the toilet seat, a warm stream of relief between my legs, I realized my hands were shaking and I didn't know whether to punch a wall, laugh, or cry. Yes, I said I would stop at one drink, just like I'd say I'd stop at one bowl of ice cream or one measured portion of pasta or one slice of triple-cream brie. If I was guilty of a behavioral crime, it's that I was a chronic dieter. Or, more specifically, a

1

chronic overeater. Which led to cycles of dieting and giving up. In short, I was a yo-yoer.

Wine was just another one of those consumables I was telling myself to limit and then embracing in a fit of rebellious pleasure. Like chocolate. And cheese enchiladas with margaritas. And champagne with cupcakes. And New York Super Fudge Chunk ice cream paired with pinot noir. *I'm not a drunk as much as I'm simply greedy when it comes to the hedonistic pleasures of food and drink. I'll concede to the term "glutton."*

Way back when I was a young twentysomething adult trying to make it on my own, I recalled a spectacularly vicious screaming match that ended with this accusation by my mother: "You just do whatever feels good!" Her comment ended the fight because I could only think, "Why, yes. *Of course* I do. Why would anyone do differently? Isn't that why we're here on Earth?"

But by the time I was solidly entrenched in my thirties—well, if I'm honest, fast-approaching forty—it didn't feel good to be single and to feel fat and unlovable. I was in a near-constant fight when it came to these behaviors, like pigging out and boozing, that, when I was younger, used to have no downsides.

I recognized that I was completely neurotic about my overeating and drinking. These habits that used to feel like fun and freedom were now so deeply ingrained that they felt like a part of me. As I tried to break free, the fun had turned into prison.

I wondered, *Does anyone else argue with themselves incessantly about what they put in their mouths?* I felt like a crazy person. So when Toni recommended the shrink she used to help her grieve her mother's death, I was hopeful that Jill could work her magic on me and help me learn how to feel normal.

*Toni and Jill are now good buddies, but the last thing I thought Jill would do was hand me the label of alcoholic without discussion and then violate my privacy by blabbing to Toni about it. Jill can go fuck herself. What kind of shrink betrays a client like that? That woman doesn't know me. She drew that conclusion out of thin air. Toni might buy it, but I call bullshit. I don't give a crap about Jill, but if Toni believes her, then I'm officially Very Pissed Off.*

As I washed my hands, I looked in the mirror. My auburn bob was flat against my head, and my pale skin was flushed from the wine. I pushed my face forward to hide my double chin as I reapplied my lipstick. As I ran my hands through my hair in an effort to fluff it up, I could hardly contain my rising anger. *Maybe I do give a crap about Jill. How dare she?*

I pulled back my shoulders and held my head high as I threw the bathroom door open. There was nobody there. I heard voices and laughter coming from the back courtyard. The party had moved outside. Rivaling my anger was embarrassment, and I didn't want to see Jill or Toni right then if I could avoid it. *I need to get out of here.* I slinked to the front door of the Brooklyn brownstone and slipped outside onto the sidewalk.

I couldn't possibly suffer an epic upset like that without stuffing the hurt down with food, so on the subway ride back to Manhattan, I fantasized about what I was going to eat. I decided on a Thai dish called drunken noodles. The name was apropos given the accusation against me, plus noodle dishes of any kind were one of my favorite soul salves.

Carbs, especially pasta, made me fat. And the more upset I was, the more physically destructive I was in my food choices. But I didn't want to think about all that just then. I wanted to escape. I picked up my cell phone and called Amy, and the tension in my body loosened one degree as her friendly voice greeted me over the phone. I asked her, "What time do you get off work? I'm craving Thai."

"It's slow here tonight. José can fill in for me at the bar if I need to leave early."

"Sorry, train is about to go underground, I'm going to lose you. Meet me at Mimi Thai in twenty minutes. Something weird happened tonight. I'll tell you about it there."

★

I emerged from the smelly, dank subway station. As I approached the restaurant, my mind reviewed familiar arguments, those deeply worn ruts that my brain was used to traveling. *This is my chance. I could change my behavior forever right now by breaking the cycle. I could go home and journal out my thoughts and feelings instead of eating my way through the hurt.*

Then other familiar thoughts hijacked the thread. *But noodles give me pleasure. What's a life without pleasure? I could get hit by a bus tomorrow. If I'm still alive tomorrow, I'll start fresh. I need this right now, just for tonight. I can't believe what they said about me. I want to feel better, and the fastest way, the only way I know how, is a steamy, savory plate of noodles.*

I wondered if after I died, it would all be clear to me. Would I be better off with a life of vegetables, never allowing myself to eat whatever I wanted? Or would God laugh in my face and say, "I made doughnuts so you can eat them, dummy!"

I wanted so badly to *not want.* It would be great if I could eat delicious and healthy food most of the time while I allowed myself the occasional treat, but I didn't operate that way. Instead I turned the flow of want on and off completely, like a valve. When I got too fat for my clothes, when I felt disgusted and uncomfortable in my body, when I worried that I was killing myself, I went on a campaign of health and cleaned up the diet.

Then when my pants loosened, when my face started to look young and fresh following a phase of healthy choices, when my belly began to flatten and look trim, the geyser of want erupted and I found myself thinking that drunken noodles were the best solution to my problems.

★

As I opened the door to the restaurant, the familiar tinkle of the bell over my head started my mouth watering, just like one of Pavlov's dogs. Amy was waiting for me at our favorite table with two glasses of cold white wine. As I sat down, I looked nervously and longingly at the glass. With what I was about to tell Amy, I suddenly wondered how to act.

Amy saw the look on my face and laughed. "I know everything. Toni called me."

"And you still ordered me a glass of wine?"

"Of course! That's ridiculous! You? An alcoholic? Give me a break. If you're an alkie, then I should have gone to rehab five years ago. Drink up."

When our waitress came by, Amy said, "Oh hey, Mimi. We'll have the usual, thanks."

A wave of calm washed over me. I picked up the wine and sat back in my chair. For the first time since I overheard Jill and Toni talking about me, I could breathe. I always felt A-OK when I was with Amy.

Amy said, "So I should probably warn you…Toni and Jill want to stage an intervention. Toni called me to see if I would lure you over to her place tomorrow morning. I told her she was being crazy."

"What? An intervention? Oh. My. GOD. I am so embarrassed!"

"Calm down, it's no big deal. I told her we're not doing it."

"And? What did she say?"

"Well, she seemed unsure of the whole thing anyway, and then she sounded relieved when I told her she's acting stupid. I think Jill pressured her into it."

"Jill. God. I never should have gone to that woman. What a bitch! I tell her my secrets and then she uses them against me? Shouldn't this be in the *Shrink Handbook of Things Not to Do?*"

"Yeah, doesn't sound right to me, but I don't know what the rules are." Amy looked thoughtful for minute and then said, "She probably thinks she's helping. What did you say to her to make her think you have a drinking problem?"

"I struggle with cravings a lot. You know how some people are food snobs?"

"Yeah?"

"I'm the opposite of that. I struggle with cravings for everything. Spinach and artichoke dip. Pasta with homemade tomato sauce with loads of garlic. Sushi. Pizza. Sugar-free Red Bull, of all things. It's possible there's nothing I don't crave. I'm obsessed with food, and to me, wine falls under that category."

"So Jill just fixated on the idea that you like wine too much."

"I gotta be honest here. I *do* like wine too much. Do I like to get a good buzz on? Yes, I do. But I always eat enough to drown out the buzz. I went to Jill to see if she could help me stop craving everything all the time. I'm tired of being fat and unhealthy. I'm wasting my life obsessing about food and my weight. I'm almost forty. Shouldn't I have this crap figured out by now?"

"You should meet up with my friend Sandy. She's really into this stuff; I mean, healthy eating and all that. She's studying to be a health coach, so I bet she could tell you what to eat. She's like a walking *MindBodyGreen* article. She'll probably take you to buy a bag of chia seeds or something."

"Oh yeah, I like Sandy. She and I chatted for hours at your birthday party. You think she'd be willing to help me?"

"Definitely. I'm telling you, she lives for this stuff. She's all about crap like goji berries."

"Whatever those are."

"Exactly. Here, let me text her for you. I'll give her your number and see if she can meet you at the Union Square Farmers Market tomorrow morning. I know she goes every week."

"How early is it?"

Amy laughed. "Are you serious, Kelly? How early is it? Would you rather we did the intervention?"

"No," I scoffed.

Smiling, Amy shook her head and texted Sandy.

On my walk home that night, I got a text from a number I didn't recognize. It read, "Hi, Kelly, it's Sandy. Want to meet at 9 tomorrow morning at Union Square?"

I texted her back, "Yes, please! Thanks so much for helping me out." Help was on the way. Finally.

# CHAPTER TWO

The next morning, I felt horrible. The noodles sat in my stomach all night, and the wine made me hot and thirsty. I stumbled out of bed and grabbed a pint of ice cream out of the freezer. As I took a bite, feelings of guilt gave way to sweet coldness, soothing my upset tummy.

At a few minutes past nine, I hustled up the hot street toward Union Square with the pint of ice cream still in my hand. I was running late, as usual. As I crossed the street, I could see Sandy with a canvas bag on her arm as she pawed through a pile of green beans in a wooden bucket at a farmer's stand.

Dainty, light on her feet, and sporting a blond pixie cut, Sandy was like a cartoon Tinker Belle brought to life. I'd met her several times over the years through Amy at the occasional party or Sunday morning brunch. From my observations, Sandy was an alien. She would accept a brunch invitation and then sit happily across the table sipping a green juice while I tucked into a massive plate of eggs Benedict and washed it down with a mimosa.

At those brunches, I saw myself as a sloppy barbarian in contrast to her glowing refinement. I could sense that Sandy didn't think about how I shouldn't be eating that or that I should slow down and chew my food properly. It was clear none of what went through my head crossed her saintly mind, but I still couldn't stop judging myself for lacking in her presence. Even now I felt embarrassed coming to her for help.

Sandy turned her bright smile toward me and waved. As I approached her, she reached her arms out for a hug. I leaned in, and the smell of her clean hair wafted around me. I pulled back and thought, *I hope I don't stink.*

"So," said Sandy, "Amy tells me you're looking for a little help."

"Yeah, just a little." I laughed. "Want some ice cream?"

Sandy said, "Just one bite." She grabbed my spoon and tried the tiniest taste. "Ugh, too sweet. Here, try this." She pulled a piece of white cauliflower out of her bag and handed it to me.

*Ick, cauliflower. Why bother? I already know what this tastes like. A whole lotta nothin'.* I took a cautious nibble. I was surprised by the fresh flavors, both bitter and sweet at the same time. Had I never had a plain, fresh piece of cauliflower before?

I licked my spoon clean and tucked it into my purse as I looked at the melted remains of my ice cream pooling in the bottom of the container. *I can't believe I ate the whole thing.* I felt revolted as I chucked the pint in the nearest trash can.

"Want another piece?" asked Sandy.

*I'm stuffed, but it's a vegetable so it doesn't count.* "Sure, why not." Sandy handed me a nice big chunk of cauliflower, and I found myself lost in the taste of it. When I was finished, I felt satisfied, something I'd rarely felt in my life.

Sandy watched me as she said, "You'd be surprised at how little food you need when you eat *real* food. Your body registers the nutrients. You get addicted to manufactured crap like ice cream that you buy in the grocery store. Then there's no end in sight to the cravings."

"But I'm so in the habit of it, I'm not sure how to stop."

"Yeah, but you can get in the habit of anything, from drugs to being a complete health nut. It's all habit-forming. When you're in a positive spiral, it becomes so clear that this is freedom, the way you're meant to feel." We started walking slowly through the market and glancing at the different displays of fresh vegetables, soaps, candles, and honey. "Amy said you want me to teach you about nutrition, is that right?"

"Well," I hedged, "not nutrition exactly. I think I know what I'm supposed to eat. It's just that I'm a little obsessed with food. I eat too much. I probably eat too often. I'm always battling cravings, and I'm sick of being fat."

"Can you remember any times in the past when you were successful at losing weight? What did you do?"

"Oh, you know, the usual. I ate less and exercised more. I lost fifty pounds by eating Special K and walking a lot."

"And then what happened?"

"I got sick of Special K and my feet got tired, and I gained it all back."

"And that's why diets don't work. You can't just 'eat less' or eat one kind of food forever. It's not that simple. It matters *what* you eat. If you only eat less, then you'll feel hungry all the time and your body will burn metabolically active tissue—muscle—and then you get flabby and your metabolism slows down.

"You want to eat plenty of healthy food. *Real* food like vegetables and nuts and chicken. Processed food is addictive and messes with our hormones and neurotransmitters. We want to eat more, even when we're full, and then we gain weight. So the real way to lose weight isn't by eating less and exercising more, it's actually by eating the right foods and plenty of them."

"Well that sounds refreshing. I can eat as much as I want?"

"Basically. I mean, you don't want to eat until you're in pain or anything crazy, but it can be pretty hard to overeat real food because the body can send you clearer messages when you're full. We're going to start gently. Start by adding more vegetables to your diet. That's it. Eat more veggies and let the veggies crowd sugar and junk like white flour out of your diet."

I didn't say anything. I wasn't sure I could follow Sandy's recommendation. *I already know what I'm supposed to do. I got it. Put down the fork and step away from the noodles. How many times in the past did I tell myself I was going to eat better?*

Sandy said, "You've gone quiet. What are you thinking?"

"I'm not sure I can stop eating bad foods. I've tried so many times…"

"Look, I get it. I can tell you what to eat to get healthy, but like you said, you probably already know a lot of this stuff. If you're abusing your body with food, then it's really soul matters that need cleaning up."

"Like what?"

"Feeling fulfilled, living a life of joy, loving yourself. You know, all the new-age, self-help, manifest-abundance crap that's all over the place right now."

I laughed nervously. "Self-help stuff, yeah?"

Sandy stopped, and her face turned serious as she looked at me and said, "I know I sound flippant, but the thing is, that stuff is important. If you don't feel okay with yourself and your life, then you slowly and passively commit suicide. In your case," Sandy glanced down at my stomach, "by overeating."

I couldn't disagree with her, but I protectively crossed my arms in front of my chest in an attempt to hide from her gaze. We turned and started walking slowly again. I said, "That sounds about right. Death by noodles."

"There's someone I think you should meet." Sandy scrolled through the contacts on her phone as she continued, "His name is Earnest. He holds these sessions that help women with this kind of thing, with living life to the fullest, losing weight, loving yourself, all that stuff. Here, I'll text you his number."

My phone blipped with the contact info. I took a peek and asked, "Why is this dude helping women? Can't he help men too?"

"I guess he could help men in theory, but Earnest is a chick magnet. He's got this super-cheesy vibe going that's somehow kind of hot. Like Billy Bob Thornton or James Franco." Sandy got a faraway look in her eye. "It's that sexy bad-boy thing. You look at him and think yuck and yum all at the same time."

I groaned. "Oh please, I really don't need to get sucked into that kind of scene."

"Oh, but you've got to see this guy. He has a ponytail, washboard abs, and he has this vague accent, definitely not American."

"Where's he from?"

"He won't say. He calls himself a 'citizen of the world,' although his students jokingly call him an 'international man of mystery' behind his back. He reminds me of a young version of the Most Interesting Man in the World from the Dos Equis beer commercials. It's comical on one level, but you just can't look away. The guy is gripping."

"That sounds ridiculous. I think I'll skip Earnest."

"Look, if you're serious about getting to the bottom of this stuff, you should go to one of his sessions and see what you think. He does them at his apartment."

"Where does he live?"

"In a dump in Brooklyn, but it's easy to get to. It's right off the L."

"All right, I'll do it. But only because you're in amazing shape and I want what you have."

★

When I got home that afternoon, I googled Earnest to see if he had a website or any information about his sessions online, but I found nothing. I looked at the number on my phone and wondered what would happen if I called it. *Will Earnest himself pick up? Will he pressure me to come to a session if I'm only calling to find out when they're scheduled?*

With the threat of an intervention hanging over my head, I dialed the phone. A sweet-sounding woman answered, "Hello, how can I help you?"

"Uh, hi, I'm calling for Earnest?"

"This is Earnest's assistant, Bernadette. How can I help you?"

"Hi, Bernadette. A friend of mine said Earnest gives classes, these, uh, sessions...to help, um, women..."

"Yes, Ducklings to Swans."

"Um, excuse me? Ducklings...what?"

"Ducklings to Swans is the name of Earnest's sessions to help women shed their emotional and physical baggage and transform into the most beautiful version of themselves."

*Is she serious?* She sounded like she was acting in an infomercial, yet her little pitch had a ring of sincerity to it. I wanted to remain cool about the whole thing, but I felt sucked in, intrigued. "Yes, that must be what my friend was referring to. Can you please tell me when the next class is?"

"We've just started a new round of sessions. Hang on, let me check the schedule. There are five sessions running concurrently. Some have already started, so you've missed the first class...Nope, that one was yesterday, that's no good...Oh, you're in luck! There's a session of classes beginning this evening at six p.m. at Earnest's loft in Williamsburg, Brooklyn."

"How much does it cost?"

"We don't need to deal with that over the phone. You can come tonight for free, and if you decide to sign up for the full series afterward, then we can take a credit card this evening. You just need to wear loose, comfortable clothing and bring a yoga mat to sit on."

As she gave me the address, I wondered if I was going to have to take my shoes off. I hadn't had a pedicure in months.

# CHAPTER THREE

That evening, I found myself trying to hide my feet under the hem of my pants as I sat cross-legged on my yoga mat on the scuffed hardwood floor of Earnest's cavernous loft. There was a shabby and broken-down red velvet couch tucked into a dark corner of the room.

Earnest stood next to a beat-up old teacher's desk as he lectured the class. Behind him, a high wall of exposed brick held a dusty green chalkboard. There was little else in the room aside from us students sitting on our mats, eight in all.

I looked around the room at the others and guessed some of the students were, like me, probably in their midthirties to early forties. Two women sitting next to each other at the front of the room looked much younger and thinner than the rest of us. There was one soft, matronly, older woman sitting in the back of the room whose long hair was completely gray.

Earnest gripped an egg timer that resembled a tiny hourglass and told the class, "Clear your head of all thought. Stop thinking. Three minutes, starting…now." He flipped the egg timer and placed it delicately on the desk. He then placed his pert tush on the desk, leaned back, and folded his alabaster forearms arms across his chest.

I looked at the dark hair of his arms against the white of his skin. My mind shifted toward his chest. *I wonder what his chest hair looks like.* Then my mind wandered farther down. Earnest called out, "Inner dialogue. What's yours saying right now?" He paused while we all took stock.

He continued, "We are always evaluating, judging, assessing. This is the nature of the mind: like a monkey, a flappy bird, a flomping hippo rolling in the mud. The mind never sits still. It's always thinking, thinking, thinking. We all have patterns of thoughts. Your parents: think of their worst qualities. I'll wait."

I thought about my parents. *They're naïve. But they're also paranoid. How is that possible, to be both naïve and paranoid simultaneously? God, they are maddening. They can be so critical. Judgmental. You know, normal parent stuff. I love them and all of their cute but annoying contradictions.*

Earnest broke the silence. "Your parents' minds trained your mind. You're slightly more aware than your parents are, because you can see their foibles. You can see how they tried to train you, and you can witness their mistakes. But know that you also have many of the same blind spots that your parents have. If your parents were judgmental and critical of you, then you are judgmental and critical of yourself."

I thought about how horrifically judgmental and critical I was of myself, more so than my parents ever were. *They don't walk around insulting my body, which is something I do in my head a thousand times per day.*

"You are here to learn about your habitual patterns of thought. You are here to study your own mind. Only by practice, by sitting in meditation and watching your thoughts, observing them objectively, can you learn what your thought patterns are. You can learn what makes you happy, sad, or angry. You can learn how to address your emotions and get your needs met.

"Now I'm going to cut to the chase. I know that you're here because you want to lose weight. You want to be conventionally beautiful. Maybe you think that if you're thinner, you'll be more lovable. Maybe you think I'm going to talk about diet and exercise. No. If that's what you want, then hire a personal trainer and a nutritionist.

"I'm here to tell you that the reason you're fat is because you eat to escape your thought patterns. You eat to forget yourself and your problems. You eat because you want to obliterate uncomfortable emotions. You eat because you can't stand to be alone with your feelings. You eat because it's easier to eat cake or drink wine than it is to change your life in ways that would actually make you happy."

*Bingo. I'm not sure what would make me happy. I don't know what changes will get me there. And rather than feel those feelings and figure it all out, I eat and drink.*

"Now what's so distasteful about your feelings that you must eat to escape them? It's because your habits of thought bring about uncomfortable emotions. You're whipping yourself into a frenzy about nonsense. Your mind is like a cat bringing you gifts of dead prey.

Instead of being discerning and rejecting those gifts, you accept them, and then you feel disappointed.

"Your thinking isn't even correct, but you buy into it wholesale, get yourself upset, and then try to eat your way out of the feelings. Some of you even get yourself upset on purpose as an excuse to eat the chocolate cake. You think things like, 'I had a rough day; I deserve the cake.' Maybe you even cause yourself difficulties in life so you get to keep on deserving chocolate cake every day."

*Whoa, whoa, whoa. Wait a minute. I have to process this.* I felt the truth of Earnest's words wash through my body with a hot flush of recognition. *How often do I blow some little upset out of proportion just so I can feel the warm tingle of a glass of wine in my belly while I soothe myself with something delicious? Every day. Sometimes more than once.*

Earnest sounded annoyed. "Okay, fine. Eat the chocolate cake. I'm not here to tell you what to eat or what not to eat. I'm only here to tell you to pay attention. Pay attention to your thoughts, and pay attention to your physical experience in this life. What's it like to inhabit your body? When eating, my simple directive is to concentrate on the sensual experience of the food in your hands and in your mouth."

Earnest pointed to a woman on the floor in front of him who resembled a pretty blond cherub in a Rubens painting. "You, come here." Eyes on Earnest, she stood up obediently and approached him with a shy smile. She stood next to him facing the class, crossed her arms, and then dropped them self-consciously to her sides. Earnest said, "Now I'm going to feed...what's your name?"

"Lydia."

"Lydia. I'm going to feed Lydia some fruit." As if on cue, a tiny brunette wearing large, cat's-eye glasses scurried into the room and handed a bowl of fruit salad to Earnest, and then she scurried back out again. I giggled.

Earnest looked straight at me while he said in a forceful tone, "Thank you, Bernadette."

I cleared my throat. "Sorry," I whispered.

Addressing the room, Earnest said, "Now I want you all to imagine that you are Lydia and that you're tasting the fruit. This is a meditation exercise, and your focus is on the fruit. The sweetness, the juiciness, the taste, the textures. Your mind is going to wander. Bring it back to the fruit. Notice your thoughts, dismiss them, always back to the fruit, over and over again. Now we will begin. Lydia, please relax, and we're going to turn our attention to the fruit."

Earnest picked up a blackberry and brought it to Lydia's mouth. She parted her lips and accepted the berry. As she chewed, I tried to imagine the tartness of the berry and the feeling of the seeds crunching between my teeth. *Ew, I wonder if his hands are clean. What if he scratched himself and now he's feeding her…fruit, fruit, fruit. I can do this. Blackberry. Some whipped cream would be nice.*

After Lydia swallowed, Earnest said, "Now watermelon. I want you to all sense the juiciness." I watched as he plucked a small, dripping piece of pink melon from the bowl and brought it to Lydia's waiting mouth. The scene reminded me of a little kid receiving her first communion from a priest at church, except that there was something sexy about this, about both Earnest and Lydia. I found myself at rapt attention as a drop of pink juice fell from Lydia's lip and landed on the rise of her breast that peeked above her scoop-neck T-shirt.

I held my breath as the juice threatened to run into her cleavage. I heard the rest of the class gasp gently as Earnest wiped the juice with his finger, then put his finger in his mouth and sucked. *Wow. I'm actually getting turned on.* Lydia's breathing had quickened, and she was blushing. She looked ready for more.

Suddenly Earnest turned to the class and said, "We've all failed the test." He looked disappointed in himself, and I realized that he meant that he too—along with us chunky flunkies—failed. He said, "We're paying attention to the present moment, but we lost the focus on the fruit. Our minds have wandered toward sex."

*Really? He thinks we were all thinking about sex? What a cocky assertion.* But then I prickled with the realization that he had me pegged, and a quick survey of the faces around the room confirmed it was unanimous. We were all sitting there making more out of the fruit scene than just fruit and a little innocent juice runoff.

Earnest regained his composure and asserted, "It's easy to make these distinctions. It's easy to have aha moments. It's really quite simple to stand here and discuss theories about our minds' restless natures, but what matters and what's hard is the practice of focus, of stilling, stopping the flow of thought, to not only stay with the present moment, but to stay with the focus you have chosen for yourself.

"You foster habits of mind. Some people obsess about what's wrong—with their families, themselves, and their physical incarnation…" Earnest made a sweeping gesture along the length of his fit, gorgeous torso. "They gossip about their friends and neighbors and complain about the government. Others obsess about their appetites and how to feed them and how to stop them, an endless cycle."

Once again, I felt hot with sheepish self-recognition. *Is he talking to me?* Another quick glance around confirmed he had found his audience. *I'm not alone here.*

"Train. Of. Thought. You are on the train. You are a passenger inside your own mind. You can wake up to the fact that you're a passenger. You are rarely the driver, the engineer, of your thoughts. But we can awaken for brief moments and steer the train. Push it in gentle increments toward where we want it to go. For most of us, the tracks were laid in early childhood. Was your mother or your father always criticizing you? That's how your train tracks were laid. Those are the well-worn grooves that serve as the train tracks of your mind. In this class, through the practices I will teach you, you are going to become powerful and steadfast like the elements, like water against rock, to reshape the landscape of your mind in order to derail the train.

"But don't think for a minute that you have total control over this process. You are going to continually awaken to the nightmare that you are the passenger, you are not the engineer, you are not the elements. But now that you know this is how your mind operates, you can wake up, steer the train, and break some rocks before you fall back to sleep.

"Recognize your pattern of thought. When you wake up, and you see you're on the train, at least look out the window: What's the scenery like? Are you worried about the condition of the houses and who must live in such a deteriorated mess? Are you worried that bandits will overtake the train and what they will do when they get a hold of you or your wallet? What green pastures does your train travel? What frightening places? What are your habits of thought? Where does your mind go when you're asleep at the wheel? Where are you when you wake up? Take note. And even more important, take note of how it drives your behavior. Our minds, with no one at the helm, drive us to do shameful things.

"But when we act as the engineer driving the train, we are acting as the Witness of our mind. When we wake up and see where the train is taking us, we become stronger. At least then we see where our tracks are laid crooked. We see we aren't in the sunny meadow we thought we were aiming for. And we continue to steer the train back, again and again.

"Now I will give you your first assignment: What are you aiming for? Where are you trying to steer your train? WHAT DO YOU WANT?"

Earnest shouted. I jumped, startled, but then I laughed as I remembered a scene from *Austin Powers* when Mike Myers said he was having trouble controlling the volume of his voice.

Oblivious to my amusement, Earnest continued, "Define your big picture. What's the place you want to occupy in the world? What's your goal? Clearly define what you want your life to be like. How do you know if you're giving in or resisting your whims when you don't even know what outcome you desire? You might want a tight ass, but what for? Do you want to be a stripper? Probably not. What are your goals for your life and your soul: focus on THAT. The size of your ass is immaterial. But overeating does matter; it hurts you, it's a dream killer. Unless your dream is to become a Sumo wrestler, then eating junk food is time and attention away from whatever your goal is. So stop thinking about food and your weight. Instead, think about what you want to do and be in your life.

"Where do you want to wake up? Do you want to feel salt air on your skin? Do you want to walk on the beach? Or does the city life call to you? Or maybe a walk in nature is a balm to your soul. Figure it out.

"The most important thing you will ever discover in this life is how to make your soul sing, how to endure moment to moment, thought to thought, how to end your suffering. How to find what you love first and then, only then, can you find your people, your tribe. Yes, it's possible for you to find people who love the same things you do. These people will be your tribe. But first, you need to figure out what you love, and then go get it.

"Don't forget the WHY. The first step is to get crystal clear on what you want your life to be like and why. Tie your why to a higher purpose. What's a bigger purpose than you? What kind of tribe do you see around you? Who do you want your peers to be? Who do you want to help?

"This helps you to clearly define what actions to take and which ones to avoid. A lot of people in this world, you would look at them and think that their goal is to never enjoy food, but to remain fat. You can't enjoy food or alcohol or sex if you've labeled it bad. Then you sneak these things and you feel ashamed of your choices, yet you confuse sneaking these things you've forbidden with pleasure. You can't experience bliss or pleasure when you're ashamed of what you're doing.

"So forget all that and just start thinking about what you want to see happen in your life, not about what you can have or should have or shouldn't have. Just focus on what you want big picture—work, friends, lovers, neighborhood, your home—and don't think too hard. We're going to learn more about all of this at the next class.

"Now I want you all to pick a buddy so you can discuss the assignment with each other outside of class..." All the other women in the class immediately turned and made eye contact, smiled, and paired off neatly. *Oh great. Just like gym class.* Earnest went on, "I want you to be each other's sounding boards and accountability partners."

Lydia was still standing awkwardly at the front of the room when our eyes met. She smiled and mouthed at me, "Buddies?" I nodded.

As we filed out of the room, I found Lydia by my side. I asked her, "Do you want to grab dinner right now? I'm starving."

"Oh good, me too. There's a great little Mexican place right around the corner, want to do that?"

"Perfect."

★

**Follow along with Earnest's assignments at home. Sign up at <u>KatieMorton.com</u> for the Ducklings to Swans Workbook.**

# CHAPTER FOUR

I was first-date nervous as I glanced at Lydia over the salted rim of my margarita glass. Lydia kept her eyes pointed at the salsa bowl as she dipped a tortilla chip and asked me, "So, what do you do?"

My stomach ached with anxiety over this question that I'd been asked thousands of times before. "I work in digital operations. My boss is a psychopath. She likes to see her employees cower, so she yells insults into their faces." *But not me. Not anymore, anyway.* I was leaving out the part where I'd blackmailed my boss, giving me tenure in a job I hated with people I had no respect for.

The fateful day I blackmailed Sadie—that awful, evil woman—was the day my work life became merely tolerable as opposed to horrifically excruciating. That was the day I slipped into the ladies' room, situated myself in a locked stall, and pulled my phone out of my pocket. I dialed Toni and listened to the line ring as the restroom door squeaked open. The click of heels sounded on the tile, then I heard Sadie whispering. I hit the End Call button and held my breath.

"Boy or girl? Are you serious? I'm gunning for a promotion here, and you're wondering if it's a boy or a girl? You listen to me. I've agreed to keep this kid for you. Now you're going to do things my way. We aren't telling a soul. If this gets out, then there's no way I'm landing this promotion. They're not giving the job to somebody with a kid hanging off her boob, they're giving it to the single guy. So keep your mouth shut, or so help me I'm getting an abortion."

The sound of my cell phone rang out and echoed against the walls. *Holy shit.* It was Toni calling me back. *Damn it!* I bobbled the phone in my hands and tried to silence it, but I dropped it to the floor. The battery cover skidded across the room and stopped at Sadie's feet. *Oh. My. God.*

I came out of the stall and came face to face with Sadie. I took one look at her expression and realized that she was more horrified than I was. She hung up her phone and stared at me. I bent down and picked up the battery cover and attempted to reattach it to my phone. After much fumbling, I finally gave up and put the whole mess in my pocket, straightened up, and looked back at Sadie.

She began to circle me. I turned to keep her in front of me because I was afraid of what she would do if I let her get behind me. My heart pounded. I could see beads of sweat forming on her perfectly white forehead. Finally, she spoke. "So. You know my secret."

I couldn't help myself as I glanced down at her belly. I hadn't noticed before, but she was wearing a blousier top than was typical for her straight-and-narrow wardrobe. I didn't know what to say. Clearly "congratulations" wasn't a good idea.

She said, "All right. What do you want? Tell me what it's going to take for you to keep quiet."

*What? This is awesome! She's letting me blackmail her? What did I want to keep this under wraps? A fully fueled helicopter and a big bag of money! Okay. Calm down. For real. What do I want?*

"I want some respect around here. I want to keep my job, of course. I want Brad to stop getting credit for everything I do." I stopped and measured Sadie's reaction. She looked just shy of homicidal. I decided to leave it at that.

"I was planning on firing you. But okay. You can keep your job. As for the rest, I'll see what I can do." Then she clenched her teeth while she raised a finger and pointed a sharp nail about six inches from my face. "I'll be watching you. You better forget this ever happened. Get it?"

"Got it."

She blew by me and out the door. I looked in the mirror and smiled so broadly I thought my teeth would come out of my head. I wanted to run and scream and laugh. I figured I'd better wait until I got outside.

When the outdoor air hit my face, I felt so light, so free, so happy. *One major problem, just like that, solved. I can stop worrying about income. Sure, I'll keep applying for jobs, but I don't have to worry about money while I do it. I can take my time and choose the right gig.*

But the rest is history. I never left. I genuinely expected to find something else to do, a dream job even, but the years slipped by and there I still sat, collecting a sizable paycheck but feeling emptier with each passing year.

*Ten years later, I'm still showing up and working for the same regrettable bunch of…sigh.* Every time my mind traveled this road, I admonished myself to be grateful. Ten years of my most neurotic fears—of unemployment and bag lady status—gone with one quick, although deranged, bathroom blackmail conversation.

I asked Lydia, "And what about you? What do you do for work?"

Through a mouthful of chips, Lydia said, "I own a cupcake bakery."

My ears perked up. "Ooh, how exciting! Which one?"

"Creamy Cake Cups over on Second Avenue."

"I'm a huge fan."

Lydia blushed and said, "Yeah, well. Thanks. But I'm getting ready to close down the shop."

"Oh no! Why?"

"Business isn't that good anymore. When we first opened, everything was amazing. The newspapers were always doing write-ups, people were coming in to check us out and then coming back because they loved us, but these days there's a cupcake shop on every block. And on top of the ridiculous competition, people are trying to get healthy and save money; they aren't eating cupcakes every day. Cupcakes have turned back into something you eat only on special occasions. And so the money isn't coming in like it used to. I had to let someone go last week, a good friend who worked in the shop for years. It was heartbreaking."

Lydia took a deep gulp of her margarita. Her eyes were wet with tears, and after she swallowed her drink, she snuffled loudly. "I'm sorry," she said. "I don't mean to get emotional."

"Oh please, it's okay. I'm not exactly happy with my work situation either. I've been trying to move on for years, but I don't have the motivation. Sometimes I think if I could find the perfect career, I wouldn't eat and drink so much to cope."

"I know what you mean. I'm really lost. I'm not sure what I'm going to do after the shop closes, so I'm limping along with it, holding it together until I figure something out. Honestly, I could go on for years like this. I'm not exactly bleeding money. I still make an okay living. I'm just not making what I used to."

"So how about this assignment? We're supposed to decide what we want our lives to be like?"

"Does he mean realistically, or like la-la fantasyland? Because I would love to be swimming in money and have a hunky boyfriend, but I'm not sure it's helpful to say I want stuff when it's not exactly going to fall out of the sky and land in my lap."

"Yeah, I'm not sure. Right now I show up every day at work and push papers around and do a little here and there, but what I want is to feel fired up about my work, I want to feel passionate about it, you know? Maybe feel like I'm making a difference while I'm making a good living, but I don't know what that would look like. I used to have this dream of being a writer. Maybe even a published author. I always wanted to write novels. But I don't know how to break into it or where to start."

"What about a boyfriend? Or a girlfriend. I don't mean to be presumptuous. Are you dating anyone?" Lydia asked.

"Oh God, I gave up on romance a long time ago. I kept getting my heart broken. I used to fall for these guys...I don't understand what went wrong. I just wanted to love somebody, but they always left me. I wanted to get married and have a family, but I'm going to be forty this year. I think it's too late." It was my turn to get emotional.

Lydia patted my hand and said, "Hey, you never know."

I tried to smile. I knew.

★

The next morning, I met up with Amy and Sandy over brunch to talk about Earnest and Ducklings to Swans. "So, what do you think?" asked Sandy.

"I'm not quite sure yet. He had us do this meditation thing where he fed this girl some fruit..."

"Let me guess," interrupted Sandy. "It got all weird and sexual and the whole class failed the assignment."

I burst out laughing. "How did you know?"

"Because I've been through the class twice already."

"Twice? You mean you didn't learn everything the first time?"

"Earnest teaches concepts that are practices. I know it seems like a lot of pop psychology, but it's actually based on ancient yogic wisdom. You'd be hard-pressed to master what he teaches, and the more you practice, the better you get at it."

"The better you get at what?"

"At willpower, basically. At training your mind. At knowing who you are, what you want, and having the discipline to get it."

"What about inner peace? I feel like a freaking mess."

"Yeah, that too. It's all part of the class. Did you pay up front?"

"Oh, geez, I forgot about that. Payment didn't even come up. How much does it cost?"

"I don't know what he's charging these days, but don't worry," laughed Sandy, "they'll hit you up for the money sooner or later."

We heard the blip of a text message, and we all reached for our phones. "It's me," I said, feeling pleased for only a moment before seeing who it was. I groaned.

Amy asked, "What? Who's texting you?"

"It's Toni. She says she wants to see me." I put my phone down and sulked. "God, I don't want to see her. It's so awkward."

"Why's it awkward?" Sandy asked innocently.

Amy said, "Because Toni was going to stage an intervention because Kelly's shrink is a freak."

I laughed. "Interesting explanation." I turned to Sandy and said, "You know how I came to you for help with food cravings? Well, I sometimes crave alcohol, too, and some people think that means you automatically have a major problem when that's the case. So my shrink—I mean my *ex*-shrink—told Toni that I need to be interfered with to save me from myself."

Amy laughed. "You did a much better job explaining it. You're safe to see Toni now. I'm pretty sure she's over the idea of interfering with you."

"Why do you say that?"

"She stopped talking about it. She hasn't mentioned Jill's name, either. I think you should go ahead and meet up with her."

"I'm not sure I want to see her. That whole scene the other night was just too embarrassing."

"What whole scene?" asked Sandy.

"I overheard Toni and Jill talking about me at a party, about how they think I'm an alcoholic."

Amy added, "Then they called me for help with staging an intervention, but I told them they're being nuts."

"Toni and I used to talk every day, but we haven't spoken since the party. It's so weird and uncomfortable! What would I even say to her?"

"Maybe she wants to apologize," suggested Amy. "What are you going to do, end the friendship? You can't do that. It would be like letting Jill win. Don't let that woman come between you guys. See what Toni has to say."

"Oh, all right," I relented. I picked up my phone and texted Toni. We made plans to meet at her apartment Monday night after work.

★

Following a relentlessly boring day at the office, I checked in with the doorman at Toni's building. He showed me to the elevator and pushed the button for Toni's floor before excusing himself to help the next person who wandered inside. I looked to see who was coming. I could have sworn it was Jill, but the elevator doors slid shut before I could get a better look.

As I rode the elevator up fourteen floors, I turned and looked at myself in the mirrored wall. I fluffed my hair and swiped on some lip balm as the elevator door opened. The frantic pounding of my heart surprised me as I poised my hand to knock on Toni's door. I took a deep breath and rapped gently. The door flew open, as if she'd been standing on the other side waiting for me.

"Kelly!" Toni beamed at me and wrapped her arms around me in a big bear hug. Then she practically dragged me across her threshold and into her apartment. She slammed the door shut behind me. "It's so good to see you. Come in, come in," she said, as she herded me into the living room and cornered me into a chair. "Here, have a glass of water."

"Uh, thanks." I took a sip and then held the icy glass gingerly with my fingertips as I looked for a place to put it down. I heard a soft knocking at the door. Toni looked startled, like she'd been caught doing something wrong. She chuckled nervously and made her way slowly to the door.

"Are you expecting someone else?" I asked, rising to place the glass on the coffee table before sitting down again.

Toni kept chuckling to herself, and it was creeping me out. I watched intently as she opened the door slowly. There stood Jill. "Oh, hiiiiiiiiiieeeeeeeee," said Jill. "Sorry I'm late. I guess we didn't get to really talk through our plan before…Oh well, never mind, let's wing it."

I glared at Toni, and my voice sounded shrill as I asked, "What is this? Why is she here?" Toni mumbled something. "Excuse me, Toni?" I barked. "What's going on here?"

Jill strode confidently into the room and said, "Toni, why don't you get out your letter and read it to Kelly."

"I can't believe this," I said, shaking my head.

As I stood up to go, Jill marched over and pushed me roughly back into the chair. Her demeanor changed, like a storm passing across her face, and she said darkly, "You sit right there. You're going to listen to what Toni has to say to you."

My mouth fell open in shock. *This is definitely not in the shrink handbook, is it? Could she lay her hands on me*, I wondered? I tried to make sense of her aggression. *Maybe force is acceptable in psychological practice, I don't know.* I thought of strait-jackets and shock therapy, victims being taken into psychiatric hospitals against their will. *Am I being held against my will? Yeah, I am.*

Jill turned to watch Toni fumble with a piece of paper. I looked at the door. *I could run. I could leap up out of this chair right now and run for the door.* I glanced at Jill, who waited calmly while Toni's shaking hands unfolded the note.

Toni cleared her throat and let out a dainty cough. She began, "Kelly, when I met you, you were a ray of sunshine. But lately, you do nothing but talk about your weight, and your plans to lose weight, and wine factors heavily into this. You're ruining our friendship, because this talk bores me. I know that if you stopped drinking…"

I stood up and marched toward the door. Jill's hand closed tightly around my elbow, and I yanked my arm out of her grip. My body flooded with rage as I said, "Don't touch me. So I bore you, Toni? I bore you? So you stage an intervention because you're bored with our friendship? Fine. Problem solved. I'm out of here. You're free to go make new friends."

"Kelly!" I heard Toni yell as I slammed the door behind me. As I hoofed it to the elevator, I heard Toni's door open. I broke into a run, afraid Jill would tackle me and take me away to the funny farm. "Kelly!" I heard Toni's voice call again.

The elevator door opened, and I stepped in and turned in time to watch Jill run up behind Toni. As the doors closed, I said, "Jill, stick a potato in your tailpipe."

# CHAPTER FIVE

As I struggled to tune in to Earnest's lecture, I couldn't stop replaying the whole ugly scene of the intervention in my mind. *Stick a potato in your tailpipe?* I was mortified. When my mind wandered back to Earnest, he was talking about the assignment he'd given us.

"What you think you want is all wrong. What you want is what you've been told you want. You don't want your bodies because the media says that real bodies are unacceptable. Your parents want that job for you so they can brag about you to their friends. Society, your teachers at school, they have all trained you to want what they think are safe options for you. They don't care if you shine. They want you to fit neatly into the boxes they've created for you. They expect you to climb in, and you're afraid to witness their disappointment if you don't.

"Lydia, what's your dream job? Is it the one you have now?"

"No, I want to be a teacher."

"But you're a baker. Why is this?"

"Because my mother and my grandmother bake, and I grew up baking with them, and I love to bake." Lydia looked down at her hands in her lap and mumbled, "And I like the hype of owning a bakery in New York. It makes me feel kinda cool."

"Then why isn't being a baker your dream job?"

"Because I'm a small business owner and I manage employees and do my own accounting. Baking is only a tiny part of what I do. And besides, I really wish I worked with kids."

"Then why don't you? Why not become a teacher?"

"Because I've already poured so much of myself into my bakery. It feels wrong to quit. And what if I disappoint my mom and grandmother? They're so proud of me for being a baker."

"Why do you care about their disappointment more than you care about your own feelings of fulfilment and happiness?"

"I'm not sure..."

"It's because you think *their* feelings about your life are more important than *your own* feelings about *your own* life. You're going to have to accept the fact that you alone are responsible for your happiness. To be happy, you must respect your own feelings. You must make choices that honor your life and your happiness without worrying that your mom or grandma might prefer you bake for a living."

My mind was reeling with ahas. *How many times have I made decisions about my own future based on what other people might think of me?* But the lesson seemed to be lost on Lydia. She didn't even acknowledge what Earnest was trying to tell her.

Lydia said, "But there's so much schooling involved with becoming a teacher. What if I spend all the money and time and effort to get my master's degree and get certified, but I realize it's not the right thing?"

"But what if teaching *is* the right thing? If you don't take action, then your world stays stagnant as the years pass you by. Next thing you know, you're on your deathbed wondering why you never tried to become a teacher. Even if teaching turns out to be the wrong thing, you'll get closer to the *right* thing by getting out there and trying things and making mistakes and being open to the results.

"Let experience be your guide in life. You're going to learn far more from experience than you ever will by sitting here listening to me talk. Let my lectures guide you into action. As much as I'd love to say I could tell you exactly what you should do every step of the way, it's my duty to tell you that I'm not the best instructor for you; the only way you're going to learn how to create a happy and fulfilling life is by experience.

"Once you create a vision—and I mean the vision your own soul has for you, unimpeded by the opinions of others—once you can *see that vision* and you create a plan to achieve it, and once you begin to act on your plans, you'll start to see gaps in your knowledge base. You're going to start thinking, 'It's too hard. I don't know what I'm doing.' Stop yourself, and simply fill in those knowledge gaps wherever you find you're lacking. Do the research. Ask people. I don't care how, but keep moving your feet in the direction of your vision.

"As we strive to reach our visions, we're bound to experience failures. Every failure is a chance to memorize what doesn't work so we never again need to relearn old lessons. Decide to treat mistakes—not as excuses to return to old behaviors—but as puzzles to be solved. Recognize that when you screw up, you're practicing and improving.

"When you do make a mistake, focus on the actual problem and how to fix it, rather than letting the issue affect your feelings about yourself. Accept and love yourself, especially in the face of weakness and failure. *Love who you are, not what you do.* That way you're free to own your failures, take responsibility for where you went wrong, and improve, without some crazy detour to Hate Myselfville.

"When faced with mistakes and failures, the only thing you need to care about is taking control and solving problems. Lydia, and all of you, you will learn more about yourself by going after what you want. Even if you don't wind up where you think you will, you will benefit by staying with the newness of the experience and seeing who you meet and what you like to do and what you don't like.

"We're going to close out today's class with a visioning exercise. I want you to take a few deep breaths, roll your shoulders, shake out your hands. Close your eyes. Loosen up and relax, and while you do this, I want you to imagine the opinions of your parents and your peers and even complete strangers rolling off you and blowing down and away like the fluffy seeds of a dandelion, swirling and blowing out of the room."

Earnest paused while we all let the dandelion seeds blow away. Then he began to speak slowly, carefully, giving us the time to see exactly what he needed us to see. "As the opinions of others leave this space, imagine your ego shrinking. You don't care what other people think. You don't care what you look like. You care about nothing but a deep inner knowing that you are enough. You are complete. And you want to live a life of pleasure and bliss and peace. You only want what your soul wants for you.

"You want activities in your life that bring you into flow, acts of creativity that make you feel alive and excited. What kind of creative outlets, hobbies, or means of expression do you enjoy? Bring to mind the activities that make your heart sing and make the world drop away when you're engaged in them. These activities are almost like prayer or meditation, and they can help restore your feelings of worth and purpose when you allow yourself to engage in them again and again.

"Imagine that you have created a life that allows you to perform your favorite activities every day. Imagine yourself one day, three years in the future. What are your favorite parts of your daily routine? Where and when do you choose to do your activities? Now that you've been doing your favorite activities every day for three years, see what's unfolding for you.

"What's happening right now in the moment that you see yourself? In this scene you're creating in your mind's eye, where are you and what are you doing? What do you hear and see? Where do you live, and how do you fill your days?

"Now visualize, in great detail, what it's like to inhabit the body of your higher self. Feel the power and energy of a healthy, happy, cared-for body. How does your body feel? Enjoy this feeling and breathe it in. In your daily, blissful life, what kind of foods do you enjoy eating, and how do these foods make your body feel? What kind of physical activities does your body enjoy, and how do these activities make you feel?

"You have many warm friendships in your life. Some of these friends you haven't even met yet. You're surrounded by love, laughter, and joy. Take in the awesomeness of your new, blissful life. Feel the warmth, the love, the giddiness, and the excitement. Imprint a burning desire for your vision into your mind."

Earnest stopped speaking, and I could hear the breath of the students around me. I felt warm and calm and happy, and it occurred to me that these were very unusual feelings for me. I wanted more, and as I started to want, the spell was broken. I knew right then and there, I would never miss one of these classes.

"After you leave class tonight, I want you to go straight home and record your blissful vision in writing. Take the time to write down the details of the amazing life that you visualized. Choose a date approximately three years in the future and write down that date. How old will you be?

"Refer back to your vision in your mind's eye and write down all of the specifics. What kinds of feelings and experiences do you want for yourself? Even if you think something seems too grand or unachievable, write down every detail. We don't want you to forget any of the finer points. Right now, you aren't concerning yourself with how—you're only writing down what you see in your vision.

"What kind of work will you be doing? What are you creating? Where will you live? What's your home like? What's your body like? What kinds of physical activities do you enjoy? Write down everything you see happening. Over time, you're going to write down more details as they make themselves known to you. Be sure to record the details each time you sense an addition or change in your vision so nothing is forgotten."

Earnest clapped his hands sharply and raised his voice. "Okay, that's it! Get going, get out of here! Go home and record your blissful vision before you forget!" We all scrambled to our feet. Earnest spread his arms and pushed the air as he walked toward us in an effort to herd us out of the room. We headed to the door, down the stairs, and out into the street. In silence, we dispersed into the night, not wanting to speak in case it could cause us to lose hold of our visions.

# CHAPTER SIX

In the calm quiet of my apartment, I laid on my side in my bed with a journal while I chewed the end of a pen. I wanted to analyze every word of what Earnest had said in class, but first I needed to jot down my vision.

I closed my eyes and took a deep breath. The images flowed easily. *I rise with the sun. I step out of my house and onto a pristine, tropical beach. My body feels incredibly strong. How did it get that way? I look down and see a pair of dumbbells sitting on the ground. Of course. I pick up the weights, and I perform my daily exercise ritual in the sand. Then I take a relaxing stroll in the wet sand along the edge of the surf.*

*Later that day, I sit in a low-slung chair on the beach. There's a laptop on my lap, and I'm intent on writing. I'm writing a novel. I smile as I type because the book is funny.* The familiar feeling of flow came back to me.

Years ago, at work in real life, I brought my laptop to every meeting. Under the guise of taking notes, I tapped away at the keyboard while I drafted a novel. It was a fluffy beach read and I didn't think anyone would respect it, but boy did I love writing it.

Then I got lost in my career and the drive to make money. Being a novelist seemed like a silly endeavor. I wanted to feel important and useful; what use could fiction be? *I guess this was what Earnest was talking about when we were supposed to let these kinds of opinions float out the door.*

*But I live in New York City. How am I going to wind up writing on a beach?* I chomped down on my pen cap harder and remembered that Earnest said we're not concerned with how this is all going to happen. I felt ridiculous imagining a life that seemed so unlikely considering where I was, but I pushed the feelings away and continued with the exercise.

I squeezed my eyelids tight and slipped deeper into the vision. *I wake up beneath a feathery, white comforter in my beach house. I stretch my arms up toward the ceiling. I climb out of bed and walk into the sun-drenched, high-ceilinged kitchen. I'm wearing silky pajamas and a robe. I pour a cup of coffee and warm my hands and sip.*

*I open the door and walk toward the ocean. I enjoy the salty breeze on my face and squint my eyes against the golden sunrise.*

★

I woke up in a puddle of drool. I peeled my face off my notebook and squinted my eyes against the very real sunrise coming into my cramped, hot, New York City apartment. I glanced at the clock. *Oh shit. I'm going to be late for work. Again.*

I ran into the bathroom and caught sight of my face in the mirror. I had an imprint of my vision written on my cheek where I'd fallen asleep on my notebook. *Awesome.* I fought the feeling of dread that threatened to overtake me every morning at the prospect of going into work. I took a military shower, reciting to myself, *Face, wee-wee, heinie, and pits.*

I scrubbed my vision off my face, wrapped myself in a towel, and looked in the mirror. I wanted to have hope for this blissful vision, for the idea that my life could change so radically, that I could escape the prison of work life as I knew it and make a living coming and going as I pleased, out in the world as a writer.

The cloud of reality descended and wrapped around me. My parents would think I was an idiot. I could imagine my mother saying, "Don't be so childish. A writer? Why don't you become a ballerina or a fireman while you're at it?" *Besides, how will I make any money? And what if people hate what I write? Snap out of it.* My mood became increasingly heavy as I got dressed and began the long, sad commute to my office.

★

When I got to work that day, no one would make eye contact with me. I shrugged it off. These people weren't exactly my friends. I sat down at my desk and opened a game of solitaire on my computer.

Out of the corner of my eye, I saw Brad, my arch nemesis, peek in my office door. Ever since Sadie and I struck our uncomfortable arrangement, I knew Brad wondered how I didn't get fired a thousand times over. When I looked up, Brad drew his head out of sight. *What the heck? Is he spying on me?*

I tried to shake off the feeling that Brad was still lurking outside my office, but I couldn't get into my game. Instead, I stumbled down memory lane to the day that I complained about Brad to the head of human resources.

★

It was ten years ago, only a few days before I'd blackmailed Sadie. I'd made an appointment to see the HR head honcho, Victoria Gannon. I'd never met her in person before, but I had seen her in the hallways. She was a woman of vast dimensions in all directions, and her suits, hair, and makeup were always pristine.

Ten years, and I still remembered every detail, probably because it was one of those self-torture mind-movies I couldn't seem to eject from my brain. Before the meeting, I'd rehearsed over and over again what I would say. I didn't want to be emotional about it, because I didn't want this to become about me. I only wanted to report the facts about Brad the PowerPoint Monkey, and how he stole credit for my work and was promoted as a result.

When it was time for my meeting, I took a deep breath, grabbed my notes, and walked to Victoria's office. Her door was open, so I knocked lightly on the doorframe to announce my presence. She looked up and smiled a welcoming smile as she said, "Come in, come in, please, have a seat."

I closed the door behind me and sat down on the edge of a chair with my knees pressed together, my hands in my lap, and my back straight. I could feel my palms begin to sweat. I took a deep breath to stem the small panic rising in my chest. I tried to look calm as I plastered a prim half smile on my face.

Victoria looked at me expectantly as I sat there sweating before finally asking me, "So. What can I do for you?"

My voice came out shaky and strange as I began to talk, and so I stopped. I cleared my throat and took another deep breath while I searched my mind for my canned speech. I was drawing a blank. I needed to start talking before this woman thought I was having a breakdown, so I blurted out, "Well, it's Brad."

Now it was Victoria's turn to force a smile. "What about Brad?"

"I caught him on more than one occasion telling other people about my work and my ideas and implying that he was the one who did it or thought of it."

She pressed her lips together tightly. She was no longer smiling, and she sat there blinking at me. *Am I supposed to keep talking, or is she going to respond?* I could feel the silky lining of my suit becoming cold with my sweat. Finally she said, "So, am I to understand you are under the assumption that Brad has claimed responsibility for your work?"

"Assumption? No, not the assumption, I know this. I know this for a fact. I've caught him."

"I see." She focused on me with this weird, scary gaze. It could have been a murderous gaze. *How does she not understand this situation? Why is she looking at me like she wants to twist my head clear off my neck and eat the innards of my skull?*

I waited for her to respond in a way that didn't entail shooting laser beams of contempt at me with her eyes. I was screaming on the inside, *I said I caught him! Shouldn't you be thirsty for details? Why won't you ask me what happened?*

After what was probably only a split second, I couldn't take her stare any longer. I had to spill the details. "Yeah, so I designed this encoding operation."

Victoria snapped at me, "*You* designed it."

"Um, yes. I designed it. And well, Brad was walking around with my diagram..."

"Your diagram? You put the diagram to paper?"

"Well, no. I mean, I designed the work flow and how all the people and the equipment fit together, and then I told Brad, and he made the diagram for me, but then he was telling everyone that he..."

"So it was Brad's diagram that, as you say, he was walking around with."

I felt lightheaded. I began to tremble, and I couldn't keep my voice from wavering. "Yes. I mean no. Well, he wouldn't have been able to make the diagram if...Look. Brad is nothing but a PowerPoint Monkey. He couldn't have an original thought if you pumped him full of LSD and threw him into the ring at Cirque du Soleil!"

Victoria drew herself up to her full Godzilla height and breathed fire at me, "Miss Ryan! That is highly inappropriate! We are done here. Please. Get out. Go. I don't want to hear any more about this. Out. Now. Leave."

I didn't say another word as I wobbled out the door of her office and hyperventilated all the way back to mine. When I got back to my office, I closed the door, sat down at my desk, and fought the urge to cry for a minute before I gave in and broke down. *That's it*, I thought. *I'm definitely getting fired.*

Everyone seemed to be huge Brad fans. Why couldn't anyone else see what I saw, that Brad was a dim-witted parasite? Then Toni finally told me about the Victoria-Brad connection, and it all began to make sense. Brad was married to Victoria. Yeah. I complained to Victoria about her darling little husband. Oops. That might have been the most awkward day of my life, and I've had a lot of those.

★

I came to the end of memory lane when I saw Brad peeking around the corner at me again. I stared directly back at him, and he scurried away. *All right, something's up.* I pushed back from my desk and looked around. *Everything looks the same to me.* I opened my e-mail.

My heartbeat quickened as my eyes landed on Sadie's name in my e-mail inbox. After all these years, she still frightened me. *Even though I'm no longer the object of her tirades, it's no less horrifying watching an executioner go to work on the victims around you.*

My stomach tightened, and I reached for the bottle of Tums I kept stashed in my desk drawer. I crunched on the chalky sweetness as I opened the e-mail.

---------------------------------------

Monday, October 6
From: Sadie Lindstrom
To: Kelly Ryan
Subject: see me in my office
Kelly,
Come to my office when you get in.
Sadie

---------------------------------------

I looked at the clock. *She's going to think I rolled in here after ten! And she'd be right. I just got here.*

I sighed heavily as I pushed my chair away from my desk and stood up. My feet felt like lead, my heart raced, and my palms were clammy. *It really is a miracle, and not a happy one, that I still work here.* I forced my feet to move in the direction of the predator's office.

I knocked gently on her door. When there was no answer after only a split second, I tried to sneak away, but Sadie threw the door open wide. Her mouth was smiling, but her eyes weren't. She looked even crazier than usual, and her dark eyes shone with that familiar, sadistic glint.

"Sit," she said brusquely.

I sat my butt down at the Conference Table of Doom, the round, four-person table that resided in a corner of Sadie's enormous office. She sat down in the chair next to me and folded her hands on the table. Her smile became genuine, which only increased my feelings of dread. *She's smiling. That means she's about to stab me in the face with a pen.*

She said, "I don't know where to begin, so I'm just going to jump right in. My daughter, Viola, has been accepted into the Young Achievers Program at Smythe University. Of course, Viola is only ten years old, so I will have to accompany her. So what I'm saying is," Sadie grinned, "you're fired!"

My hands went numb, my vision dimmed, and I could hear a rush of blood in my ears. *I'm going to faint.* I forced myself into consciousness as I focused on the words coming out of Sadie's mouth.

She chortled, "I'm leaving! I've written my resignation letter, and getting rid of you was my last task before I quit." She looked down and shook her head, her smile looking almost sweet as she said, "Oh, how I've dreamed of this day."

*Wow. I'm part of Sadie's blissful vision. Sadie achieved her dream. Her dream of firing me.*

I got up from the table, trembling and swaying. *I'm not sure I can make it out of here, but if I lose consciousness in front of her, she'll definitely murder me.*

I tried to rally some adrenaline so I could escape as Sadie said, "There's a security guard waiting at your office. You can pack a box and the guard will escort you out. Ta-ta!"

I lurched toward the door, my steps fast and then slow. *I can't control my legs.* A look of hatred and rage returned to Sadie's face as she yelled, "Get OUT!" and slammed the door behind me.

When I returned to my office, I could hardly believe my eyes: a security guard really was waiting for me. This was not some elaborate hoax.

There was a piece of paper on my desk: a termination letter. I looked up and Victoria was standing outside the door, her arms folded across her massive chest. Her eyes held the same glimmering look of hatred as Sadie's. "I need to witness your signature," she said.

I nodded, picked up a pen, and left a scribble on the signature line above my name. I handed the paper to Victoria. She rolled her eyes, snatched it from me, and placed the paper back on my desk. She held out her hand and barked, "Pen!" I handed it to her and she held it tightly as she quickly penned a neat signature to fully execute our agreement to banish me from the secure world of employment I'd known for the last ten years. Then she picked up the sheet and left without another word.

I looked doubtfully at the single box I was given and then at everything I'd collected in my office over the years. *What will make the cut?* I selected some books, several pairs of heels, which I kept stashed in my bottom desk drawer, and my trusty bottle of Tums. I abandoned the rest.

I kept my eyes on the carpet in front of me as I made the long walk of shame through the building. Employees stopped to gawk as I struggled with the box, the security guard useless at my heels. He left me outside and then turned and went back inside the building.

As I stood blinking on the sidewalk, a khaki-wearing tourist bumped into me. I struggled to hang onto the box. "Sorry, excuse me!" smiled the clean-cut, corn-fed young man. "Hey, do you need a hand there?"

I looked away. I had to get home, away from these streets full of people, so I could let myself fall apart and cry.

# CHAPTER SEVEN

Oh, and I cried. Alone in my bed, I wept. I sobbed. I hyperventilated and then caught my breath so I could sob some more. I went through wads and wads of tissues as fear played my brain like a piano, filling the air with dirgie little ditties of pending financial destitution.

When I could cry no more, I opened my journal and read the words I'd written only the night before. It felt like a lifetime ago. I caressed the pages and allowed hope to creep in to the edges of the room, temporarily dulling my brain-song of disaster. *Getting fired is like the Universe speaking to me. The massive obstacle of my job is out of the way. I can go write.*

Reason spoke up next. *I need to pay my rent.* The debate began: *But I have savings. At least for a little while, I could pay rent out of my savings while I pursue my vision.* Reason came back stronger, *How long is it going to take you to make a living as a writer? It's probably going to be seven years, if you're lucky. Some people never make it. You need a job.*

I needed to get out of my own head. I picked up my cell phone and called Amy to tell her what happened.

She said, "Thank God."

"Excuse me?" I thought I misheard her.

"Thank God! You're free!"

"What?"

"You're free! Kelly, you've been miserable in that shithole for years. I can't believe it took them firing you before you could get out, but whatever. You're out! I'm so happy for you!"

"Huh? Happy?" My brain felt sluggish. I struggled to figure out what she could possibly mean.

Amy sounded impatient. "Don't tell me that not even a *tiny* part of you can see what a blessing this is."

I was silent.

"Kelly, you should feel relieved that you never have to be around those toxic people ever again. Those people were nothing but nasty to you. I can't believe you put yourself through that as long as you did."

I could feel the sunrise of recognition stealing into my mind. She was right, of course. But still, I couldn't shake the feeling of utter destruction of my ego. *Those horrible people got rid of me. Those people, those lower life forms, bested me. My paychecks are no longer coming. They won. I'm gone.*

Amy's words woke me up out of the fog. "Come out with me tonight."

"Okay. When? Where?"

"Let's go have dinner, and then we can hit up a club in the meatpacking district. My treat."

★

I looked in the mirror and smeared foundation onto my red, puffy face. I wasn't sure if the dark circles under my eyes were from a lack of sleep or from the mascara that had mingled with my tears all afternoon. I blotted out the darkness with concealer, and then lined my upper lids with a black kohl pencil. I stepped back to survey the results.

*I'm not impressed. Keep going.*

I reapplied my mascara, slapped on some blush, then swiped on lip balm and prune-colored lipstick. I picked up my wine glass in one hand and tousled my flat hair with the other. I took a sip and watched myself in the mirror. *Good enough.*

I drained the wine glass and set it on the counter. I mentally tallied how much wine I'd already had. *Two glasses. But they were big ones, so maybe more like three. Two and a half. Whatever. Okay, what about dinner? I'll probably have a drink while I look at the menu. Then I'll have two drinks to wash down the meal. Then there'll be more drinks at the club. Wait. How many drinks is this going to be?*

I was worried that if I got wasted in my current mental state, I was going to turn into a blubbering, weeping, sobbing maniac. I also didn't like the idea of nursing a massive hangover at the same time I was shouldering the fresh devastation of unemployment.

I stood up straight and breathed. *Limits. I'm going to set some limits on how much I drink tonight. I'm already buzzed, so I could have one with dinner. Then I'll have water at the club. There. That's a much more reasonable amount.*

I stepped outside and into the gutter, raising my hand to hail a cab. I felt like I was watching myself up on a movie screen, emotionless and disassociated from what had happened to me. A cab rolled up, and I climbed in. "Empire Diner, please." The cabby's face looked at me in the rearview mirror with a blank expression. "Oh sorry, Tenth Avenue and Twenty-Second Street." Without another word, we sped off.

I stared out the window at the dark streets and the faces of the people as we drove past. *What do all these people do for a living? Where are they going? And are they all drinking too? One drink. One drink. One drink, one drink, one drink, one drink.* I held it in my head as a mantra. *I will only have one drink with dinner.*

When the cabby pulled up at the restaurant, my mind chewed on a fear nugget. *I have to pay the driver. Dollars will leave my hand when I have no way to bring dollars back into my possession.*

I entered the small restaurant and saw Amy waving at me from a booth. On the table in front of her was a wine chiller with a bottle of champagne poking out. *Oh crap.* As I sat, she leaned forward and gave me an air kiss. Then she filled a champagne glass with bubbly and pushed it toward me. I gestured at the sparkling wine. "What's this?"

"We're celebrating your freedom!" I smiled a tiny bit. How could I not?

Amy held up her glass and said, "Cheers to the end of this miserable, horrible career chapter." We clinked glasses and took a sip. "And let's toast your future. Your gorgeous, wide-open future."

My heart took an anxious jump as I thought, *My big, empty, broke future.* I took a long, drawn-out swallow this time. In no time flat, Amy topped off our glasses and asked the waitress to bring another bottle with our dinner order. *Okay, so obviously one drink with dinner isn't happening.*

A tiny voice in my head said, *You really could have one drink with dinner. You don't have to keep sucking it down, ya know.* But I pretended I couldn't hear the voice. I drowned it out by saying loudly, and maybe a bit overenthusiastically, to Amy, "Wow, this champagne is really good! I love it!"

"I want you to get it in your head that we need to celebrate your new life. Honestly, Kelly, it disturbs me a little bit that you got so upset about losing this shitty job. You can find another one. It's not that big of a deal."

*It's a huge freaking deal. I can't even begin to explain how little these cheap, pointless sentiments mean to me. You want to celebrate my new life? What new life? All I can do is try not to hyperventilate every time I think of the uncertainty and instability of my financial situation. I have no job, nowhere to go, and no idea how this story is going to pan out.*

I sucked back the next glass of champagne in an effort to push down the rising panic. Amy was staring at me. "You don't look happy. What are you thinking?" she asked.

"What do you expect? I'm panicking, you know, like normal people do when they get fired. How do you know I'll find another job? What if it's not that easy? What if I have to accept a terrible job out of financial desperation?"

Amy smirked. "A terrible job? Like what?"

"I don't know, like emptying the trash for a fishmonger. Which would completely destroy my résumé, of course."

"Right. A fishmonger. I don't think you have experience in fishmongering."

"I know! What if *no one* will hire me? What if I can't make ends meet and I get evicted from my apartment? I could wind up living in a cardboard box on the street!"

"Look out a dirty window, see a gray day."

"Excuse me?"

"I said, 'Look out a dirty window, see a gray day.'"

"What's that supposed to mean?"

Amy pursed her lips. "I've been meaning to tell you this for a long time." She sighed.

"What?"

"Now, please. You need to know that I say this out of love. But you have a set of pessimistic blinders on. You have the really bad habit of gathering unrelated pieces of 'evidence,'" Amy gestured with air quotes, "and conflating them into your story, which is usually an absurdly negative interpretation of reality."

I let out a long breath and leaned back in the booth. As much as I wanted to be angry at Amy, I could feel a mist of truth coming over me. I looked at her in the eye, steeled myself, and said, "Okay. Give me an example."

Amy smiled and relaxed. She rubbed her hands and said, "Okay. Let's talk about your ex, Patrick."

I groaned and rolled my eyes. "Oh, THAT douchebag. Every time I hear his name, I think about the shitty way he dumped me."

While Patrick and I were in Paris for a long weekend, I hoped he would pop the question. He'd never given any indication that we were nearly as serious as that, but I held on to the delusion all the same.

41

I woke up anxious the morning we had plans to visit the prime engagement spot, the Eiffel Tower. I was with the man I loved in a romantic city. I was more than ready to give my life to him, but I knew he didn't feel the same way.

Patrick and I slogged umbrellaless through a downpour on our way to the Eiffel Tower. I was cold and soaked by the time we neared a quaint café about halfway along our route. I suggested we stop for a hot tea so we could dry off while we waited for the rain to let up. Patrick called me a lazy whiner, and I told him he could continue on his forced march without me. We were miserable in Paris. We were primed for destruction.

"I couldn't get out of bed for a month after he dumped me. I'll always hate that douchebag."

"Exactly. I mean, this is exactly the kind of thing I'm talking about. That was, like, eight years ago. Patrick really wasn't a bad guy, I mean, after all these years, you have to concede to that. He was a decent human being."

I looked down at my hands and grumbled, "I guess so."

"I know he didn't want to commit, and that you hurt you."

"Deeply," I shot back.

"Yeah, deeply. I get it. Don't you have *any* new perspective about him after all this time? You used to think he was always trying to cheat on you, but he spent every single day with you. He'd be up late playing a video game, and you had yourself convinced he was on the computer chatting with another woman."

"Yeah, I have to admit, I was pretty paranoid as far as Patrick was concerned."

"But you were like that with every guy before him too. You accused every boyfriend you had of cheating."

"But that's because I was cheated on, twice in a row, by two different boyfriends."

"Yeah, because you dated a couple of jerks. We've all done that. But it doesn't mean everyone you ever date is going to cheat on you and your life's mission is to catch them in the act. I mean, that's what you were doing. You were constantly collecting these 'clues,'" there she went with the air quotes again, "that these guys, these—I'm sorry, but these *really, really nice* guys were cheating on you!"

"And then they left me!"

"Of *course* they left you, Kelly. What else could they do? They weren't proving to you that they were jerks. They were proving that you were totally paranoid and impossible to be around."

*Oof. That stings.* I fought back the tears that rose to blur my vision. *She's right.*

"Kelly, I'm so sorry if I'm being too blunt or nasty or…"

"No, no. You're right. I need to hear this. It's good to get this perspective."

"I mean, we've had this conversation before. You remember when you were dating Patrick, and you guys had that big fight over the video games? He was just trying to blow off steam after a long workweek. And you told me that the second you turned thirteen, your mom started doing this to you. She would seek and hunt for evidence that you were bad, that you were a slut or that you were on drugs or whatever, when you weren't doing anything. She was paranoid, and she was always looking for evidence to support these nonexistent crimes. And you remembered that and you saw that you were doing the same thing to Patrick."

I nodded. I could feel my mind reopening to the realization. *My own mother didn't trust me. I couldn't trust her. It's impossible to trust anyone. That's why I gave up on love.*

Amy said, "Have you ever heard of the negativity bias?"

"No, what's that?"

"Sandy told me about it. She said the mind clings to bad things that happen, and it looks for evidence that they're going to happen again. It's a self-protection mechanism, but it means that as we get older, we all grow more pessimistic and paranoid. And it's actually not a realistic way to view the world. I mean, lightning isn't necessarily going to strike twice. But we all walk around looking up at the sky, as if worrying about it is going to prevent bad things from happening. Which they *won't* necessarily. I mean, we *think* they will, and this pessimism invites bad things in. Like with you and your boyfriends. When you're so suspicious and negative, of course they're going to leave."

"Okay, Amy, you've made your point."

"But I'm just getting to my point. The opposite of what we're afraid of can also be true. Sandy told me that what matters, and what shapes your destiny, is what you pay attention to. You go where you're looking. You get proof of what you think. And so, on the job thing: you're smart. You're capable. The fact that you're stressed about finding a new job, or that you think you won't be able to make ends meet, this is crazy business."

"Yeah, maybe."

"And anyway, don't you have like a gazillion dollars saved up?"

"By now it's about two gazillion." We both cracked a smile at that.

The waitress plunked our plates down in front of us, and we tucked in to our meals. As the cheesy, starchy heaven of macaroni and cheese slid down my throat, I could feel my mood lifting higher. *Amy's right. I have at least a gazillion dollars saved up. I'm going to be fine.*

After dinner, we hopped in a cab and rode farther downtown to a club. After a short wait at a red velvet rope, we pulled out our licenses and handed them to the bouncer. Since there was clearly no way we were underage, he graciously played the game and inspected our IDs, then nodded and opened the door for us. As I entered the bar area, my eyes adjusted to the dim mood lighting.

Amy said, "I'm grabbing a drink. What are you having?"

*Screw it. I'm not even going to pretend I'm drinking with restraint after downing all that champagne with dinner.* "White wine, please."

Amy waved a twenty-dollar bill to get the bartender's attention while my eyes roamed the room. *Man, when did New Yorkers get so young?* I corrected myself, *When the heck did I get so old?* I greedily accepted the glass of wine from Amy and took a deep gulp.

Amy said, "I hope you don't mind, but this guy I like is going to meet us here."

"Oh yeah? Who's the guy?"

"His name is Guillermo. He's a model and an actor. And he's *gorgeous.* I mean, I cannot handle how ridiculously good-looking this man is." Amy fanned her face dramatically with her hand while she swooned.

"How'd you meet him?"

"A couple weeks ago, at Car Bar. He works there. We've met a few times since then, but only late at night after our shifts end. He'll text me, and we'll usually meet up for, uh, you know, nighttime activities." Amy giggled. Then she looked serious for a moment. "Sometimes I worry about being just a booty call. I mean, it would be nice to go on a proper date for once, you know, dinner and all that. But I'm pretty sure he likes me. I sure like him!"

I wasn't sure what to say. I wanted to tell her she deserved better. She didn't have the best romantic history either; she tended to gratefully accept pitiful scraps of attention from whoever would feed her. *She's enjoying herself. Let it go.*

"Oh, there's Guillermo!" Amy shouted. She stood on her tiptoes and waved frantically at a tall, dark, and handsome man who was slowly checking out the room as he made his way toward Amy. Without even looking her in the face, he pulled her body close to his before bending down to kiss her on the mouth.

I looked away for a moment to be polite, and when I turned back around, they were playing air hockey with each other's tongues. *Oh, okay. All right. That's enough. Any day now.* I sighed and sipped my drink. *Okay, take your time.*

My mind wandered back to our dinnertime conversation, about how Amy said I was looking at everything so negatively. My mind flitted back to my financial concerns and my job-hunting fears. *What if I imagine things unfolding the way I want them to? What exactly did I want to see happen?*

I thought back to my journal entry about my blissful vision. *I really do want to be a writer. I love to write. I love it when ideas and sentences form beneath my fingertips. Can I really make a living doing something I love? Or am I tangling money and writing together when they need to stay separate?*

Amy bounced into view and shouted in my face, "We're gonna go dance now!" Guillermo was literally bringing up the rear, with his eyes and hands fixed to Amy's rump.

*We all know how their night is going to end.* "All right, I'm going to head out. Catch me up on this," I pointed at Guillermo, "tomorrow."

"All right, chica, be safe!" said Amy before disappearing into the crowd with Guillermo firmly attached to her butt like a barnacle. I poured the remaining contents of my wine glass down my throat and sashayed out the door.

# CHAPTER EIGHT

The next morning, I awoke to the thud of my heartbeat jackhammering away at the front of my skull. *Oh God. I am so hung over.* I tried to move around to get comfortable, but every twitch, every tiny little movement, sent shockwaves of pain through my head.

My mouth was watering and I felt as if I might throw up, but the thought of getting out of bed and moving toward the bathroom seemed like a vast, impossible undertaking.

I tried to get the hamster in my head to get on the wheel and start it spinning so we could get an idea of how to fix this misery, but I'm pretty sure the hamster died of alcohol poisoning. All I could do was lay there, my limbs and brain flaccid, until I fell back asleep.

When I woke again, hours later, I felt a smidge better. My brain hamster was alive too, and it hopped on its squeaky little exercise wheel and began formulating ideas for a hangover cure. I took down the messages he beamed at me: *General Tso's chicken, lo mein noodles. No, wait— Mexican food and margaritas. No, no, no, scratch that. There's no way in hell hair of the dog's going to help. It might kill me. Thanks, hamster, we're done here.*

*Thank GOD for delivery. I don't even need to brush my teeth or shower to get food into my mouth. I only need to dial the phone.* I placed an order for Chinese food and then sank into a chair in my living room to wait while the minutes ticked by without mercy.

Later, as I shoveled noodles and sweet fried chicken into my sad, disgusting, hung-over face, I thought, *I will never drink again. What's the point? I feel like shit! This is so stupid! What in God's name would make me think that drinking that much would ever be a good idea?*

I took out my journal and scrawled across the page: I WILL NEVER DRINK AGAIN.

Then I enjoyed a long, painful afternoon of lying on the couch while I flipped through magazines and half paid attention to the television. As the shadows grew long, I thought, *I could eat again. I'm not exactly hungry, but my tummy is still upset. Maybe eating some more will help. I should go out to dinner. Why not? I can't stay inside any longer. My brain is still scrambled, so I can't do anything else. Might as well go eat.*

I took a quick shower and threw on a pair of jeans and a loose-fitting black top, which I hoped would disguise my bloated stomach. I stuffed my journal into my messenger bag and headed out the door.

Once my feet hit the sidewalk, I allowed the cool air to caress my face and relieve my nausea. I took a moment to dream about what food would be the most delicious and satisfying. *Italian? Nah. Thai? Nah.*

My earlier craving for Mexican blipped onto the radar. *Yeah. And a nice, sweet, sour, and salty margarita! Oh wait. I said I would never drink again. Well, "never again" might be a little dramatic. I can have one marg,* I rationalized, *because that's the perfect thing to wash down some cheesy enchiladas. Frankly, I can't imagine drinking anything else with enchiladas.*

I walked the three short blocks to my local Mexican restaurant, a dingy hole-in-the-wall with a huge, plastic cactus adorning the outside of the establishment. The hostess gestured to the nearly empty dining room as the international signal for "sit anywhere." *I love eating this early. I have my pick of tables, plus I can eat whatever I want without worrying about side-eye from other diners.*

A waitress set a basket of chips and salsa on the table and then took my order. My margarita was brought to the table almost immediately, and before the liquid even stopped moving in the glass, I was licking salt from the rim and attaching my lips to the straw for a taste. *Mmmm. All is right in my world.*

I took out my journal. Underneath where I'd written "I WILL NEVER DRINK AGAIN" I wrote in tiny, flowery letters: "I feel better now." As I flipped the cover shut, I noticed the edges of some yellowing papers poking out from between the bound pages of my journal.

I tugged the papers into full view onto the table in front of me. My hand flew up to cover the pleased little "oh" coming from my mouth when I identified the papers. *My high school report cards. How the heck did they get inside my journal?*

My desk at home where I kept my journal was a teetering mess of papers: old mail, bills, and benefits paperwork mostly. I couldn't imagine how my almost-twenty-five-year-old report cards got tangled up in the mess. *But here they are.*

As my eyes roamed the columns of letter grades, subjects, and long-forgotten teachers' names, I expected to feel a surge of pride. After all, I'd been inducted into the National Honor Society and I'd been awarded some college scholarships. I wanted these report cards to show me how smart I was.

Instead, every grade that wasn't an A felt like a tiny fist-punch to my gut. After getting pummeled by a series of Bs and one or two Cs (littered with plenty of As, which I roundly ignored), I felt a donkey kick: a D in algebra.

*I don't remember getting a D. I must have blocked it from memory. What must my parents have said about their daughter bringing home a D? The carnage, the horror!* I thought, without even a twinge of irony.

As I skimmed the names of my teachers, the familiar, haunting feelings of shame mingled with stress crept over me, the way I felt all throughout high school. I was always hunched over, and I remember wondering why I couldn't straighten out my posture. Now I knew: I was ducking that feeling of clicking tongues and heads shaking at me in contempt, always the question hanging over my head, *Why doesn't that girl work up to her potential?*

Back then, I didn't know. But now, sitting in that Mexican restaurant, looking at those report cards, it all made sense: high school academics were mind-numbingly, soul-suckingly BORING to me. I'm sure they were boring to everyone around me too—I'm not saying they were boring because I was somehow special. High school was boring because I was forced to memorize massive amounts of bland information that had nothing to do with me or real life and for no tangible reason.

Oh of course I was given plenty of "reasons." I was told at every turn that my grades mattered so much that they would impact my future levels of success for the rest of my life. I was force-fed (and I believed) the lie told by my parents, my teachers, and fellow students. We all sincerely believed that the caliber of college I attended would have complete, total, one hundred percent impact on my ability to get a job and make money (or not!) until the day I died.

The pressure I felt was unspeakable. Every grade I earned was a struggle because none of the information I was taught mattered to me. I believed every grade I got was pushing my future around on some imaginary plane. Every A grade meant I could live a regular life. Every grade less than that was a downgrade in earnings, in status, in the potential for normalcy in a life that could—or couldn't, depending on my performance—contain a job and a home and a car.

In that moment, sitting in a Mexican restaurant with an icy margarita glass sweating a few inches from my hand, the way I felt throughout high school washed over me again and again, crashing waves of shame and stress. I remembered how I had to expend herculean effort to force myself to do my homework and to study for tests. I knew it would merely soften the glares of disapproval, but it would never eliminate them entirely. Dirty, constant, and heavy: disapproval is what I felt to this day, heavy across my shoulders, tight in my throat, and in the ache of my heart, head, and belly.

I'm sure that in actuality many of my teachers were warm and forgiving, and I was only projecting these awful feelings of shame and inferiority onto their dealings with me. But I knew of at least one teacher who did see me as someone to be kicked around.

One day I entered her classroom late, right after the sound of the bell, and she immediately gave me a detention. I tried to explain why I was late. The button had popped off my wraparound skirt, and I had to borrow a safety pin. Miracle of miracles, another student produced one for me in the bathroom where I was able to repair my skirt and preserve my honor. I don't know how I would've otherwise navigated the school's halls with an armful of books and my skirt flapping open.

But upon entering this woman's classroom only a moment late and with what I thought was a bulletproof excuse, she gave me detention anyway, and without even entertaining the story I was trying to tell her for even a moment. I sassed back at her, "You'd rather I ran down the hall naked?" She gave me a second detention for talking back. *Maybe I deserved that one, but still, what an asshat.*

It's no wonder I had stress headaches every day and I was popping Tums for my nervous stomach, even back then. I also had stress-induced cystic acne when I was in high school, but I didn't know the cause until well into adulthood.

I took a sip of my margarita as I recalled how I felt about my peers and my desperate-yet-hopeless wish to fit in. Sometimes I would see little love notes written on desks like, "Valerie Catalano is hot." So one day I'd written my name neatly in blue ballpoint pen on a desk during study hall. It would be a full twenty-four hours before I returned to that desk in that classroom to find out what nice things people wrote about me under my name.

I hoped they would say I was hot. Or at least cute. Or maybe they would say I was smart. I didn't know, but I couldn't wait to find out what they thought.

When I returned to that desk, my heart swelling in anticipation, underneath where I'd written "Kelly Ryan" it said "is a dork." My heart shattered. I fought tears as I wet my finger in my mouth and then smeared away the unkind results of my anonymous graffiti collaboration. *It could have said much worse.*

The familiar swirl of shame wrapped itself around me like a wet blanket. I chugged the rest of my margarita. When the waitress brought my enchilada, I asked for another marg on the rocks with salt.

*The feeling of disapproval is still with me, no matter what I do. No matter how much stress I put myself under. No matter how much I try to be better at life. No matter what I eat or drink. Whether I go to work every day, or I get fired. This feeling is still following me everywhere, and I need to learn how to shake it.*

*What if it's not possible? What if shame and disapproval and stress are my cross to bear for the rest of my life?* But at least these feelings were no longer invisible to me. After looking at that report card and reliving the feelings in full force, I could now distinguish that shame was here—whether in the loud rush I'd just felt, or in shame's normal, workaday, dull roar. I knew somehow that noticing the feeling of disapproval hanging over me was the first step in getting rid of it.

# CHAPTER NINE

I sat enthralled, soaking up the words as they came from Earnest's beautiful mouth. All of us were at rapt attention as Earnest dove deeper into his lecture.

"So far in this class, we've learned about some factors that affect our feelings of self-worth that reside outside of ourselves, like our parents or society. But one of the most damning is right inside our own heads. It's the part of the brain responsible for emotions—the amygdala, or 'lizard brain' according to Seth Godin.

"It wasn't long ago in the history of the human race that we relied on tribes for survival. We pulled together to stay alive. We hunted and gathered together. Some members made clothing and shelter for protection against the elements. The whole tribe minded the children and defended against predators. If you were kicked out of the tribe, you wouldn't last long out there on your own. And so it was essential for survival to fit in with the tribe.

"And so we evolved to care deeply about the opinions of others. When our parents or our peers express displeasure about some aspect of ourselves, our lizard brain freaks out and starts asking, 'What if we get cast out of the tribe? We're going to die out there! We better do something to look lovable. Our survival depends on it.'

"This lizard-brain thinking makes us want to mold our behavior to fit the status quo. We organize our lives around the opinions of others because our lizard brain thinks we're going to die if we don't.

"This is why bullying is akin to torture; people who are bullied are being told that they don't belong in the tribe. The lizard brain thinks, 'We're being rejected. This means we're going to die.'

"The lizard brain makes us worry that we're damaged, flawed, broken, or unworthy of the tribe's love. Once upon a time, this might have helped us try harder to fit in so we could survive , but in today's world, this aspect of evolution leaves us feeling unsettled and uncomfortable in our own skin, as if being rejected, judged, or criticized is akin to death."

I thought back to the words written about me on the desk: *Kelly Ryan is a dork.* I remembered the hot flush of embarrassment in my face and the heavy feeling of shame burning my stomach. *No wonder that little rejection felt so horrible.*

Earnest continued, "However, we don't need to believe the lizard brain! If a bully thinks your choice of footwear looks stupid, you will survive just fine thankyouverymuch. If our parents think we need to go to a traditional church that we find morally offensive in its judgments of modern relationships, our lizard brain might nag at us to comply, but we have the power to politely decline. In today's connected and transportation-rich world, we can be comfortable knowing that—even if we are ejected from the tribe—we can find our own tribe, a new tribe that suits us perfectly.

"If there's a career path we'd love to take, but we worry, 'What will people think,' we can rationally dissect that thought and decide that it's irrelevant what other people think about our chosen careers."

I thought about my chosen career: becoming a writer. *Can I really do it? Can I stop worrying about what other people think? Even my parents?* I was so familiar with their voices of disapproval in my head that I sometimes caught myself confusing their opinions with my own.

"Our lizard brains can make us hang onto trauma long past usefulness. When something traumatic happens to us, whether it's an accident, physical violence, or mental or emotional abuse, our lizard brains replay these stories in our minds. We stay fearful for years after the threat of danger has passed. When we realize that it's our lizard brains making us fearful, we can reclaim control over these stories. We gain the knowledge that, regardless of what anyone put us through in the past, our inherent self-worth is still very much intact.

"The part of us that can reason away the irrational fears of the lizard brain is called the neocortex, and it's responsible for conscious thought. When we're aware of the impact of the lizard brain, we're better able to stand back from ourselves as if we're at a distance from the drama created by our inner lizards.

"Think back on interactions with your peers that hurt your self-confidence or made you doubt your self-worth. What lizard-brain messages might you have internalized from your interactions with your peers? Based on past or current experiences, in what ways does your lizard brain fear that you don't fit in?"

*Kelly Ryan is a dork. What if I try to become a writer, but everything I write is dorky and everyone in the world finds out I'm a great big dork?*

"We have the power to stop believing negative messages about our self-worth. Like most of these exercises, this is a practice, not a one-off deal. First, you will figure out what these unconscious messages of inferiority are. Then you will practice disputing the messages you've received from others and from your lizard brain about your self-worth."

*I'm not a dork! Not a dork, not a dork, not a dork!*

"Oprah Winfrey once said, 'Do you believe that you are worthy of happiness? Do you believe that happiness, success, abundance, comfort, fulfillment, peace, joy, love is a part of your birthright? Is that what you believe? Or do you believe something else? Because you will manifest the life that you believe.'"

I thought about the life I had manifested for myself. It wasn't a bad life, on the surface. I lived in an exciting city. I had lots of money saved up. But I was lonely. Lonely and empty. My mind pleaded, *Fix me, Earnest.*

"If deep down we believe we are unlovable, we will continue to act like we don't love ourselves. We will continue to operate in a split fashion between our accepted face-to-the-world personality and our Shadow. We deny the Shadow part of ourselves that's steeped in shame and rejection. We blame ourselves and our Shadow for everything bad that happens to us and for every time we're mistreated.

"Then we disown the part of ourselves that feels unworthy. We sabotage ourselves, our health, and our well-being when we don't hold a deep knowing that we are worthy. When we feel ashamed and uncomfortable in our own skin, our entire life is negatively influenced.

"Today we will learn how to accept all of ourselves. To do so, we must acknowledge that we don't need to be perfect to deserve love. Once we see that we don't need to be perfect, we can stop undermining our own success. When we feel bad about ourselves, we act out against getting our deepest wishes for our lives fulfilled. We act in shameful ways when we feel shameful or uncomfortable. Unfortunately, this prolongs and deepens our bad feelings about ourselves.

"When we feel good about ourselves, and we're accepting of all of our traits in an honest light—the good and the bad—and we offer ourselves love, compassion, respect, and kindness, then we act in ways that align with these feelings. We take our health seriously because we value our lives and our bodies—not because we're worried about how we look to other people. We choose work that fulfills us spiritually and financially—not because the job is a way to impress other people.

"Where did your feelings of unworthiness come from? When I was sixteen, I got dumped by my first girlfriend. Soon after that, I lost a student council election. I didn't realize it at the time, but my mind began searching for evidence that people didn't like me, and hey—look at that. I got dumped. I lost the election. Also unbeknownst to me, I began to split off from that carefree teenager who was open and up for anything. I became closed off and depressed. That happy boy was gone forever. Or so I thought.

"I continued to have experiences in college that confirmed for me that I wasn't likeable. The nastiest kid alive was my roommate as a freshman in college. Let's just say that living with a sadistic psychopath for an entire year in a room the size of a shoe box did nothing positive for my sense of self-worth. My mental health was seriously injured quite a few times at a very formative stage of my young adult life. As I retreated further and further from my open and happy essential self as a means of protection, I became unrecognizable to myself."

*I love hearing details about Earnest's life. I want to cuddle him and make him feel better. It's okay, you sweet, sexy man. I'm here for you.*

"Put your notebooks away. Sit quietly and close your eyes." Earnest spoke slowly, pausing between each sentence. "Create a mental image of your younger self. Remember some of the delightful qualities you had when you were younger that you might have rejected when you were hurt.

"Concentrate on her. Love her. Accept all of her. Accept her failures. Accept how she looks. Smile at each other. Embrace and merge together. Together as a team, you're more joyful and powerful. Enjoy this time together."

*There I was, that awkward, chubby kid with the feathered hair, ugly glasses, and crooked teeth. I get it: that awkward kid is still sitting on my shoulder wherever I go. I can see how embarrassed I am by that part of myself.*

I smiled at her. I hugged her. *I'm sorry, honey. You're okay just the way you are. I love you.* I felt tears roll down my face. Part of me felt ridiculous for falling wholly into Earnest's spiel, but I felt the exercise working. I felt whole and strong and accepting of the most gawky, embarrassing part of myself.

When I opened my eyes, Earnest was looking at me. *What is that look?* I glanced at the bulge in his pants. He was looking at me with desire.

*This is amazing. I can't believe he wants me. I've never been so turned on by a man in my life.*

At the end of class, I wanted to run from the room and hide, but Earnest said, "Kelly, I'd like to see you for a moment." The rest of the women filed out, some shooting jealous glances over their shoulders as they departed.

When it was just the two of us, Earnest said, "Kelly, I noticed you seemed moved by the exercise. I'd love to hear what's happening with you."

My mind swirled with details. I stammered, "I'm not sure where to start. I…" I took a deep breath and blew it out while Earnest stood looking at me patiently but expectantly.

"Go on," he said.

"I got fired this week, which is *huge* obviously, and I decided I want to be a writer. And I also realized that I'm carrying a lot of shame and…I guess feelings of unworthiness around with me. I found my old report cards and all these awful feelings of stress and pressure came back, and it was pretty relevant to your lecture tonight. I never realized it before, but I feel unworthy. Like, all the time. And I want to be a writer, but what if I'm not worthy?"

Earnest gathered me to him and pressed my head to his chest. He rubbed my back while he hugged me and said, "There, there. You're going to be okay."

I wanted to laugh. I wasn't exactly feeling overwhelmed with emotion in that moment, so I found it exceedingly funny that Earnest was trying to comfort me. But I also loved that Earnest was paying attention to me. *He smells so good. I could settle in here with my face on his chest forever.*

To my disappointment, he grabbed me by the shoulders and placed me back at a respectable distance. He said, "So you've lost everything, and now you have everything to gain. No job. This is the best thing that's ever happened to you. Now you need to drop your ego."

I felt a rush of anger. "I'm sorry, ego? Ego is hardly my problem!"

Earnest looked bemused as he said, "No, no. Not ego like you're used to hearing it. Your ego is the part of you that worries about what everyone else thinks and what everyone else is doing. Your ego is wrapped up in judgment. It's judging you, by your accounts, quite harshly and frequently.

"To drop the ego means to move into the role of the Witness. You can step outside of these thoughts and feelings of unworthiness and observe them. Don't judge the thoughts as bad, or then you're slipping right back into ego. Instead, say, 'Huh. Look at that. It's happening again.' Simply watch. That's where your freedom lies."

"My freedom? I don't understand."

"Imagine someone who goes ahead and does what she wants—let's say she wants to become a writer, like you. Her ego fears judgment. It's a natural human tendency. The ego isn't all bad; it prevents us from leaving the house wearing nothing but rain boots, a tutu, and suspenders."

I giggled while Earnest continued, "So this writer is afraid that people won't like what she writes. But freedom awaits her when she understands a few things: that everyone is afraid of what others think; that she can feel this feeling of fear and she can write anyway; and that she can see her fearful thoughts from a distance and look at them practically without engaging with the thoughts or believing them. There's no lion out there that's going to eat her. She might have an odd fear or a feeling like she shouldn't be writing, but she can observe that feeling and choose to dismiss it and she can write anyway. It's when we start believing everything we think that our lives circle the drain."

I smiled broadly. "This makes perfect sense. Thank you."

"I'm glad. Kelly, I would love to take you out to dinner."

"Oh!" I said in surprise. "Oh, that would be great. Nice. Very nice. Thank you. Yes. Please. Thanks. I would like that." *Dork, dork, dork, shut up!*

"Fantastic. I will have my assistant call you to schedule our date."

# CHAPTER TEN

On my way home, I was freaking out, in a good way. For the first time in my life, I understood the cliché feeling of floating on air after a romantic encounter. I was floating above all my petty concerns about career and money and what people thought of me, because, OH MY GOD, EARNEST ASKED ME ON A DATE! I was mentally punching the air with glee.

I could hardly contain myself, so I texted Amy: "Is it okay if I stop by the bar?"

She texted back: "Go for it. FYI, Sandy is here keeping me company."

That was perfect. I couldn't wait to tell Sandy that Earnest asked me out. *She's going to be shocked!*

When I arrived at the bar, I was grinning from ear to ear. Amy immediately picked up on it and said, "Well, well, you look like the cat who ate the canary. What's up?"

Sandy greeted me with an air kiss and said, "Amy told me you were pretty upset about losing your job. I'm glad you recovered so quickly!"

I laughed. "Yeah, I was pretty upset until after Earnest's class tonight."

Sandy said, "Oh my gosh, I remember having so many mental breakthroughs, especially the first time I took his class. You must have had a big aha tonight. What was it?"

I tried to suppress my smile, but there was no point. I burst out, "Earnest asked me for a date!" I waited for Sandy to squeal with glee and jump up and down while she hugged me, but instead she stayed very still, except for her jaw, which I was going to have to pick up off the floor if she didn't close her mouth soon.

Amy sat there looking from Sandy to me, not saying anything. As the silence grew more awkward, I said, "Geez, don't everybody congratulate me at once."

Sandy closed her mouth, and I could tell she was gathering her thoughts before speaking. I waited. She said, "I didn't expect this so soon."

"So soon?" *What on earth could she mean? Did Earnest tell Sandy he likes me? Did she know he was going to ask me out?*

"I wasn't going to say anything, but obviously I have to now." Sandy looked uncomfortable and like she was forcing herself to say the words. "Earnest is always dating his students. He usually waits, though, until the class is farther along and his students have a grasp on the concepts, and…" Sandy trailed off.

"And what?" I asked.

"And almost everyone has lost quite a bit of weight."

My face burned. "Oh. So you're surprised he asked me out because I'm still fat?"

"No, no, Kelly, I didn't mean that. It's just that I should have warned you sooner."

"Warned me?"

"About Earnest, that he…he's kind of a manwhore."

"Oh. Well. I like him," I said, my voice breaking. I fought back tears.

"Of course you do, Kelly. Earnest is dashing. He's handsome. He's exciting. But he's constantly dating multiple students of his, whether they're current students or former."

I felt a sudden stab of jealousy. "Did you ever date him?"

"No. He never asked me. I probably would have if he did, but now that I've heard the stories and seen so many people get hurt, I'm glad I didn't have the chance to date him. I know it wouldn't have ended well."

I imagined myself brokenhearted after Earnest was done with me, and I felt defiant. "I don't care. He asked me to dinner, and I'm going."

"I don't blame you, Kelly, but don't fall for him."

*Too late.* I forced a fake smile and said, "Thanks for warning me."

Amy said, "Now you look like you need a cocktail. How about a pumpkin martini? I've been perfecting my recipe. It tastes exactly like pumpkin pie."

"Sure, that sounds great," I said.

As Amy mixed up the martini, my mind was spinning. *Sandy's jealous that Earnest asked me out and not her. I hate that she rained on my parade. I was so incredibly happy only a minute ago, and now my stomach hurts. Why can't they be happy for me? A hot, incredibly compelling man with a sexy accent just asked me on a date! All I want is for Sandy and Amy to celebrate with me.*

Amy placed the drink in front of me. I slurped at the rim of the glass and thought glumly, *I'm going to celebrate. I'm going to feel as happy as I want about this. I don't need no stinking warning. Thanks but no thanks.*

Sandy said, "I'm sorry, Kelly."

"No, you're fine," I snapped. I didn't want to sound hurt, but I couldn't help it. I took another sip of the martini and said to Amy, "I think you've outdone yourself on this one. It really does taste like pumpkin pie."

Sandy said, "Okay, well. I'm going to head home. I've got an early morning yoga class. Thanks for the water, Amy!"

"Don't mention it. Have a great night," said Amy, as she leaned across the bar and kissed Sandy on the cheek.

Sandy looked sheepish as she raised her hand in a quick wave at me. "Bye, Kelly. I really am sorry."

"I know you are," I said, a little softer this time.

A rush of cool air blew past me as Sandy left the bar. I shivered.

"Man, fall is blowing in quick, isn't it?" asked Amy.

I was grateful for the change of topic. "Yeah, I need to get some new long-sleeved tops. Everything from last year is too small," I admitted. I looked down at my gut and sighed. Then I tossed back the rest of the sugary-sweet martini.

"Do you want another one?"

"No thanks, Amy. I need to think through some things alone. I wanted to feel happy and excited for my date, and well, now I want to try and forget everything Sandy said. I'm going to head home."

"Okay, but let me know if you need to talk about stuff. I'm here for you."

*Good old Amy. Lord knows I helped her through quite a few broken hearts, so I guess she owes me one. But I don't want to believe that things with Earnest are going to happen that way.* On that day at least, ignorance was bliss. "Thanks, Amy, I appreciate it. I'm gonna go now. Gimme a kiss." Amy gave me a loud, exaggerated, smacking kiss on the cheek. I laughed. "Thanks!"

"All right, take care of yourself."

I didn't like what her words implied, but I said, "I will."

On my way home, my body tensed up against the cool breeze and I tried to pull my paper-thin sweater closed around my neck. My head felt indescribably awful with, not a headache exactly, but tortured nonetheless with everything Sandy had said about Earnest. *I want so badly to forget.*

I passed a brightly lit store with both neon and handwritten signs in the window. I glanced up and read: *Get ready! Beaujolais Nouveau Day is coming soon!*

*Mmm, wine. Yes. This is what I want.* My step became lighter as I entered the shop.

I was greeted by a smiling, frizzy-haired older woman who asked, "Can I help you find something?"

"I'm looking for a nice pinot noir, something easy to drink." The whining vocals of the song "Red Red Wine" played in my head, and I smiled to myself. The sales clerk led me down the narrow aisle to the reds. I selected a cheap (*unassuming,* a wine snob might call it) bottle.

As the clerk ushered me to the cashier to pay, the little voice in my head asked, *Are you sure you want to bring that home with you?* I shook off the question and pulled out my wallet. As I walked home, the voice prodded me again with a tiny bit of doubt, but I only gripped the paper bag tighter around the neck of the wine bottle.

When I got home, I felt uneasy as I opened the door to my dark apartment. I quickly flipped on all the lights to dispel the shadows. I walked the few short paces to my tiny kitchen and placed the bottle on the counter.

I opened the drawer that held the corkscrew. When I didn't see it right away, I peeled the paper down from around the bottle and noticed a screw cap. *Brilliant.* I felt the satisfying click of the cap release beneath my hand.

I grabbed a gleaming wine glass out of the cabinet. I tilted the bottle while I watched the dark-ruby wine swirl into the glass. I took a whiff. *Heaven.* Then I took a sip.

*Does wine really taste good? I mean, sort of, and of course I really do love the taste. But if I were an alien from outer space and I visited planet Earth without understanding all the pretension and affectations that Earthlings have when it comes to rotten grapes, I would think we've all gone mad. If an alien compared the taste of wine to fresh-squeezed lemonade, wine basically tastes like ass.*

I placed my glass on the end table next to my easy chair while I rooted around in my messenger bag for my journal. The heavy feeling that had been hurting my head lifted as I remembered Earnest's words to me: *I might be afraid to write, but I can do it anyway. I don't need to worry about what other people think of me. And I don't need to worry about what Sandy thinks of Earnest. I like him, and that's all that matters.*

I sat down and opened my journal to the first clean page. I took a sip of wine and uncapped my pen. I stared at the blank page and waited. I knew what I wanted to write. A short story, a little bit of fiction. I hesitated. *What's the point?*

I repeated Earnest's message: *Write. Do it anyway.* I put my pen to paper and the words flowed.

*I was sitting in my recliner with a saucy plate of pasta in my lap, mindlessly shoveling twirled forkfuls into my mouth, when my carb-trance was broken by a knock at the door. I put my fork down and debated. Should I answer it? The knock came again, more insistently this time.*

*I picked up the plate and lowered the footrest of my chair so I could place the plate on the coffee table. Then I grabbed a napkin and checked my reflection in the mirror. I wiped the sauce from my face and chest and balled the napkin in my hand before answering the door.*

*He was gorgeous. Long, dark hair fell about his shoulders. His dark eyes locked with mine, and he didn't say a word as he advanced into my apartment. He grabbed me with one arm and shut the door with the other. I melted into his firm embrace as his warm, moist mouth closed over mine.*

*I felt his kiss in my loins . . .*

*Moist mouth? I felt his kiss in my loins? Eeeeewwwww. And the whole pasta thing is gross anyway. But this is just for me. I need to write. I have to start somewhere, and I will get better with practice. And no one ever needs to see it except me.* I took another sip of wine and kept writing.

An hour passed, and then another. As time flowed by, I was enraptured with this practice of putting a story to paper, no matter how weird or silly. As the wine bottle got closer to empty, I felt more euphoric and manic. *I'm a writer! I might even be good!*

I was incredibly proud of myself. I wondered, *How many people actually get out of their own way and allow themselves to be creative? Not many, and I'm one of them.* My ego, in the traditional sense, was soaring.

*I don't even need to worry about whether I'm drinking or not drinking. Maybe a glass of wine while I write is exactly what I need. Maybe it's helping me be creative. I don't know, and I don't care. I don't want any more criticism, shame, or negativity to weigh me down. I want to feel proud of myself for once in my life.*

As I attempted to cling to this rare high, that familiar feeling of doubt came creeping back, and I shifted into my standard level of anxiety. *How am I going to make money? Should I really be spending hours on end writing when I don't even have a job?*

*Maybe I should start blogging. I could get a designer to make a really cute website, and—oh great, genius, put your weird stories out there so everyone can know what a freak you are. And how could you think about spending money on this silly hobby when you don't even have a job?*

As my mood fell further and faster, I couldn't think clearly. I had the sensation that I needed to sort out my life and my options for making money, but my brain felt like wet cement. *I need to get some sleep. Maybe it will all make sense in the morning.* I shoved the empty wine bottle into the recycling bin, placed my glass in the sink, and went to bed.

★

When I woke up the next morning, I felt confused at first, like I was forgetting something. *Was it a dream?* I searched my mind for what happened, and the disorientation was replaced with a rush of memories and a mess of emotions.

My mood soared as I remembered that Earnest asked me out on date, and then crashed as I pictured Sandy saying, "…well, he's kind of a manwhore." Then my feelings rose again as I remembered writing for hours, and then the swell crashed back into a pit as I remembered I don't have a job and I had zero idea of what I was going to do next.

I tried to comfort myself. *But you have so much money saved up!* The voice of reason—or voice of doom—answered, *Yeah, but your rent is over two grand a month! It won't be long before your stash of cash is totally decimated if you don't get a job.*

I dragged myself out of bed and got into the shower. I needed to clear the brain fog. I felt confused again as I wondered, *Why do I feel so foggy?* Then the bottle of red wine, accompanied by the song "Red Red Wine," once again played in my head. *Oh yeah. I drank a whole bottle of wine. Well, that was unnecessary,* I scolded myself.

As I washed my hair, I heard the phone ring. My heart thudded as I tried desperately to rinse the shampoo from my eyes. *What if it's Earnest calling? Come on, rinse, damn it!* I willed my weak shower spray to disperse the suds faster. I gave up as I realized there was no way I was going to make it to the phone in time.

*It's okay. It's best not to seem so eager. If that's really Earnest calling, it's better that he gets my voice mail. He'll think I'm busy. This is a good thing.*

*Wait a minute. Earnest said his assistant would call to schedule the date. What if she doesn't leave a voice mail? What if she crosses it off the list that she called me? What if she doesn't schedule the date and then it doesn't happen and I see Earnest at the next class and he changes his mind and then this whole thing goes away and I never get to have dinner with the man of my dreams?*

*Okay, deep breaths, calm down. You're being ridiculous.* But I still finished the shower as quickly as possible and then barely dried myself off before running to the living room to check my phone. My hands shook as I fumbled with the buttons. *Missed call and a voice mail from…my heart sank. Sandy. Oh, that's just fucking perfect.*

I sighed as I put the phone to my ear and listened to her message. I softened a bit as I heard the tone of regret in her voice. "Hi, Kelly, it's me, Sandy. Look, I want to apologize for yesterday. It was out of line for me to share that, and you know, things could be different. It's been a while since I've seen Earnest, and it's best to give people the benefit of the doubt. I'd love to make it up to you, but the only thing I have to offer is free coaching. So I hope you take me up on it. Give me a call, okay? Okay, thanks, bye."

*Free coaching. Actually, that's exactly what I need. I know she's supposed to be a health coach, but maybe Sandy can help me figure out my next move careerwise. I don't want to discuss the whole Earnest thing with her again, but I'm definitely willing to ask her advice on making money.*

I called her back, and she sounded relieved that I was willing to meet up with her. She asked me to come to her apartment that afternoon.

# CHAPTER ELEVEN

As I rode the M15 bus up First Avenue to Sandy's apartment on the Upper East Side later that day, I tried to imagine how our conversation would go. *I want to keep it strictly career related. I won't hear another word about Earnest. I don't even want to hear another apology.*

*But what if Earnest's assistant calls to schedule the date while I'm with Sandy? I will say firmly to Sandy that the call is about a private matter and I'll take it in another room. I won't tell Sandy who called.*

*Or maybe I should lie and say it's my mom calling. No, no, then she's going to think the only person who calls me is my mom and who takes a call from her mom in the other room while she's with a friend? No, I can't say it's my mom! She'll think I'm a loser. I'll just say it's private.*

When I got off the bus, I felt a leap of excitement in my belly. *Sandy is going to help me figure out how to make money!* I suddenly couldn't wait to hear what she'd say as she buzzed me in to the building and I tromped up the stinky old stairwell to her apartment.

Sandy smiled at me as I came down the dark and narrow hallway toward her front door. "I'm so glad you could come! Please come in."

Sandy ushered me past the threshold, closed the door behind me, and enveloped me in a warm hug. I stiffened suddenly, waiting for her to apologize again about the Earnest thing, but she didn't bring it up. She gestured at her espresso-colored, rustic, beat-up kitchen table and said, "Have a seat. Here, let me get you a glass of water."

I got as comfortable as I could in the hard chair and gratefully accepted the glass. I pulled my journal and pen out of my bag and waited as Sandy poured herself a glass of water and sat down next to me.

I said, "I'm not sure where to begin or how this really works…"

Sandy held up her hand and said, "Don't worry, I'll lead the way. I see you brought your journal, that's perfect. You can open it up and start on a clean page. I'm going to ask you some questions, and I want you to write down the first thing that comes to mind. Don't think too hard, okay? Ready?"

I nodded with my notebook open and my pen poised in my hand.

Sandy asked, "What beliefs do you have that you think are holding you back?"

"What do you mean?"

"We all have limiting beliefs. Like one might be, 'I'm too old.' Or 'I don't know how,' or whatever. It's the discouraging stuff we say to ourselves. I mean, there's a reason we do that. It's because change is scary, and it's scary to put ourselves out there and take risks. So we all make up these stories about why we shouldn't try or why it's a waste of time, or how we shouldn't bother making an effort when it won't amount to anything. That sort of stuff. What kind of things do you tell yourself?"

"I'm not sure. I guess I think, 'Why should I bother getting another job when I know I'm going to hate it?' I hate feeling trapped in an office all day. And I hate feeling how my livelihood is in someone else's hands. I want to have more control over my own income and time. I really don't want to ever get fired again. That was the worst feeling in the world."

Sandy nodded. "Okay now we're getting somewhere. These aren't actually limiting beliefs, but these are really important preferences you have. It's important to know what you want and what you don't want. So you don't want another office job. And you want to control your own income and time, meaning you want to start your own business?"

"Not my own business, exactly, but I want to be my own boss. Like you. You're a coach. You don't have to go to an office, and you get to name your rates and choose your clients."

Sandy laughed. "Sometimes my clients choose me rather than the other way around, and there are some people I'd really like to work with who don't want to hire me. But yeah, for the most part, I've got a pretty sweet gig. But I do have to let you in on one secret. I don't make a living yet as a coach. I'm actually a freelance production assistant as my main way to bring in money."

"What's a production assistant, exactly?"

"They do all sorts of things, but I work for a company that makes commercials for the Internet. You know how when you're watching a video on YouTube, and you have to suffer through a thirty-second advertisement? Well, I help out on commercial video shoots doing whatever the higher-ups, like the executive producers or the directors, need. Sometimes it's crap like going on a coffee run, and sometimes it's more fun, like scouting out sets or booking talent."

"That would be a cool job. You probably get to be on all kinds of sets and locations and meet all different kinds of people, and you work with actors…that's something I could do. Are there any openings that you know of?"

"Right now we're looking for someone to host a series of videos for Tast-ee brand plastic wrap. It's going to be like a fake cooking show, and the host will demonstrate how to prep food ahead of time. She'll use Tast-ee Wrap to package everything up for the fridge and freezer."

"Oh, I could totally do that." I laughed. "Throw some food around and wrap it up? That's a dream job right there."

Sandy got a faraway look in her eye. She said slowly, "Yeah. Your dream job. You know what? I'm going to put in a good word for you."

"What? No. Wait, really? Are you kidding me? *Me?* But I'm so…" I wanted to say fat, but I didn't dare insult myself so horribly out in the open. Sandy would call it a limiting belief, and I'd have to pretend I didn't mean it, so instead I said, "Inexperienced."

Sandy said, "That's actually what makes you appealing. They're having huge budget problems on the shoot because they blew all their money creating this amazing kitchen set and buying all this cooking equipment, and now there's next to nothing left to pay for talent. Sorry, I know you came here looking for ways to make money, and this isn't exactly lucrative, although…"

I felt a surge of excitement. "Sandy, that would be amazing."

Sandy said, "I'll see what I can do. If you get this job for such a well-known brand, then you could have a reel created and you might be able to get more commercial work. So maybe it's a good way to get your foot in the door."

"Wow, this is so unexpected. I came here thinking I was going to talk to you about my dream of being a writer, but this is way better."

"Oh, you want to be a writer?"

"Yeah. I've always wanted to be a writer."

"I don't mean to distract you with this video stuff then, let's stay focused on how you can become a writer."

"No, no, the video stuff sounds really exciting! I would get to be on camera! That's the coolest. I could wind up with fans! And my mom would definitely have something to brag about, her daughter the TV chef, or Internet commercial chef, really, but whatever. It would be such a nice change to get in front of the camera. I've never done anything as glamorous as that before. I wonder if they would have a professional makeup person do my face? And what about wardrobe? They could pick out something flattering for me to wear. That would be awesome."

Sandy looked uncomfortable. "First of all, we don't have budget for stuff like makeup and wardrobe, but also, didn't Earnest talk about how we shouldn't chase careers or activities because of how we'll look to other people?"

I could feel my ego deflating a smidge. "Yeah, he talked about that a lot. But let me try this out. What if I'm good at it and I like it? Regardless of what other people think. It can't hurt to try."

Sandy smiled and relaxed and said, "Yeah, you're right. It can't hurt to try; I'll see what I can do. But let's get back to limiting beliefs. I want to give you some more perspective so you know where we're going with the exercise. Whatever you don't like about your life right now is a result of your thoughts. What you believe influences what you think about all day long. And what you think about all day long influences your actions. And of course when we act a certain way consistently over time, then that's how we build our life. So let's come at this backwards. What do you hate the most about your life?"

"My weight. Definitely my body. I'm so tired of being heavy. I hope the Earnest stuff helps me, but I'm still eating and drinking too much." I blushed as I admitted, "I drank a whole bottle of wine last night. By myself."

Sandy didn't even flinch. She said, "Look, I've been there. I bet you didn't know I used to be really unhealthy and overweight."

"You did? Really?"

"Yup. And I used to drink a lot too. Now I only have a glass of champagne at really special occasions, like a wedding once in a great while, and that's it."

"Wow, how did you do it? I mean, change your habits and lose weight and everything."

"I changed the way I think because I realized that I had all these limiting beliefs. Here, I'll get out my notebook and you can see how my thinking changed." Sandy walked her perfectly adorable little legs over to her bookshelf, grabbed an old journal, and opened it on the table in front of me.

She rifled through the pages and then pointed to a page and said, "See? I made these columns and rows of what I expected—which is how my life was in the first column—and the thoughts, attitudes, and beliefs that got me there. Here, read it. This is what my life was like."

As I examined the page, I could hardly believe that pixie-like little Sandy could have thought this way.

| EXPECTATIONS | THOUGHTS | ATTITUDES | BELIEFS |
|---|---|---|---|
| Fat | I can't/don't want to quit | Lazy | I can't. |
| Unhealthy | It's okay to be fat. | Closed-minded | Too hard. |
| Broke | Money is such a struggle. | Whiney | Why bother? |
| Bored | How will I fill the afternoons? | Ungrateful | Wine is it. |
| Struggle | I can't plan and cook dinners. | Confused | Not worth it. |
| Overwhelmed | There aren't enough hours. | Impulsive | No time. |

WHAT I'VE GOTTEN OUT OF THIS:

× Fattest EVER: 197 pounds on the scale yesterday! I saw my reflection in a store window...I am BIG. No way to hide it. Numb feet. Don't feel well.

× Under-earning! Leaving money on the table!!!

× Lame afternoons...I could be shopping and cooking every day!!! I could look up a recipe and go cook it instead of wasting all my money on wine, junk food, and takeout.

× Fog. Confusion. Grain brain. Too much sugar. Wine too often.

× If I would stop wasting money, then I could use it to complete my coach training certification and then I could make more money.

She said, "This exercise is what really sparked the turnaround in my life. It was the second time I took his class. The first time I took it, honestly, I wasn't acting on what I knew. I was still self-sabotaging, and I couldn't figure out why. But then Earnest talked to me privately about limiting beliefs. I mean, I'd heard of them so many times before, but when I wrote down everything I was thinking and feeling about myself and my life, then it made perfect sense why I would act that way. And I saw the pain I was causing myself. I had to stop blaming other people or circumstances for what I was actually responsible for."

She turned the page. With only the slightest glance at the next sheet of paper, I could see the Sandy I knew in the words she'd written there. I said, "Wow, you really liked exclamation points. How did you go from *that* to *this*?"

"I was so sick of myself by the time I did this exercise that I was really motivated to change. I was ready. My life was going nowhere, and I felt so fat and unhealthy that I was afraid I was on the brink of a health crisis. I was beyond even caring that I felt unattractive—I was scared half to death of cancer or a stroke.

"And frankly, my finances were so bad that I was starting to think fighting for my life would be a nice distraction, which is, you know, pretty sad. But the thing is, right under the surface I had this feeling of hope, this feeling that I knew I could turn everything around. I needed to change how I was thinking and what I expected of myself. So then I wrote down what I knew could be true for me if I really wanted it to be."

The page was set up the same way, but the picture it painted was vastly different.

| EXPECTATIONS | THOUGHTS | ATTITUDES | BELIEFS |
|---|---|---|---|
| Winning! | I can do this! | Joyful!! | I can! |
| Fit! | I want to do this! | Enthusiastic! | This is doable. |
| Healthy! | I will be fit and fabulous! | Grateful! | It will pay off. |
| Clear-minded! | Cook dinner every afternoon. | Excited! | This is fun! |
| Joyful! | There's enough time. | Happy! | I choose wisely. |
| Consistent money! | I can create a schedule that works! | Hopeful! | I'm smart. |

WHAT I WILL GET OUT OF THIS CHANGE:
×   Enthusiasm for life, a great attitude, and happiness.
×   I will draw people and opportunities to me, and I'll attract good things when I feel good.
×   I will get my health back, and I will have unlimited energy to do everything I want to do.
×   I will learn how to cook healthy meals so I can save money and get healthy.
×   I will choose my daily activities based on what I want my future to be like.
×   I will make more money by working consistent hours.
×   I will stick to a schedule that will include exercise, my production assistant job, coach training (and eventually coaching clients), grocery shopping, and cooking dinner every day.

I stood there staring at the paper for a long time. Sandy had pretty much started out where I was at that moment. I was fat, unhappy about it, worried about money, and I had no daily routine or schedule to speak of, except maybe one that revolved around eating and drinking crap.

She'd been one step ahead of me, though. I was so deep in the habit of eating out at restaurants that it never even occurred to me that I should cook my own dinner. *Maybe I should think about it. Oh, but I love restaurants. Damn it.*

Sandy broke the silence. "What are you thinking? Does it make sense to you?"

"Yeah, but I guess I'm not clear on how writing all of this stuff down would get you to magically start taking action and turn your life around. It seems like kind of a leap. Am I missing something?"

"It's the emotions involved. So while you're looking at this, you might feel like you relate to some of it or that you understand what I wrote on a logical level, but when you do the exercise yourself, in order for it to be effective, you have to really get into the emotions of feeling dissatisfied with your life.

"You also have to have an understanding of how you caused the problems, and how you could fix the problems. It's about feeling the pain of the status quo at the same time that you feel exhilarated that you can take back the reins. You have to let yourself know deep down that you can actually have a massive, positive effect on your own life. It's all about taking responsibility for why things are the way they are now, and taking responsibility for how your life will be different when you make the effort."

"I feel so stuck, though. I can't imagine having so much hope that I actually get excited. I've tried to change so many times, but nothing seems to work. Like this job thing. You can't tell me I'm responsible for becoming unemployed. Sometimes shit happens."

"Look, I hear you and I've been there. So much of our issues are blamed on circumstances outside of us, but we can't fix our lives if we're unwilling to be responsible for ourselves. If there's anything I've learned from coaching, it's that people hate being accountable for their problems. It's like their ego is on the line if they had to admit that anything is their fault.

"But you can never live the life of your dreams if you don't hold yourself accountable. If you don't take responsibility for yourself, then you give all your power away. Sure, you might get to feel better temporarily when you point fingers for the way things are, but you're still left with a messy life."

She was getting really excited now. She went on, "Most of us walk around in a haze thinking that we don't have control over anything, and we feel like our problems landed in our laps. But your life is an accumulation of past choices and beliefs and emotions that you cultivated over time.

"You have to realize that you can create your future, starting right now, based on what you're going to think about, how you're going to act, what you choose to believe, and what attitudes you choose for yourself.

"You can steer how you spend your time little by little so you can slowly move your life in the direction you want to go. As change takes hold, it becomes clear that you're the one driving the bus. You start to see proof that you're in charge of your life.

"No matter what's happened to you in the past, you can understand that right now it's your choice whether to manage your life well or not. There's something thrilling in that, in giving yourself permission, in handing yourself the power. Rather than always defaulting to 'I can't,' or 'It's not worth it,' or 'It's too hard.'"

While I appreciated Sandy's impassioned speech and I agreed with everything she was saying, I felt slightly defensive. *This is all my fault? Really? Well, yeah. She's right. I sat in a job I hated for ten years instead of finding a career I felt passionate about, or at least finding people I liked working with. I'm the one who chose to be upset instead of happy when I got canned, even though it didn't feel like much of a choice. I'm the one who was choosing wine and noodles and ice cream at every turn. While I hate to admit it, she's right about all of this. The choice is mine: remain unhappy with my life, or take responsibility for it and clean it up.*

Sandy looked at her watch and said, "Oh, jeez! It's almost time for my next coaching appointment. I'm so sorry, Kelly! The time flew by. I have to get going. I'm meeting my client at her office in Midtown."

I gathered my notebook and bag and said, "Okay, no problem. Thanks so much for the session, Sandy. I learned a lot."

"My pleasure, Kelly! I'm so glad you came." She strode toward the door and said, "Here, I can walk you out."

As we descended the uneven stairs of her apartment building, my mind swirled with everything we'd talked about. I felt a little wave of excitement when I thought about the on-camera job. When we reached the sidewalk, I said, "Sandy, thank you so much for helping me, and also for looking into the Tast-ee plastic wrap gig for me." *I don't want her to forget about that.*

"No worries. We'll have an answer for you soon because the shoot is supposed to start in a few days. What's your schedule like this week?"

I grinned from ear to ear. "Free as a bird. I'll wait for you to call me."

She squeezed me in a warm embrace and said, "Great, Kelly. Have an awesome day!" Then she turned and bounced down the street. I stood and watched her vibrant, tiny figure until she was out of sight.

Just then my phone rang. I hoped with all my might that the caller would be Earnest. My heart hammered in my chest as I answered, "Hello?"

"This is Earnest's assistant, Bernadette. I'm calling for Kelly Ryan."

I tried to sound cool and calm as I said, "This is she."

"Kelly, Earnest would like me to schedule dinner for the two of you. How's Saturday following that evening's Ducklings to Swans session?"

"Perfect! That's great. Okay. Yes. I'll put it on my calendar. Thank you so much for calling."

"No problem. Have fun."

"Oh, I will! I can't wait! This is so exciting!" *Oh my God, what am I saying?* I slapped my forehead and cringed.

"Okay, bye now." I imagined Bernadette smirking at me over the phone.

*Oh my God, between the possibility of this Tast-ee job and the date with Earnest, I can't stand the excitement. I am flipping out! I can tell Earnest all about the shoot on our date Saturday. He's going to be so impressed.* Even though it was a complete mess, my life had never felt so perfect.

# CHAPTER TWELVE

I spent the entire afternoon strolling the streets of New York while I fantasized about the days to come. A little part of me believed in *The Secret* and manifestation. I thought, *If I visualize the outcomes I want, I'll get them.* I imagined myself totally killing it during the video shoot. My hair, makeup, and outfit were perfect, and I was expertly jabbering away at the camera. My performance was so brilliant that the camera crew burst into wild applause at the end of the shoot day.

As I strolled past storefronts and restaurants, I could see Earnest in my mind's eye over our romantic, candlelit dinner. He held my hands across the table and hung on my every word as I told him about my burgeoning career as an actress.

In my fantasy, he knew immediately that I was a keeper and that he must woo me and cherish me forever. *Lest other men come and steal me away from him, because I'm such a highly desirable and successful actress. At the end of our date, he pulls me deftly into his arms and kisses me tenderly but passionately.*

Then I smelled bacon. I glanced in the window next to me and saw a man with his fork poised over his plate while he gulped his beer. I looked up at the sign over the restaurant and read: BarBacon. *Oh yeah. It's on.*

But then I remembered everything I'd been fantasizing about, and I thought, *Wait. Just for a few days, I need to reel it in. I don't want to be all bloated and enormous from chugging beer and eating salty bacon when I go out with Earnest. Oooh, I know! I can go on a crash diet and lose a few pounds so I feel slimmer for my date.*

*Yes, yes, yes! A crash diet!* I kind of loved crash diets, in a weird way. Every once in a while I would have some big event coming up where I wanted to look good, and so I would get super motivated to limit my intake and maybe even do a little exercise. And it would usually pay off, a little bit anyway. Of course once the event was over, I would gain it all back and then some.

I walked on and thought about my midtwenties, which was the last time I was at a healthy weight. *What was I eating and drinking back then? Well, I was broke for one thing, so I wasn't buying alcohol. I drank coffee for breakfast. I ate a normal meat-and-potatoes-type hot lunch in the cafeteria at work. And then dinner would be cheap eats that I made at home, maybe eggs and toast or a carefully measured two-ounce portion of pasta. I was hungry a lot. Man, was I broke!*

I remembered at age twenty-four, staring longingly at the frozen diet dinners in the grocery store and thinking they cost an outrageous sum for a single meal. *Now I'm easily paying three or four times that amount for every meal I eat in a restaurant. And I have no job. These restaurant meals must stop. Sandy's right. Cooking healthy dinners at home is where it's at. And then I can eat the leftovers for lunch.*

I could feel a plan coming together. I felt the weight and structure of my hardcover journal in my bag, and a burning need poured though me to get home and write out my diet plan for the next few days. I hopped on the nearest subway and rode downtown, wishing I could pull out my notebook on the crowded train to get started.

Once back at my apartment building, I skipped up the stairs two at time, only to arrive huffing and puffing at my door. The huffing and puffing went on for quite some time after I got inside. *Am I really this out of shape? Note to self: add exercise to the plan.*

When I was done jotting down my plan of virtuous deprivation, I decided to treat myself to a writing session. I opened my notebook to a blank page and stared into space. Then it hit me. *I'll write down my fantasy of how I want the next few days to go.*

*I'll shop for some cute dresses—one for the video shoot in case Sandy calls, and of course one to wear out with Earnest. Oh crap, wait. I can't wear a dress to Ducklings to Swans because we sit on the floor on our yoga mats, and a dress would look ridiculous.*

I frowned as I chewed my pen cap. *Most of the women wear yoga pants to the sessions, not that any of us actually practice yoga. All right, I'll have to figure out something cute to wear on my date that won't look silly or overdressed at class.*

*Okay, fantasy time.* I wrote out a highly detailed scenario for how I imagined the Tast-ee shoot going. I was the shining star on set, with all eyes on me as the lights blazed, with the scene culminating in the aforementioned wild applauding by the crew.

Next I wrote out my best date scenario with Earnest, which also ended with wild applauding by the restaurant staff as Earnest bent on one knee and pulled a ring box from his jacket. Even the cooks and the executive chef emerged from the kitchen to clap for us, which was a big deal because we were eating in a four-star restaurant and they were very busy. The next day, a photo of us would appear on Page Six, with the caption "Budding Actress and Guru to Wed" in bold beneath a shot of Earnest's proposal.

I was having such a great time writing that I decided to pen a few more short stories. I was proud that I was writing without a glass of wine to help my creativity. When I stopped for a break, it occurred to me that I could have a glass to reward my hard work. *No, no. Don't even go there.*

My mind strayed to what it would take to get myself a glass of wine. *I have a bottle in the fridge, but it's been open for a few days and I doubt it would taste very good. Good for me! I actually let a bottle of wine go bad. I can pat myself on the back while I pour it down the drain. I could go out and buy a bottle, but that's a bit of a hassle.* Then I remembered: *I want to look as good as I can for this date. No wine!*

Now that the thought of wine had entered, it was chewing at the corners of my brain. I wanted to escape that nagging feeling. I looked at the clock. *Is nine o'clock too early for bed?*

*A girl needs her beauty sleep. Might as well.* As my head hit the pillow that night, I wondered: *Am I escaping a craving with sleep, or am I actually tired? And am I a dysfunctional jackass, or am I on the verge of an amazing life?*

★

The next morning, I was awakened by the ring of my cell phone out in the living room. I threw back the covers and shuffled across the cold hardwood to where my phone sat on the counter. It was Sandy. I never thought I would be so excited to take a call from her.

"Hello?" I answered.

"Hi, Kelly, it's Sandy. Is this a good time?"

"Yes! Of course. What's going on? Did I get the part?"

"Yes! You did!" Sandy sounded almost as happy as I felt.

"Oh my God, oh my God, Sandy! This is so amazing! Thank you, thank you!"

"Hang on, there's only one catch."

"Okay." I took a deep breath and tried to slow my heartbeat. "I'm listening."

"The director said this is a big gamble and he'll only trust my judgment to a degree. They accepted you without a reel or headshot because it's a rush job and they're out of money, and so they agreed to take you on as kind of a trial. We're going to have you do a run-through of the script on camera tomorrow. Then the client, meaning the head honchos over at Tast-ee, will review the footage and offer their approval of you before we go any further. Does that sound okay?"

I felt only slightly deflated as I said, "Yeah, that's great. No problem."

"Okay, cool. The studio is on Broadway in Times Square. Meet me at my apartment tomorrow afternoon at one o'clock, and we can walk over to the shoot together. We start shooting at two."

"That all sounds perfect. Is there any way I can see the script before the shoot? I'd love to give it a read so I'm not going in cold." *I hope I sound like I'm using producer lingo. "Going in cold" seems like something a producer might say.*

"Sure, no problem. I'll e-mail it to you right now. You should do your best to learn the script really well, but you don't need to memorize it word for word. They're going to have cue cards for you on set to prompt you through it. They said the most important thing is to act perky. They want someone with really high energy. Do you think you can do that?"

"Oh, awesome. Yes, totally." *How hard could it be? It's only a thirty-second commercial.*

"See you tomorrow, Kelly."

"Thanks, Sandy. See you tomorrow."

The moment I placed my phone on the counter, my e-mail indicator binged. I went straight to my computer desk so I could print the script and read it over a cup of coffee. As I sat down in my easy chair with twenty sheets of paper containing the script, I felt myself starting to sweat. *Twenty pages? This is not thirty seconds' worth of copy. This is more like a full-length TV show. How is this possible?*

As I began to read, I felt horrified at the bumble-hick language they expected me to use.

"I'm Kelly Ryan with *Weeknight Dinners Made Easy*. Today I want to tell you about two big-batch recipes. The first recipe is roast chicken. Duh quote of the day: Chicken is versatile. Soups, salads, pasta, stir-fry—the world is your oyster! I should really say the 'world is your chicken' because you can do whatever you want with it." *Really? The world is your chicken? Oy vey.*

After reading the script through once, I decided to go out and buy myself something cute to wear on set. I took a quick shower, and then headed to Bloomingdale's. I figured their sales clerks would be the most helpful, unlike some of the snooty boutiques around my apartment. On my walk to the subway, I imagined a clerk asking, "Can I help you find something?"

"Oh yes," I'd say. "I need something for a video shoot. I'm doing a cooking show." *No, that's not right. She might steer me toward the aprons.* I would say, "Yes, I'm going to be on camera tomorrow. I'm acting in a commercial." *A commercial. Does that sound glamorous enough? Well, it is what it is.*

I was smiling like an idiot as I rode the escalator up to the dress section of the store. I thought, *I can't wait to say I need something to wear for my acting job,* as I wandered the racks and caressed the fine fabrics. A praying mantis–like clerk suddenly popped up from behind me and whipped the fabric of a dress out of my hand.

"Can I help you?" she hissed at me, her face twisted into an ugly snarl.

"Oh!" I stepped back. "I, I, yes, well, I need a dress," I said, as I gestured at the rack next to me. "There's a commercial, and I need to try some things on, and…"

"No! You can't try that on. You'll *tear* it. *Your* department is upstairs." She turned on her heel and marched away from me. Tears started to pool in my eyes, and I took deep breaths, willing myself to hold it together.

*Your* department? Whatever could she mean? I made my way back to the store directory that was posted next to the escalator. *Women's, one level up. This level is misses. Okay,* I seethed to myself, *first of all, I do fit into misses sizes. Secondly, I don't care if I'm bigger than anything they sell in the whole store—who does that ass-clown think she is, and where does she get off treating me like dirt?*

*Okay, calm down. Breathe. I don't know which I want more, a drink or a fight. It's funny how getting viciously shamed for my weight by a stranger makes me want a drink. Well, first I could punch her and then I could go to a bar for a post-knockout brewski.*

While I had a bone to pick, I also had a script to memorize. *I guess I was procrastinating with this whole dress shopping venture anyway. I have a blouse in my closet at home that I could wear with a black skirt. Sigh.* I stepped onto the escalator, rode back down, and then shuffled back out of the store and onto the sidewalk.

# CHAPTER THIRTEEN

I didn't feel like going back underground to the subway, so I walked to a downtown bus stop instead. Once on the M15 bus, I pulled out my phone and read over the script again: "Let's talk about make-ahead meal prep. Why? If you carve out a small block of time on the weekend to prepare some foods ahead, it's going to save you time and mess in the kitchen all week long. Your weeknights will be more like a barrel of monkeys and less like a bag of rattlesnakes." *Jesus. What?*

*How on earth am I going to sound natural saying that your weeknights won't be like a bag of rattlesnakes? Who talks like this?* I started to sweat again. I could see clearly now that I'd gone to Bloomingdale's because I didn't want to study the mess that was this script.

*You know what would make this way more fun to learn? A bottle of champagne. Damn, but I feel like I'm getting a cold. I don't want to drink today for several reasons, the biggest of which is my weight. And if I'm coming down with something, I have a better chance of staying healthy if I drink a lot of water instead of wine. It's settled. No drinks.*

*Uh-oh. I can feel my nose getting stuffy. And my throat feels scratchy. Can I do a commercial with a stuffy nose? Oh no. I'm doomed.* As the bus got closer to my apartment, I stared out the window, looking for a drug store. *I need the good stuff, stat.* I liked the kind of cold medicine that made me jumpy and high, like another person altogether. *It's the only stuff that keeps my nose clear and like I can get out of bed and function in the world. Even though it makes the world feel like an alternate universe.*

I saw Block Drug Stores, a tiny little store that's crowded up to the rafters with remedies. I pressed the stop indicator on the bus. I hopped down to the sidewalk and popped into the store to score my cold meds. Once back outside, clutching my white paper bag with the goods, I decided to walk the rest of the way home.

I hadn't gotten very far when, *Oh hey, would you look at that: Wine & Liquors. It couldn't do any harm to pop in and look, could it?* And before I knew it, I was back out on the sidewalk clutching a second paper bag, this one brown and containing a big, fat, one-and-a-half-liter bottle of chardonnay. *It's more economical that way*, I reasoned, feeling oddly virtuous about the decision.

*Why did I buy it? Just in case. I'm undertaking something big. It makes me feel more secure to have a ripcord at my fingertips. I don't have to drink it.*

When I got home, I took my cold medicine then sat down to study the script. "When you're through making your big-batch meals, portion them out, seal them up with Tast-ee plastic wrap, and store them in the fridge. Then when weeknight hassles come aknockin', you can blind them with chili and beat them over the head with delicious roast chicken." *What? No, seriously. WHAT?*

I looked up at the bottle of wine on the counter. Then I absentmindedly put it in the refrigerator. *Just tidying up.*

*Okay, let's get serious about this*, I thought. *I need to practice.* I stood at the kitchen counter and set my phone on its edge with the camera pointing at me. Then I hit record and practiced smiling and saying, "I'm Kelly Ryan with *Weeknight Dinners Made Easy.*"

Once I felt convincing at that, I decided to try longer and longer portions of the script, pausing between each take to review my work. I detected a crazy look in my eyes, no doubt a side-effect of the cold meds.

After a few hours, my sinuses and throat felt the benefits of the medicine wearing off. My on-camera persona became monotone and sluggish, as opposed to perky and smiley. I took another dose. The crazy eyes came back, but at least I appeared happy and energetic.

When I felt reasonably confident that I knew the script and that my performance was resonant of TV chefs and commercial actresses, I decided I deserved a break. It was dark outside, and I hadn't even noticed when the sun went down. I wanted to see Amy to catch her up on all the excitement of the last few days, so I walked up to the bar.

As I approached the door, I looked in the large, plate-glass window at the front of the bar. It was always a comforting sight to see Amy standing in a commanding position with her hands on the bar, warming the space with her inviting smile, always ready to take away all my cares and worries.

As I pushed open the door, she shouted, "Kelly! Where have you been?" She poured a glass of white wine and pushed it toward me as I walked in and sat down. *Oops. I wasn't going to drink today. Oh well.*

"I've got so much to tell you."

"Did you have your date with Earnest?"

"Not yet. That's Saturday night."

"What are you gonna wear?"

"I'll get to that in a minute. First, I've gotta tell you, Sandy got me an acting job!"

"An acting job! That's awesome!"

"Yeah, we're shooting a commercial for Tast-ee Wrap tomorrow. It's like a cooking show format. I went to Bloomingdale's today because I wanted to get a dress to wear, but the saleslady—get a load of this—wouldn't let me try on a dress. She said I would *tear* it."

"What the hell? What a bitch!"

"I know."

"So what did you do? I hope you told her manager."

"No, I left. I needed to study the script anyway."

"So, what are you gonna wear?"

"Ha, you keep asking me that."

"Come on, you gotta look the part."

"I'll pull something out of my closet."

"No, no, no. Let me help you. What time is the shoot?"

"I'm meeting Sandy at her apartment tomorrow at one and we're walking over to the studio together."

"Perfect. I'll meet you at your place tomorrow morning at ten, and we'll go to one of those cute little boutiques nearby. We'll get you something to wear to the shoot and for your date with Earnest."

"Amy, you're the best."

"My pleasure, sweetheart. You're gonna kick butt."

"Enough about me. What's new with you? How's Guillermo?"

"Oh, you know." Amy looked away.

"Are you guys finished?"

"No, it's not that. It's just that everything's still the same. We're not progressing. It's all booty calls and no dates."

"Ugh. Get rid of him. Who needs it, Amy? If it's making you feel bad…"

"Yeah, but I like him so much. I'm happy when I'm with him. We have the most amazing time."

"In bed."

"Yup. That's about it. I don't know. I keep thinking things are going to change."

"Then give him an ultimatum. Start taking you on dates, or you're outta here."

"No, I could never back it up. If he said no, I'd still stay. It's like I'm addicted to this guy."

"I've been there. That's tough."

"Change of subject! Toni came in here earlier. You just missed her, actually."

"Thank God."

"I can't believe you guys aren't talking. This is so weird to me."

"I know. It's weird for me too." As I said the words, I wasn't sure it was true. *I haven't been thinking about Toni. Toni was my voice of reason for years, and now all of a sudden she's out of my life. The only feeling I have about it is a sense of freedom. Like I'm suddenly free from a nagging mother figure. I can finally explore adulthood on my own.*

"I think the whole Jill thing is going south."

"What do you mean?" I was careful not to look too excited, but I was salivating for details.

"The shine of the relationship is wearing off."

I strained to sound casual as I sipped my wine. "How so?" *Gimme the goods.*

"Jill talks to Toni about all her clients, breaches patient confidentiality left and right. At first, Toni liked being her confidante. I think it made her feel important because Jill would unload and Toni felt like she was helping the therapist come up with solutions for her clients. But now it's starting to feel like one big gossip fest."

"That's gross." I felt smug.

"Yeah. Toni said that Jill feels so damn superior to all her clients. She revels in it."

"Ew." *I can so relate. I feel so damn superior to Jill right now.* I was reveling in this juicy bit of dirt. I took a big gulp of wine. "So what's Toni going to do?"

"Nothing, from what I can tell. At least not yet. She said that when Jill starts going off about her clients now, Toni tries to redirect the conversation onto something else. But she said Jill is like a dog with a pork chop about it. She won't let it go."

"I *knew* Jill was bad news."

"Yeah, and Toni is starting to get it."

I felt validated. *Maybe once Toni sees how nasty Jill is, she and I can go back to being friends. But for now, the rift between Toni and me is good for me. It's good for my boundaries. Maybe I'm making mistakes, but they're my mistakes, and I'll learn from them.*

The word *responsibility* rang in my ears from my conversation with Sandy.

*I can stop blaming everyone else if I screw up. These are my decisions, and mine alone. I feel good about owning my life.*

As I sucked down the last of my wine, Amy asked, "Want a refill?"

"No thanks. I better get some sleep. Big day tomorrow."

"Oh yeah! Your place, ten a.m. Let's shop!"

"Yes, let's. Thanks, Amy."

"No problem, see ya tomorrow."

★

The next morning, Amy came through for me. She held my hand in the stores, spoke for me to the clerks, confidently leafed through the racks, and came up with some brilliant outfits. She got me a simple, red, A-line dress for the shoot. For the date with Earnest, she picked out another A-line dress, but this one was a sexy black number with a keyhole neck line.

I'd protested the purchase of a dress for my date, explaining that it would happen immediately after class. Wearing that sexy dress to sit on the floor for the lecture would be wildly inappropriate. But Amy waved my concerns aside, stating that it was much more important to look sexy for my date than it was to look appropriate for class.

At the thought of Amy controlling my wardrobe choices, my mind asked tentatively, "Responsibility?" *Not right now*, I thought impatiently.

Back in my apartment, I put on the red dress so I could record a dress rehearsal on my camera phone. As I watched the video playback, I realized I looked flat and lifeless. *What's missing? Oh yeah, the crazy eyes.* I was feeling much better when I woke up in the morning, so I hadn't taken my cold meds.

I needed to be perky, so I popped some pills out of the blister pack and washed them down with a drink of water. About halfway through the next practice run, I felt myself coming back to life. The manic smile returned, and I felt like laughing and dancing my way through the script.

I looked at the clock. *One hour until I leave for Sandy's.* My heart began to pound as the reality of what I was about to do—stand in front of people and deliver a twenty-page script written for a deranged hillbilly—

hit me square in the chest. I tried to calm down by taking a few deep breaths, but I felt like I was going to hyperventilate.

*Oh my God, oh my God. I can't believe I'm doing this. Everyone is going to be looking at me.* I smoothed the front of my dress with my sweaty palms. *Do I look fat? What if I forget my lines? What if I deliver the lines just right, and they sound exactly as ridiculous as I think they do?*

*Hair! Makeup! I have one hour to glam myself up. Okay, fifty-five minutes after my mini panic attack.* I balanced my makeup bag on the teeny-tiny sink vanity in my dimly lit bathroom and peered into the mirror. I pulled my eyelid taut and attempted to apply eyeliner, but my hand was shaking. *Oh my God, I'm still freaking out.* I straightened up and looked at my shaky handiwork. *Yikes.*

*Okay, calm down. You can do this.* I picked up the eyeliner again and had a go at the other eye. I turned this way and that, trying to pretend it all looked passable. *Not a chance.* I pulled out some makeup remover wipes and tried to clean up the mess, but my hands started to shake so hard that I was poking myself in the eye.

I actually scared myself as I shouted at the mirror, "Oh my God, CALM DOWN!" *Um, that didn't help. Surprisingly.* As my heart continued to hammer in my chest, it dawned on me that my manic-happy cold-med pills might not be all sunshine and rainbows.

I left the bathroom and sat down in my easy chair. *Breathe. Breathe.* I caught another glimpse of the clock: *forty minutes left. Holy shit. I'm running out of time. And I can't stop panicking. What the fuck am I going to do?* My heart hammered harder. "Shhh. Shhhh. It's okay," I whispered to myself. "Let's figure this out."

*Ripcord. I'm going to pull the ripcord.*

I jumped up and practically ran to the refrigerator. My hands were still shaking as I jabbed the corkscrew into the bottle. I poured a small glass and took a sip. *Phew. That's better.* I carried the glass into the bathroom and set it on the back of the toilet. *There, that can keep me company while I do my makeup.*

As I sipped and painted my face, I could feel myself mellowing out. *Thank God. I'm going to be okay.* When I emerged from the bathroom, it was time to leave for Sandy's.

*Wait. Can I really leave my security blanket behind? That doesn't seem like such a good idea.*

The little voice said, "It's probably not a good idea to bring a bottle of wine to your job."

I silenced the voice while I put a pack of the red happy pills in my bag. *They want perky. Perky comes in pill form. But I can't go around freaking out and hyperventilating.* So I grabbed a large metal water bottle out of a kitchen cabinet and I filled it with wine.

*There. Problem solved.* My portable mood regulators were coming with me.

# CHAPTER FOURTEEN

On the walk over to the set with Sandy, I asked her, "Why's the script so long? I thought this was supposed to be a thirty-second spot."

"Oops, sorry. I totally forgot to explain that. The video is going on the Tast-ee Wrap website. It's more like an infomercial than a regular commercial."

*Who the heck is going to the Tast-ee Wrap website to watch an infomercial? No one is ever going to see my on-camera debut. I'm not sure whether that's comforting or a letdown.*

When we got to Times Square, I expected to make a grand entrance beneath flashing lights inside some majestic, marble lobby. Instead, Sandy brought me to a side entrance that led into a long, dark, concrete hallway. At the end of the hallway was a tiny, bulletproof glass window. Behind the window, which was lit with gleaming fluorescent lights, was a person-sized booth containing a security guard.

*I can't imagine sitting inside a vertical coffin all day long. I feel claustrophobic just thinking about it.* I wanted to ask the guard, "Are you okay in there? Can you breathe?"

Sandy instructed me to slide my ID across the counter, under the slit in the window. The guard checked my ID against a list of names and slid it back to me. Sandy flashed the badge hanging around her neck, and then we walked through a series of bleak corridors until we reached an elevator.

We rode up in the elevator in silence, facing forward, as people do. *That's weird. Why don't people talk in elevators? Why don't we face each other and have a conversation? Bing! Whoa. That was fast.* The doors opened.

*Walk, legs! Go, go, go. Catch Sandy. She's fast. Ha-ha. Wow. I feel weird. Act normal. Okay. I'll do my best! Heeeeeeeeeee.*

We entered the studio. The dark, back half of the room was covered in black soundproofing material. The front of the studio was brightly lit and contained the kitchen set, which was fantastically realistic, except for the tacky factor. No one in their right mind would decorate a kitchen to look like it came out of *Deranged-Hillbilly Kitschy-Kitchens Digest*.

I tried to act somber and cool as Sandy introduced me to the crew, most of whom were wired with headphones and carrying armfuls of cable. I nodded at each person, but their names and faces all floated right over my head.

Sandy whispered to me, "Are you doing all right? You're acting kind of weird. Are you nervous?"

I pondered the question. *Am I nervous?* "YES!" I answered. Sandy looked worried for a moment. Then she was called away by a man I presumed was the director. Those two had their heads together, and I was left standing there in the middle of the room, still holding my bag, unsure of what to do.

I decided to stand behind the kitchen counter, since that was my spot for the day. The counter blocked everyone else's view of my bag, which I opened on the floor in front of me. I felt nervous as I studied my water bottle full of wine and my cold medicine. *No one will know. It's only a water bottle. It's only cold medicine. It's fine. No big deal.*

As I felt a hand close on my shoulder, I jumped ten feet into the air. When I came back down, I put my hand on my heart and took a few deep breaths as I turned to see who was trying to get my attention. It was Sandy; she looked anxious. I watched her lips move, but I was unconcerned with what she was saying to me. *Concentrate*, I urged myself.

The words came into focus. She was saying, "…the cue cards are ready. Do you want to do a practice run while looking at the cue cards to make sure they say what you need them to?"

"Yeah, that's a great idea!" Sandy looked at me strangely, but she didn't say anything as she backed off the set and onto a stool placed on the side of the room. She put on a pair of headphones and stared into a monitor that held a camera shot of yours truly standing there on the set.

The room was silent. All eyes were on me, and the eyes that weren't on me were on monitors that contained video of me. I could tell everyone wanted to see how the rookie was going to do. How would I sound? What would my delivery style be like?

A young man stood in front of me holding a cue card that read: EASY WEEKNIGHT DINNERS. ROAST CHICKEN. VERSATILE.

I wracked my brain. *Something about rattlesnakes. Right? No. Oysters.*

"The world is your chicken!" I shouted.

*Nailed it.* The crew laughed quietly and maybe a little nervously.

The man I presumed was the director said with authority, "Cute. Let's cut the jokes and get right into it. This is a rented studio, and we need to be economical with our time. Let's skip the practice run and go straight to our first take. Rolling."

"Rolling," I heard a voice say from somewhere in the dark.

"Weeknight dinners, take one," said the director.

A guy popped up in front of me with a black-and-white movie slate that had "Weeknight Dinners, Scene 1, Take 1" written on it. *Wow, they actually use those things.*

"Weeknight dinners, scene one, take one," said the slate guy as he clapped the little arm with a loud snap!

*Wow, this is so authentic. Just like I'm on a real set.*

"And...action!" said the director as he pointed at me.

*Holy shit.*

From somewhere in the recesses of my brain, the script came forth. "I'm Kelly Ryan with *Weeknight Dinners Made Easy.* Today I want to tell you about two big-batch recipes. The first recipe is roast chicken. Duh quote of the day: Chicken is versatile. Soups, salads, pasta, stir-fry—the world is your oyster. I should really say the 'world is your chicken' because you can do whatever you want with it. If you roast enough chicken on the weekend, you're going to be able to stretch that into three or four meals during the week with a little strategery."

"CUT!" shouted the director. "We don't do political jokes here!"

I stood there blinking into the bright lights. "Political jokes?" I said weakly. *What the heck is he talking about?*

"You said *strategery.*"

"Oh. I meant strategizing."

"Then say STRATEGIZING. Rolling!"

"Rolling," said the anonymous voice in the dark.

"Weeknight dinners, scene one, take two!" shouted the director. The guy with the clapperboard popped up in front of me and did his song and dance, and then the director yelled, "ACTION!"

*Once again, holy shit. Could this be any more nerve-wracking?* With a combination of adrenaline and endorphins coursing through my veins, I somehow held it together and got through a whole scene. I was no longer feeling the effects of any wine or cold meds because my body must have flushed them right out in my panic.

As we did scene after scene, and okay, take after take, we started making a little progress, but my nerves were shredded. It was hot. I had been standing for hours and my feet hurt. My throat felt cracked and my voice sounded reedy from speaking for so long. My brain was fried from reaching for lines. I could sense the director's patience, which was thin to begin with, unwinding like a spool of thread and piling on the floor around him. It was hell for both of us.

Between takes, Sandy pulled me aside and said, "Your energy is flagging. Look, I know it's a long day. But the director said you better bring 'perky' to the next take or we're done."

"Okay, give me a second to pull it together," I said. As Sandy scurried back to her stool, I squatted down to pull some cold meds out of my bag. I washed them down with a big gulp of wine, then I straightened back up.

"Places, everyone!" the director shouted to the crew packed into the hot studio.

*Man, how the heck does this guy yell all day long. Does he say nothing in a normal tone?*

At the top of his lungs, he bellowed, "ACTION!" at me.

I stood there blinking at the bright lights. *The cold meds are going to take a few minutes to kick in. I need to pull it from somewhere.* I smiled. "I'm Kelly Ryan with *Weeknight Dinners Made Easy.*"

"CUT!" The director pulled his hair with his fists. I looked at Sandy, and she looked back at me. I tried to read her expression, which was somewhere in between pleading and apologetic. The director clenched his teeth and looked at me fiercely. "I need you to BRING IT! MORE ENERGY!"

*I wonder where the director is getting all his energy from. He should totally be the one up here. His energy is less "perky" and more "homicidal rage" but at least he would BRING IT.*

My body was spent. I could feel the pills trying to make a comeback. My heart began to beat a little bit faster. I began to sweat a little bit more. But I felt weak and lifeless. I could hardly force my face into a smile. *This is never going to work.*

The director looked hopeless as he said in an almost-normal tone of voice, "Rolling."

"Rolling."

Over the course of the day, the slate had slowly morphed from an adorable novelty into a dreaded instrument of torture that calculated and reported my failures. The guy holding the slate sounded exhausted as he said, "Weeknight dinners, scene three, take fifty-nine."

"Action," said the director with an eerie calm.

From the depths of my soul, I tried to bring it. I pulled my spine up straight, took a deep breath, and smiled broadly. I could feel the crazy eyes coming back as I said, "I'm Kelly Ryan! And this is dinners! I mean, weeknight dinners! Easy weeknight dinners! Weeknight dinners made easy!"

"FUCK! CUT! That's it! Wrap it up, people!"

"It's a wrap?" called a voice from the darkness.

The director answered, "It's not a wrap. We're scrapping it. We're getting new talent. Miss Ryan, thank you for your time, you are dismissed."

I felt relieved, followed quickly by tired and sad, and then rejected and ashamed. It really hadn't occurred to me that failure was an option. In all my imaginings, I wondered what level of success I would rise to, what levels of glamor I would experience, how far would I go. I never considered that they wouldn't approve of my performance. Even after the day had gone so horribly, I was still shocked in a small place in my brain, the place where I held visions of grandeur.

I was too tired to even cry. Sandy came to my side and said, "I'm so sorry, Kelly. I'll walk you down." I picked up my bag and followed her out of the studio, down the elevator, back through the cement corridor, and out amid the twinkling lights of Broadway against the dark night sky. Once on the sidewalk, Sandy grabbed my hands and said, "I'm *really* sorry, Kelly."

"You're sorry? Sandy, no. Why would you apologize to me? You're the one who got me the gig. I'm the one who fucked it up."

"Yeah, but of course you did."

"Excuse me?"

"I mean, this is not an amateur's gig. It's not a thirty-second commercial. It's like a full-length show. You've never even done this before. It takes a ton of stamina and energy to stand up there and deliver that much material. Even pros can struggle to get enough endurance to pull off a shoot like that. And the director, man. He didn't even let you do a run-through..."

"A run-through wasn't really going to help me, now was it?"

Sandy cracked a smile. "No, I guess not."

"I'm not cut out for this, am I?"

"No, probably not. Did you at least enjoy it, maybe a little bit?"

"No," I admitted. "It's really not how I imagined it. I thought it would be fun and easy. I thought, 'It's just regurgitating a script into a camera. How hard can it be?'"

We laughed and said together, "Very hard!"

Sandy said, "I'll be honest, it *is* easy for some people. Some people are naturals. And for others, they need to work at it. But the ones who work at it practice their asses off and they take acting classes and they act every chance they get because they love it. If you don't love it, Kelly, then don't look back. You tried. It didn't work out. Don't beat yourself up, okay?"

"Thanks, Sandy."

"I gotta go help the crew pack up. Bye, Kelly." Sandy squeezed me in a bear hug and then turned and ran back inside.

I felt numb all the way home. When I was finally alone in my easy chair, I burst into tears. I was deeply embarrassed and ashamed. I remembered Sandy's words. *So acting isn't for me. No big deal.* But I couldn't handle the feeling of failure that was pressing its weight against my chest, and the fact that I drugged myself for the shoot felt deeply disturbing to me. *I think I might have a problem.* I needed to see Amy, mostly because I knew she would tell me I didn't have a problem.

I scraped myself together and headed in the direction of the bar. When I got halfway there, I thought better of it. I knew Amy was going to pour me a glass of wine and tell me I was fine. *That's the last thing I need.* I turned around and headed back home.

# CHAPTER FIFTEEN

Saturday morning, I woke up feeling excited for my date with Earnest that night. Yet beneath the excitement, I could detect a feeling of uneasiness, like something was wrong.

As I shuffled to the living room, I debated with myself. *Should I tell Earnest what happened with the shoot? Should I tell him I think I have a problem? If anyone could help me, it's Earnest.* But there was no way I wanted to show him those cracks in my armor on our first date. It would kill the romance right off the bat. *No. I need to be cool.*

As I waited for evening to fall, I killed time by reading, alternating with writing short stories in my journal. *God, I love writing. The only time I forget myself—or maybe even feel good about myself—is when I'm writing fiction. What if I try to get some of these stories published? Nah. Too scary. Then I'd have to read the reviews. Well, if I were lucky enough to get reviews.*

As the sun set, I got up and looked in my closet. *There's the dress. The little black number with the keyhole neckline. I'm probably going to look ridiculous wearing it in class, sitting on the floor surrounded by yoga pants, but I don't care. I need to impress Earnest. Thank you, Amy, for picking it out and pushing me to ditch the yoga pants.*

As I slipped on the dress, the cool satin lining warmed against my skin. I zipped it up and gazed at my reflection in the mirror. *I look fabulous. This dress is absolutely perfect.* It skimmed my curves, nipped in at the waist, and flared out over my hips. It highlighted my best feature with a little cleavage peeking out of the keyhole. *Hot.*

I pulled on a pair of thick, opaque tights. *As I sit down and get up from the floor in class, I can spare everybody an eyeful of wardrobe malfunction. It's the least I can do for my fellow classmates. They're going to wonder why the heck I'm so dressed up.*

As I grabbed my keys out of the bowl near the front door, I almost shoved them into my usual messenger bag that held my journal, but I thought better of it. *Nope. An evening bag will do for tonight.* I selected a tiny silver clutch and transferred only the barest of essentials into it. Then I practically skipped out of the house to the subway.

When I arrived at the classroom, I realized I'd forgotten my yoga mat. *Well, maybe not forgotten, because there's no way I'm dragging a yoga mat with me on our date.* But now as I looked for a place to sit, I was afraid I would get my dress dirty or snag my tights on the worn hardwood floor.

I spotted Lydia sitting toward the back. I asked her, "Hey, do you mind sharing your mat with me tonight? I'm a bonehead. I forgot mine."

"Of course! No problem." Lydia hopped up and turned her mat sideways so there was room for us to sit next to each other side by side while we stretched our legs out in front of us. After we were seated and the other students filled in the spaces around us, she turned to me and said, "Wow, you're dressed up. What are you doing tonight?"

I blushed. "I have a date with Earnest," I whispered.

"Get out!" she said as she shoved my arm. She giggled, and some of the other students turned to look at us.

"Shh," I whispered. "I know. Crazy, right?"

"Who asked who?"

"He asked me."

"You lucky dog."

"I know." I glowed. "I'm so excited."

"I bet you are. Good for you!"

"Thanks."

Everyone quieted down as Earnest strode into the room and took his place in front of the class. He made the briefest eye contact with me and then he smirked.

*Wait. Was that a smirk, or did he smile at me? Did he smile because he thinks I look hot in my dress, or did he smirk because I'm ridiculously overdressed for class?* As usual, I struggled to still my mind and pay attention to what Earnest was saying.

"As human beings, we're always trying to protect ourselves from pain, whether it's physical or emotional. And so, in a roundabout way, it's natural to feel afraid to become wildly successful in achieving our visions because our minds find convoluted ways that this could cause us pain.

"Why is this? What do we fear could happen if we stop holding back and we stop keeping ourselves small? What might happen if we get out there, hit the big time, or start expressing ourselves? We fear that we might be judged or criticized. We fear our success could cause our lives to become full of overwhelming obligations we don't know how to manage. If we succeed, we fear we could lose it all and that would be painful.

"I'm not going to lie. Success can bring love, happiness, and excitement, but it can also bring pain. Whether we play big or stay small, pain is an unavoidable part of life. The Buddha says that once we accept pain as an inescapable part of life, we end our suffering. Pain is inevitable; suffering is optional.

"If we want our lives to expand in ways that are rewarding and blissful—if we are to live our lives to the fullest so we can die knowing that we didn't hold back—then we need to let our guard down and put ourselves out there. You're not making yourself any more or less vulnerable to pain by expanding your experience of life.

"Until we come face to face with exactly what our fears and hang-ups are, our Limiting Beliefs lurk in our minds. They prevent us from fully engaging with the world and our talents. Limiting Beliefs keep us unsure and therefore prevent us from taking action."

At Earnest's mention of Limiting Beliefs, I remembered Sandy's journal. *This is the lecture that turned her whole life around.* I leaned forward in an effort to drink in Earnest's words.

"A Limiting Belief many of us have is that the criticism and judgment of others means something. We mistakenly think that it's important that other people approve of us.

"As a child, I was fearful of my mother's opinion of me because her negative judgments would, in all actuality, deeply impact me. Her opinion really did matter because she had the power to punish me and make my life unpleasant. Into adulthood, I took with me the Limiting Belief that other people's judgment of me would deeply impact me.

"By the time we're adults, other people's criticisms and judgments of us don't matter. They really don't. But we're conditioned as children to believe that our survival depends on having other people judge us positively. And so as adults, we engineer our lives and our actions to avoid criticism or negative judgment. Or we do things because we think we're going to look cool, or because we think we're going to impress somebody. We want to be liked. We all desperately want to be liked.

"Is this a problem? Yes and…mostly yes. Because we don't take our own proclivities into consideration. We don't go out there into the world and do what would make us feel happy and fulfilled with our lives, because what if it's not good enough for our parents? What if it's not cool enough for our friends? What if our choices aren't good enough for everybody else?

"But know this: no matter what you do, you will never escape judgment and criticism. Don't even take this as bad news. It just is. It's what people do. They can't help it. You're getting judged either way, so you might as well do what makes *you* happy.

"Part of the process of exercising your creativity and breaking out of the status quo of your life is getting over your fear of criticism. Everyone who's successful raises the ire of insecure people who want to tear down others in order to feel better about themselves. But there's no point in staying small to avoid negative opinions."

*This makes perfect sense to me. This is why I don't take my writing seriously enough to publish it. God forbid someone criticizes it.*

Earnest continued, "You may fear disapproval from loved ones. Your friends and family might worry about your decisions. They might condemn or criticize whatever it is that you want to do.

"But you need to remember that living a happy and satisfying life is *your* choice to make. It's *your life on the line.* When it comes to these decisions about what to do with your life in order to feel fulfilled, neither conventional wisdom nor other people's opinions are your friend. You have to learn to trust yourself and take steps in the direction you feel is right, the direction that will lead to happiness and peace.

"You have to put aside your fears of criticism and scrutiny while you continue to figure everything out. Otherwise, a fear of what others think can paralyze you. You might have to very consciously tell yourself, 'Who gives a crap what anyone else might think? It's not their life!'"

*Yes! Yes! Yes! I love it when Earnest gets passionate during his speeches. My God, he's hot. I want to jump the man right here and now.*

"We all have thoughts about ourselves that limit what we're capable of. These Limiting Beliefs serve as *excuses* to avoid follow-through. Here are some common examples of Limiting Beliefs. See if you identify with any of these:

"I'm not good enough.

"I don't like myself.

"I have no discipline, no willpower, no self-control.

"I don't deserve unconditional love from myself; I would have to be perfect before I could be worthy of such a thing.

"Things are getting too good. I better put on the breaks and sabotage myself.

"You can't trust anyone. People are crazy.

"Trying hard and putting in sincere effort makes you look like a fool.

"Be quiet and stay in line or you're going to get hurt.

"If I do what I want, I'll disappoint someone.

"Being proud of yourself will cause you to get you cut down to size.

"I'm too tired.

"I don't have enough time.

"I don't have enough money.

"It's all too much. I can't keep up.

"Pursuing my dreams is too daunting and complicated.

"It's not my fault. I'm not responsible. I'm not in control.

"I don't matter.

"I'm deeply flawed or broken.

"I'm too old, young, fat, thin, rich, poor, ugly, beautiful.

"I'm afraid of what my family, friends, coworkers, and even the checkout lady would think."

*Yes to all of that. Except for the thin, rich, and beautiful part.*

Earnest said, "When you get home tonight, I want you all to do a journaling exercise. You're going to write down all of the Limiting Beliefs you think you may have. When you think about living the life you were meant to live and being the person you know in your heart you most want to be, what are the Limiting Beliefs that stop you? Write them all down. Then write down all the ways in which your Limiting Beliefs are *not* true.

"After that, you're going to choose Success Mindsets—these are simply positive, motivating beliefs that resonate with you and directly counter your Limiting Beliefs. In choosing your Success Mindsets, ask yourself what beliefs make you feel more peaceful, happier, more secure, or free to pursue your dreams? Write them down. Make a nice big list. Look at the list and choose the beliefs that feel better to you, are more helpful, more powerful.

"Then for each of these Success Mindsets, write down reasons why they're true. Of all the Success Mindsets you choose to adopt, pick three of these to focus on. Write them out nicely on paper and place them somewhere you'll be able to see them often. When you meditate, choose a Success Mindset as a mantra. Grind it in. Rewire your brain.

"That's it for tonight, ladies. Go forth and journal."

As the class scrambled to gather their belongings and rise to their feet, I felt my heart begin to pound. *Oh my God, this is it. Date time.* I stood up next to Lydia and said, "Thanks for sharing your mat with me."

She grinned mischievously and said, "Nooo problem. Have fun tonight. You lucky dog." I tried to stifle my smile and act cool, but it was hopeless.

# CHAPTER SIXTEEN

After Lydia left, I looked around for Earnest, but he was nowhere in sight. *Uh-oh. Did he forget about our date?* Soon the room was empty except for me. Just as I began to despair, Earnest emerged from the shadows.

"Oh! I thought you'd left."

"No, I was…hiding out. In order to avoid questions from the other students. You understand, don't you?"

"Yes, of course." *No, not really.*

"I thought we could go to Tao."

"My favorite! I love Tao! I've been to the Uptown location, the newer downtown restaurant, and even the one out in Vegas." Any weirdness I'd felt about Earnest's hiding completely dissipated as I thought about Tao's giant fortune cookie dessert.

We walked in silence to the Marcy Avenue M train. We waited for the train in silence. We rode the train in silence. And then we walked ten minutes to the restaurant—yup—in silence.

My mind whirred frantically the whole time. I thought about witty things to say, deep thoughts to reveal, funny observations, and gossipy crap things I'd be too embarrassed to say. I tried not to, but I also thought about what Sandy told me concerning Earnest's manwhore ways. I imagined for a brief moment confronting Earnest with Sandy's suspicions, but…*no, I could never.*

As Earnest pulled open the heavy, red door to the restaurant, he said, "After you."

*His first words since we left the loft. Maybe he spent the whole way over pondering how awesome my dress is.*

The first thing I noticed when I entered the restaurant was a woman wearing the same dress I was. And then another. And another. And another. *What in God's name? And they're all taller and thinner than I am. Every last one of them.*

As we checked in at the hostess booth with yet another woman who was wearing the same black dress with the keyhole neckline, I finally figured out that I was wearing the uniform of the staff at Tao. *Oh, that's just perfect.*

The hostess looked at me and said flatly, "You're late."

Earnest pressed me to the side and said, "No, actually, we're exactly on time. Our reservation is under…"

My ears perked up. *What is Earnest's last name?*

"Earnest and guest."

*And guest? Really? Am I that interchangeable?*

As we got settled at our table, I couldn't stop staring at the model-thin waitresses as they moved gracefully around the room wearing my dress.

"So…," said Earnest.

"So. I'm wearing the same dress as everybody."

"Yup."

"Do you think anyone besides the hostess noticed?"

"Yup."

I pursed my lips, trying to think of a comeback, something funny, something to lighten the mood, something to show that the whole dress thing didn't bother me in the least, but I was coming up empty. I thought, *The waiters are wearing pants, and you're also wearing pants. Nope. Not saying that.* We sat in silence while we stared at our menus.

I felt relieved when the waitress came. *Hello, a drink. At least that might relax me.*

"Welcome to Tao. What can I get you to drink?"

"Prosecco, please."

She turned to Earnest, "And for you, sir?"

"Water, thanks."

*Water. Wait. Does he not drink? Should I not have ordered booze? Oh crap.*

Earnest looked at me and smiled. He grabbed my hand and squeezed it. "Kelly, you're fine. Just relax. I'm feeling a lot of nervous energy coming from you. What's on your mind?"

"Oh, ha-ha, everything. You know." *Oh my God, can he read my mind?*

"No, I don't know. Tell me. What's going on in your life? You're sitting here with a guru. Take advantage of this moment. Let me be of service."

I thought about my little problem, about how I brought wine to the set. *No way can I tell him about that.*

"Here, let me help you," Earnest said. He turned my chair so my back was facing him and he began to rub my shoulders in a deep massage. My head dropped forward. I closed my eyes and tried to relax, but, *Oh my God! Earnest is touching me!*

"You're very tense. Just breathe into your shoulders, breathe all the tension away." I finally relaxed enough that he stopped the massage and turned my chair back. I was disappointed it was over, but at least I actually felt calmer. "Let's start simple. Tell me what you did this week."

"I did a commercial video shoot."

"I see. You did a commercial video shoot. What does this mean? Explain."

"My friend Sandy, oh, you might know Sandy. She was a student of yours. She got me an on-camera job. I had to memorize a script for a cooking show. Well, it was a commercial, an advertisement. An infomercial. But it was set up like a cooking show."

"Oh yes, Sandy. The production assistant. And how is Sandy?"

"She's great! I mean, she's amazing. She's a health coach now too. In addition to her other job."

"Good for Sandy." Earnest got a faraway look in his eye. "I knew she had potential. A special spark. I always wanted to get to know Sandy a little better. But so many students, so little time."

*Ugh. Really, Earnest? I'm trying so hard to believe you're not a manwhore, but you're making it difficult.*

The waitress came with our drinks and took our dinner order. Crispy Thai pork for me, and the miso roasted black cod for Earnest.

"Excellent choice, sir," smiled the waitress.

*Hey! What about my choice? Huh? Isn't my choice good too?* Earnest looked at her a little too long and smiled at her a little too much. She looked fantastic in my dress and I couldn't wait for her to leave.

After he watched the waitress until she disappeared from sight, Earnest turned his laser focus back to me. He said, "Tell me about your video shoot. Did you enjoy yourself?"

"Um, no. I expected it to be fun, but it was really hard. I don't think the director liked me very much." I tried to shoo the screaming face of the director from my mind's eye.

"And have you done this sort of thing before?"

"No, first time."

"I see. Why did you agree to do it?"

"Oh, a bunch of reasons. I thought maybe I could parlay the shoot into a career, and I thought my mom would be proud of that. I thought it would be really cool to be on video, to maybe even have some fans if I picked up some better jobs after this one. I thought the crew would treat me like a star, but that sure didn't happen."

"Mm-hmm. Kelly, do you pay attention in class?"

"Yes, of course. I love your class."

"I see." Earnest sat there looking at me. "How do I put this?"

"Put what?"

"You are clearly missing the entire point."

"The point?"

"Yes, the point. The point of my class is to teach people to do what moves them, what makes them come alive, to do the things that put them in flow, the things that make the world drop away. Do you know why?"

I blinked a few times. *Do I know why?* "Um, because it's fun? No wait, because I won't eat as much if I'm distracted?"

Earnest sighed. "Because this is how you discover what you love. When you discover what you love to do, you will slowly become proficient—even brilliant—at it, but this will only happen when you give yourself the time to practice and hone your craft, to make love to your own genius."

I tried to imagine Earnest making love to his own genius. I wasn't sure exactly what that would look like, but I knew it would be hot.

He went on, "Once you have honed your talent, you can begin to uncover your gift. Do you know why they call it a gift?"

"No, why?"

"Because it's your gift to the world."

The waitress placed our meals in front of us and said quietly, "Bon appétit."

Earnest answered, "Merci," then he picked up his fork and began picking at his food. I mirrored his actions as he said, "Your gift to the world is how you will use your talent to make the world a better place. Once you're making the world a better place, you have found your purpose, your *raison d'être*, your reason for existence. Your drive, your ambition will come alive! You will have no need to overeat. You will have no need for food, alcohol, or any other outside substance to alter or numb your emotions because you will feel exhilarated and driven and ecstatic to practice your craft and to unleash it on the world."

I was sitting on the edge of my seat. My breath quickened, and Earnest's excitement flooded my body. I tried to regulate my breathing as I sat back in my chair. *I don't want to look so...taken.*

"What are you thinking, Kelly?"

"That I'm really far from where you're trying to get me."

"And why is that?"

I thought about telling him what I did, that I brought wine and cold medicine to the shoot with me, but I was mortified. I could feel heat and color leaking across my cheeks, giving me away.

"You're blushing, Kelly. Don't be afraid. Tell me what is it you want to say." Earnest leaned forward and fixed me with his gaze.

I blurted out, "I took meds! I drank wine! For the shoot! I needed to be perky because they said the most important thing was perky, but then I was hyperventilating and so I had a little wine to calm down, and..." I hid my face in my hands.

Earnest sat back and smiled. "Kelly, it's okay."

"It's okay?" I looked up at him. *That's the last thing I expected him to say.*

"Yes. It's okay."

"How is it okay? I mean, I was trying to 'alter my emotions' or whatever you would call it."

"And what do you think this means? You are obviously assigning some grave meaning to this."

"Huh?"

"What do you think this means that you used wine and cold medicine to alter your emotional state? What does that mean?"

"It means I have a...uh..." *Oh God, don't make me say it.*

"A what?"

"A problem." I sighed loudly.

"Yes, you do have a problem. But it's not the problem you think you have." I just stared back in confusion. "Kelly, your problem is that you worry too much about what other people think. You say they wanted you to be perky. And on your own, without the cold medicine and wine, were you perky?"

"No. That's why I took that stuff."

"I see. So you weren't what they were looking for. They wanted you to be perky, but you found you couldn't be perky without chemicals."

"Yeah, I guess. I mean, maybe I should have tried harder."

Earnest held up his hand and said, "Shh. No. You should not have tried harder. They wanted you to be perky, but you needed chemicals to accomplish this. Do you know what this means?"

"No."

"This means you aren't perky."

I couldn't even imagine where he was going with this, so I just sat there in dumb silence.

He went on, "They wanted perky, and you're not perky, so you're not what they wanted." I continued to sit and stare, saying nothing.

"Kelly."

"What?"

"They didn't want you."

"Because I'm not perky! I get it!"

"No, you don't get it. The problem is that you wanted them to like you. You cared so much what they thought of you that you drugged yourself in an attempt to give them what they wanted. Your problem is that you're so obsessed with avoiding rejection that you drugged yourself."

I considered his point. "But I drink at other times. See, look, I'm drinking right now." I took a sip of my Prosecco.

"Yes, I see. Why did you order this drink?"

"Because I needed to relax."

"Why did you need to relax?"

"Because I was nervous for our date." *Oh my God, you dork, why did you admit that?*

"Why were you nervous for our date?"

"Because I want you to like me." *Sigh. He's winning at this game.*

"Your problem isn't alcohol. It's fear. What makes you think you need alcohol? You're afraid that people won't like you. You're afraid you aren't good enough. There are two Limiting Beliefs at work here. The first Limiting Belief you have is that it even matters what people think of you. The second Limiting Belief you have is that people don't like you. Who gives a shit on either count?"

*Yes, who does give a shit?* "Wait, how could I *not* give a shit? Doesn't everybody give a shit?"

"No. I don't give a shit. You give two shits, perhaps even many, many shits, because for some reason you don't love yourself unconditionally. You don't accept yourself as you are, and so you want other people to validate you, to offer their approval of you. The third Limiting Belief at play here is that your emotions aren't okay as they are. You feel the need to alter them instead of feel them. It's a trick: you don't need people to like you anyway, so alcohol is useless. It's an antiquated social custom, nothing but a poison that impairs your brain.

You think you feel better because you suddenly stop caring what people think after you've had a drink. But you need to understand that it doesn't matter what people think. The problem is that you think other people's opinions are important. There's only one person whose opinion matters."

*Whose opinion? My mother's? Earnest's? Who?*

In response to the puzzled look on my face, Earnest said, "It's your own opinion. Your own opinion of yourself is the most important. You need to accept and love yourself. Do you remember the exercise we did, when you embraced your younger self?"

*How could I forget? That was right before you asked me out.* "Yeah."

"That exercise is about unconditional love. No matter what you do, no matter what you say, and no matter how you feel, know that you are worthy of unconditional love. That means stop judging yourself for lacking. Stop criticizing yourself. It's only when you love yourself that you can stop giving a shit what other people think. When you did that exercise, I was offering you my unconditional love. I fell in love with you just a little bit at that moment."

*A-hubba-wha?*

"I don't mean that I'm telling you I love you in the conventional, romantic sense. What I'm saying is that the divine in me sees the divine in you. We are both magnificent. We are both eternal. We are both worthy of unconditional love. Kelly, I need you to know this." Earnest grasped both my hands, stared into my eyes, and said, "Kelly, you are worthy of love."

I just about melted and flowed right off my chair into a puddle onto the floor. Earnest let go of one of my hands and brushed a piece of my hair back from my face. "Kelly, I would like to kiss you now."

"Uh-huh."

He placed one finger delicately under my chin and his lips met mine. Then his lips parted slightly and his tongue gave my mouth a gentle and brief prod, like a small hello, before he closed his lips and sat back. "Thank you, Kelly."

"Uh-huh."

"Kelly, what do you think your gift is?"

I sat there, stunned. "I…I dunno."

"What's your talent? What is it that you like to do? Did something come out of the first visioning exercise we did, the one about creating your blissful life? Is there a creative activity that you love? Is there something you'd like to do more of?"

"I like to write."

"You like to write. What kind of writing?"

"Fiction. Short stories, mostly." I took a bite of crispy pork. *Oh my God, this is so good.* I chewed quickly and ate another forkful.

"And do you practice your craft diligently?"

"No, I wouldn't say diligently. More like sporadically," I said through a mouthful of food.

"How does the craft of writing fit into the blissful vision exercise that we did? How do you want writing to impact your life?"

I felt embarrassed as I told him, "I want to be a novelist. I want to make a living at it."

"And have you written a book before?"

My face flushed as I admitted, "Yes, but it's just a fluffy beach read."

"That's okay, Kelly. So you've written one book. There are many who will go their whole lives saying they'd like to write a book, and they never do. What will your next book be about?"

"Oh jeez. I haven't even thought of that. I hadn't written in years before I took your class. I just started doing it again."

"This is good. You're making some great first steps. And thank you for sharing that part of your blissful vision with me. Just one small warning: Never share your dreams with small minds. Only with like minds." Earnest tapped his temple. "With others who want to share their gift."

"Okay, got it." *I totally don't get it.*

As we finished up our meals, the waitress came back to clear our plates. "Would you like any coffee, dessert?"

*Giant fortune cookie! Giant fortune cookie!* I chanted in my head.

"Kelly?"

"No thanks, I'm good."

"The check, please. Thank you."

After we got up to leave, Earnest placed his hand on the small of my back and guided me expertly through the restaurant to the door. I had to stop myself from pushing back against his hand to reinforce his touch, to feel his hand through my clothes.

As he opened the door for me, my normal routine would be to start freaking out over end-of-date logistics. *Is he going to kiss me? Should I say I'll call him?* With all of my might, I forced myself to chill. I would simply follow Earnest's lead.

# CHAPTER SEVENTEEN

As I reached the sidewalk, I half expected to turn around and see a cloud of smoke because Earnest may have worked some escape artist trick to disappear and fly off into the night. But what happened next wasn't even close to what I expected.

"Kelly, I would like you to invite me to your apartment."

"Oh, okay." I smiled uncontrollably. I searched my brain for a mental image of my apartment as I'd left it. *Are there any empty takeout containers lying around? Did I leave my underpants draped over the lampshade?* "I'm just south of here. And east. Southeast. I live on the Lower East Side. Probably best to take a taxi."

Earnest stepped from the curb to the street and raised his hand, instantly summoning a driver. As the cab pulled up in front of me, Earnest opened the door and ushered me inside. The cabby looked at me in the rearview mirror while I recited my address, then he sped off at warp speed. Earnest pressed his thigh against mine. The moment was surreal. *I can't believe this is happening.*

When the taxi arrived at my apartment building, Earnest paid the driver while I awkwardly scooted across the seat and climbed out of the car. Then Earnest was at my side, again with his hand at my back. "Where to?" he asked.

I pointed up at my bedroom window. "Right up there." I led him to the beat-up metal door of the building and dug into my clutch for the key. *I only had one glass of Prosecco.* I tried to remember a time I brought a man home when I wasn't half in the bag, and I realized this had never happened before.

I suddenly froze. *Can I do this? Can I actually have a man—I mean this is Earnest, not just any man—over for sexy-time without even the slightest hint of a buzz? I can offer him a nightcap. Oh yeah. No I can't.*

As we trudged up the stairwell to my apartment door, I became self-conscious about the peculiar odor of my apartment building. It was a mixture of stale cooking smells on top of a couple hundred years of God knows what. Earnest seemed to think the whole thing was a field trip to a history museum.

"Klein Deutschland."

"Say what?"

"Klein Deutschland. It means Little Germany. Your neighborhood is known for buildings like yours, former tenements that housed Jewish immigrants. But before that, it was known as Klein Deutschland. Ironic, don't you think?"

I tried to think of a response. *Yup? Nope? Okay?*

As I opened the apartment door, I was greeted by the sight of a pair of underpants on the floor in front of me. I deftly kicked them behind my easy chair then looked at Earnest to see if he'd noticed, but his eyes were busy roaming the apartment. I closed the door and locked up.

"This will do," said Earnest.

"What will do?"

Earnest turned and enveloped my body with his, his mouth on mine, his hands everywhere on me at once. I was stunned into submission. Without interrupting the embrace and our mouth-to-mouth contact, he practically dragged me over to the chair. I dropped my purse on the floor and thought, *What the hell, why not?*

He pushed me roughly into the chair, then thought better of it and hauled me out of it again. *I've never seen him second-guess himself before.*

"Bedroom. Now," he said.

I walked ahead of him, my eyebrows raised in shock but with a smile on my face. He clearly wanted to wipe that silly grin off my face as he grabbed a handful of my hair close to the scalp and guided me forward onto the bed until I was on all fours. Still holding me by the hair, he pushed his hips against my rump and I could feel his erection.

*Holy shit, Earnest, do you do this to all your students?*

He pulled me forward by the hair, forcing me to crawl. Then he climbed onto the bed behind me and stood there on his knees, pressing himself into me through his pants. He let go of my hair and pushed my face and shoulders down on the bed, my rear end still in the air.

*This is so exciting!*

Then he gripped my hips and rubbed his crotch in a circular motion all over my business. I wanted to laugh, but I was also getting incredibly horny. His nails raked my back, and I moaned. He pulled back from me for a moment, then swat! He slapped my butt cheeks.

He grabbed my hips and flipped me over onto my back. He leaned forward and pinned my wrists to the bed on either side of my head. He stared into my eyes as he rubbed his hard dick against my crotch. "I think you'd better get ready."

"Get ready?"

"Remove your clothes." Earnest abruptly got off me and stood up. "You may use the bathroom. Freshen up, if you'd like."

I was used to feeling off-balance around Earnest, but *Jesus Christ. Way to up the ante, dude.* I ducked into the bathroom, stripped, peed, and then "freshened up" down there with some toilet tissue and a little water from the sink. *I think that's what he meant, anyway.* When I was convinced I was fresh, I emerged, feeling shy as I walked naked into the bedroom with my hands folded in front of my crotch.

Earnest had freed himself of his clothing and was standing there waiting for me with his boner at attention. His white skin glowed, and his perfectly flat abs created a ninety-degree angle with his you-know-what. He pushed my hands away and looked at me. "Yes," he said. "Beautiful breasts." He cupped them for a moment, then suddenly slapped them.

You know that game you played when you were a kid where one person holds her hands above the other's, and the kid with his hands on the bottom suddenly slaps the hands of the person on top? Yeah, that. But with my boobs. And I was okay with it. Shocked, but definitely on board.

Earnest grabbed two handfuls of my hair and guided me on my back onto the bed as he climbed on top of me and, all in the same motion, opened my thighs with his legs. Then he produced a condom from somewhere—like he was a magician pulling a coin out of a kid's ear. He wrapped his schlong, reached between my legs to check me for readiness (all systems go), and we were off to the races.

As he moved frantically inside me, he would alternately offer a light slap to my cheek, place his hand on my throat, pull my hair, or pin down my wrists. I'm not going to lie, I was getting off on it. When he was finished, he rolled off of me and then grabbed my hand as he lay there panting. I loved the contrast of the rough sex followed by the tender hand-holding.

*This is it, we're getting married. I can totally put up with the weird sex, enjoy it even. I wonder how many women must have run screaming from the room before. It's*

*okay, Earnest. You've met your match. I'm cool with your kinky sex fetish. You
don't have to hide your true self any longer. I'm here for you.*

# CHAPTER EIGHTEEN

When I woke up, Earnest was gone. *Did that actually happen? Or was it all a dream? I'm buck naked and there's a condom wrapper on the floor. It happened.*
On my way to the shower, it occurred to me I might not want to wash off the evidence. *Maybe I should luxuriate in the stink for a little while. Ew. Don't be disgusting.*

After I got dressed, I texted Amy: "I need to talk, where are you?"

"Having brunch at Essex with Sandy. Come meet us."

*Dang. I don't want to do a tell-all brunch with Sandy. What would she think?* Then I remembered Earnest's words, and I revised my stance to not giving a shit. *This story needs to be told, and it needs telling right now, innocent bystanders be damned.*

The whole way over there, I rehearsed what I would say in my head. *Earnest has a commanding presence in bed. He took control of the situation. He's a powerful lover. Oh forget it. Earnest is a kinky fucker.*

Once at the restaurant, I made my way to Amy and Sandy's table and pulled up a chair and said, "Hey, ladies! Thanks for letting me crash your brunch."

Amy said, "Oh, no problem. We would have invited you, but I know you had your date with Earnest and I figured you'd call me the second you wanted to tell me about it."

"You know me too well."

Sandy offered me a weak smile. *Whatever. She might think Earnest is bad news, but the sex was worth it.* Then I remembered the shoot and realized she could have suffered fallout after my royal failure. "Hey, Sandy, I hope things went okay for you with the crew and director after I left. Did I get you in trouble?"

"Yeah, maybe a little. I'm off talent-scouting duty for a while."

"Ugh, I'm sorry, Sandy."

"Thanks, Kelly. It's not your fault, though. I should have known better. I hope you don't mind, but I told Amy what happened."

"No, it's fine. Saves me the breath."

Amy said, "Tough break, Kelly."

"It's okay. I've moved on to other things, seriously."

Amy said, "So tell us about your date!"

"Where do I start?"

"Start with the good stuff: did you get any?" A sly smile crossed my face. Amy playfully pushed my shoulder and said, "You did! Details. Spill 'em."

"It was dirty. I'm not sure I can adequately describe what happened."

"Try," urged Amy.

I noticed that Sandy wasn't saying anything. I focused on Amy and said, "Well, I got spanked. And there was hair pulling."

"*Really?* Go on."

"And maybe some light slapping and pretend choking."

Amy's eyes got big. "Are you serious?"

I tried and failed to stifle a grin. "Yup."

"Wow, I wasn't expecting that."

"Me neither!" I laughed.

"Was it good?"

"Oh yeah. The best I've ever had."

"The best? Better than…"

"Yeah, hands down."

"All right, Earnest! Nice job. Are you going to see him again?"

"I would assume so. I'll definitely see him in class."

"No, I mean are you gonna go on another date? Is he going to call you?"

"I don't know. He was gone when I woke up this morning."

Amy flinched, "Oooh. Poor form."

"Eh." I shrugged. "It's Earnest. He probably had to go meditate."

"Or greet his adoring fans," suggested Amy.

"Or scale Mount Kilimanjaro on the back of a mystical spirit animal."

"Well, are *you* going to call *him*?"

"Nope. Don't have his number."

Amy wrinkled her nose. "You don't have his number? Didn't he call you for the date? Isn't it on your caller ID?"

"His assistant set it up. If I called the number, she's the one who would answer."

"Ew, weird!"

"Why, what's so weird about it?"

"You had sex with the guy, but you can't even text him to say hi? Texting each other is half the fun of a new relationship!"

"Relationship? I wish."

"You don't think this could turn into something?"

Sandy cleared her throat. Amy and I both looked at her while we waited for her to say something, but she just sat there with a concerned expression on her face. Amy and Sandy resumed eating their breakfasts, and we all fell into a comfortable silence until the waitress came and said, "Oh, I'm so sorry, I didn't realize you had a third. What can I get you?"

"Nothing for me, thanks." As the waitress walked away, I patted my belly and said to Amy and Sandy, "I'm trying to lose weight. For real this time."

Sandy came alive and said, "Kelly! Starving yourself is going to make you *gain* weight, not lose weight!"

"How so?"

"So many reasons. You'll lose muscle, which slows your metabolism. Oh, and simply not eating lowers your metabolism anyway. Plus you change your hormones in ways that make you put on fat."

"Like how?"

"If you don't eat when you're hungry, you raise cortisol levels, which makes you store belly fat. You raise the hunger hormone ghrelin, which will make you eat more later to make up for the calorie deficit and then some, which leads to raised blood sugar and additional insulin production, which promotes fat storage. Plus, skipping meals can negatively impact neurotransmitters like serotonin, which can lead to emotional eating."

"Wow."

"Yeah. Eat when you're hungry. Don't eat when you're not hungry." Sandy flagged down the waitress and then pointed to me.

"I'll have the fruit plate."

"Kelly, get the veggie omelet," urged Sandy.

"But there's so much fat in an omelet!"

The waitress sighed and said, "I can come back."

Sandy said, "Okay, thanks." Then Sandy turned to me and said, "Kelly, are you serious about losing weight?"

"Yes, of course."

"Then let me help you."

"Please do. I need all the help I can get."

"Okay, tell me what you eat on a typical day."

"After my coffee, I'll usually have a bowl of cereal with skim milk for breakfast with fruit. Then some rice and veggies for lunch, and fruit for a snack. And then for dinner, a big pasta salad with whole wheat pasta and a load of veggies. I try to use less oil on the salad."

Sandy laughs and says, "Is that actually what you eat, or is that what you think I want to hear?"

I pouted. *She caught me.* But rather than come clean, I lied, "That's what I eat. Seriously."

Sandy said, "No wonder you're struggling with your weight. That sounds like a diet plan straight out of the eighties. Low-fat, high carb. Yikes. That's exactly the kind of diet scientists would feed rats to promote obesity for experiments."

Amy laughed, and I gave her a dirty look. Sandy went on, "Our grandmothers knew that starches made people fat. If you've ever read articles or books by Gary Taubes, you'd know that some bad science got publicized, the media ran with it, and now everyone's confused. If you're trying to lose weight, a very vague and general rule of thumb is: pastured chicken is good, grass-fed meats are good, starches like bread and pasta are bad, and fat is required—the right kinds in the right amounts. Fat will make your meals digest slower, and that promotes feeling full for longer. You need to eat good fats, especially for brain health. There's only one thing that all nutritionists seem to agree on: vegetables are good."

I had only seized on one idea out of everything she said, and it infuriated me. "What do you mean, pasta is bad? So I can never have pasta again?"

Sandy said, "Sure, if you don't mind eating something that makes you sick and fat. Look—you're confusing happiness with pleasure."

"I'm confusing happiness with pleasure?"

"It's harder to be happy when you don't have your health. Your liver needs help. You're eating way too many starches and sweets."

"My liver needs help?"

Sandy pointed at my puffy stomach. "Too many starches and sweets can stress the liver. If the liver is kept busy like that, then it has a harder time clearing out toxins, and that makes you a candidate for cancer.

Besides, when you're in the habit of eating starches and sweets, you can easily become addicted."

"Does wine count as a sweet?"

"Sure does. The goal, Kelly, isn't weight loss. That will be a side effect of getting healthy. The goal, especially for you as you're starting out, is to keep your blood sugar stable. That will get you off the roller coaster of cravings and overeating. And to do that, you need to eat plenty of protein like chicken and eggs—yes, whole eggs for the fat and the nutrition in the egg yolks. Eat plenty of vegetables, and stick to healthy fats like olive oil, coconut oil, and grass-fed butter. Remember: eat meat, eat fat, and eat vegetables. You don't have to eliminate them entirely, but cut way back on starches and sweets. That's all you need to know for now. We can get into the finer details later."

"You make it sound so easy."

"I never said it's easy, but it's not complicated. You can have a great variety of foods eating this way. Plus you'll have steady energy. Don't deprive yourself and let yourself get too hungry before eating."

The waitress came back and said, "Are you ready to order?"

I smiled and said, "I'll have the veggie omelet, thanks."

★

On my walk home from brunch, I thought about what Sandy said: *Your liver needs help. You're a candidate for cancer.* I took a few deep breaths in an attempt to calm my quickening heartbeat. *Eat meat, eat fat, eat vegetables. Calm down. This is totally doable.* I stopped in at the Essex Street Market and bought some chicken breasts and a head of broccoli.

When I got home, I cooked it all up in a frying pan with olive oil and salt and pepper. *There. Chicken, fat, vegetables, enough for the next few days. No problem.* I packed it all up in containers and put it in the fridge so it would be ready for me when I was hungry.

Then I sat down to write, but I was restless. It was an unseasonably warm and sunny day, and I didn't feel like being cooped up inside. I put my notebook down and went back outside for a stroll. As I reached the sidewalk, I could hear Earnest in my head: *Do you practice your craft diligently?*

I felt ashamed as I remembered telling Earnest: *No, not diligently, more like sporadically. Get out of my head, Earnest.*

Only a few feet into my walk, the thought hit like a lightning bolt: *Ugh, I should really get a job.* I'd managed to avoid ruminating about my unemployment since Sandy had gotten me the Tast-ee gig. *I deluded myself into thinking I was launching a new career. Now I'm back to square one.*

An uneasy feeling grew in the pit of my stomach as my mind replayed my humiliation at the shoot. I tried to shake it off as I looked in the windows of the shops and restaurants along my route. Then my mind volunteered, *My liver needs help. I'm a candidate for cancer.*

*Deep breaths*, my imaginary Earnest said in my ear. This time I welcomed the mental interference and decided to run with it. *What would Earnest tell me to do right now?* His words from the first lecture came back to me. *Watch your thoughts. Be the Witness.* I attempted to back up mentally out of the chattering fog, to rise above, to detach. I felt peace for a few gorgeous seconds before the sugary smell of cupcakes baking assaulted my nose in an almost-welcome violation.

I stopped and rubbernecked at the window of the cupcake shop, one of Lydia's competitors. I stared at the thick, pink icing that formed delicate, crunchy peaks at the tops of each little cake. *All of those innocent little confections, so adorable, so sweet, waiting to be taken.* I was really channeling Earnest now.

Then I switched to pouting. *I can't believe I'll never be able to eat this stuff again.* I began to feel irritated at Sandy. I imitated her words, mocking her in my fit of resentment. *Sure, if you don't mind eating something that makes you sick and fat. Look—you're confusing happiness with pleasure.*

*Confusing happiness with pleasure.* I hated myself in that moment. *Sandy wants to help me. Why do I have to be such a whiny bitch?*

My phone's text indicator sounded—*sweet distraction. It's Amy.* Her text said, "Hey, I'm bartending this afternoon. It's dead. Will you please keep me company?"

"Hell yes!" I texted back. I knew this wasn't going to end well. I knew Amy was going to feed me drinks, and I knew I wasn't going to stop her. I didn't care.

★

I woke up in the middle of the night and was made intimately familiar with the term *splitting headache.* I'd never given the expression much thought before, but now it dawned on me why they called it that.

*I heard that if you concentrate on the spot where you feel pain, it will dissipate. I'm willing to try anything.* I focused my attention on the center of my forehead. It pulsed. *Pounding headache. Which is this, splitting or pounding? Can it be both? Maybe I'm having a stroke.*

I forced myself out of bed so I could use the bathroom. I held onto the walls to fight against the vertigo that was trying to spin me to the floor. *Oh God. I want to die.*

I peed and climbed back into bed. I barely slept the rest of the night through the atrocities of that headache.

The next morning, I scrunched my eyes shut against the intense sunlight encroaching the boundaries of the blinds. The headache was still there in all its terrible glory. I cataloged the sins of the previous night. *Four martinis. And a salad for dinner.* I was trying to be good by ordering a salad, but it occurred to me that salad plus martinis equals murderous headache. *Besides, there's no such thing as "being good" when martinis are involved.*

I tried to go back to sleep, but I could feel the headache growing more painful, as if that were possible. *I need something to eat.* I trudged into the kitchen and yanked open the fridge. *Chicken and broccoli out the wazoo. No fucking way.*

I don't know how I managed, but I went to the bodega across the street and acquired a sausage, egg, and cheese on a roll. Once back in the apartment, I unwrapped my sandwich and nearly wept in pain as I ate it. *Diet shmiet.*

Earnest was lecturing that night. I felt a small pulse of excitement, followed by a groan of misery. I knew that if I felt like grim death, I probably looked like it too. I didn't want him to see me like this, but there was no way I would miss his class for a hangover. *I need Earnest's help.*

For the rest of the day, I sat in my easy chair, staring at the television. I wanted to pick up my notebook for a writing session, but I was absolutely useless. I kicked myself. I couldn't even write. Not only was the day wasted, I suspected it was entirely possible this hangover was going to be a two-day affair.

# CHAPTER NINETEEN

Later that evening, I fought to keep my eyes open and to sit upright on my yoga mat while Earnest spoke to the class. I wanted to look interested and engaged. Most of all, I wanted to look like someone Earnest would have sex with after class.

Earnest lectured, "Oftentimes when we want to improve our lives, we see what's on the surface that doesn't look quite right to us. We think our bodies and our homes should look a certain way. So we go on a campaign of self-improvement. And this campaign might sound like: I'm going to lose weight. I'm going to make my home spotless. I'm going to manage my time perfectly. I'm going to give up all of my vices and become the most perfect Barbie Doll ever to live in the most perfect dream house.

"This is the definition of a red herring: you have your focus on the very things that you don't want in your life. The vices, the messes, all the things that you think are problems or that need improvement. A red herring diverts your attention toward the very things that you don't want and away from what's actually important in life.

"During this campaign of self-improvement, we spend a lot of time and energy thinking, 'Don't eat that. Don't do that. Control yourself. Stop it. Pull yourself together. Behave.'

"What you focus on is what you get. If you spend a whole lot of time obsessing about wine or porn or fancy dinners out, or anything else that you're trying to cut back on, your two feet are going to have a hard time not marching in the very direction you're trying to avoid.

"A study was done by Harvard University psychology professor Daniel Wegner that proved asking yourself *not* to think of something is going to trigger your mind to return repeatedly to the forbidden thought. While well-documented as a common strategy, Wegner proved that thought suppression fails miserably as a tactic.

"When we have a bad habit we're trying to break, it's only natural to attempt to suppress our thoughts in an effort to curb ourselves. But now psychologists know that thought suppression actually brings about thoughts of the very thing we're trying to avoid. So how the heck are we supposed to break bad habits? How do we leave our red herrings behind?

"Focus on what you want, not on what you don't want. The solution lies in moving our fixation to where we want to go as opposed to what we're working to avoid. Instead of furtively trying to avoid thoughts, think like you mean it. Actively focus your thoughts on the direction you want to go, rather than peering in the rearview mirror at whatever you're trying to run away from.

"Weight loss—having a sexy body—should *not* be what you're living for. Giving up a vice like drinking or junk food shouldn't be your main focus. The solution is counterintuitive. When we're trying to clean up these messes we've made for ourselves, the answer is this: Think about what you *want*, not about what you don't want.

"Think back on the visualization exercise you did, and recall what you *want* your life to be like. What kind of hobbies and work do you engage in? What kind of people do you want to surround yourself with?

"This class will help you develop a higher consciousness that allows you to live in ways that go beyond wanting to feel good personally. You won't care so much about short-term pleasures. You'll learn to live a more profound and meaningful life.

"As you get deeper into the work of creating a life that's amazing, you won't want to self-medicate with food, drink, or other time wasters. You won't pine for that red herring—junk food or wine or whatever— that's making you miserable. When your life is amazing, you won't want to escape it.

"Red herrings are unsolvable issues. We chase our tails, focusing on an issue that would become a nonissue *if only we would let go of it.* However, we do get something out of trying to solve these unsolvable puzzles.

"We use red herrings to avoid listening to our hearts and taking action. Going for the bigger life always involves risk. And it's easier to stay mired in addictive, repetitive behaviors than it is to risk our tiny, shallow lives in search of something bigger and deeper.

"When you stay focused on your red herrings rather than listening to your heart, then you never have to face your fear of the unknown. Instead, you get to continue dealing with the fears you already know about. These fears, such as the fear that you're harming your health or otherwise wasting your life, will eventually become your reality—the downhill slide you'll face if you stay on the same old path, wrestling with red herrings for eternity. Your red herrings will keep you stuck to those fears and the raw deal that you already know about.

"Sometimes we turn to bad habits day in and day out because there's something big missing from our lives. While your red herrings protect you from the unknown and they help you numb your feelings of disappointment, they also prevent you from living the amazing life you deserve.

"When we dismantle old habits and replace them with powerful new habits, it can help us reach our blissful visions. It's important to remember that our habits are here to serve us and to make our lives fulfilling. We need to avoid getting overly vested in habits themselves, but rather what they can help us achieve.

"Red herrings present an interesting conundrum. When we wrestle with them, we're distracted from living a bigger life. But if we let these bad habits run amok, we can destroy our health, our minds, and therefore our chances of living a bigger life. Therefore we must strike a balance of working to change these habits *at the same time* that we pursue our blissful visions.

"I will use the lovely Kelly Ryan as an example. Her blissful vision involves her becoming a writer. But Kelly has confessed to me that she's a drinker."

All eyes in the class turned toward me, and my face burned with shame. *Oh my GOD, Earnest! Shut UP!*

He seemed oblivious to my embarrassment as he continued, "Writers are notorious for destroying their lives and careers with alcohol. Don't let the myth of the drinking writer fool you. For every famous writer who drinks, there are thousands upon thousands of writers, perhaps even millions, languishing in obscurity; drinking writers whose hopes of ever succeeding are dashed against a massive collection of empty bottles.

"So should Kelly worry that she drinks? No. That's a waste of time. She should only worry about writing. And when drinking stands in the way of writing, then drinking stands in the way of achieving her blissful vision of becoming a successful novelist. Only then will she learn to hate drinking."

I already hated drinking at the onset of that killer headache. But Earnest was driving the point home. I couldn't write when I was hung over, and that was a deal breaker. Finally, I was getting on board with the idea of shoving booze over the side, for real this time.

"Many of you have shared with me your goals of losing weight and getting healthier, and you have red herrings of your own that stand in the way of that. Maybe your vision for your life involves a thinner, fitter body. Getting in shape. That sounds simple enough. Lots of people, every day the world over, resolve to lose weight. Why don't they succeed?

"Because they look at a whole host of habits that impact their weight and they try to change all of them. They try to cut back on the amount they eat, to cut back on junk food, and to start exercising simultaneously. They fail, sometimes spectacularly, over and over and over again. People waste years of their precious lives on this. And they might lose weight temporarily, but when any one of these habits begins to veer back into old territory, their whole new system collapses. They gain all the weight back. And then they either start over or they give up.

"If you want to change your life, begin with your toughest habit. You probably have a habit that negatively impacts your ability to improve any of your other behaviors. For example, once upon a time, I was an oenophile, a great connoisseur of wines. When I had a glass of wine with my dinner, I wanted to eat more, I didn't sleep as well, and then I didn't want to exercise the next day because I felt tired.

"If you want transformation, you have to give something up. Now that I don't drink, it's easier for me to eat well, sleep well, and enjoy the energy that exercise gives back to me. When wine went by the wayside, I was able to sleep more soundly, which positively impacts my motivation, my stress levels, and therefore my willpower."

I found it hard to believe that Earnest had ever let alcohol impair his functioning. He seemed like such a well-oiled machine. I felt like a complete mess in comparison as I rehashed all the pain and inconvenience of my colossal hangover. *Earnest is absolutely right: I'm never going to become a best-selling author when I let drinking stand in the way of my writing.*

Earnest went on, "Because of this trickle-down effect on my life, I call drinking my Apex Habit. It's the habit at the top of the pyramid that has an effect on all my other habits. Once I experienced a win in this difficult area, I felt certain that I could overcome any other habit I wanted to change.

"When you succeed in changing one habit, you strengthen the processing capacity of your prefrontal cortex—the part of your brain associated with restraint and higher thought processes. Regular meditation also strengthens your prefrontal cortex, which makes it easier to conquer your Apex Habit.

"You're going to choose one habit that you want to focus on changing for a significant period of time. It's important to allow yourself some slack in other areas as you focus on your Apex Habit. If you're quitting or giving up drinking for a time, you might let your weight go for a month or more while you practice restraint around alcohol. If you're focusing on the foods you eat or on getting exercise, let the other habit changes you want to make fall by the wayside while you master just one of these.

"As we embark on this journey of changing our habits, we need to master the art of follow-through, and we need to master the art of valuing each small decision. We have to fight that tendency of feeling too comfortable when we go through a period of ease. We need to be conscious that, just because it feels easy now, it won't always feel that way. When things seem easy, we need to be mindful of the tiny decisions that are fueling our success.

"When we discount the small decisions and we think they don't matter, they add up over time. It's those small decisions, strung together moment to moment and day after day over the course of our lives, that actually make a difference and pave the road to our success or failure.

"We can master the arts of follow-through and of valuing tiny decisions by focusing on one habit to change over a meaningful length of time. That way we can learn how to persevere in the face of difficulties, complications, and distractions.

"We might feel bored or like we don't need to commit to a meaningful length of time to focus on one habit. But if we actually want to succeed at changing a habit, we're going to have to fight through the threat of boredom by committing to a singular focus for even longer than we think is necessary.

"Our habits must bring us pleasure, or they won't stick. When changing a habit, it's essential that we associate the cue—our reminder to take action—with the pleasure of the reward. This way our brain will crave the habit and make it stick. As you focus on your Apex Habit, how will you remind yourself of the pleasure your new habit will bring?

"Be forewarned. When you begin to create or change a habit, before and perhaps even after you've formed new neural pathways, your brain will try to get you back into your old, well-worn ruts and habits via a stream of sabotaging thoughts or excuses. Witness the excuses your brain generates from a detached mental state.

"Then you will create an Excuse Neutralizer. The idea behind an Excuse Neutralizer is to recognize your needs and to write up a list of alternate behaviors; when I feel *this*, I'm going to do something to get my needs met—instead of your former default behavior, which perhaps was to give in to cravings.

"I want you to write down the excuses as they come and recognize them as the lies your brain generates to keep you on the old path. When you resist over and over again via your Excuse Neutralizers, you begin to form new patterns and habits. Your brain will eventually cooperate with your new reality. In time, you will notice your brain contributing thoughts and impulses that support you in sticking to your resolution, and the changes will become easier and easier to abide by.

"Time and again you will feel the impulse to go back on your word. When you feel this happening, take note of the excuse you invented. Appreciate how clever, convincing, and truly ridiculous the excuse is. Keep a growing list of all your excuses. Examine each excuse, and one by one figure out what your actual need is. Write down the actions you will take to get your needs met. These actions are called Excuse Neutralizers.

"Review your list of Excuse Neutralizers daily until the stream of excuses slows down to a more manageable trickle. When you notice unhelpful thoughts and impulses, continue to counter them with more helpful truths about your needs and the actions you can take to fulfill them.

"Ladies, as you go forth in the world, I want you to remember this: if you've consistently struggled with something in the past, you'll probably struggle with it in the future. We can rewire our brains for new habits, but the old neural pathways are still there, waiting to be reactivated.

"When your willpower feels ironclad, don't make the mistake of thinking that you'll always feel that way. Willpower waxes and wanes. We tend to mistakenly think we're going to have more self-control in the days ahead, or later in the day, or later in the year, than we will. This I know: we're all going to feel weak sometimes, well into the future.

And so I urge you, do favors for yourself to help yourself succeed in the future, even if you think you won't need it. I call this the 'Don't Buy Chocolate' rule. If your weakness is chocolate, keep it out of the house for now. That's all. You may go."

# CHAPTER TWENTY

A s the rest of the class scrambled to their feet, I stayed rooted to my mat. I'm not sure I could have gotten up even if I tried. As the rest of the women shuffled out the door, Earnest exited stage right. I knew that he would come back out to see me once we were alone, and I was right.

He crept back into the light and said, "Kelly. What are you still doing here?"

"Oh, I thought…" *What am I still doing here? Not exactly the warm embrace I was expecting.*

"Come, to your feet."

I slowly crawled to a standing position. Earnest approached me, looking regretful and like he didn't want to come too close. He loosely held the tips of my fingers in his hands in an awkward, ambiguous gesture. Despite the fact that we were touching, the obvious distance he was putting between us felt unbearable. He finally broke the silence, "Kelly, you look terrible."

"Gee, thanks." I desperately longed for the vibe of intrusive intimacy from our date.

"You're green."

"I'm hung over." And then, like it was out of my control, I started blathering and whining at Earnest. "Oh my God, I feel so bad, oh God, I'm dying!" I willed myself to stop talking. Not only was I hung over, I had officially humiliated myself.

Earnest dropped my fingers and scolded me, "Kelly, you're like a small child who drags God's creation through the mud and then complains to God that it's muddy. You need to learn how to cherish your body and stop treating it that way."

"I know, I'm trying," I whined.

"No, you're not 'trying.' Either do it or don't do it. Be decisive. But stop complaining to God when you're the one who hurt yourself." I wanted Earnest to hold me, to kiss me. I hated feeling like he was angry with me. He asked me abruptly, "What's your Apex Habit?"

"Drinking." *Duh. Obviously.*

"Thank you for sharing this with me. Because you care so much what others think, accountability will be key to your efforts. Tell your friends, especially those who engage in this habit with you."

"Okay." I didn't look forward to telling Amy. I knew she would argue with me. *But it has to be done.*

"Choose a period of time to give up alcohol. Forever would be great, but when you're starting out, it helps to move the psyche in the direction you want it go by putting a limit on the experiment. How long will you go without drinking?"

"A week?" I could tell by the look on Earnest's face that this was the wrong answer. "A month?"

"At minimum. Thirty days."

"Okay. I'll do it."

"Thirty days is a nice start. But remember this: if you return to old habits after thirty days, you'll get what you've always gotten. Now, we need to prepare you for your response to cravings. Have you tried meditating? Have you been the Witness of your thoughts?"

"Yeah, yesterday. My brain was going off like crazy, and so I stopped and witnessed it."

"And? Did you feel peace?"

"For, like, a second maybe."

Earnest clapped his hands like a little kid and shouted, "Kelly! This is wonderful! Keep this up. It will serve you well."

"Wow, um, okay."

"Why do you sound hesitant?"

"Well, I guess I didn't realize that my little moment of peace was such a big deal."

"Of course it is, Kelly. Becoming the Witness of our own minds gives us insight into God consciousness. When you can step outside of your mind's chatter, you can see your thoughts how God sees them, and you can hear the wisdom he has for you. We can see into the Soul of the World, as Paulo Coelho so eloquently calls it in *The Alchemist*. We can read the omens."

*The omens. I can't even begin to fathom what that means.* The Witness was nowhere to be found in that moment. I couldn't help myself as I begged, "Earnest, will you please come home with me?"

"You are in no condition to enjoy my aggressive style of lovemaking. When you learn how to cherish your body, we will resume our intimate relations. Come to me when you've achieved your thirty days with your Apex Habit."

I was crushed and then hopeful. *In thirty days, I can have Earnest.*

★

At home with my journal that night, I wrote, "Apex Habit, no alcohol. Thirty Days." Oh man. What about visiting Amy at the bar? I chewed my pen cap as I remembered Earnest's words. *Remind yourself of the pleasure your new habit will bring. That's easy. After thirty days, I'll get a porking from Earnest.*

Excuse Neutralizers. How did these go again? I notice an excuse to drink. Then instead of drinking, I figure out what I need. I knew I could come up with a few of these right off the bat.

I started writing. "Amy hands me a drink. Oh look, free drinks!" *Okay. So maybe I don't need anything. But I could ask her for water instead.* I tapped my pen on the page. *When else do I drink?* I wrote, "When I think about being unemployed and getting a job." *Ugh. I need a drink right now. I hate thinking about this. Okay, focus. What do I need? I need to face this issue and figure this out. I need to look for work and stop hiding from the problem. I just have to start somewhere.* I took a deep breath. I wrote, "I'll start asking around. I'll start putting together some writing samples."

*All right, back to the exercise. What are my excuses for giving in to cravings? If a butterfly sneezes in Mexico, I want a glass of wine. Tired, overwhelmed, bored, low energy...* I documented every cockamamie excuse that my brain invented, and then I came up with solutions and answers to each one.

Then I made a long list that contained the solutions to my excuses. *Call Sandy if you feel like injecting sugar into your eyeballs. Make a pitcher of iced tea if you're tired and you can't nap. And if you can, then go to bed. Watch a comedy when you're bored or sad. If I'm overwhelmed or stressed out, I can make a to-do list and knock off some priorities.*

I kept my list of Excuse Neutralizers handy and dutifully read them every day. Over the next few days, I surprised myself by resisting temptation over and over again. I could feel new patterns of behavior forming, like sitting down for a glass of iced tea in the afternoon and updating my to-do list, rather than unraveling in a heap, wishing for death, and then going out for noodles and booze.

★

Three days later, I woke up feeling excited and inspired. *Thirty days without alcohol? No problem! I got this.* I leaned over the side of the bed and dragged my journal up with me. While I was on a roll, I would make some resolutions.

*I want to keep myself busy and clean up my life.* I took out my pen and jotted down all the changes I was going to make:

1. Write every day.
2. Journal my feelings and my Excuse Neutralizers.
3. MONEY. Find a way to make some.
4. Start exercising every day.
5. Diet; reel it in!
6. Clean up the apartment, and keep it tidy.

Earnest's voice came back to me. "You're going to choose one habit that you want to focus on changing for a significant period of time. It's important to allow yourself some slack in other areas as you focus on your Apex Habit…let the other habit changes you want to make fall by the wayside while you master just one…"

*Really? Only focus on not drinking? This seems crazy to me. This seems like chasing a red herring if all my focus is on that one thing. I'm overweight and unemployed, and my apartment is a wreck. I really feel like I should be doing more.*

I scribbled down a diet plan. I resolved to find a job. And I'd go to the library to check out some exercise DVDs. For thirty days, I was going to live like Barbie in my dream home, or at least I would try.

★

That afternoon, as I marched up the steps of the New York Public Library, I tried to breathe deeply to prevent myself from getting winded. It didn't work. I had to stop and catch my breath before going inside so I didn't disturb all the readers with my wheezing and panting. I placed my hand on my belly and remembered Sandy's words: *Your liver needs help.*

*Your liver needs help. What does that mean exactly?* I got the sudden urge to google symptoms of liver disease, so I made my way to the computers. After a frightening journey through Google images, I shut the browser window and stumbled to my feet. I felt ill. *Do I feel ill because my liver's damaged, or because I've been looking at graphic medical photos?*

*Wait. Why am I here again? Oh yeah, exercise videos.* As I made my way to the health and fitness section, I placed my hand over my liver again. *It feels puffy. Is it just my chubby belly, or did I have a fatty liver? Oh my God, stop it.*

I picked up a DVD that was decorated with a photo of a smiling woman wearing a leotard with leg holes cut up to her waist. *At least that photo successfully distracted me from my liver hypochondria.*

I browsed the titles. *Buffer Than You* boasted a bicep-exploding, bun-tightening strength workout. *That one has potential. Who doesn't like tight buns?*

*Dance Your Ass Off* promised a heart-pounding aerobics extravaganza. *Sounds fun, but after getting winded by the library steps, it's clear that* Dance Your Ass Off *would kill me.*

*Body and Mind Yoga* sounded relaxing, but I doubted it would help me lose weight. And the scowling, sweaty people gracing the cover of *Booty Bootcamp* weren't exactly encouraging. *Those people look pissed off that they were forced to do* Booty Bootcamp. *The tagline should read: "Booty Bootcamp: Get seriously peeved that you have to exercise!"*

I settled on *Buffer Than You.* I had some dusty old dumbbells on the floor of my closet. It would be nice to take advantage of the investment that I no longer remembered making, it was so long ago.

As a thin, older lady-librarian checked out my DVD for me, I felt embarrassed as I wondered what she thought of my selection. *With a figure like hers, she probably gets her fair share of exercise.* She smiled and told me, "It's not due for six weeks!" *Thin Older Lady-Librarian approves.* I felt slightly less awkward as she handed me the box and told me to have a nice day.

As I walked down the sidewalk, my DVD tucked into my messenger bag, I felt a twinge in my upper belly. *Is that liver pain? My liver is scarred. I'm sure of it. Cancer. Toxins. Sugar. I need to get away from all that junk. I need to start treating my body like a temple.*

*I'll make an appointment to see a doctor. I'll make sure my liver is okay. And then I'll exercise every day and eat chicken and broccoli and get healthy and go back to the doctor in a year, and she'll be so amazed that I healed my body!*

I went home, googled a doctor, and called to make an appointment. "It's your lucky day! We just had a cancellation," the receptionist told me. There was an available appointment the following morning. Yes, this was the new me, someone who actually went to her annual physical.

# CHAPTER TWENTY-ONE

The next morning, sitting in the doctor's waiting room, I tried to stop the fluttering feeling in my chest every time I thought about all the horrible things I'd done to hurt my health over the years. I put my hand on my puffy belly. My liver was torched, I was sure of it. *So many cupcakes. So much champagne! Why did things that tasted so good have to be so bad for me? WHY, GOD WHY?*

I needed a distraction. I looked above my head and saw a clear plastic case full of pamphlets on the wall. "Kidney Disease: Know the Signs." *Okay, I'll bite.* I stood up and pulled down a pamphlet to read while I waited.

- **Fatigue and Weakness.** *Why yes, I am feeling tired. And weak. Definitely. Maybe the weight workouts will help with that.*
- **Insomnia.** *Always. Yes, oy, the insomnia.*
- **Decreased Mental Sharpness.** *Yup. I feel like an idiot most of the time.*
- **Swelling of Feet and Ankles.** I wiggled my toes in my shoes. *I'm definitely feeling claustrophobia of the toes.*
- **Persistent Itching.** *Uh-oh. I'm racking up quite a few of these symptoms. I'm very itchy.* My fingers traveled from my scalp to my face, to my back, to my thigh, to my belly, to my armpit, and back again. *I'm going crazy with the itching. How had I not noticed this itchiness before?*
- **Shortness of Breath.** *Oh my God. I have that! My kidneys. My poor, poor kidneys.*
- **Loss of Appetite.** *Nope. Definitely not. Phew!*

*Okay, wait, do I need to have all of these symptoms to have kidney disease, or only some of them? Does my raging appetite mean my kidneys are okay? This is so confusing.*

*I think I'm dying.* My heart hammered in my chest, and I struggled to catch my breath. *Oh no, not another panic attack.* I started sweating and trembling. *Maybe it's a heart attack.* I looked up at the other pamphlets and saw "Heart Disease: Know the Signs." *Do I dare look at it? No, stop, you're going to convince yourself you have another disease.*

*I'll pray to God. Yup. That's exactly what I'll do. If anyone can help me get out of this, I'm pretty sure it's God. It will be the first time I've prayed since I was a little kid, but I can't stand the anxiety any longer. I need to strike a deal with someone who can solve all of this.*

*God? God, please forgive me, for I have sinned. I've been treating this body you gave me like a heap of shit. I eat whatever tastes good, no matter how bad it is for me. I also eat or drink every time I feel the slightest bit emotionally uncomfortable. I'm pretty sure I've wrecked my liver, and quite possibly my kidneys. Please, I pray to you. I'm so scared. I think the doctor is going to say I'm dying. If you heal me, I promise that I will never, ever do bad things to my body again. I will join the movement to quit sugar! Just let me live, please, please, please. Amen.*

*There. Is that a deal? Did God agree to let me live if I stop being such a jerk to my body?* I looked at my watch. *Man, how long am I going to sit here? I saw on Facebook the other day that a study came out that states that sitting leads to immediate death. Or maybe it said that people who sit are one hundred percent more likely to die than people who don't sit. I hate waiting. I'm starting to feel snacky.*

"Miss Ryan, the doctor will see you now."

*Oh thank God.* I practically ran across the tiled lobby and past the nurse, who was holding open a door to a carpeted hallway. Right inside the door was a scale.

"Please step onto the scale, Miss Ryan."

*Oh damn.*

I kicked off my shoes and removed my heavy sweater, hoping to fool the scale into a lower appraisal. Then I hopped on and frowned as the nurse slid the weights across the metal bar in front of my face and stopped at an all-too-high number. "I'm wearing my heavy pants today. And a very heavy shirt. And bra. And socks and undies." It was nice of the nurse to laugh, even though I didn't mean to be funny. *She probably hears crap like that all day long,* I reassured myself.

A few minutes later, I was naked under a paper gown and seated—*sitting kills you!*—on crinkling paper covering a padded table. I decided to use the time while I waited for the doctor to pray some more, or really, to beg God for mercy.

The door opened with a rush of sunshine and rainbows as the doctor breezed in and said brightly, "Good morning, Miss Ryan. And how are we feeling today?"

"Great, thanks," I lied.

"And are we here for a well check?"

*A well check? No. I wouldn't be here if I thought I was well.* "I, I…have some concerns."

The doctor switched her sunshiny demeanor to frowny face. "Oh, I see. Tell me what's bothering you."

As I began to talk, the doctor started to do doctorish things, like feeling the glands in my neck and looking into my ears with a tiny flashlight viewer. "I feel okay, I guess, but I'm worried about my liver. And my kidneys."

The doctor pulled back from her activities and looked at my face. "Oh? And why is this?"

I patted my belly and said, "My friend told me my liver needs help."

"She did, did she?" said the doctor as she gently guided me into a lying-down position. Then she looked at the wall in front of her as she palpated my stomach. "Does this feel tender? Let me know if you notice any soreness as I feel your liver."

"It feels fine to me. Good even. Kinda like a massage." The doctor smiled and her eyes crinkled. *I like her.*

"Your liver feels fine." She pulled out my chart and took a look at the notes the nurse had written. "Do you have any other concerns today?"

*I'm afraid I'm dying. She seems so breezy, and I'm nervous about walking out of there without impressing upon her how drastic a case I am.*

"I'm trying to lose weight!" I blurted out as I sat up and folded my hands in my lap.

"That's wonderful, Miss Ryan."

"Call me Kelly."

"Okay, Kelly. Talk to me about your lifestyle. What behaviors are you working to change?"

"I drink wine and I eat sugar. And I need to exercise more."

"How much do you drink?"

*I want to be honest.* "Usually one glass of wine a day, sometimes even two or three when I go see my friend Amy." *Oops. I stopped short of total honesty because I left out the part about how Amy and I occasionally go out to dinner and to clubs, and then it's more like four or five. Okay, eight once in a blue moon.*

I watched the doctor's face, expecting to see a look of horror, or at least some serious disapproval, but she looked as happy and breezy as ever. "How are your stress levels?" she asked.

I felt my bottom lip begin to quiver and tears sprang to my eyes. *Oh no, this isn't happening.* I looked at the ceiling, trying to keep the tears from falling. The doctor put her hand on my shoulder, and I fell into all-out sobs. "Well, this is embarrassing," I sniffled.

The doctor's frowny face had returned. She stuck out her bottom lip and said, with authentic concern, "Aw, Kelly. I know, I know. Stress is so tough. What's got you so stressed? Is it work? Family?"

I chuckled through my tears. "Oh wow, now this is really, really embarrassing. No job. No family." *Why am I so stressed? What right do I have to be stressed, without even the normal stressors of people?*

"Unemployment is stressful. And no family." She looked at me with pity.

*Am I leaving her with the impression that I'm an orphan? I mean, I have family, I just don't have a husband.*

She asked, "Do you have a support system?"

I nodded. "I have friends. Amy and Sandy." *And I used to have Toni, before stinking Jill stunk up the place.*

"Let me give you some pointers on stress. Observing your physique, I think your friend meant well, but it's likely she noticed the distribution of fat on your body and is perhaps confused about your condition. Stress can cause high levels of cortisol, a stress hormone, which leads to fat storage in your belly. Do you drink coffee?"

I nodded.

"Every day?"

"Yup."

"Do you have trouble sleeping?"

"Yes."

"And you said you're trying to cut sugar. Do you have sugar cravings?"

I laughed through my tears. "All the time."

"Okay, I think I'm getting a clearer picture of what's going on here. You need to learn to manage your stress and lower your cortisol levels, and then I think you're going to find relief from your concerns. You need to cut alcohol and caffeine, because both raise cortisol. It's very easy to wind up in a cycle of feeling stressed and not sleeping well, using caffeine to wake up in the morning, and then using wine to calm down at night. All of these factors will continue to raise your stress hormones and increase your desire for sugar."

"Cut coffee?" *Oh boy. It never occurred to me that I'd have to give up coffee along with wine and sugar. I think I need a new doctor. Holy crap, can I have nothing that gives me pleasure?* I heard Sandy's voice in my ear: "You're confusing happiness with pleasure." *Fine. FINE. I'll do it.*

The doctor said, "I recommend cutting back on caffeine gradually to reduce the likelihood of withdrawal headaches. You can reduce the amount you drink over a few days, and you can start to swap in black tea to replace coffee. Black tea contains an amino acid called L-theanine, which can help you feel alert, but calm."

"That sounds nice." *Okay, black tea. I like tea. Maybe this won't be so bad.*

"And you can try chamomile at night in place of wine."

"Chamomile. Okay."

The doctor's happy face was back. "Are we all good here, Kelly? Is there anything else I can do for you today?"

I smiled. "I feel better, thank you. It's good to finally figure out what's wrong with me."

"There's nothing wrong with you, just some stress. You might consider finding some ways to relax like meditation, yoga, some light exercise. Lifting weights will help you sleep better and improve muscle tone. But nothing too strenuous. Overexercising can also raise cortisol."

I laughed. "Nothing too strenuous. No danger there!"

"Great, Kelly, have a nice day!" And the doctor blew out of the room, taking her rainbows and sunshine with her.

# CHAPTER TWENTY-TWO

A few days later, as I sat in Earnest's class, I tried to ignore the gnawing lump of nervousness in my belly. *I can't believe I gave in to a craving, even after I struck a deal with God. I only needed to go thirty lousy days without wine before I could have sex with Earnest again, and I gave in.* My disappointment in myself was directly proportional to how badly I wanted Earnest to ravish me.

*Maybe he'll assume I'm on track and he won't ask how I'm doing. Maybe I can pretend everything is going according to plan, and in a few weeks I'll be basking in his attention in a fancy restaurant and bouncing around in his lap for dessert.*

My heart almost jumped out of my chest when Earnest asked, "How well did you all do with your Apex Habit? Pull out your journals, please, and write down where you succeeded and how you failed. Write down what excuses you made to give in. Write down an Excuse Neutralizer, or what you will do instead the next time you hear yourself make that excuse. Did anyone here do perfectly? No errors in the past week?"

One hand shot up at the front of the room, and then another hand, Lydia's, tentatively crept into the air. The rest of us looked at our toes or at the back of the person in front of us, avoiding eye contact with Earnest. "Very good, Monique. I expected as much from you. Monique is a longtime student of mine, back for a refresher." I felt a pang of jealousy. *Did he sleep with Monique? Is she back for "more"? Wink, wink, nudge, nudge?*

Then Earnest approached Lydia and purred at her, "Veerrrry good, Lydia." He walked slowly up to her, and I could have sworn he was trying to look down her shirt. He ruffled her hair at the nape of her neck, and she leaned into his leg, like a Golden Retriever getting her ears scratched. *Oh my God. What exactly am I seeing?*

"To the rest of you, have heart." Earnest shot a look in my direction, and I quickly turned my head to avoid his glare. "We will do some exercises and mediation today to help shore up your will so you'll have the chance to improve your performance. But right now, go ahead and start writing about how you did the past week. Give yourself credit for your successes, and see how you can do better next time when you have moments of weakness."

I tried to tamp down my envy as I concentrated on my notebook, but mean, sickening thoughts kept intruding. *Did Earnest bone Lydia? Do they have the same thirty-day agreement?* I took a deep breath and let it out between pursed lips. *Focus, damn it.* I wrote down my performance in several areas during my thirty-day challenge, deliberately flouting Earnest's advice that we focus on our Apex Habit.

The first three days of my challenge were awesome. I knew Earnest's class was helping me, because I'd never experienced such a feeling of willpower and control over my behavior before. I meditated, I fought cravings (and won!), I wrote daily, I took walks when I needed a break, I surfed the Internet for jobs, and I almost got started decluttering my apartment.

I also did my exercise DVD three days in a row. I was too sore to move by the fourth day, and then, miracle of miracles, I started up again on day six. "You guys," I wanted to shout to the whole room, "I exercised for three whole days in a row!" That was a huge improvement—no, it was *life shattering*—as far as I was concerned.

*Diet? Eh. So-so. Not terrible. Better than usual, that's for sure. I had a few run-ins with pizza, and I made myself pasta. But it was whole wheat. And I did start making myself some healthy smoothies to drink after I exercised, which can only be considered a victory. I thought I would have lost at least a little bit of weight by now, but no dice. Now if I could just make myself start cooking dinner every night.*

*Okay, fine. I will address the drinking. It wasn't a lot, no. But after staying away for three days, I showed up at the bar to see Amy (okay, maybe it was to "see Amy," if you get my drift) and I didn't confess to her that I'd made a promise to myself to stop drinking for thirty days until she placed the second glass of wine in front of me. She felt bad, but it was okay. Two glasses of wine in a week is actually pretty good for me, and I have to give myself credit where credit is due. I really should have told her beforehand, though. Excuse Neutralizer: I need to tell Amy what my plan is and ask her to help me.*

Earnest continued on with the lecture, "So many of us think, 'My life will start when I get my behavior under control.' But we have it backwards. Our behavior comes under our control when we start living the life we're meant to live.

"In *The Book of Awakening*, Mark Nepo writes, 'Transformation always involves the falling away of things we have relied on, and we are left with a feeling that the world as we know it is coming to an end, because it is.'

"As you change your life, you might want to fall into comforting behaviors to relieve the disorientation that change brings. You might get wrapped up in fighting against these comforts instead of focusing on the positive directions you're moving toward. Don't obsess about these behaviors. Instead, live your life. Live into the change. Allow yourself to bloom without thrashing and fighting the process.

"Now, keep your journals and pens ready. We're going to do a lot of writing in today's class. For the first exercise, we are going to revisit our blissful visions. You are going to ask yourself, 'What does my ideal life look like?'

"My first question for you is, *Why do you want to change your habits?* The reasons why you want to change will help you succeed. Do you want to be on this earth longer so you can have more time to love your children before you die? Do you want to be able to influence large groups of people, and you know this will be easier to do within an energetic, fit body? Dig deep. Close your eyes and picture it. Then journal ways you'd like your life to be bigger or more fulfilling. What fantastic things will you experience?"

*Ooh, I love this question. I do want to influence large groups of people.* I closed my eyes and imagined myself on a stage, speaking to a full stadium. I was wired with a microphone headset, and I looked up into the crowd, beaming. *I look great, physically fit. Strong. Performing like this, speaking to a crowd on a huge stage, feels effortless because I'm in such great shape. I'm not sure how a novelist would wind up doing such a thing, but still, this is what I see, and I love it.*

I also imagined laughing and chatting with glamorous reporters during TV appearances to promote my book, what would eventually become the novel of the year, translated into twenty-one languages. The reporters looked beautiful as they always do, with gorgeous, polished outfits, perfectly coifed hair and dramatic makeup—and so did I. My hands felt electric as I scribbled what I saw in my notebook.

Earnest said, "Next question: *How do you want your life to feel?* Do you want it to feel exciting? Expansive? Playful? Peaceful? Full of love? Laughter? Friendship? Family? Write down at least ten adjectives or feelings that describe how you want to feel, or what you want your life to be like, and then write down ten things you might do to get these feelings into your life."

Earnest paced the room as we wrote, glancing down at our notebooks. *Or maybe he's glancing down at our cleavage. Probably a little of both.* "Perhaps you want to join a club, or travel more, or explore new career options. Maybe you want to write a book or become more creative every day." I looked up at Earnest, and he winked at me. My face flushed, and I buried my face in my notebook.

"Perhaps you long for a tight group of loving friends, or a large group of rowdy friends, or a combination of the two. Maybe you want to work for yourself so you can have control over your time and activities. Or maybe you want to live in a city, by the beach, in the mountains, or the desert. Don't let these suggestions constrain your ideas. Think big and wide. Answer now and get something on paper, but never consider these answers final. Over time, let your mind play with these questions."

*I want to feel energetic, creative, and confident. I want adventure, abundance. I want freedom, ease, and clarity. I want self-discipline. I want to be able to return Earnest's looks without feeling like my head is going to explode. And I want to feel like I'm making a difference in the world, to inspire other people. Okay, fine, and I probably want at least a few of these things because I want to impress Earnest. Hmm, what kinds of things could I do to get these feelings?*

*For energy, I can eat foods that give me energy, and I can keep exercising. Creativity...this one's easy. I need to write every day. To feel confident, the combination of physical exercise and writing could help with that. Adventure, abundance? Well, I need to make some money to get those going, so I guess I could get a job. Or maybe even self-publish that old book I wrote, and see if it sold at all.*

*And how can I find freedom, ease, and clarity? I still feel trapped eating and drinking nasty stuff, and if I can fully get away from those habits, then life will certainly feel freer, easier, and I'll have more mental clarity. No doubt. Self-discipline: if I do what Sandy did, which is to create a daily schedule that fulfills all these needs and stick to it, then I'll certainly have the feeling of self-discipline.*

*To make a difference in the world, I need to write useful books. I know I love to write fiction, but there has to be a way to make the books inspirational, at least for some people.*

My journaling reverie was interrupted by Earnest as he told us, "I want you to create a narrower focus for all of these thoughts and feelings. Out of everything you wrote, what are three goals you could go ahead and start pursuing right away? Tie each of your adjectives to your goals to make sure you're pursuing the right objectives."

*Only three goals? Okay, let's see.* I scanned what I'd written and I realized that I could easily lump all of these aspirations into three goals. I wrote,

*Goal 1: Lose thirty pounds with diet and exercise. That way I'll tackle confidence, freedom, ease, clarity, and self-discipline all in one go.*

*Goal 2: Write a novel by sticking to a daily writing habit. That's more self-discipline, confidence again, plus creativity. (And abundance and adventure, if I'm lucky.)*

*And speaking of abundance, Goal 3: Start making money. Get a job.*

*Sigh. That one really doesn't grab me, but ya gotta do what ya gotta do.*

Earnest said, "Now I want you to choose at least three actions you can take this week to get the ball rolling on each of your goals."

*Good idea, Earnest. Let's make this real.* I could sense Earnest looking over my shoulder as I wrote down what actions I could take. I tried to make my handwriting as neat as possible. *See, Earnest? My handwriting is so amazing it makes you want to have sex with me!*

I wrote,

*Action #1: Meal plan and eat healthy foods.*

*Action #2: Write every day.*

*Action #3: Get a job. Oh God. Do I have to?*

Earnest said, "When you get home, I want you to put these actions in your calendar. Place other reminders in plain sight that will ensure you take action. It's easy to write these things down and forget about them, so I want you to arrange your environments to help you.

"Kelly wants to do a meal plan and eat healthy foods. One way to bring this action into the real world is to print out a meal plan and a shopping list and keep it on your kitchen counter. Keep the meal plan simple. Grocery shop so you have all the foods you need on hand. I want you all to consider how you are going to bring your hypothetical plans to life in your homes.

"Okay, moving on. I'm now going to enlighten you about the choice you all need to make. The choice involves two paths for your life: failure or desire. I'm going to tell you a story about how I made the choice in my own life to pursue the path that leads to desire.

"Early in my career, I felt a sense of embarrassment and failure following a public event I hosted that went poorly. Following this public failure, I turned to numbing behaviors to cope by drinking and eating. As a result, I packed on some more weight on top of what I'd already been trying to lose."

I tried to imagine Earnest as a fat man. *Nope. Can't do it. I can't possibly believe that this man standing in the front of the room with his shirt hiding his washboard abs could have ever had a body fat level above pure and total hotness.*

"However, I was able to regain my footing, thanks to a mental exercise I'd done months prior. I had imagined what life would be like if I kept turning to my old numbing behaviors. Then I contrasted that scene with my vision of the new behaviors that would propel me toward my blissful vision. Remembering the results of that exercise helped me to recover relatively quickly and retain my persistence in working toward my vision of what I wanted my life to be like.

"I call the exercise Two Paths: Failure or Desire. Failure means you numb out and forfeit your blissful life. Desire means you keep the desire for your vision alive. We're going to imagine two different scenarios. In one scenario, you do the work to better your life and reach for your blissful vision. In the other, you engage in harmful habits and snub the possibility of change and a better life.

"Often we think nothing of a few glasses of wine at night, or we stay up late watching TV or surfing the Internet. Or we procrastinate in achieving the goals we know would improve our lives, thinking we'll do better the next day or sometime in the future. But when we follow a bad habit all the way to its conclusion, it often turns out to be a lot less innocent than it seems.

"Failure-Desire takes a closer look at seemingly harmless choices, those tiny decisions we make every day that can push our lives into long trajectories of either ecstasy or wreckage. I'm going to take you through an example of the detrimental effects of a seemingly harmless decision.

"Let's say you have a couple drinks at night, or maybe you enjoy a large and hearty helping at dinner and you eat until you're stuffed. Either of these will negatively impact deep sleep. Deep sleep helps our brain recover from the day, so this means the day after we indulge, our brain function is impaired, which means our decision-making ability is compromised. This makes it likely we'll make more poor choices again the next day. And the next.

"Human growth hormone is secreted during deep sleep, so those alcoholic drinks or that big meal will also impact your body's ability to maintain muscle tone. Lack of muscle slows down the metabolism, which leads to fat gain.

"There's yet another problem caused by a less-restful night's sleep: elevated cortisol levels. This leads to feelings of stress, which may make us feel even more likely to pick up a drink or sweets the next day. Plus, elevated cortisol makes it harder to sleep well at night, which can lock you into a cycle of poor sleep, high stress, and drinking or eating to relieve that stress—while drinking or eating too much are actually the very things that keeps us locked into this cycle of stress via disrupted sleep!"

*It sounds like Earnest and I have the same doctor. I like hearing all of this coming from Earnest. Maybe I'll take it more seriously. It occurs to me that maybe it's slightly deranged that I'm more likely to follow advice from Earnest than a doctor.*

"Imagine the negative impact all of these hormonal reactions are having on your body and your organs. These behaviors over time lead to some of the top causes of mortality in this country. Heart disease. Cancer. Stroke. Kidney disease. Obesity. Alzheimer's disease. Diabetes. Kelly, alcohol use contributes to all of these conditions." I wanted to crawl under my yoga mat. *Jesus Christ. Is he trying to embarrass me to death? Because it's working.*

"Now, these are merely the biological impacts on your body, your weight, and your health. Imagine the very real impact on your day-to-day life, your choices, and your feelings of demotivation, stress, and anxiety. Think about what that impact can look like over days that lead to weeks, months, or years. Your feelings of wellness, energy, happiness, motivation, and fulfillment suffer greatly.

"What might seem like a flippant decision in the moment—oh, I'll just have one more drink or a second helping—can absolutely have a massive impact on the quality of your entire life."

I felt my resistance rising. *I don't want to believe that having one drink could really derail me.* After everything I learned, I still kept sliding back and forth between inspired and reluctant to change. *Why does this have to be so difficult? Why am I so indecisive about taking charge of my health?*

Earnest paused and looked at each and every one of us to make sure we were absorbing the gravity of his message. It was incredibly uncomfortable. I tried to shake it off as I thought, *I know, I know, I've heard it all before. It's unhealthy, blah, blah, blah.* I wanted so badly to dismiss what he was saying. But at the same time, it was sinking in. For real. Connecting my small, flippant decisions with my eventual death. *Yeah, we're all going to die, but do I need to speed up the process?* Earnest's dramatic pause was working on me.

Earnest turned and walked to the chalkboard. As he picked up a piece of chalk, I willed myself to stop staring at his perfect little ass. *Mine has to be at least three times its size.*

He said, "On this chalkboard, I'm going to replicate the Failure-Desire exercise as I did it in my own life."

He began by drawing a line down the middle of the board, then he turned to us and said, "The column on the left contains bad habits that I used to regularly engage in." He wrote "Failure" above the left hand side. "The column on the right shows the habits and steps that led to my blissful vision." He wrote "Desire" above the right-hand column.

"Each column is a progression. One step, habit, or thought feeds into the next. The two different columns show what happens as I engage in these activities. The columns represent the two possible paths I could take, side by side. As I write, I want you to read down each column, one at a time, to view the two different progressions."

Earnest began to write furiously. Instead of watching the words appear on the board, I concentrated on his body. *I'll read it when he's done.*

| Failure | Desire |
|---|---|
| Drink wine | Eat healthy dinner |
| Eat unhealthy foods | Sleep well |
| Feel guilty, bloated | Wake up feeling refreshed |
| Weight gain | Morning workout. mental clarity |
| Sleep poorly | |
| Fuzzy thinking the next day | Research & write with clear head |
| Derailed motivation | Journal & meditate, relieve stress |
| Tasks undone, unfulfilled goals, guilt | Sleep well at night |

| | |
|---|---|
| *Wine to numb anxiety &* *guilt* | *More energy, work is easier* |
| | *Good feelings encourage* *creativity* |
| *Tired & unmotivated* | |
| | *I love my work, my life of* *freedom & bliss* |
| **Failure** | |
| | **Desire** |

We all sat and stared at the chalkboard for a long time. When Earnest seemed certain we'd read every word, he broke the silence. "You're now going to explore how your own decisions impact your life. I want you to close your eyes as I talk. Concentrate on my words and use your imaginations. Put your pens down." Earnest clapped his hands and said, "Notebooks away. You'll do the written exercise later when you're at home. Now it's time for our closing meditation."

We all complied. When the rustling of the room settled down and we were all sitting quietly with our eyes closed, Earnest began the meditation. "I want you to look at your life and consider which habits you have that may be holding you back from a life of well-being and ease. Do you eat too much food or unhealthy foods? Do you drink more than is healthy? Do you gossip or complain about other people's perceived shortcomings? Do you numb out or procrastinate via watching TV or surfing the Internet? Think about any lifestyle factors you have that are detrimental to your blissful vision.

"I want you to mentally follow these behaviors all the way down the path toward their logical conclusion. Answer the following questions in your mind. What are the risks for you if you keep engaging in these behaviors? In what ways will the quality of your life suffer? Will you impact your income, your levels of fulfillment, the amount of love and engagement with others that could be available to you?"

My face burned with shame as I thought about my recent hangover and how I begged Earnest to come home with me. *I didn't write for a couple days after that.* I thought about all the years I've wasted obsessing about my diet, and then giving in and eating junk.

Earnest continued, "Are you negatively impacting your health, leading to preventable medical emergencies in your future? For example, do you eat poorly, increasing the likelihood you could suffer a stroke, cancer, heart attack, or diabetes? What would these medical issues be like for you and your family to endure? What would this cost you in terms of money, quality of life, and fulfillment? What about the effects on your body? Are you shortening your life? How are you negatively impacting your quality of life by hurting your body?"

My heart thumped in my chest as I thought about all the aches and pains I try to ignore almost every day. *I feel bloated and sick more often than not. Why am I walking around like this? Why am I doing this to my body?*

"Now I want you to visualize what will happen if you continue with your sabotaging behaviors. If you keep going like that, what's going to happen to you? What will it feel like when you go to the doctor and you are handed a life-threatening diagnosis? I want you to see really see and feel what this is going to be like for you when it happens, should you keep treating your body poorly.

"If you're a gossiper or a complainer, I want you to imagine what it's like to face those friends or loved ones or in-laws the next time you see them, knowing that you've been spewing vile words about them behind their backs. If you think they don't know, you're kidding yourself. Imagine all the love and goodwill you're repelling with this abhorrent habit of gossip."

I thought about Toni and Jill and how their gossip had hurt me, whether they thought they were helping or not. Had I gossiped about them too? I wasn't sure. But I suddenly felt uncomfortable with the wall that was up between Toni and me. *Toni was my dear friend for years.* I felt a surge of yearning for Toni and our old level of closeness. *Maybe we could be friends again someday.*

"And if you love complaining, whether it's about people or events in your life, imagine all the stress hormones you're sending through your body every time you carry on whining instead of fixing the issues or coming to terms with them.

"I want you all to see very clearly how you're hurting your body, your health, your levels of wellness and vitality. I want you to imagine what it really means to shorten your life by these habits that are under your control. What will it be like on your deathbed, saying good-bye to loved ones as you leave them too soon because you didn't make a change?"

I heard the sound of a gasping cry. I opened one eye, ever so slightly, to sneak a peek at whoever was weeping. It was the oldest woman in the class, probably in her late fifties or early sixties. It occurred to me that I wasn't *that* much younger than she was. *Wow. Mind blown.*

"And even before that stage, imagine as the days and years roll by, feeling helpless and guilty that you aren't taking control of your life to make it better. Imagine every negative result that's going to befall you if you don't shake up your current life and make changes. If you *don't* take action toward your blissful life, what will your health be like? How will you look and feel?"

*Like Jabba the Hutt.*

"What about your work and your levels of fulfillment? How will you spend your days if you don't pursue your blissful vision, and how will this make you feel? Are there any other negative impacts you expect?"

*If I don't keep writing every day, if I don't allow myself to become a published novelist, I'm going to feel like a loser for the rest of my life.*

Earnest was quiet for a moment before he said, "Now, finally, when you get home, I want you to write down your own version of the Failure-Desire exercise. Create two columns and write down what will happen if you engage in sabotaging behaviors versus what will happen if you engage in behaviors that are driven by your desire for a blissful life. That is all. You are all dismissed."

I watched Earnest as he strolled toward the front of the room. Right before he dipped into the shadows, he looked right at me and winked. Then he was gone.

# CHAPTER TWENTY-THREE

I stayed where I was on the floor as the women stood around me and rolled up their yoga mats. I waited as they chatted and laughed and headed for the door. I knew from Earnest's wink that he expected me to wait for him, and he wasn't going to come out until we were alone.

Lydia stopped next to me and said, "Aren't you coming?"

"Yeah, in a minute. I need to think about what he said."

"Oh. Well, I can wait for you, if you want to walk with me to the subway."

"No, that's okay."

"Are you sure? We could get something to eat after."

"No thanks, I'm good."

"Yeah?"

I didn't answer. I hoped if I just sat there in silence, she would get the hint and skedaddle. *And yet she's still standing here. I have to get rid of her.* I snapped, "I'm sorry, Lydia, but I really need a minute alone here. You're making it hard to think."

"Jeez, Kelly. Sorry. I didn't mean to make it hard to think," she said sarcastically.

I hardened my face and seethed silently. *We're done. I need her to Get. Out. Of. Here.* Finally, she headed toward the door. I could hear the reluctance in her slow steps. *What the fuck? Hurry the fuck up, Lydia!* I shouted at her in my head.

A moment after I heard the door close behind her, Earnest came out of hiding. I stood up as he walked toward me and said, "Kelly, tell me. How is it going for you?"

"It's hard, to be honest. I mean, I had a pretty good week. I exercised, and I didn't eat too badly. I only had two glasses of wine. But

I keep swinging between these extremes of feeling like I have it all handled—like it's really easy and kind of a no-brainer, but then I go and give in to a craving. I don't know what my problem is."

"When Sigmund Freud was eighty-three years old, Hitler took Vienna. Freud fled to London. He was free of Nazi rule. He liberated himself. And do you know what his reaction was?"

*Oh boy. Earnest, you weirdo.* "No, I can't imagine."

"Freud wrote, 'A triumphant feeling of liberation is mingled too strongly with mourning, for one had still very much loved the prison from which one has been released.'" Earnest stood there looking at me with a glint in his eye.

I looked back at him, knowing that if I stayed silent, he would make his point in plain English.

"Kelly, Freud's point is that we love the prisons we impose on ourselves. You said last week went well. You ate a little better. You exercised. How did you do this? What did you think to yourself to resist temptation?"

"When I got cravings, I used my Excuse Neutralizers. I made a big pitcher of iced tea. I took walks. I thought about my future as a novelist. I wrote more last week than ever, and I used writing to distract me from going out to eat so much. I went to bed early just about every night because the thought of staying up and having a snack or a glass of wine wasn't making me feel so happy anymore. And then I had more energy during the day for exercise."

"So you've made a massive amount of progress, yet you still think the occasional craving is a major problem. Kelly, you need to adjust to your freedom. You have essentially broken free from your prison, but you're still pining for it. You need to mourn your poor choices. Kiss them good-bye delicately, sincerely. Dote on them for a time, but then release them so you fully release yourself from your prison, both mentally and physically."

"I'm not sure how to do that. I mean, I've doted on my bad habits for years. That's what got me into this mess."

"No, you don't dote. You devour. You've been stuffing yourself and gulping food without appreciating it. You can't savor food—eat it slowly and deliberately—and overindulge at the same time. Savoring is about the pleasantness of the full experience, and overindulging leads to displeasure. When you savor, you stop yourself before you get to the point of over-fullness. You need to taste your food. You need to see it for what it is. It's nourishment. It's not a magical elixir that will take you to fairyland."

"Well, sometimes I think wine is a magical elixir that will take me to fairyland."

Earnest smiled. "But it's not, is it? How do you feel after you've had wine?"

"Well, I feel great at first. But then I feel fat and foggy."

"Fat and foggy. And is this how you want to go through life? Fat and foggy?"

"No, of course not."

"But when you want wine, you're not thinking, 'Oh good, if I drink this, I'll stay fat and foggy.'"

"No, that's definitely not what I'm thinking."

"Well, maybe you should start. If you pull the blinders off, you might be less likely to indulge. Kelly, I'd like to take you to dinner again"—my heart soared—"but as a student this time, not as a date." And my heart crashed and burned.

"Dinner? As a student? What for?"

"I noticed when we went to Tao that, even though you were served scrumptious food, you didn't take the time to savor the food. When you savor food, it's impossible to overeat. I'd like to teach you how to savor your food."

"Oh. Um, okay, thanks." *He's taking me to dinner to teach me how to stop eating like such a pig? Ugh. This is horrible.*

"My assistant, Bernadette, will be in touch."

"Thanks for everything, Earnest."

"Good night, Kelly."

★

When I woke up the next morning, I pulled my journal up into bed with me and opened it to the page where I'd done the Failure-Desire exercise the night before. On the one hand, I was faced with an early death in obscurity. And on the other side, life was magnificent, huge, and bright.

*When the choice is so obvious, why do we struggle?* I wondered. It made no sense. I pulled out my pen to write up my plan for the day. I stopped and sighed deeply. My heart hurt, and I felt like crying. I couldn't believe Earnest's invitation. A small part of me felt relieved. He was right, of course, and he was excellent at pinpointing exactly what I needed to learn. But I was also humiliated at the insinuation that I didn't know how to eat like a lady. *Why did he bother having sex with me if I'm such a disgusting animal?*

I leafed through my journal to find the notes I'd taken from one of Earnest's earlier lectures. He'd said: "When you make a mistake, focus on the problem and how to fix it, rather than letting the issue affect your feelings about yourself. Accept and love yourself, especially in the face of weakness and failure. Love who you are, not what you do. That way, you're free to own your failures, take responsibility for where you went wrong, and improve, without some crazy detour to Hate Myselfville."

*Wow. I just took a crazy detour to Hate Myselfville.* Remembering how Earnest's in-class meditations made me feel calm and safe, I decided to try one myself. I took a deep, slow breath and closed my eyes. I imagined a warm, white light over my head that was pulsing with love. I let the love-light shine down through my head to fill my whole body. *I am loved. By myself, at least, and at last. I'm still sad, but I'll be okay.*

My meditation ended abruptly as I put my pen to paper. *I need to write out my plan. I want to look as thin and fit as I can for my dinner with Earnest. I have no idea when Bernadette will call to schedule. Do I have days to prepare? A week? I want him to think he's wrong about me, that I'm already a dainty eater who appreciates her food. Now that I know the problem exists, surely I can solve it myself.*

I wrote out a meal schedule that included a chocolate protein shake blended with greens for breakfast, a veggie omelet for lunch (based on Sandy's brunch recommendation for me), a piece of cheese or a hard-boiled egg and some cut-up veggies for a snack, and then I would cook a healthy dinner for myself each evening.

*How hard can this be? Plenty of protein and fat, not too many carbs. My meal plan looks satisfying and healthy. I mean, the shake probably isn't ideal compared to eating real food, but I know I'm not going to cook myself breakfast. This is a decent compromise, especially since I'll pack the blender with spinach.*

It turns out, it was very, very hard. I was starving all day. I didn't understand. This seemed like a decent amount of food. I was eating things like eggs and cheese, for God's sake. How could I possibly be hungry?

That night, I thought, *Screw it. I'm eating pasta.* I cooked up a huge batch of angel hair and drenched it in olive oil and butter. Then I stuffed myself. I don't think I savored even one bite as I twirled large nests of noodles around my fork and crammed it all into my pie hole.

The good news was that I didn't beat myself up about it; instead, I decided to give myself credit for sticking to my meal plan for the better part of a day. As Earnest said, I was free from my prison, but maybe I was just mourning my old ways. I didn't even consider drinking wine that day, when normally, in order to eat such a naughty dinner, I would have needed a glass of wine first in order to numb the guilt. *At least I made dinner myself instead of going to a restaurant.* I was making progress, and I refused to feel guilty.

As I slurped down the last of the pasta, I thought, *I'll make an adjustment to the plan to eat a healthier dinner the next night. All is well here.* When I was done eating, I pushed myself up from the table and rinsed my plate in the sink. Just then, my text indicator binged at me. It was Amy. "Hey, girl, hey. I'm going to a party tomorrow night. Wanna go? Sandy's coming too."

*YES. I so want to go.* I wanted to chew Sandy's ear about what went wrong with my diet plan. And okay, fine. I wanted a glass of wine, and going to a party seemed like as good a time as any to have one. *I'm human, damn it, and that's okay.*

I texted Amy, "I'm so there! Whose party? When and where?"

A full minute went by with no response, so I went back to washing my dinner dishes. When my text indicator finally binged again, I dried my hands and read, "Toni's apartment. You already said you're coming, so no backing out. That's an order."

*Seriously?* I texted her back, "Fine. What the hell. I'll go." *It's about time Toni and I buried the hatchet anyway. I'm starting to miss my friend.* I was changing. I had bigger dreams for myself than ever before. I was slowly learning self-discipline, slowly, oh so slowly. I wanted Toni to see the new me. Even if you couldn't tell by looking at me that anything was different.

I went to bed that night imagining what it might be like to see Toni again. I couldn't come up with any scenario that wasn't awkward. I knew I wanted to look good, breezy, like I didn't care whether things worked out between us or not, because really, I didn't. Of course on some level I wanted things to go back to the way they were between us, but deep down, I knew that our relationship would never be the same.

For one thing, Toni wasn't into all this self-improvement-Earnest stuff, while I had fallen irretrievably down the self-improvement rabbit hole. Toni didn't seem to need this stuff. She never seemed the slightest bit troubled by life. Well, except for that time her mother died. But besides that, Toni seemed unflappable, and that perturbed me.

*Is everything so perfect in her inner world? Or is she lying about who she is and what's going on under the surface? I feel like I'll never really know her.*

# CHAPTER TWENTY-FOUR

When I woke up in the morning, I felt nervous for the party. I also felt fat and bloated after eating all that pasta the night before. I hadn't seen Toni in months, and I wanted to look like I'd changed. Like I'd improved. Like I had my shit together, and like I didn't need her to tell me what to do anymore.

*I'll stick to my diet today. It was hard yesterday for sure, but at least I was able to do it until the evening. I'll do it again, because I know I can hang on long enough to talk to Sandy about it.*

*Maybe I'll go out and buy myself a cute outfit to wear so I can feel super confident. I saw an adorable top at the boutique when I went with Amy, but it cost an offensive amount of money. I'm pretty sure I can afford it, though.*

After I showered, I stood in front of my computer desk and logged on to my bank account. I hadn't checked my balance in months, probably since I was fired from my job. *I've gotta have at least twenty or thirty grand left in there.*

When I saw my balance, I gasped. I had three thousand dollars left. *After I pay rent next week, it'll be closer to one thousand. Oh my God. Where did all my money go? I've been robbed. Someone hacked into my account.* I sat down and clicked around to look at my account history.

I read the list of charges that had been debited from my account. The boutique down the street. Dozens upon dozens of charges at my favorite restaurants. Amazon out the wazoo. I logged in to my Amazon account and saw that there had been two hundred and fifty-three orders placed in the last six months. *This is outrageous. Someone hacked my Amazon account, I'm sure of it!*

I scrolled through my Amazon orders and saw my beloved and pricey Estée Lauder face lotion, my printer ink (*necessary, of course*), plus a five-pound bag of chia seeds that I hadn't even opened yet. *A purchase I made when I was channeling Sandy that one time.* My striped pajamas that made me look like a round Christmas ornament. *I don't care because they're comfy and no one is going to see them anyway.* I saw books, makeup, purses; a random assortment of things that I hadn't even used that I certainly didn't need.

*Oh my God! All of those purchases are mine!* I hyperventilated. *The good news is that I'm not even tempted to chug from the bottle of wine sitting in the fridge. And how much did that stupid thing cost? The bad news is that I spent myself right out of my comfortable unemployment. I have to get a job. This is no time to be picky! And I have to stop spending money!*

*Damn it. What the hell am I going to wear to this party tonight?* I pawed through my closet and found a blouse that might look cute. I pulled on jeans and struggled to button them up. These jeans rolled my fat up my body so it ballooned over the top of my pants like bread dough rising out of control.

I put the blouse on. It was a miracle that it hid my bread-dough middle, but when I looked in the mirror, I noticed my big bosoms straining the buttons to get out, and it was sexy, like Grandma-chin-hair sexy. I tried pulling the top's fabric forward from my shoulders to give my boobies more room, but I had to stay perfectly still to keep it that way. And when I turned around, I realized that the top had ridden up over my giant ass. *Sigh. This clearly isn't going to work.* I tried a few more items from my closet, all with similar results.

*Look, no need to panic.* I sat down in front of my computer again and searched for a nearby thrift shop. *I can stop shopping myself into poverty, and instead I can be sensible and buy some used clothing. I can even bring a bag of all this ill-fitting stuff I have packed into my closet, and maybe they'll give me a few dollars per item.*

My mind began to spin big dreams: *Maybe I can even make money off the transaction! I can sell more than I buy, make some room in my closet, get a few items that look great and are new to me. This is so easy! What was I even worried about? Maybe I won't have to take the first job that falls into my lap. I can start selling my belongings instead. My place is too cluttered anyway.*

I pulled my go-to baggy black shirt over my bread dough and checked myself in the mirror. I could still see *it* through my shirt, so I put a pink cardigan on over it. *Acceptable.* I added a long necklace with a sparkly pendant for added distraction. I smiled in the mirror. *I look great, actually. No one will know about the bread-dough rising up from my pants.*

I decided to explore the thrift shop empty-handed because I wanted to see what rate they paid for consignments before handing over my belongings. I put on my parka, which wouldn't zip over my middle. As I stepped outside, a polar wind whipped around me, and I held my coat closed with one hand. I trudged the ten blocks to the thrift shop, staring down at the sidewalk the whole time to keep the wind from stinging my watery eyes.

When I arrived, I perked up as I pulled the door open. I stepped inside and rubbed my hands together for warmth as I glanced around. *Housewares, straight ahead.* Then I noticed a handwritten sign above the cash register in sloppy red marker: "Today's special! All clothing 50 percent off." My anticipation grew. Another sign beneath that read: "Currently accepting donations." *Donations? They aren't going to pay me for my stuff? I guess that makes sense. Too many people have too many things. Space is at a premium, but belongings aren't.*

My dream of starting a side business by selling my stuff swirled down the toilet. *But I can sell on eBay. No, I know I won't bother with that. Craigslist? Okay, maybe. I'll think about it. I'll have to figure out how to avoid getting murdered, though.*

I looked around the housewares section. On freestanding shelves scattered about, there was a chia pet, a broken waffle maker, and about a million coffee cups. *A chia pet! I would have something to do with my five-pound sack of chia seeds!* Then I saw four adorable glass ice cream dishes for thirty cents apiece. *Oh, I so want those!* Then a mental image of my stuffed cupboards came to mind. *Stop spending money on crap you don't need. But, chia pet…NO! Damn it. Fine.*

I sulked over to the clothing section, but it was both intimidating and off-putting. All I could see were racks upon racks of clothing in no discernible order. I noticed a dress so large it would fit a redwood tree hanging next to a little black dress so little that it would only fit a toddler.

The musty smell of deep-rooted body odor from decades of unwashed clothing began to fill my nostrils as I walked through the store. I pulled a few garments aside to look at them. They all bore indelible marks of wear. Pills, holes, stains. *Gross.*

I looked around at my fellow shoppers. *Why are they here?* A mom spoke in a foreign language to her kids as they browsed. An old woman pushed a cart containing a smattering of finds.

I stopped and watched the workers in the back of the store sort through bags of clothing donations. They listened to music and smiled as they worked. Their hands moved rapidly through the clothing as they talked and laughed with each other. They bopped in time to the music and they made the work look light, fun, and easy.

*I'm being a brat. I've been ungrateful for the income I'd been given. The other people here either want to be here or they have no choice. Well I don't want to be here, and I have a choice. I can get a damn job.*

★

When I arrived at the party that night wearing my black top and pink cardigan, Toni's apartment was packed with people holding cocktails and chatting in small groups. A high peal of laughter, like a cross between a sheep's *baa* and a man's voice, split the air. *Oh my God, what is that annoying sound?* I heard it again, and looked around to find the source.

Then I spotted her: Jill, standing next to the wellspring of that noise, which was coming from a normal-looking man wearing normal-looking clothing, which happened to be jeans and a sweater. *He's not dressed like a barnyard animal or a clown. Yet he's making that noise. It really is his laugh. And he laughs a lot.* My fear of Jill was temporarily dulled by my fascination with this character.

I could tell he thought he was very, very funny. He was the only one talking among the tight circle around him. He was loud, he gesticulated with his hands while he talked, and then he would let out that blood-curdling sound at the end of every anecdote. *Holy annoying, Batman!*

The trance was broken as Amy sidled up to me, gave me an air kiss, and said, "I'm so glad you made it!"

I jerked my head toward the laugher and asked, "Who the heck is that?"

Amy rolled her eyes. "Oh, that guy. That's Jill's husband. He's one of these guys who completely confuses insults with jokes. Like, he literally doesn't understand the difference. He says horrible things about people and then laughs."

"Well that's awkward. And Jill married him? She seems so humorless."

"Exactly. That's why they're the perfect couple. She probably doesn't realize he's not funny."

I felt smug. *Jill is married to an asshole! I might be single, but at least I'm not with that guy.*

I said, "So give me the lowdown. Who are all these people?"

"I knew you wouldn't come if I told you beforehand, but it's a joint party given by Toni and Jill."

"Jesus Christ, Amy! Jill is ready to haul me off to a facility. Do you really think this is a good idea?"

"Don't be so dramatic. I'm sure she's over it by now. Besides, you've got me, and Sandy is here somewhere. As for the rest of the crowd, pretty much half are Toni's work friends, and half are psychotherapy types."

"Oh, great. Well, I'm not in the mood to be analyzed, so how do I know who's who?"

Amy scanned the room. "Just pretend you're normal. You'll be fine."

"Isn't that what everybody does?"

"Pretty much. Oh, there's Sandy." Amy waved her over. Sandy smiled and strode toward us.

I said, "Hey, Sandy, you're looking perfect, as usual."

"Oh, Kelly, you make me blush. Thank you."

Amy said, "I'm going to grab a drink while you two catch up. Do you want anything?"

"Nothing for me, thanks," said Sandy. *Of course.*

"White wine for me," I said. *Of course.*

Sandy smiled her genuine, sweet smile as she looked into my face attentively and asked, "How's it going with you, Kelly? You look nice. I like your pink sweater."

I rolled my eyes. "God, this thing. It was hard getting dressed today. I feel like none of my clothes fit. I've been working out, so I don't understand it."

"What's your workout like?"

"I got a strength-training DVD from the library."

"Well, sometimes my body retains water when I do a lot of lifting. How's your diet?"

"Ooh, glad you asked. I want to talk to you about that. I feel like I have a decent meal plan going, but I'm having a hard time sticking to it because I'm starving by the afternoon."

"What are you eating?"

I rattled off my daily intake of shake-omelet-cheese-veggies-dinner.

Sandy said, "The bottom line is, if you're starving by dinnertime, you're not eating enough of something, probably fat, protein, fiber, or all three. Look over all of your meals and see where they need to be balanced with more vegetables. And rethink protein shakes; you might want to eat real food rather than relying on a processed drink. And if you insist on using protein shakes, remember a shake is going to digest quickly because it's liquid, so that might not be tiding you over. Blend in some avocado or some chia seeds—fat and fiber will keep you feeling full longer."

I felt triumphant. "Chia seeds! I have those!" *Boy, do I have those.*

"If you want to try something even faster than a shake, eat some cheese, nuts, carrots, fruit…things that are easy to keep on hand so you can grab them in a pinch."

"Carrots and fruit? I heard those are really high in sugar."

"Oh my God, if one more person complains to me about the amount of sugar in carrots or fruit…" Sandy sighed in frustration. "I'm sorry. This question comes up a lot. You know I'm a big fan of Gary Taubes and I think it's great to eat low carb, but how many people do you think became obese because they couldn't resist eating cantaloupe? I have one client who told me she refuses to eat carrots, corn, potatoes, and fruit. But then she thinks nothing of drinking seven margaritas on a Friday night at happy hour, or scarfing chips and crackers in front of the TV."

I suddenly had to urge to hide my glass of wine behind my back as I asked her, "Do you eat fruit?"

"Yes, but I don't eat fruit every day—only once in a while, in moderation. Some people do though, and it works for them. You have to figure it out for yourself, see how it makes your body feel. I might recommend eating cheese or nuts but if you're lactose intolerant or allergic to nuts, then you have to do what works for your body."

"I heard dairy is really bad for you."

"That's another one that gets me all riled up, people who run their personal campaigns against dairy. If you don't like how dairy makes you feel, then fine—don't eat dairy. But don't tell me I can't eat it. We're all different here, and we need to pay more attention to how different foods make us feel. Sorry. I just get pissed at all the crazy food rules that get passed around. Everyone needs to stop listening and start feeling it out for themselves. If you don't mind my asking, how long have you been on your current meal plan?"

I felt sheepish. "Well, yesterday, but then I attacked a plate of pasta. And today, up until now," I said as I raised my glass.

"Oh, okay. It's always going to be harder at first when you change your eating habits, and then if you can hang on after about four days of total compliance to your plan, your body should adjust as long as you're eating enough."

"Four days. I think I can do that."

"Just keep in mind you're going to face a little discomfort to lose weight in the form of resisting cravings, but don't think of it as a diet, and don't let yourself get too hungry. You have to eat in a way that you think you could do this forever. It can't feel extreme to you, and it has to be pleasurable. Oh, and avoid foods that are triggers for bingeing for you, like pasta."

I felt a hand on my shoulder, and I turned to see Toni. My heart started pounding, and I tried to smile as I said, "Oh, hey, Toni. Thanks for having me at your party." It suddenly occurred to me that I might not even be invited.

"No problem, glad you could make it." She seemed to read my mind as she added, "I was relieved when Amy said you were coming. I was worried you'd stay away. I miss you."

"I miss you too, Toni." Even as I said it, I wasn't sure it was true. Toni always made me feel less than, and that night was no exception. And here it came.

"So Amy said you're just writing. No real job?"

"Just writing? No, I mean, yes, but the writing is important, it's what I want to do. I want to write novels. Or maybe be a comedy writer. Or a sitcom writer, I'm not sure; I'm working out the details." *What? Where are these options coming from?* I didn't know, but they sounded interesting as they tumbled from my mouth. *Yes, I'll entertain all of these ideas. Why not?*

Toni feigned a half smile and said, "Okay, I guess you need to get this out of your system before you get a real job."

I felt slapped. And then it dawned on me, what Earnest had been trying to tell me at dinner when he said, "One small warning: never share your dreams with small minds. Only with like minds." I could see Earnest tap his temple in my mind's eye as he said, "With others who want to share their gift."

As far as I knew, Toni always wanted to be an accountant. *Is that her gift? Is that what she feels called to do? Maybe she doesn't feel called. Maybe she likes her life exactly as it is. Maybe she's normal and I'm a daydreaming freak. Or maybe, like Earnest said, she's one of those small-minded people with whom I shouldn't share my dreams. And what about Amy?* I felt irrationally furious that Amy had obviously told Toni what I was up to. Part of me blamed her that I endured Toni's insult.

Toni snapped me out of my internal monologue by saying, "Well, let me know when you're ready to make some money, because we need someone for a really easy QA job. You wouldn't even have to come into the office. You can sit at home and test web pages."

"Uh-hubba-wha? Money? Stay at home?" I smiled. "Toni, are you telling me that someone would pay me money to stay home?"

"Yeah, basically. They don't have enough desk space in the digital department to cram in a quality assurance team, so they're hiring people to VPN onto the network from home. You basically look at web pages all day and make sure they work okay. I don't think the pay is great, but the work is really easy and you can do it in your pajamas."

Thank God I'd gone to that disgusting thrift shop that day. Thank God this job was landing in my lap on the day that I realized I was financially broken, because I wouldn't have accepted it otherwise. As much as I hated to admit that I needed a "real job," Toni was right. I needed a real job that paid actual dollars, not future-fantasy money.

"Toni, I could kiss you. Yes, I'll take it, if they'll have me. I was just thinking today that I've got to get something. This is perfect timing!"

"Okay, great. I'll give your name to the team lead, and he'll hire you. No problem." *What was all that negative stuff I thought about Toni, small minds and whatnot? I take it all back. Toni is awesome.*

Then my stomach dropped as Jill sidled up to Toni with a mean twinkle in her eye. She looked pointedly at my glass of wine and said, "Oh, hi, Kelly. What brings you here?"

"Uhhhh." *What brings me here? The subway?*

Toni tried to smooth over the awkwardness by saying, "I was just telling Kelly she can work with our QA department."

Jill said, "Oh? Is that a skilled job? Will she be doing anything interesting? Like writing?" Jill smirked at me. *Oh this is nice, being openly mocked by a psychopath.*

Toni acted like there was no hint of condescension in Jill's question as she said, "No, it's pretty basic work. You just…"

Jill interrupted her, "I was eavesdropping. You just sit at home and stare at web pages." Jill rolled her eyes and said to me, "I don't know why you think that's such a great idea."

I stammered, "I…I'm not sure what you mean?"

"Haven't you ever heard of Rat Park?"

"Rat what?"

"Rat Park," Jill said, with a tone of duh-oh-my-God-everybody-knows-about-it-but-you. "A psychology professor had two sets of rats. Some rats were kept isolated in cages and they easily became addicted to morphine. He put other rats in a place he called Rat Park. It was a utopia where the rats could play and exercise and mate. The rats with social opportunities didn't want the morphine." She folded her arms across her chest and looked smug.

"I don't know what you're getting at," I said. *I'm pretty sure I know what she's getting at, but I want to annoy her in any way I can, and forcing her to explain herself is the only power I have.*

Jill narrowed her eyes and condescended. "Well, since you're so prone to falling into addictive patterns, it seems terribly ill-advised for you to put yourself into a situation that boils down to a cage in isolation. I think you're going to see your addiction worsen." A self-satisfied, closed-lipped smirk flickered across her mouth.

I glared at Jill in an impotent rage while Toni let out a nervous little laugh and chirped, "One person's cage is another person's utopia!"

Toni's defense of me, if that's what it was, gave me courage, and I said, "Yeah, what makes you think I don't want to work alone?"

Jill turned away from me as she said in a sarcastic voice, "Suit yourself. Just trying to help."

A woman I'd never seen before approached Jill and said to her, "Is that the patient you told me about over lunch?"

*Murder. I want to murder her.* As I swallowed the last of my wine, Toni pulled me into the kitchen and said, "I'm so sorry about Jill. *Please* don't take it personally."

I laughed maniacally. "How can I *not* take it personally? It's me, personally, that Jill was mouthing off about to her therapist friend over lunch." I was beyond offended by all of it: by Jill's assertions about me, by her lack of decorum, her big mouth, and her sneering insults.

Toni looked at my glass and said, "Can I get you another one?"

"Yes please."

Toni grabbed a mostly empty bottle of white wine from the counter and poured the last of it into my glass as Jill sauntered into the room. As Jill watched Toni shake the last drops of the bottle into the glass I was holding, a look of rage distorted Jill's face. I felt panicky as Jill, huffing and puffing, marched over and snatched an unopened bottle of wine from the collection crowded on the counter.

My fear gave way to curiosity as Jill clenched her teeth, grabbed a corkscrew out of a drawer, and stabbed the cork violently with it. She gave the corkscrew a few angry twists and then forcefully yanked the cork from the bottle with a pop. Then she filled her wine glass to the rim. *I've never seen anyone fill a wine glass all the way to the top before.* She leaned over and slurped at the glass to bring the liquid level down before picking it up. The whole performance was downright bizarre.

I looked at Toni, whose mouth was open as she watched Jill. Toni's eyes met mine and she said nervously, "Okay, I'm heading back to the party!" I silently trailed Toni out of the kitchen and back to the relative safety of the living room.

Frankly, I was so freaked out at that point that I wanted to put my glass down and get the heck out of there, but Amy collared me and said happily, "Oh, there you are! I want to introduce you to Tom." The handsome fellow at Amy's side held out his hand to shake mine as Amy said, "We're going kayaking on the Hudson tomorrow! Tom's an instructor. Isn't that awesome?"

I smiled and said, "Yeah, that's cool. I've always wanted to try that."

Tom said, "You should! Come on down anytime."

I was startled as Jill appeared at my side, and her sheep-*baa*-laughing husband materialized at my other side. As the five of us stood there in a tight circle as if we were all normal, sociable partygoers, I stared hard into Amy's eyes with a look that said, "Don't you dare leave me alone with these maniacs."

Amy tried to pretend I wasn't staring at her with crazy eyes as she smiled and said, "Hello, Jill, why don't you introduce us to..."

"Henry," Jill snapped. "This is my husband, Henry."

Amy held out her hand and said, "How are ya, Henry?"

Henry shook her hand and said, "I'm awesome! Better than you chumps." We all stood there with half smiles on our faces.

I noticed that Amy didn't bother to introduce Tom. *Smart move.* I wondered if anyone would protest if I ducked out and ran down the hall, never to be seen again.

Fear rose in my throat as Amy started to excuse herself, but Henry grabbed her upper arm and said, "Do you think I'm handsome?"

Amy laughed awkwardly and said, "Uh, sure."

Then Henry turned to me and said, "Hey you, what about you? Do you think I'm hot?" He pumped his arms and gestured like he was humping the air. "Would you bone me?"

*Holy shit, what the fuck is this weirdo getting at?* Jill caught my eye, looking like she was going to kill me, or maybe just eat my face clear off my skull, I wasn't sure. Maybe she'd already called the men in white coats to come get me and this whole Henry shtick was Jill's way of stalling for time.

I looked around and realized that the whole of the room, all of the shrinks and all of Toni's friends—everyone was silent, awaiting my answer: *Did I think Henry was hot? Would I bone him?* The psychotherapists all looked at me like they were holding imaginary notebooks so they could write down my answer to Henry's question. Then they could all huddle afterward and analyze the interaction.

As time stood still, I considered my options. *If I say, "Yes, Henry, I would bone you," it'll look like I'm hitting on Henry, and then Jill will stab me.* So I said the only logical thing I could think of. I said, "No." I didn't hear anyone gasp, but it still somehow felt to me like the whole room inhaled.

People tried to return to their conversations, or at least they pretended to. Henry dismissed himself from our little group and walked behind me in the direction of the cheese platter. I began to relax, thinking it was all over. Then Henry hissed in my ear, "When's the baby due?"

I was slow to understand what Henry meant. I turned with the innocence of a baby deer curious about why a hunter would fire an arrow. I smiled and said, "I'm not pregnant."

His eyes shone with meanness as he glanced down at my belly and said, "Coulda fooled me." Jill smiled and looked back at me as she linked arms with Henry.

*Bazinga. He got me.* My body betrayed me with a visceral reaction to what he said. I gulped as tears sprang to my eyes and my heart ached. I didn't know why it upset me so much. Maybe because yes, I did have a big belly, but I had hoped it wasn't so obvious.

*And how dare he? How dare he take such a cheap shot? I'm a woman, damn it, not a piece of meat. My body isn't here to be pleasing to Henry's eye.*

My mind was swinging between shame and feeling indignant as Amy closed in and whispered to me, "It's okay. We can go."

As the door closed quietly behind us, I said, "But what about Tom?"

"No worries. We're going kayaking, and I'll see him in the morning. Are you okay? You look really freaked out."

"Didn't you hear what Henry said to me?"

"No, what?"

I didn't want to repeat it. It was embarrassing. But I wanted Amy to know what a terrible person he was, so I told her. "He said, 'When's the baby due?'"

Amy didn't seem to know what a big deal this was. She shrugged and said, "Oh, well, he *had* to be joking."

"No, he didn't say it so everyone could hear him. I mean, thank God for small favors. But he *wasn't* joking. He didn't laugh. He whispered it to me, in my ear."

"What a dick."

*What a dick indeed.* But that reaction still wasn't enough for me. I wanted Amy to be furious. I wanted her to punch a wall. I wanted her to violently uncork a wine bottle and fill her glass to the top! We rode the elevator down in silence, and when we reached the street, Amy asked, "Do you want to go grab some dinner? Maybe you need to vent some more."

I was changing. In the-not-too-distant past, between Toni's comment about getting a real job, Jill's dirty looks and all-around crazy factor, resisting the bowl of tortilla chips, Henry's exacting insult—any one of these instances would have triggered an excuse to wash down noodles with wine.

*But not tonight.* While I absolutely considered getting piss-drunk and bloated with carbs, the thrill was gone. I said good night to Amy, went home, drank a glass of water, and went to sleep.

# CHAPTER TWENTY-FIVE

The next morning, I was startled awake by the phone. It was Bernadette. Let me rephrase that. OH MY GOD IT'S BERNADETTE! She wanted to know if I would have lunch with Earnest.

"Today. Yes. Of course. Whatever Earnest wants me to do, I'll do it." *If he wants me to fly to Paris to mow his lawn while he vacations in Hawaii, I'll do it.*

Later that day, dazed, star struck, and wearing my black top and pink cardigan sweater because—as extensively documented previously—nothing else in my closet fit me, I was sitting across from Earnest at some crappy diner in Brooklyn. I didn't care that he downgraded me from a dinner date at a fancy, pricey restaurant in Manhattan to a whatever-the-heck-this-was lunch at an outer-borough greasy spoon. I only cared that he still wanted to sit across a table from me and eat food while he talked to me.

*This is all that matters. Income? Who gives a shit. Still fat? So what. Me, Earnest, lunch. This is my whole world.* I was riveted by his mere existence. *His face is in the same room with my face.* It was beyond stupefying that it was because *he* arranged it.

Earnest asked me, in his usual, intense way, how my life was going and what was on my mind. I mustered the courage to tell him about Henry's comment regarding my pregnant appearance. Then I detailed Jill's sociopathic behavior, and the new job courtesy of Toni. "That's what's on my mind. In that order, more or less."

Earnest told me it was commendable that I was able to be completely honest with him about what I was thinking and feeling. In spite of the ridiculous pettiness of my complaints, I felt impressed with myself. He said that a lot of people are thinking about crap like this, but they pretend to care about things that sound more important. *He really greased the wheels with that comment. I'll be more honest than the two of us can handle.*

Earnest said, "So. It's Henry's comment that has bested you. That's driving you crazy, as you say. What do you think this means? That Henry made a disparaging remark about your body."

I thought for a moment and said, "That everyone knows how fat I am. It made me realize that I go around thinking that no one knows I'm chubby. But it's plain to see. Anyone can look down at my stomach and see how fat it is. My clothes aren't hiding anything. I guess I thought I looked thinner than I do. I thought I looked…normal at least. Not fantastic. But I didn't think I looked so fat that I look pregnant. And I didn't think I looked so bad that everyone was thinking it."

"And you think that because Henry made that remark that everyone is thinking that way about your body."

"Well, maybe not, but it made me realize that the evidence is there, if anyone cared to look. They'd see that I was fat. And I'd been fooling myself about that. And yeah, okay, I'd like to feel attractive…no, I'd like to *be* attractive. Look, I'm just going to lay it all out here. I've been single for a long time, and I thought I was okay with that, but that comment made me think that I'm going to die an old maid, as disgusting and outdated as that concept is, to be clear, but his comment made me feel desperate and I realized I still want to get married, and who wants to marry a woman with a big fat belly?" I couldn't believe I told Earnest I wanted to get married. I wasn't completely aware of the fact myself until I told him.

"There are some truths I'd like you to consider. One is that you don't love your body the way your body deserves to be loved. A comment like that wouldn't upset you if you knew your true worth, and the size of your stomach, and any other body part, has nothing to do with worth. Your body is deserving of unconditional love, and if you knew that in your heart, then Henry's comment would have slid right off you, like bird poop hitting greased window."

I hardly had time to consider that visual before Earnest continued, "Your fantastic body got you here to meet me. Your body is relatively young and strong. Just because you can't walk down the street without seeing very young, gazelle-like models with stick-like legs that reach up to their armpits doesn't mean that people like Henry deserve to have their opinions deliberated."

"Ummm…"

Earnest plowed ahead, "That man isn't fit to make small talk at a party. He's an imbecile. Why are you taking stock in the opinions of an imbecile? Your body, no matter what it looks like, is here to be loved. All of you, extra pounds and all. I'm willing to bet that you would find a suitor if you would accept your body and decide for yourself that this body of yours is lovable. And even if you don't wind up with a suitor in the traditional sense, regardless, you would benefit from more thorough self-acceptance."

"Mm-hmm," I said, not really believing a word about his self-acceptance speech.

The waitress, who happened to have stick-like legs that reached up to her armpits, came to take our drink order—iced tea for both of us. Earnest admired her figure while she smiled a toothy smile and told us all about the specials in great detail.

*What is it with Earnest and hot waitresses? Maybe I always have hot waitresses and I don't notice until I'm with Earnest. Or maybe hot waitresses fight over our table because they want to wait on Earnest.*

When the waitress left, Earnest said, "It's highly possible you haven't seen or experienced enough tragedy in your life to believe me."

"Believe you about what? What do you mean tragedy?"

"You don't know what it's like to endure chemotherapy or radiation and to claw back to life from the brink of death. You've never suffered a stroke and been without speech or the ability to write or to walk. You've never experienced what it's like to abuse laxatives until your intestines are no longer absorbing the nutrients from your food, something that has happened to more than one of my students; you don't know the damage that does to your body and your mind. You take your body for granted. You virtually ignore everything your body is capable of, all the joys your body gives you every day."

"I...I never thought of it that way before."

"And I bet you never knew that it's important you give your body joy in return."

"Hmmm," I murmured as I stared at the menu.

"I noticed that you ordered iced tea as opposed to an alcoholic beverage. How's that going for you?"

"Going great. I'm writing every day. I like being sharp in the morning, so I've cut way back. I had a glass and a half at a party last night, but it was no big deal. As long as I get my writing done, ya know?"

"That's wonderful. What do you want to eat?" asked Earnest.

"What do I want to eat, or what am I going to order?"

"They aren't one and the same?"

I laughed. "I'm getting the veggie omelet." I closed my menu.

"Interesting. And where did you get the idea that you should order a veggie omelet? It doesn't sound like the idea originated with you, since you implied it's not what you want to eat."

"Sandy," I said triumphantly. I thought Earnest would be proud of me for keeping such good company.

"Sandy. Mm. Yes. Sandy. And…she's been telling you what to eat?"

"Yeah, isn't it great?"

"No."

My face fell. "No? Why not? She's really good at this stuff."

"Your body is best at this stuff."

I laughed bitterly. "My body? This?" I said as I pulled viciously at my belly.

"If you're trying to indicate that your body is somehow unacceptable, you can point to your mind as to why that is."

"Look, Earnest, I got called 'pregnant' at a party. There's more than what's happening in my head going on here."

"You misunderstand me. You try to make decisions about what and how much to eat with your mind, rather than your body. And then your body rebels. And then you have an eternal tug-of-war happening between your body and mind. You restrict your eating because your mind tells you to, and then your body overeats because it's been restricted. You need to stop this nonsense. Don't listen to your mind, and certainly don't listen to Sandy's mind. Ask your body what it wants to eat. What do you want to eat, in your heart? What looks good on that menu?"

"French toast," I admitted sheepishly.

"Then order the french toast." Earnest looked at me intensely as he said, "*Deny your body no pleasure.*"

I willed myself to ignore the potential sexual innuendo in that command. "But then I'm going to pig out, and when I eat too many sweet and starchy foods, I get sleepy. And fat."

"Kelly, if you really want to lose weight, there are only three rules to remember. Eat when you're hungry. Don't eat when you're not hungry. Stop when you're full. Or in other words, do not eat to over-fullness."

"But it's so delicious! It's impossible *not* to overeat!"

"You overeat because your body thinks it's never going to get french toast again. Order french toast whenever you want, and then perhaps you won't feel the need to gorge yourself. And if you order french toast regularly, and it still makes your body feel sleepy or unhealthy, then maybe you'll order something else next time, but not because your mind thinks you shouldn't. It will be because your body doesn't want it."

This sounded insane to me. I was so used to worrying about fat grams and carb grams and calorie counts that ordering french toast just because I wanted it seemed deranged.

*Damn it, the hot waitress is back.*

To my horror, Earnest told her, "Eggs Benedict for me, and french toast for the lady." Then he shooed her away with a wave of his hand and a singsongy "thank youuu!"

The waitress frowned and scooted out of arm's reach as Earnest came dangerously close to physically hustling her along. Then Earnest looked at me and asked, "How are you feeling? Are you anxious at the thought of eating something so decadent?"

"Well, yes and no. I mean, I'm used to eating decadent things, obviously."

"But you haven't allowed your heart and mind to relax about the decision to eat these things."

"Nope. I always feel pretty conflicted about it. My mouth wants it, but my mind thinks it's a terrible idea."

"And so how does it feel to give yourself permission to eat french toast?"

"Well, I haven't, actually. You gave me permission. And it makes me tempted to give myself permission."

"I urge you to do so. I urge you to let your heart rest. To allow your body this pleasure without judgment. Close your eyes and take a deep breath."

I did as I was told.

Earnest switched to the quiet, soothing voice he used during meditations in class as he said, "We are going to take a moment to feel grateful for everything that's good in our lives. It's common across cultures to say a prayer of thanks before eating. When we're filled with awareness of the goodness in our lives, we don't feel the need to stuff down existential feelings of angst and fear. Instead, we enjoy the pleasure and nourishment that food brings us.

"A meditation on the grace of God, the Universe, fills our souls with hope, faith, and love. We understand how blessed we are to be alive and to experience the joy and pleasures available to us on this physical plane.

Let's concentrate now on counting our blessings. Let's give thanks for our health and our strength.

"Thank you for our friends and loved ones. Thanks for the work that exercises our hands and minds and brings us all the monetary wealth we need in each moment to flourish. Thank you for the sun and moon and sky, the stars, the flowers, the trees, and the grass. Thank you for the beauty and contrast of the ice and snow in winter, so we don't take for granted the warmth of summer. Amen."

"Amen." When I opened my eyes, Earnest was staring at me.

"How do you feel?" he probed.

"Relaxed."

"Good. Remember this feeling. This is how you should feel before you eat. Always take a moment to center yourself. Never eat when you're sad or angry."

I reveled in the feeling of relaxation, and then my heart fluttered a little. *I'm going to eat french toast!* I reminded myself to breathe and relax until I was calm again.

Earnest studied my face and said, "What are you thinking?"

"I'm kind of swinging back and forth between feeling excited and breathing to relax."

"Okay, this is good. Let's practice this. As you concentrate on your breath, imagine your heart opening, like the petals of a flower blooming."

As I did it, I said, "It feels a little scary. To open my heart."

"Yes, because we're all used to being guarded. We think that our fear protects us, and we use it to close our hearts. But we can get hurt whether our hearts are open or closed. It's best to live with the heart open. If it stays open, even when hurt, it will heal faster. Shutting down never solves anything; it keeps us bitter and fearful. Always, throughout your days, practice the feeling of opening your heart. Feel the petals unfurl and breathe into the sensation."

I took deep breaths, and for the first time in forever, a calm, natural smile spread across my face. I noticed the distinct absence of tension in my face, especially my forehead. *Oh, if only I could feel this way forever. This is why I love being with Earnest. All is right in the world when I'm with him.*

When our food arrived, Earnest said, "Now, the first thing we must do is appreciate the appearance and aroma of our meals. Eating is a multisensory experience. Take a look. What do you see? Does it look appealing?"

"No," I admitted. "It wasn't what I expected. I thought the french toast would be a stack of thick, fluffy, golden pieces of bread, dusted with powdered sugar. Instead, I got these burnt, soggy, wrinkled triangles. That strawberry garnish looks mostly rotten. And instead of a cute little pitcher of syrup on the side, my dish already has syrup on it." I looked enviously across the table at Earnest's magazine-ready plate.

Earnest said, "Now, let's sniff our dishes."

I put my face next to the plate and took a whiff. I wanted to inhale a rich, buttery aroma that was laced with sweet maple syrup and cinnamon, but it didn't smell like much at all, except for a burnt smell.

Earnest waited until I picked up my head and then said, "And now let's get a feel for the texture. Pick up your knife and fork, and as you cut a bite, notice what tactile sensations your food reveals. Does it increase your eagerness to eat your meal?"

I anticipated the way the bread would yield easily to my knife, but instead it was tough and rubbery. I stopped and looked at my knife to make sure I was using the correct edge. *Yup.*

Earnest asked, "And how is this exercise going? Do you still feel excited?"

"Kind of. Maybe. Okay, well, maybe not. I think this stuff's been sitting in a chafing dish in the back getting dried out. It seems kind of…old."

"Okay, and now we're going to take our first bite. And as you do, I want you to pay close attention when it first hits your tongue. Concentrate on all of the flavors and the feel of it in your mouth. As you chew, I want you to notice how the taste changes and how the texture softens as it mingles with your mouth juices."

*Mouth juices. Oh, Earnest. You freakin' weirdo.* I tried stifling a smile as I brought my first bite to my mouth. *Yuck. That wiped the smile right off my face.* I said through a mouthful of subpar french toast, "I think they put honey on it instead of syrup. That was *not* what I was expecting."

Earnest took a bite of his food and looked up at the ceiling in ecstasy as he let out an emphatic, "Mmm!"

*Son of a bitch. I definitely got the wrong thing.*

As I chewed the leathery, honey-covered bread, Earnest reveled in his meal. Earnest paused and said, "Now. I want you to chew slowly, count your bites, and notice at what point you feel like you've finished eating."

I said, "I think I'm done now."

"Is it really that bad?"

"Yeah, it's really that bad."

"I'm sorry I ordered it for you. I wanted you to have a good experience."

"No, don't be sorry. This actually was a good experience. I think if you weren't walking me through the steps, I probably would've done what I always do."

"And what's that?"

"I wouldn't have paid much attention. I probably would've eaten a lot of it and ignored how terrible it was. I would have eaten until I was full. I wouldn't have noticed that it was rubbery. I probably would have noticed the honey, though. That was pretty bad. I mean, I like honey, just not on my french toast. I wanted syrup! But anyway, I would've eaten a lot of it and then regretted it afterwards. I would have wished I hadn't eaten it at all."

"Okay, this is good. I want you to practice the rest of the exercise later then, when you're by yourself, perhaps with a meal you know you'll enjoy. I want you to concentrate on feelings of hunger and fullness as you eat, and I want you to stop eating when you're full. Do you think you can do that?"

"Yeah, I can do that." Even as the words escaped my mouth, I wasn't entirely sure I'd follow through.

Then Earnest said, "And I want you to report back to me about your experience."

*Okay I'll do it, as long as it means I have an excuse to talk to Earnest again.* I started to feel wistful, anticipating the end of our date. *I mean, our non-date-teacher-student diner experience.*

Earnest said, "Are you still hungry? Would you like to order something else, or should I get the check?"

I didn't want to be a bother. Even though it went against my inner yearning to spend as much time as possible in Earnest's presence, I donned a veneer of being low maintenance. "Nah, let's get the check. I'm good."

Earnest raised his hand slightly and the waitress swooped over to our table. As she bent down to gather Earnest's empty dish, I watched him stare at her cleavage. She paused there, like she was waiting for Earnest to insert his nose in the space between her breasts. Then her boobs jiggled as she gestured toward my mostly untouched french toast. "Didn't you like it, sweetheart?"

"Oh, it was fine. I'm not that hungry."

Earnest said, "She told me it was tough and rubbery, and it had honey on it instead of syrup." I wanted to slide down the booth under the table and onto the floor.

"Oh no! Let me get you something else."

"No thank you, it's fine, seriously," I protested. *My attempt to appear low maintenance is spiraling even more out of control than our waitress's boobs.*

Earnest seemed to notice my discomfort and said, "We'll take the check."

"All right, but I'm not gonna charge you for that dish."

"Thank you," Earnest and I said in unison.

Earnest looked serenely off into the distance as we waited for her to come back. I imagined he was taking these empty moments to meditate by repeating a mantra in his head, while I sat there with my mind spinning. *How will this non-date wind up? Should I embrace him? Shake his hand? Tell him I'll see him in class?* I didn't want our time together to end, but I felt so painfully awkward sitting there with him in silence that I knew it would be a relief to be alone again.

The waitress came back and placed the check on the table, then leaned down and made a big show of crossing the french toast off the bill and retallying the total. With each movement of her hand across the bill, her boobs shook and wiggled in her shirt. Earnest was entranced. *So that's what he'd been meditating on. I can't stop thinking about those Jell-O Jigglers my mom made me when I was a kid.*

As the waitress finally turned to go, she knocked the pen to the floor and then turned to pick it up. Time slowed down as she performed the following move: Ass to our table, she spread her legs slightly, then hinged at the waist. She very slowly (it seemed at least) made her way down toward the floor to get the pen while her keister and undercarriage were aimed at us.

My mouth dropped open. When I turned to look at Earnest, he had the same expression on his face, except his eyes were bugging out of his head like he was trying to see harder. When he sensed me looking at him, he closed his mouth and regained his composure. The waitress plopped the pen on the table and said, "Sorry about that!" With a big grin, she flounced off and said over her shoulder, "You two have a great day!"

When I turned back to the table again, Earnest was fussing with his pants and I realized he was trying to rearrange his erection before standing up. He stopped, looked at me with watery eyes, and said,

"Kelly, there are other pleasures besides food I'd like to show you today. Will you please invite me to your apartment?"

The sound of blood rushed in my ears. Earnest cleared his throat.

I said, "Earnest, will you come to my place?"

"Yes," he said hoarsely. He grabbed me by the wrist, threw a wad of cash on the table, and tugged me outside where his hand shot up into the air to hail a cab.

# CHAPTER TWENTY-SIX

O nce in the cab, Earnest instructed the driver while he grabbed a handful of my hair at the back of my head, close to the scalp. He applied a gentle, steady pressure to the back of my head while his other hand lightly closed around my throat.

I noticed the cabbie's eyebrows go up in the rearview mirror, and I put on a smile that said, "Nothing to see here."

The cabbie's eyes returned to the road, and Earnest grabbed my wrists, pinned them to the headrest behind me, and straddled me. He began kissing my face and neck before giving me a deep french kiss. He eventually released one of my hands so he could grope my breast. I wasn't sure what to do with the free hand, so I placed it lightly on his back. He searched my chest and sucked my face until we got to my apartment.

He opened the door to the cab, tossed some bills at the cabbie, and shoved me out of the car. He appeared by my side, pushing me toward the door to my apartment building. As I unlocked the door, he breathed, "Hurry," into my ear.

He propelled me up the stairs with his hands on my waist and his face dangerously close to my big butt. When we were barely inside the apartment, he demanded, "Strip. Now."

I wanted to clarify the question. *Should I go into the bathroom? Do you need me to clean down there?* But the look on his face stopped me, and I did as I was told. When I was completely naked, he pulled his pants down. His boner bounced off his stomach and rested at a ninety-degree angle, aimed at me. He again grabbed me by the wrist, practically dragged me into the bedroom, and said, "On your back." I scooted onto the bed, knees raised, legs slightly parted.

He widened my legs so he could sit in between them. He cupped my groin in his hand, and then with his thumb, he gently circled the area near my clitoris. After some light exploring, he gradually applied more pressure and sped up his motions.

As he thrummed my womanly bits, I began clock watching. I felt uncomfortable, but not because what he was doing didn't feel good. Earnest knew his way around my anatomy better than I did. But I wasn't used to having someone fixated on my pleasure. *What if he gets bored? What if things don't look pretty down there? Shouldn't I be reciprocating instead of just lying here?* I tried to sit up, but Earnest pressed my shoulder back down onto the bed.

Earnest sensed my whirring mind and said, "Surrender is your mantra. Your body is surrendering to the pleasure. Empty your mind and fill it with the mantra. Surrender. Surrender. Surrender. Keep repeating it. And if a thought intrudes, return to the mantra." I did as I was told until I reached a zone of mindless pleasure.

What happened next can only be described as sacred. God entered my body at the cellular level and infused me with light and angels and music and it was only interrupted by a strange noise I heard intruding at the edges of the experience. I tried to shut my eyes harder to block it out when I realized it was my own voice shouting, "I'm coming! I'm coming! I'm coming!" And then the light and music vanished, leaving behind a faint trail of pleasure, and when I opened my eyes, I was in Earnest's arms and he was smiling down at me, like a mother cradling an infant.

I began to flip into neurotic-old-me mode. I couldn't believe I let go like that, but Earnest said, "You did well," as if it was everything he expected of me. "You used the mantra to enter a holy space." I felt stunned that he used the word *holy* when that's exactly how this had felt. *Halleluiah, halleluiah.*

We rose from the bed, gathered our clothes, and began dressing. Earnest said, "Kelly, if you have more time this afternoon, I'd like to sit with you and talk about surrendering."

"Of course." I couldn't believe my luck. *That happened, and now this?*

Earnest fluffed up some pillows at the head of the bed and sat with his back leaning into them. He patted the spot next to him and motioned for me to sit, so I did. He took a deep breath and sighed it out, slowly. I waited like a lamb, wondering what he'd say and anticipating how I would drink it up.

"Kelly," he began, "Most of us on this Earth live in a perpetual state of anticipation. We wait for things to improve in our lives. We hope and pray for the perfect job to turn our lives around. We ignore or barely endure our lives until we can go on vacation. Many of my students come to me thinking their lives will begin after they lose weight. Then they think life begins once they find a partner.

"When we constantly pray for change in our lives, we discount everything we already have. We want more success while we ignore everything we've accomplished. And because we live in the future our whole lives, waiting for a time when we think things will be better, we're perpetually dissatisfied. Many people only realize on their deathbeds that this is the way they've lived, wasting each precious moment by wishing it were different."

*As usual, Earnest has me pegged. At least he framed it that everyone thinks that way, so I won't feel embarrassed that he figured me out. Or maybe a lot of people do think that way.*

He went on, "There's nothing wrong with anticipation, with enthusiastically working toward goals. There's nothing *wrong* with hope. Hope is a virtue of the human experience. However, when we never learn to surrender to the present, we live in hope at the expense of joy. Because we can only be happy in the present moment—and we spend all of our time trying to escape the present for an imaginary future—we never learn to enjoy ourselves. It saddens me when I think of how many people never learn to let go and release the tension in their faces and bodies; they never learn how to feel freedom and joy.

"One of the most important realizations we can all have is that, while we will never be done praying and hoping and wishing—the real gold of life is always right where you are in the present moment. There is always something to be cherished, treasured, and grateful for.

"Now, I know that you're hoping to be a successful writer one day. But what is it in your life that deserves to be treasured? Describe to me the myriad things you have to be grateful for right now."

"My friend Amy. She loves me unconditionally, and I'm only starting to understand how important and special that is. And a job. My friend Toni said she's getting me a job so I can work at home and start bringing in money again. Writing, of course. Even if I never hit the big time, I love to do it. That's a joy to me. And the ability to feel strong in my body. That's never happened before."

"Strength. Yes. That's a wonderful feeling. Tell me, what's changed? Why do you feel strong?"

For the first time, I feel like food and alcohol have loosened their hold on me. I mean, the fact that I was going to order an omelet and iced tea instead of the french toast and a mimosa today, and it wasn't even going to be a difficult decision…and I'm starting to genuinely enjoy exercise. I believe it's possible for me to get healthy, and now I'm making choices that reflect that. For the first time in my life, I *know* I can get healthy. I believe it now. And I'm starting to understand that I will act in line with what I believe.

"I've never been so sure before that this is what I want, to take care of my body without feeling that conflicted draw toward eating foods that hurt me. It's like I love myself and I want to take care of myself, and eating healthy is simply part of that. Weight loss, if that's going to happen, will merely be a symptom of feeling loving toward myself rather than the goal itself."

"And how does this differ from past attempts to lose weight?"

"In the past, losing weight was the main driver. I hated my body. I was embarrassed by it. And dieting and exercising were ways to punish myself. But now I like exercise. I like to feel stronger and more powerful every day. And eating well—eating enough healthy foods to satisfy my body's natural appetite—is a pleasure in itself.

"If someone were to say to me, 'Loosen up, eat this chocolate cake,' I wouldn't have this conflicted rush of emotion about it, and I wouldn't stuff myself full of cake. I might enjoy a little, or I might not. It would depend on whether I felt like doing it, but I certainly wouldn't do it to drown out my feelings, like I used to."

"And how do you manage your feelings now?"

"I journal a lot. I write down the thoughts that are causing the feelings. I'm finding there's always more than one way to see a situation. I can either shift my perspective, or I can find a solution to a problem. But there's never a reason to eat or drink over something that's bothering me. I never realized it before, but eating and drinking to cover my feelings adds a layer of confusion and frustration and negativity to any problem. Trying to ignore stuff always makes it worse."

"And to what do you owe these changes?"

"Reality. I stopped arguing with reality every step of the way. I can face problems instead of ignoring them or complaining. I'm beginning to accept that my choice is to stay in the struggle and to keep arguing against the reality that booze and junky foods make me feel fat and unhealthy—or I can accept it and move on and eat what I know is good for me."

"And how did you get in touch with this reality, this newfound sense of clarity?"

"It's from meditation. I practiced watching my thoughts from a distance. I don't argue with myself anymore, and I also don't believe everything I think. It's like I'm tapped into a smarter version of myself."

"Yes, your higher self can communicate and receive the wisdom of the Universe, once you quiet your thinking mind—the part of you that argues with yourself and makes you struggle to accept reality. This is wonderful, Kelly. You've grown a lot under my tutelage. But remember: surrendering to the now is a lesson we all must learn many times over, every day, every moment of our lives. The next time you have a problem that's emotionally upsetting, it might be difficult to surrender to what is. May the heightening of your emotions remind you that surrender is always an option. Surrender might be hard to find sometimes, but it's there, waiting to be accessed."

"Do you mean I shouldn't solve problems? I should surrender instead?"

Earnest chuckled. "No, no. That's not what I'm saying at all. What I mean is that sometimes the problems that cause us the most grief aren't so easily solved or dismissed. Sometimes we might see a solution that won't be so quickly reached. We might be in a situation we don't like and so we resolve to address it, but we might remain stuck in unpleasant circumstances for a time before we can execute on a solution or come to a true shift in perspective. These are the times that we must empty our minds, breathe deeply, and truly surrender to the present moment, rather than struggling against what is. As Eckhart Tolle would say, we must be in our bodies. We must simply inhabit ourselves rather than projecting into the future or worrying about the past. We must do what we can to resolve the issues, and then throw all that extra energy and attention into being here now, of breathing into your lungs and seeing with your eyes and feeling what it's like to be alive, rather than striving toward distraction."

"Okay, I'll keep it in mind." *I hope I don't need to remember that advice any time soon.*

"Kelly, one thing is troubling me. You said your conflict with food and alcohol seems to be resolved. But you admitted in the diner that, had we not been practicing mindful eating, you would've eaten the french toast quickly and mindlessly. What do you think of this contradiction?"

I blushed and stammered, "Look at me, trying to act all enlightened."

"No, no, Kelly. I wasn't trying to catch you in a lie. But I don't want you to fall into the trap of thinking you're done growing and done making mistakes. You may still give in to urges, even though you think you won't."

I felt indignant and a spark of rage surged. *How dare he predict that I'm going to fail?* I couldn't stop myself from snapping, "Well, obviously *you* gave in to an urge! Do you think *you're* done?"

Earnest chuckled again. "I do have a weakness for beautiful women. So much so that I violated our agreement. I said you must go thirty days without alcohol before we engaged in intimate relations, but I was overcome with desire."

*Desire for me or for the waitress who made him horny?*

"Kelly, my point is that none of us will ever be done learning or growing spiritually. There are infinite levels of expansion and ascension. And mistakes will be made. I don't want you to make a mistake and then jump to the conclusion that you were wrong about your capabilities and learnings thus far. This is a common reaction to humans' seeing they've made a mistake. They lose all faith and backslide completely, erasing all of the gains they've made. We often throw away previous evidence of progress as a fluke. We think we're hopeless. We give up on whatever we were striving for. In fact, many of us use mistakes as an excuse to stop working toward what we want. We use mistakes as an excuse to return to our lowly comfort zones."

I was calm again, humbled by my outburst, and determined to take his advice about mistakes to heart. "Okay. I think I get it. You're saying that one day, I could get upset and, instead of facing the issue, I might put a spoon into a carton of ice cream and start shoveling. It doesn't mean I'm a failure or that I've learned nothing."

"That's right. You can learn from your mistake."

"What could I learn? I already know not to do that."

"If you're repeating a mistake, then there's more to learn. You need to get curious about the subtleties and intricacies of what drove you to that point. Had you little sleep the night before? Did you skip too many meals, and you became ravenous? Did someone make you angry, and maybe you don't yet have enough experience opening your heart and exploring the emotion of anger, and so you took your anger out on your body instead? Usually there are myriad causalities behind such slips. You must open your eyes wide to the circumstances that led you to this point so you may learn more about the secrets of your willpower. You must continue to study your own mind from a distance."

I laughed inside, a knowing Buddha laugh, because I understood what Earnest meant about studying my own mind from a distance. In the past, I would have giggled like a childish dolt at the ridiculousness of the phrase, but now I basked in the warm glow of knowing.

I was jolted from my reverie when Earnest asked, "Kelly, are we done here?"

My insides dropped. *I don't want you to leave. I want you to belong to me.* But I couldn't think of a compelling reason to make him stay. I mustered up a smile and said, "I'm good. Thanks for hanging out with me today."

"You're welcome, Kelly. The pleasure was all mine. Seeing one of my students surrender the way you did today is one of my greatest joys." I willed myself to ignore the plurality in that statement; I couldn't bring myself to imagine which of the other students had surrendered to Earnest. *Please, God. Let me be the only one.*

# CHAPTER TWENTY-SEVEN

After I closed the front door behind Earnest, I took a running leap onto my bed, kicked my feet in the air, and squealed. *This is the best day of my life.* I wanted to lay there and replay the events of the day in my mind, but I was interrupted by the phone ringing. The voice on the other end asked, "Is this Kelly Ryan?"

*I can't stand telemarketers.* With a cold edge to my voice, I said, "This is she."

"Oh, is this not a good time?"

"Who is this?" *I'm losing time! I must commit each tiny detail of my fantastic day to memory before I forget anything.*

"This is Rex. Toni told me you were interested in the QA position?"

"Oh God, I'm so sorry, Rex! I thought you were a telemarketer." Rex let out a laugh, and I could feel the tension dissipating.

"So are you interested?"

"Yes. Definitely. With every fiber of my being."

"Well okay then. That's more dedication than I was expecting. Let me tell you a little bit about the job first, and then we can confirm whether it's still something you want to do." As Rex droned on about the interface I'd be using to measure the different qualities I'd be evaluating on each web page, one ear listened to him, but my mind was a thousand miles away.

As I sensed Rex going deeper into detail, I snapped away and pulled out my notebook so I could process what he was saying on paper. The pay was hourly and the rate was much lower than what I was used to making. *But still—sitting at home! Working in my pajamas!* "I'll take it."

Rex asked, "Can you start right away?"

"You mean like right now?"

Rex laughed again. "No, I'll need to get you a contract and your W-9 and all that. Can you start as soon as HR has all your paperwork processed?"

"Oh." I laughed at my own stupidity. "Yes, this week should be fine."

"Great. Can you join a two-hour training over the phone tomorrow?"

"Absolutely."

As I hung up, my heart was bursting with joy. *I'm going to make money again! I can still work on my writing in my free time. And Earnest. Oh, Earnest.*

I picked up my cell phone and texted Sandy and Amy, "I have news!" *I need to talk about all of this goodness.* "Dinner at my place," Sandy texted back. Amy and I replied one after the other, "Yes!"

★

When I arrived at Sandy's apartment building, she buzzed me in and I hoofed it up the stairs to her unit. Her door was left open a crack, so I stuck my head in and said, "Hello?"

"Hey, Kelly! Grab a bowl, help yourself to some salad, and come join us in the living room."

*Salad? For dinner? That's it? Yeah, I'm getting better at my food choices, but I still like to think of dinner as a bigger event than a bowl of lettuce.* But then I saw the salad.

Nestled into a wooden bowl on Sandy's kitchen table, I saw pecans, chunks of avocado, goat cheese, chicken, and roasted pears over crisp romaine lettuce, all glistening with dressing. *Okay, this is my kind of salad.* I grabbed a hearty helping, tipped a pitcher of ice water into an empty glass, and walked into the tiny living room. "Amy! Sandy! This salad looks amazeballs. Thanks so much for having us over."

I put my glass down on the coffee table and plopped in between them on the couch as Sandy laughed. "Oh, my pleasure. I wasn't in the mood to go out tonight, so it was selfish of me to have you girls over."

As I sank into the couch and drove my fork into my bowl, I tried to stop myself from smiling. Amy caught me smirking and said, "I know that look. Spill it. I want details."

I giggled and covered my mouth as I chewed and said, "I don't know where to start."

Amy put her bowl down and said, "Start at the beginning. I'll wait."

Okay, fine. I put my fork in my bowl, placed it on the table, and then took a swig of water. Amy's foot jiggled up and down. "Still waiting."

"All right, all right. Okay. So I went out with Earnest today."

Amy yelled, "What? Get out!" A smile played on her lips as she said, "Where? Someplace fancy?"

"Nah, just a shitty diner." I looked at Sandy and said, "I was going to order the omelet, but Earnest made me get the french toast."

Now it was Sandy's turn to freak out. "No! Why?"

"He wanted to teach me about mindful eating."

"And you guys couldn't have done that with an omelet?"

"I don't know, I think he wanted it to be something really decadent, something I'd want to savor. Oh, wait. I did tell him that I would've ordered french toast if I wasn't watching what I eat. And then he ordered it for me."

Sandy looked concerned. "Wait a second. But since you *are* trying to eat healthy, it blows my mind that Earnest, of all people, would pressure you to go against that. What was he thinking?"

Amy said, "Enlighten me. Why the big deal over what she ordered? And when do we get to the sex part?"

Sandy said, "It's a big deal because Kelly has shown some signs of food addiction. What Earnest did was akin to ordering a vodka martini for someone struggling to stay sober."

I said, "Well, I wouldn't go that far. I mean, I didn't even want alcohol."

Sandy said, "No, I was just…that was not what I meant. I mean, look at breakfast syrup like they have in a diner. It's mostly corn syrup, liquid sugar at any rate. Sugar triggers your brain's natural opioids. When you eat sugar, you can get addicted to the release of opioids. It's the same thing that happens when people take morphine or heroin."

"Actually, they put honey on my french toast by accident. It was pretty gross."

Sandy was getting frustrated. "Look, I'm not getting my point across. What I'm trying to say is that your body has been craving sugar for a long time and you've been trying to make choices that will help put an end to those cravings. I would hate to see an order of french toast put you back on the wrong path. It can be a slippery slope—at any time in the game, for anyone. Processed foods are highly addictive. It's so easy to fall back into a cycle of cravings and giving in."

I felt smug. "Oh, you really don't need to worry about it. The french toast was nasty and stale. I hardly ate any of it."

Amy burst out, "Will you guys stop talking about the fucking french toast? I want to hear about the sex!"

"We actually didn't have sex."

Amy threw her hands up in disgust. "Then why are we even here?"

"No penetration. He did make me come, though."

"*What?*" They said in unison.

"Yeah. It was a meditation exercise."

Amy said, "Whoa, whoa, whoa. He gave you an orgasm."

"Yes."

"Hands? Mouth?"

"Hands."

Sandy asked, "And this was a meditation…how, exactly?"

"He gave me a mantra."

Amy said, "Okay, I'll bite. What's the mantra?"

"Surrender."

Amy clapped her hand over an open-mouthed grin. "Oh my God, shut *up*! He is a kinky fucker!"

"No, it wasn't like that. Well, maybe a little bit when we were making out in the cab on the way to my place. But then it was, like, sacred."

Sandy's face had shifted from fascination to disapproval and back again before asking, "And how does this affect you? When Earnest comes on to you like this."

"Well, it's thrilling for sure. But it's also given me this sense of worthiness I've never felt before. To have someone that powerful pay attention to me, it's electrifying. And the effects last. I hold my head a little bit higher. I love myself now more than I ever have. I feel bulletproof."

Sandy said, "Okay, I'm going to play devil's advocate for one second. What if he's messing around with other women in the class? Do all these good feelings come crashing down?"

"God, I hope not." I took a deep breath and squared my shoulders. "No, no," I shook my head. "Something has fundamentally changed inside me. I always used to feel inferior to other people. I don't feel that way anymore. I have unconditional love for myself now. And for others too. It's not about comparing or judging or being less than or better than other people. I really get, in here"—I patted my chest with my palm—"when Earnest says we are all magnificent and we deserve to live a magnificent life. I really believe that now. He's told me so many times that I'm worthy of love. Now it feels ridiculous to feel any differently. As strange as it sounds, since this all came from being around Earnest, for the first time, I don't need a man to feel loved. It's in here. For good."

Sandy looked doubtful, while Amy looked captivated, the usual when I talked about anything to do with Earnest. I let it all slide right off me, and then I realized this was a much more assured reaction than I would have had in the past.

Amy said, "I'm psyched for you. I've never seen you this confident before. Is it really all Earnest, or is it also because you're done with that soul-sucking job?"

"It's also because I'm writing every day, and I know I'm getting better at it. And speaking of jobs, it looks like Toni got me one! Working from home. I start this week."

Sandy said, "That's fabulous, congrats."

"Thanks, I'm pleased."

Amy said, "That's awesome, girl. See, you don't need to be a fishmonger's trash collector after all."

Sandy looked confused.

"Never mind," I said.

"Amy, what's the story with Tom? Did you guys go kayaking?"

She rubbed her hands together and said, "I thought you'd never ask! It was awesome. We're going again tomorrow."

"Seriously? That's a lot of kayaking. Or is kayaking a euphemism for sex?"

"Nope, just kayaking so far. But I'm getting hooked on it. I love being out there on the water, looking back at the city. It's so peaceful. You've got to try it."

Sandy said, "I might try it, maybe. When the weather's a little warmer."

Amy said, "You can wear a wet suit, and then it's not so bad. You pee inside and it keeps you warm."

Sandy and I yelled, "Eeeew!"

"Whatever. You guys are wimps."

# CHAPTER TWENTY-EIGHT

The next day, I dialed in to Rex's training conference call. The job sounded mind-numbingly easy. You looked at a dashboard, evaluated each web page based on a few different stats, and hit a button to categorize each page you reviewed.

*A monkey could do this job. And they're giving me money. It seems too good to be true.* I faxed my paperwork and photo ID over to HR after the call, and that was it. I could start working immediately.

The first hour, I whistled while I worked. It was kind of fun to feel like I was the Judge of the Web Pages, damning some of them to hell and letting others pass based on their merits.

Hour two, I longed to get up and stretch. I checked the refrigerator. I peed. I paced. I wondered, *If I'm not busy clicking pages, is someone aware that I'm not working?* I imagined some guy sitting in a dark control room, watching over the dashboards of each remote worker, grading us on our speed and accuracy. Red lights flashed. *Kelly Ryan isn't working!* I looked at the clock. *Can I bill for the fifteen minutes I wasted?* I felt paranoid and sat back down to work.

During the third hour, I was going crazy. I got up and made popcorn, purely for the entertainment factor. But it was hard to click web pages when I had salt and butter on my fingers. I began to scarf handfuls of popcorn with one hand while I attempted to work with the other.

As the week wore on, my mood quickly morphed from blind enthusiasm to *FUCK THIS SHIT.* I snacked constantly to dull the searing boredom. I couldn't write because I was supposed to be clicking on web pages for eight hours a day, and the thought of sitting in front of my computer to write either before or after that was just...no. Besides, my brain was fried. The work was easy, but mind-numbing turned out to be the perfect description for it.

I began slacking off more and more, and so I tried to talk myself into writing because at least it would be a better use of my time. But I felt too guilty to write when I hadn't gotten my work done. I willed myself to work, and I mostly disobeyed my own orders.

All of my newfound good behaviors slipped from my grasp. This job was quickly driving me insane, and the constant eating would surely kill me. I couldn't understand why I was unable to motivate myself to regain control of my diet, to start exercising again, and to keep working on my writing.

Why were all of my behaviors rapidly backsliding into old territory? I worried that it would soon be like I'd never met Earnest. All of my enlightenment was slipping through my fingers. I began to feel tempted to sit in front of the TV and drink wine, like the good old days. I resisted, but I thought about doing it almost constantly.

I talked myself into keeping the job every day. *I can't quit. I need the money. Maybe I simply need to get used to the work, and then it will all be fine.* I didn't want to make a decision. I wanted it to all go away.

The following week held similar bouts of procrastination and agonizing. Rex finally called me. I winced as I picked up the phone, because I knew he was going to call me out. He said, "Kelly, I'm a little concerned. I've been checking the system, and I noticed that your productivity is very inconsistent."

I didn't know what to tell him, so I pretended I had the flu. He sounded apologetic and rushed off the phone. I thought about drinking wine.

I hated to admit it, but Jill was right. I was like a rat in a cage. I was sitting around in isolation, like a rat hitting a lever. I could put wine at the other end of the lever if I wanted. I could make this job bearable. But I didn't. Instead, I barely worked, barely got paid, and came up with increasingly thin excuses every time Rex called.

Weeks went by and I spent every day in a coma of frustration. My journal got dusty. I longed to write, but my well of creativity felt dry.

Amy texted me, "I haven't heard from you. Come to the bar and see me! Let's catch up." *Thank God.*

I didn't even shower. I pulled my coat on over a stained T-shirt and practically ran up the street in my yoga pants and sneakers. I walked into the bar frazzled and miserable and bemoaning how irresponsible I'd been.

Amy said, "Then quit!"

"Quit? I just got this job, a job that's supposed to be perfect for me. It's supposed to let me stay home and write and avoid office politics."

"But you're not writing. You said when you walked in here that you're eating yourself to death and you hate the job. I don't understand why this is so hard for you."

"Because I need the money."

"But you're not even doing the work, and you don't get paid if you don't do it. So what's the point in staying?"

"I don't know." I put my head in my hands. "I don't know what's wrong with me. It's not in my DNA to leave a job."

"Fine. Don't quit. But you better get your ass out of your apartment before you go nuts. I'm going to the YMCA tomorrow. Come with me."

"The Y? Why the heck would I go to the Y? And you know, as discussed, I need to work. Tell me how I'm supposed to work, not how I should take a field trip to the Y."

"You're not working anyway, you're holed up and losing it! I'm going to help you get out, get you some human contact. Get a little exercise with me. Come on, it'll be fun."

"All right, I'll go."

"Cool, we can do my dance aerobics class. It's the nerdiest ever, but it's so fun, you'll love it."

*Amy's right. I need to get out and break up the monotony. Maybe she can help save my sanity.* On the walk home that night, I envisioned what it would be like to do dance aerobics, wiggling around doing goofy moves while a flock of ladies bobbed along with us. *Yes, this is going to be fun.*

★

The next morning, Amy checked me in at the front desk of the Y as her guest as I looked around at all the bodies coming and going. The diversity was striking. All races, ages, and sizes paraded in and out of the facility.

When we got to the classroom, we were stuck with the only spots left in the room, front and center. We'd be breathing down the teacher's neck once she got the music started and took her place in front of us. The teacher was an ample blonde in her sixties wearing black tights and purple leg warmers; you'd think she'd be all smiles and lightness, but she was stoic as she warmed us up with ridiculous hip circles and crotch thrusts.

She placed her hands on her hips and gyrated her ass one way while her boobs swung around her body in the opposite direction. Then we switched course and gyrated our upper and lower privates going around the other way.

I was delighted by the lewdness of the moves in combination with the stern, grandmotherly figure ordering us around. She was like a grizzled old madam teaching her younger charges how to be seductive. She shimmied and dipped, her grandmotherly rack jiggling in a frenzy. She frowned hard against our smiles as we followed suit. Amy caught my eye and started cracking up. I didn't dare acknowledge her or I would've fallen apart laughing.

After class, Amy said, "Well, what do you think? Would you join? Just think: you can do dance with me every week!"

I laughed. "Oh my God, why didn't you warn me? That was hilarious. And fun. I loved it. Seriously. It was exactly what I needed."

"So are you gonna join?"

"How much is it?"

"I dunno what they're charging right now, probably fifty bucks a month or so."

"Let me think about it."

"No. If you go off and think about it, it'll never happen. You had fun, you dialed down the crazy, come on. What do you have to lose?"

"Money. I'm not sure I can stay in this job, and I'm about to be broke."

"If you come here with me every day, it'll be way easier to sit down to work afterwards, I promise. Talk to someone in membership. Maybe they can give you a discount. Please?"

"Fine."

I was soon sitting across a table from Jessica, the Y's membership consultant. She watched me squint as I moved my finger down the paper, examining the pricing she had scribbled. "What are you thinking?" she asked.

"Well, I need to come here to blow off steam from my job because it sucks, but...what if I quit? Is it easy to get out of my membership?"

"You know, we're always hiring. If you get a job here, then membership is free."

"A job here?" I looked around and my heart beat a little harder in excitement.

"It's an option, if you see a job in our listings that interests you."

"Yeah, that does interest me. It would be fun to come to work here. No desk job. Getting some exercise. Talking to people. What kinds of openings do you have?"

"We're looking for a water aerobics instructor right now."

"Oh, I don't have any experience in that."

"I noticed you did our dance aerobics class today, and you kept up very well. We can train you. Why don't you talk to our aquatics director and see what you think?" I gave my name and number to Jessica to hand over to the aquatics director.

As Amy and I left the Y, I felt giddy as Amy said, "I can't believe they recruited you to work here. You're such a job magnet."

"I know! I'm super excited. This could solve all my problems. I could come here and laugh the day away. And I'd probably get in good shape too."

★

That afternoon, as I puttered around my apartment avoiding work, the phone rang. "Hi, Kelly, it's Samantha, the aquatics director at the Y. Jessica tells me you're interested in applying for the water aerobics instructor job."

"Yes, very interested. Thanks for calling me so quickly."

"Great. I'd love to have you come in for an interview on Thursday at six p.m., if that works for your schedule."

"Perfect. I'll see you then."

*Whoo-hoo!*

I went online and googled salaries of water aerobics instructors and I found some instructor's blogs. I came back down to earth when I saw how much—or I should say, how little—money they made. I read a blog post written by a young woman who said she no longer teaches multiple classes per day because it's too hard on her body.

I put two and two together and realized that there was no way I could make a living at this. *Certainly not living in Manhattan, that's for sure.* Still, the allure was there. *So maybe I could teach a few classes per week, get my free Y membership, and pad my earnings a tiny bit in the process.*

I convinced Amy to bring me back to the Y to do water aerobics the next day so I could gather intel for my interview.

★

As Amy and I stood next to each other in the pool, the instructor fiddled with an ancient boom box. We waited for the class to start while an old man flirted with his eyes and a shy smile.

As the class began and I made out the lettering on the instructor's name tag, I realized with embarrassment that Samantha, the aquatics director, was the one teaching. I didn't think that her seeing me bob up and down next to the ancients in the class would help my chances, so I prayed that she wouldn't recognize me when it was time for our interview.

As I jogged and jumped through the class, it dawned on me that I probably fit right in with the rest of the class, rather than looking like an odd standout. Amy, on the other hand, was way younger-looking and fitter than the rest of us.

After class, as Amy and I toweled off in the locker room, she asked me, "So what do you think? Could you teach a class?"

"I think so. It looked easy enough to me." Famous last words.

★

On Thursday, I strolled into the Y for my interview. I'd only ever interviewed for desk jobs before, so I was baffled when it came to choosing an interview costume for this one. I wore pants that were ambiguous; they looked like they could be sporty or dressy, like something Sporty Spice would wear to a nice restaurant. I wore black athletic shoes and a black T-shirt with a blazer over the top so it didn't look like I forgot I was being interviewed.

Samantha met me at the front desk and said, "Are you ready to teach?"

I tried to make the fear in my eyes look like excitement. "Teach? Oh boy. That sounds like fun." When we got to the pool deck, the wet heat and chlorine smell hit me in the face and I began sweating profusely. I ripped my suit jacket off and looked around for a place to put it. The pool deck was more wet than not, so I found a tiny dry square of tile and lowered my jacket into a puddle.

The class was gathered in the pool watching us. I recognized all the same faces from class the other day. My heart hammered inside my chest.

"Did you bring your own music, or do you want to borrow mine?"

"Yours, please. I want to see what your sound system is like," I lied. I was terrified. I didn't care what came out of my mouth. I only needed to avoid having a panic attack and I would consider the interview a success.

As Samantha pulled a CD out an envelope, it bounced out of her hand and landed in the pool. I was seized by the adrenaline that had been building in my system from the moment I realized I had to teach. I dove onto the pool deck like a baseball player and plucked the CD out of the pool before it sank.

*That was epic! I doubt the blue-haired class attendees ever put their heads under water, so if that CD sank, what disaster would befall all of us? There would be a CD in the pool! Irretrievable at the bottom!* I was a hero in my eyes.

After I gallantly handed the CD to Samantha, I waited for her profuse thanks. Instead, she grabbed it from me without looking, wiped it off, and stuck it in the CD player. Not even a nod of appreciation at my baseball slide across the pool deck. *Don't I get any credit for saving the class?*

She hit Play, and as the music echoed over the tiled walls, she said, "You go ahead and warm up the class, and I'll watch."

*Holy shit.*

Samantha walked around the deck to the opposite side of the pool, where the cute male lifeguard was perched on a guard stand. She struck up a flirt session while the music blared and the class continued to stare up at me. I wracked my brain for moves that Samantha had done in class the other day, but I couldn't remember a single thing. Then my mind turned to the dance aerobics class. *Maybe I could steal some moves from there.*

"Okay, everybody," I said. I couldn't hear my own voice above the music bouncing off the walls. I stepped from side to side, clapping my hands. The class look confused. As I watched them, I realized they weren't sure if they should clap under the water or above the water. They glanced around at each other as some of them splashed at the surface and others were frustrated by the impossibility of clapping one's hands underwater.

"Okay, like this!" I dropped the clapping and began walking forward. I could only take two tiny steps before I was balanced at the pool's edge, so I tried walking backwards. The whole class looked at me with an expression that read, "You clearly don't know what you're doing."

I panicked and began channeling lewd grandma. I did some big hip circles. I saw one woman shake her head and mouth, "I'm not doing that." The rest of the class did it while they glared up at me.

I snuck a glance at Samantha. She was smiling and laughing with her lifeguard friend. Then she caught me looking at her as I hula-hooped my hips. The sight of her class standing stationary in the pool while they wiggled their fun parts made Samantha snap to attention.

She raced around the pool and shouted, "No! You've got to get their heart rates up! I said *warm them up*!" When she reached my side she said, "Haven't you ever done this before?"

"Nope! First time," I smiled.

"Oh, jeez. I thought you had some experience. Okay, look. No problem. I'll teach, and you follow along next to me. You shadow me and do everything I do, and then I'll be able to tell if you can keep up, okay?"

I nodded. *Thank you, sweet Jesus, for having mercy on my soul.* I calmed down and aped everything the teacher did for the rest of the class. Even when it involved lying on the floor in a puddle and kicking my feet like an upended turtle.

When the class was over, I was free to go home. I might have bombed the interview, but I was undeterred. I wanted my enlightenment back. *This Y could be my Rat Park.*

# CHAPTER TWENTY-NINE

"When I first arrived in London, before I was accepted for my course of study at Oxford, I used to ride the Tube aimlessly around the city every day. I had submitted my application and there was nothing to do but wait. I had never wanted something so badly, so desperately before. I thought that if I was accepted, my life would have a clear and positive direction. And if I was rejected…well…" Earnest chuckled. "I felt I couldn't be responsible for my reaction. I wasn't sure what it would be, but I knew it would be self-destructive."

Lydia leaned over and whispered, "I bet it would involve Irish whiskey and lots of women." I raised my eyebrows and looked sideways at her. *Is she making a silly joke, or is she somehow privy to Earnest's history?*

"Mind the gap," said Earnest. "This is what the conductors on the London Underground would say as passengers moved between the train and the platform. Mind the gap. I've heard this admonition thousands of times. And it began to take on a deeper meaning to me. Mind the gap.

"I wasn't minding the gap. I had fallen *into* the gap. I was dwelling rather uncomfortably in the gap, the gap between how my life actually was and how I wanted it to be. I wanted to be a scholar. But for the time being, I was nothing but a bum with nowhere to go and nothing to do. I had made my wishes to the Universe clear, but the Universe acts on her own time, not on my schedule.

"The wait was maddening. Quite literally. I left parts of my sanity on the London Underground. And many of us will do this to ourselves. We form our blissful vision of how we want our lives to be. We take the first few steps in that direction. In my case, it was completing and submitting my application. You are all taking these first steps toward your visions." Earnest winked at me as he said, "In Kelly's case, it's writing every day."

Lydia elbowed me, hard. *Like she's mad that Earnest winked at me.* I blushed. *I haven't written since I started my new job.* I wanted to sink into the floor and disappear.

Earnest seemed to ignore our interaction as he continued, "This is a risky time in your quest. You must mind the gap. You can see where you want to be, but you risk trying to leap over the gap, carelessly, desperately. The waiting is killing you. You hate to see the contrast of how your life is now versus what you want it to be. You make hasty decisions. You begin to feel off-kilter. You don't take your financial realities into consideration. You are ungrounded, floating toward your vision while ignoring the very real details of existence that must be tended to.

"Others of you will sabotage yourself equally as well, but in the opposite way. You will see that there's a gap, and you'll mind it too well, at the expense of your dream. You will mire yourself in the details of your current circumstances. You will get sucked into your job. You will stay in the drama of your relationships. You will cook yourselves elaborate meals and you will watch endless TV shows, and you will find ways to stay on this side of the gap. You will stay so focused on your present that your vision becomes a distant memory. You refuse to take the daily steps required to reach your vision because you're entirely lost in day-to-day living.

"You must strike a balance. You must keep one foot grounded in your current life, and you must stride forward carefully, purposely, with the other, without losing your balance, without falling into the gap. How do we do this? Practice. Each day, you must practice gratitude and appreciation for the present. We only ever have the present moment. We can make the mistake of wishing our whole lives away, or we can take the time every day to feel glad for *this* day, exactly how it is, even when our vision hasn't come to fruition.

"Yet we also must live in hope. While we have to appreciate the status quo, we must also work to improve the status quo. The whole Universe, all of the God system, is working, toiling, striving toward evolution. The angels never rest. They are busy placing clues and omens at your feet every moment, a path of breadcrumbs for you to follow in order to reach the highest incarnation of your being.

"Of course, we don't need to *do* anything to access bliss and the sacred. Reaching our ambitions won't make us happy. We can simply choose to be happy right now. We only have to open our eyes to the wonder of life on Earth at this very moment, and every moment thereafter. We can drop into a wordless state. Once the ceaseless whirring of our minds grinds down to silence—once we separate out the worries and the discord and the dissatisfaction from who we really are— we can finally just be.

"But you are here because you feel a pull in your soul. A pull toward being or doing something in this life. And you have repeatedly ignored that pull, until now. You have dulled that calling with food or alcohol or other worldly distractions. And you don't want to live that way anymore. You want to open your heart to your calling. And this involves action in this world. It involves taking steps.

"And taking these steps, to go from where you are to where you feel pulled, is one of the most difficult aspects of the journey. Because you think, 'If only I could be there.' But what you don't realize is that once you get there, your work doesn't end. If you are to have any hope of retaining what you've earned, you must continue to hone your focus and to grow. Otherwise you wither and it all slips away. The journey doesn't end once you arrive at your blissful vision.

"Kelly, let's say you publish a book. And it does well. You feel complete. But only for a time. When the accolades fade, and in the following year, there's a different, younger, more celebrated author of the year, how will you feel? Remember, we're reaching for these visions not to stroke our egos, but to obey the call of our souls.

"Your soul has determined that fiction writing is your dharma, Kelly. Not selling books. Of course it's nice to sell books. But you are here on this Earth to write. Remember that when praise ebbs and flows like the tide, so you will remain unaffected. You write heedlessly. You write across the gaps. You don't fall in, hoping and praying for a book deal or to reach a certain number on some list that represents someone else's manufactured and branded notion of success. No. You write. And you keep writing to heed the call of your soul.

"But be forewarned. In these quiet, early days, when you start to make progress, when you start to see success, you will sabotage yourself. The voices in your head, the Shadow side of yourself, will ask you, 'Who do you think you are? Who do you think you are to get out, to change, to bloom? Do you think you're better than everyone else?'

"You might not even hear this voice so clearly, so directly, but when you begin to bloom, the change will feel disquieting. And that feeling of unease in your body and soul can begin to feel like a nagging in your gut.

And for comfort, you may slip into old habits. Soon, it will be like we never met. You will be back to all of your old complaints and behaviors and ways of thinking and being."

*Oh my God. Is this what happened to me? Is this why I stopped writing? Am I sabotaging myself by pretending this new job is so terrible?*

"Get your footing. Climb once again. Fight these feelings of discomfort and open your heart to the possibility of wonder. To help beat this sabotage, to help you mind the gap, keep your eyes on the platform and the train, the present and the future. Every day, work on both. Don't let one crowd out your sight of the other.

"Make a plan to do the work. Stay flexible as to the outcome. As you work toward your vision, you may find yourself in unexpected places. This is okay. As long as you keep doing the work and enjoy yourself in all endeavors, you will reach higher ground.

"You must design your day-to-day life to be as pleasurable as possible as you strive to achieve your vision. As we make plans for the way we live, one of the most important things to remember is to sustain gratitude for your life, right now, as it stands. Don't constantly view your life as something that needs to be fixed or molded or overcome. Your life is meant to be enjoyed.

"As you push the limits of what's possible for you in pursuit of your blissful life, you may deal with unpleasant experiences—and those are a part of life, no matter what kind of life you live. But I want you to keep in mind that, as you explore exciting new possibilities, the present moment is here to be appreciated and enjoyed."

*Can I really enjoy my present existence?* I felt a sudden spark of hope that was at risk of being snuffed out just as quickly. *Can I enjoy sitting in front of my computer for eight hours a day while I work? And how will I get myself to sit down to write on top of my work hours?*

"Throughout the entire process of bringing your blissful vision to fruition, it's important to stop and look around and remember that right now is your life and that you are always exactly where you're meant to be. Every day, your eyes will flit back and forth between the future and what's inside you in the present moment. While hope for the future is an important part of the experience, it's also vital to appreciate what's inside you: the stillness, the peace, and the joy that you hold within you.

"Each moment of your life, there's no place else you need to be. Your life is amazing right now, and we want to keep it that way throughout the entire journey toward making your blissful vision your reality.

"When we're bringing our visions into reality, we have to remember that we're creating our daily lives, the process, and all that entails—even some unpleasant parts. Obtaining your blissful life will always require more work and more blood, sweat, and tears than you imagine at the start. Sometimes along the road to bliss, we might wonder, 'What the heck did I get myself into?'

"We imagine a neat and sparkling home, but we don't visualize the part where we're on our knees scrubbing mildewed grout with a toothbrush. We imagine having a beautiful, fit, and toned body, but we don't imagine the part where we turn up our noses at chocolate cake or set an early alarm to exercise. We imagine being our own boss, but we don't imagine the part where we might need to get up at four a.m. to work on our dream business.

"Personally, I like to imagine a clear dining room table, but I tend to skip the part where I imagine myself putting things away and policing that surface to make sure it remains clear. I don't imagine the part where I bring the mail in the house and immediately sort it. And so what happens in reality is that I walk in the door with the mail and dump it on the table."

*Earnest has a dining room table?* I peered past the lit area of the classroom into the darkness. *This room is huge. Does he really live here? Eat here? Sleep and bathe here? Does he...bring women here?*

"When creating your blissful life, there will be effort and sacrifice involved. Know that as difficult as the process is, there's love in the process. The process is your life. Not the end result—there is no end, there is no 'there' to get to. All we have is the process of living.

"Embrace the process, because once you reach your goals, you won't leave the processes and the habits and the character you've developed behind. They will become part of you, because the daily grind, the process, and the habits you engage in from day to day—that's what encompasses your time spent here on Earth.

"You can choose habits that make you feel good physically, proud and happy mentally, and comfortable knowing that you are doing the right thing, the thing your soul wants, the steps that, little by little, will take you up the mountain to your goals and your blissful vision.

"We'll never be done. It's not like you can lose a bunch of weight and then think, 'Oh, thank God that's over with. I can finally sit down and eat Fritos while I catch up on my soaps.' But this is how humans tend to operate: Let's get the hard part over with so we can sit back and slack off.

195

"In the past, before I knew that the value is actually found in the process, I've taken months where I've watched my diet like a hawk and I slaved away at the gym—and then when I realized that I chose a lifestyle that was devoid of all pleasure, I stopped doing those things and my physique declined into a weak softness. I had no balance in my life, because I wasn't focused on the process; I was only obsessed with the end goal of having a fit body. When I realized that I chose a lousy, joyless process, the pendulum swung back to Lazy-No-Brainer Town.

"When we ignore turning the process itself into part of the blissful experience, we get tired of trying and we give up. We have to keep renewing our commitment to ourselves and our blissful lives. When you feel your attention waning, it's not time to relax! It's time to make your process more pleasurable. You might need a change, but it's not back to where you've been in those old, unhealthy habits."

"Spend as much time as you need creating an enjoyable lifestyle. We need to create a healthy and fun lifestyle that we enjoy in order to make sure that it's sustainable. This isn't about depriving ourselves and working ourselves to the bone to keep all the balls in the air. It's finding out how you can engineer your lifestyle and your habits so you can be consistent and peaceful, rather than always struggling to maintain a punishing regime.

"When we're used to our old ways of doing things, and especially when we're first starting out on the path of change, we're going to experience pain—that getting-over-the-hump pain of adjustment. I call it Beneficial Pain because it's simply that pain that we need to feel in order to make changes for the better.

"Let's take beginning the habit of jogging, for instance, something I did recently in order to improve my cardiovascular health. I noticed that the first few times I went jogging, I experienced pain. I felt hot, breathless, and my heart was pounding. A lot of times, when we feel this pain, the voice in our head says things like, 'I HATE this! Exercise feels HORRIBLE, who in their right mind would DO such a thing?'

"However, when we keep in mind that some level of pain is beneficial while we adapt to a new habit, we're able to shut out that wimpy inner voice. When we turn up the music and decide that we're going to power through, we're treated to the pleasure of endorphins. When we're done jogging, we feel elated and accomplished. Our brain starts to associate jogging with pleasure, which actually makes us crave exercise. But if we never embrace Beneficial Pain, we won't form the habit. When we see Beneficial Pain as simply a part of change, then we reap the rewards.

"Whenever we try to do something different, we're going to experience Beneficial Pain. The voice in your head is going to try to talk you out of the new habit. It's going to go on and on about how unpleasant this new undertaking is.

"The solution to the negative inner voice is to go wordless. When I jog and I start to hear that complaining voice, I turn to images in my imagination. These images are wordless. I might picture Manchester United running on a soccer pitch. I might imagine myself running along the side of a highway at the speed of a car.

"I don't listen to the voice or engage with the voice, which is trying to convince me to quit. Instead, I tune into images that are motivating and engaging, and the voice instantly disappears. I'm left in a happy place while I pound the pavement, and time moves ahead without my noticing.

"I've noticed that the complaining voice amplifies feelings of pain. Moving into wordless scenes in my imagination gives me pleasure. This gives me a chance to improve my endurance in the absence of pain. Now jogging is a part of my daily routine, and it's something I crave."

I wondered if I could do my work in a wordless state. *Possibly? At any rate, I'm going to have to find a way to start writing again. My life depends on it. No, my eternal soul depends on it.*

"When we create new habits so we can create our blissful visions, an important part to remember is that if a habit we create isn't pleasurable and thus rewarding, it's unlikely to stick. But when we strive to create habits we love, we're more likely to be successful. Maybe you'll never like jogging. Then walk instead. Walking is easy, accessible, and free. And it's effective." Earnest looked around the room as he said, "For those of you who have been resisting exercise, I urge you to start walking. Stop worrying about spending money and time at the gym. Simply walk. It's good for you. It's good for the soul.

"I want you to meet up with your buddy after class. I want you to talk with each other and discover where you're discounting the process—meaning, where you've been thinking that you need to engage in an unpleasant process in order to reach a goal—so you can create habits that are rewarding. I want you to help each other find ways to make your current daily schedules pleasurable so you may enjoy your life as it is, while you work toward your blissful visions."

# CHAPTER THIRTY

On the sidewalk after class, Lydia said, "Should we do that Mexican place again, or…?"

I wanted to make a better choice, and the thought of a cheesy enchilada accompanied by a boring glass of water held no appeal. I was starting to see that I liked a drink with my meal only as long as the meal was fattening. Alcohol dulled the guilt of eating foods that hurt my body. When I ate a meal that was light and healthy, like a salad, a glass of water with lemon sounded tasty.

*But then again, to add a check in the box next to Lydia's suggestion, I enjoy margaritas. The salted rim of the glass giving way to the sweet liquid and then the lovely sour pucker that pinches at my mouth as I swallow…and I love how alcohol cuts the grease of naughty food.*

I considered the other nearby options. *I don't want to go to some cafeteria-style restaurant to eat a packaged salad. Yuck. But, but, but! Sigh. Why do I have to make such a big fucking deal about this decision? Why can't I enjoy a drink with my meal—or not—without making a federal case out of it?*

Because I could see that the idea of a drink had the potential to conceal so many layers, which may or may not apply to me, and I was certain of absolutely nothing. Did a drink with dinner mean a slippery slope? Did it mean I was hiding from my life? Was I trying to escape my emotions? Was I simply embracing pleasure and the present moment? Or was I destroying myself?

When I awoke from my mental debate, Lydia was opening the door to the restaurant. We'd walked there in silence. It reminded me of my first date with Earnest, except this time the silence seemed normal, necessary even.

*But what was Earnest thinking as we traveled to the restaurant together on the night of our first date?* I had assumed that he was in a monk's contemplative silence. But after what happened that night, I now wondered: *During that silence on the way to our date, was he debating whether he would sleep with me or not? Am I his guilty pleasure, or a pleasure that he feels sanctioned to enjoy? What's the difference? Where do we draw the line between harmless pleasure and compulsive, destructive behavior?*

As we sat down and opened up our menus, I decided: *Okay, a margarita, in order to be present to the pleasure of it, minus all the heavy baggage of meaning.* I closed my menu and focused on Lydia as I asked her, "So what did you think of the lecture? Are you 'in the gap' or whatever Earnest was talking about?"

Lydia looked radiant as she said, "I'm in love!"

"You are? That's so great! Who's the lucky guy?"

"Well, it's, uh, no one you know, but anyway…" She fanned her face with her hand and looked down and away. I watched her make an effort to turn the corners of her mouth downward. I recognized that look of trying to hide a smile, because I wore that look after my trysts with Earnest. I looked at her more carefully. Her eyes sparkled with joy. Her smooth, blond hair framed her blushing cheeks and her pointy little chin was so cute and dainty. I smiled at her. She was beautiful and in love. *Good for her.*

The waiter popped up next to our table, scribbled down our order, and scurried back to the kitchen. When he left, Lydia said, "About the gap…yeah, I guess you could say I'm in the gap. I really haven't given any thought to becoming a teacher. I'd need to get a master's degree. And I dunno, the thought of grad school, and entrance exams, and school loans…and starting over from scratch. I mean, I've put so much of myself into the bakery. It seems insane to walk away from it." She shredded the corner of her paper napkin into a tiny pile next to her fork.

"I can imagine. It's scary. Especially when you don't even know how things will turn out. Do you think maybe you could run the bake shop while you go back to school, or do you definitely need to close the bakery?"

"I dunno if I want to go back to school. The shop has been doing better. When I began to think more seriously about closing it down, I started to appreciate it more. And now that I have a boyfriend, I'm enjoying my life as it is. I'm happier with my customers and my employees. The dream of being a teacher seems less urgent, unnecessary even. I mean, I'm finally happy where I am. Maybe I just needed to meet the right guy. I don't see the point of shaking things up. What about you? Are you in the gap?"

I put my head in my hands. "You could say that."

"Oh no! What's wrong?"

I picked my head up as the waiter placed our margaritas on the table in front of us. In a moment of silence, Lydia and I each took a deep sip, then we sat back in our chairs with satisfied smiles.

"Okay. The gap. Where was I...? Well, first of all, I don't think I told you, but I got fired..."

"Oh my God, I'm so sorry! Earnest mentioned something to me about that."

*What? Earnest told Lydia I got fired?* "Huh? No. Wait. I mean, that was a while ago. That's not why I'm in the gap now."

"Oh, sorry. Okay, why are you in the gap?"

"I took on another job. I thought it was going to be perfect for me. I work from home, no office politics, just me, myself, and I. Alone in my apartment. All day, every day. I'm bouncing off the walls, bored out of my mind. I never thought I would say this, but I need people. I like people. And I want to be around them. But the right people, ya know? I've spent most of my work life around people who make my skin crawl. I don't want to get another job where I'm pulling a lottery ticket out of a hat when it comes to who I work with, and then I'm right back to dealing with a bunch of psychopaths."

"Oh, I hear ya. That's partially why I opened a bakery, so I could pick the people who work with me. I won't lie, it's pretty awesome."

"But anyway," I shook my head, "that's not even the worst of it. I haven't been writing at all. When I started this job, I completely stopped working on my stories."

"Why? Why can't you write? You're home all day, might as well."

"Yeah, that's what I thought, but I can hardly do the work, and it doesn't seem right to sit down at my computer to work on my own stuff when I'm not even doing what I'm supposed to be doing. And so instead, I do a whole lot of nothing. I'm afraid I'm going to run out of money, and I will have absolutely nothing to show for any of this. And I've started stress eating like it's my job. I'm getting, like, no exercise...I'll stop now. I'm sure I sound completely pathetic." I dropped my head onto my arms on the table.

Lydia reached over, patted my hand, and said, "Oh, we are so going to solve this. I'm, like, the master of employee motivation."

I picked my head up and laughed. "What do you mean?"

"I employ people. If I want people to get their work done, I need to make sure they're happy. I break up their shifts the way they like it. I have one woman who works a longer shift because she leaves in the middle to go to her yoga class. There's a guy who likes the first shift because he needs to pick up his kid from school every day. I like to do everybody little favors. I always make sure my staff is fed, because nothing makes a worse employee in a bake shop than someone who's hangry. I can't have that. And I've noticed a little music goes a long way to keep everybody smiling. Like fifty times a day, somebody starts dancing around like a goofball and laughing. We can figure out what would make your workday happy. Let's change it up to make it so you like it."

I had a mental flashback to the workers sorting clothing in the back of the thrift shop. *That place smelled so bad. They were probably paid next to nothing. Yet still they were smiling and laughing and moving to the music as they worked.* I said, "Yeah, music. I bet that would help."

"Okay, now let's talk about your shift. Who says you need to work eight hours in a row? You don't have a boss standing over your shoulder."

"Yeah, they never said I had to do it that way."

"So you aren't exercising and you aren't writing. Why don't you break up your shift so you're fitting those in? Two hours of work, an hour of exercise. Another two hours of work, and then take a writing break. Work, eat. Work, take a walk."

"That sounds a lot more doable than staring at my computer for eight hours straight. But what about people? I'm starting to feel…" *Lonely.* I couldn't say the word out loud. *It's too embarrassing. Too pitiful.*

"You need an Internet connection, right? Do you have a laptop?"

"Yeah, I have a big old clunker stuffed in the back of my closet. I need to make sure it works, but I could probably dust it off and get it going."

"Then why don't you work for part of the day in a coffee shop? Get out of the house, become a regular somewhere. Make some friends. You know, the bake shop has Wi-Fi. We serve coffee. We have a couple of tiny tables in the back. Why don't you come by sometime?"

"Yeah, that sounds awesome." I felt a renewed sense of hope. *I can do this.*

I took another sip of my margarita as the waiter came by to drop off our plates. "Ooh, your enchiladas look so good!" said Lydia. The steak and peppers for her fajitas sizzled and smoked on an iron pan in the center of the table. We went silent again as Lydia busied herself assembling a fajita, and I tucked into my food.

As I ate and drank, the world fell away and I felt like I had come home in my mind. I realized I hadn't let myself enjoy a meal since the compulsive snacking that accompanied my new job had begun.

As I reached the end of my margarita, I paused and looked at my plate. I was only a third of the way through my meal. *I don't want to keep eating without another drink. But do I really want another drink? Am I even still hungry?*

Lydia started talking about her boyfriend…something about going on a picnic. I nodded and tried to listen while I debated with myself about how to proceed with my meal.

*Another margarita to wash down the rest of this food would be so good. But I'm not really hungry anymore. I could stop eating right now. But look at Lydia's plate. She has so much left and she keeps talking and we're going to be here all night. I might as well keep myself entertained. But if I have another margarita, I'm not going to sleep well tonight. I'm not going to think clearly tomorrow. And all these changes I'm trying to make are gonna go right out the window. I'm going to keep feeling crazy…no, I'm done feeling fat and confused and full of cravings. This is why the decision to have a drink was such a big deal. Because here I am, debating with myself about what to do next. It's not really about one drink, it's about the next one, and now I'm wasting time even thinking about this. This is so annoying. I'm done.*

"…and I think we might take a trip to Ireland this summer. He said he has family there…"

I smiled and took some deep breaths. I imagined having another drink. I imagined the hangover and my bloated belly. Not writing. Not solving my work problem. *Delaying bliss.* I imagined Earnest's disappointment in me. *No. It's settled.*

# CHAPTER THIRTY-ONE

The following afternoon, I lugged my laptop up the street to the bar. I'd blasted pop music while I forced a few hours of work out of myself, and now it was time for a break. Even more important, it was time to write. *But first, a little human contact and a change of scenery.*

As I entered the bar, Amy said, "Kelly! Yay! What a surprise! I didn't expect to see you here. What's going on? What can I get you?" Amy picked up a wine glass and rotated it in her hand as she wiped around the rim with her bar towel.

I held up my hand and said, "I'll have a water."

"Water? I'm impressed." As she filled a water glass with her soda gun, she asked, "So you have to tell me how your interview went at the Y. Have you heard anything?"

I blushed with the memory of my interview. "I don't think I'm going to hear back. I realize now that I was going completely crazy when I applied for that job. I needed exercise and human contact and that seemed like the fastest way to get it. But I talked with Lydia last night, and she gave me some great pointers to make my current work situation a little more fun."

"Oh yeah?"

"That's why I'm here. I needed to get out of the apartment."

Amy scoffed, "Well I could have told you that. In fact, I *did* tell you that."

"Yeah, I know. You were right. So I'm joining the Y. I'll get some exercise, but the whole idea of me teaching water aerobics is crazy."

"I didn't want to rain on your parade, but I didn't think you were an exact fit for that job."

"What do you mean?"

"I think it's great to go to the gym every day. I love it. But teaching water aerobics?" Amy wrinkled her nose.

"Yeah. It's great for some people, but not my thing. Listen. I think I'm ready to take on the thirty-day challenge again. No alcohol, thirty days. Do you want to do it with me?"

"Yes! This comes at such a perfect time. Tom and I are kayaking a lot more now that the weather's warming up. He loves to go early in the morning to see the sun rise as we put our kayaks in the water, and man, those days when I've had a drink the night before…whew! Painful. I think I would go with him more often if I took a break from drinking."

"All right, we're on. Let's seal the deal." Amy and I did a pinky swear over the bar, then she began stocking the bar for her shift as I settled in to write. I tapped the keyboard slowly, searching for words, unsure of myself at first, out of practice. I wondered how to pick up where I left off.

Little by little, my writing gained momentum. I picked up steam as ideas came to me and my hands began to fly over the keyboard once again. *Now I really know what home feels like. It's wherever I'm writing.*

★

Over the next several days, I hit a rhythm. *Get up, work to music. Get out of the house, get some exercise. Work some more. Eat some lunch. Talk to Amy. Write. Back to work again. Take a walk.* It was peaceful. I had reached a truce with my life. But I couldn't lie to myself. It was far from perfect.

Those times that I was working, I fought feelings of resentment. *Why can't I just spend all my time writing? Why can't I somehow get paid to do what I love? Why must I spend hours of my life every day doing something that feels meaningless? So I can pay for a roof over my head. Thank you, God, for the roof over my head. But couldn't I please get that roof by writing?*

It felt so unfair that life had to be this way. Now that I figured out what I loved to do, it's all I ever wanted to do. Once I started writing, it was hard to force myself to take breaks. I didn't want to stop writing even long after my hands were tired from clacking on the keyboard, and even when my writing started to suffer because my brain had sputtered and conked out after so many hours of work.

After one such mental tantrum, I packed up my laptop. I couldn't face another moment in front of a screen. I needed some fresh air and to feel the sun on my face. *I have to get out of here.* When I reached the sidewalk, I slung my bag across my body and then stretched my arms up and breathed in the beauty of a clear blue sky.

As I walked up the street, I thought about Lydia and wondered how things were going with her and her bake shop. I wondered if she was still crazy about her boyfriend. I wondered if she would ever become a teacher, or if that was a long-lost whim that would never come to pass.

My thoughts were interrupted when something clinked against my shoe. It was a tiny bottle cap. I looked up and saw a woman standing in front of a Starbucks. She held a mini bottle of liquor, the kind they serve on airplanes, in one hand and a cup of coffee in the other. She didn't notice me as I watched her pour the contents of the bottle into her coffee cup. She looked around furtively before dropping her hand toward the ground and releasing the bottle onto the pavement.

When I reached the bottle, I picked it up and read the label. *Sambuca. Ew. If you've gotta dump poison in your coffee, couldn't you at least pick something that doesn't taste horrible? Like Bailey's. I would almost understand if it was Bailey's.*

I squeezed the bottle in my palm as I hurried to get closer to the woman. *I want to see who would do something like that. Maybe I can write a story about her.* She was on the move, her long legs striding at a pace that was hard to match as she weaved through people on the sidewalk. *What's her life like that she's putting liquor in her coffee on the street? Is she doing this to get through the day? Is she just entertaining herself? Is she trying to get over a hangover? I need to see her face.*

I spotted her waiting at the next crosswalk. She was well dressed in a white coat, black dress pants, and patent leather heels. Her black handbag looked expensive. As I approached, I read "Kate Spade" on the label. *She's not at all what I expected. I guess I expected a stereotype. She looks like she could be anyone I know, people I used to work with, people I go to parties with. We all have problems, don't we? I wonder if she's okay.*

When there was a break in traffic, the group of people standing on the corner moved in unison across the street. I moved faster through the crowd so I could catch a glimpse of her face. I was next to her now as she brought her coffee cup to her lips. I stared at her intently. *Will she grimace against the taste of the Sambuca? Or will she drink it down like it's nothing?*

After we'd crossed and our feet touched down on the sidewalk on the other side of the street, the woman rolled her head in my direction and slurred slightly as she said, "What the fuck are you looking at?"

I gasped and stepped back. "Jill?" She stared at me, mouth slightly open. Time slowed as her eyes moved from my face to the bottle held loosely in my palm.

She stiffened and strode ahead, wobbling, but pulling it together as she gained speed. I chucked the bottle in the trash can on the corner and tried to catch up with her. "Jill? No. I didn't mean...I wasn't trying to come after you with the bottle. I wasn't shaming you, I..." She quickened her pace even more, turned a corner, and ducked into an office building.

I needed help processing what I saw. *And screw it, maybe I want to gossip about it. It was fucking Jill, of all people!* I remembered Jill's angry, crazy pour of wine at Toni's party. *Toni. I'm not far from her apartment.* As I walked there, my mind chewed on the slippery details. *Did I really see what I think I saw? Was it Jill outside Starbucks? But her reaction...she was slurring...and she had the coffee...it was definitely her.*

When I arrived, the doorman called Toni's apartment for me. *What if she's not home? Maybe I should pretend this never happened. It's really none of my business. But maybe Jill needs help. Maybe Toni will know what to do.* Toni was home. The doorman sent me up in the elevator, which I rode in a surreal fog.

Toni opened the door, smiling, happy to see me. As we hugged, I felt like my head was floating off into her living room. As she guided me to the couch, she said, "Oh, Kelly, I'm so glad you came for a visit. I can't even begin to tell you how much I miss you. I need to apologize for that whole intervention thing."

We sat close to each other, butts perched on the edge of the couch, knees angled toward one another. I smiled politely and nodded. *I need to tell her about Jill! But she's apologizing! Okay, let's slow down and take it in. This apology is like gold to me. Let's enjoy it. Two old friends reconciling.* I beamed. My heart opened. *Jill can wait.*

She went on, "I guess I never understood what it's like to be you." She took a deep breath. "How do I put this?" She paused.

I waited while she navigated uneasily through whatever she was trying to say. *It will take as long as it takes. I want to hear this apology. I need this.*

"I guess the crux of the matter is that my thinking is organized. My wholeness is intact. I'm put together. My self-esteem is decent."

*Where is she going with this?*

"But I've been really, really judgmental. I don't understand what it's like to be you. To feel messy and vulnerable and like you're always one thread pull away from completely falling apart. When I first met Jill, I have to admit, I was impressed by her. Jill's like me. She wants friends who are mentally healthy. I mean, yeah, I get annoyed by you. And it's not only you; it's a lot of people. It's like a badge of honor lately for everyone to be such a freaking mess all the time. I don't like this new culture of oversharing. It makes me feel really itchy and uncomfortable."

"Um, I thought you were apologizing, or…?"

"Oh yeah, I guess I'm apologizing. I'm sorry for the intervention. I think this is just who you are. You seem to thrive on not having your life together. I mean, Amy told me you're having sex with this Earnest character? The guy who's supposedly helping you straighten yourself out?"

*Amy! Jeez Louise. Really? Does everything I do have to get back to Toni?* Obviously discretion was not Amy's strong suit. I loved Amy because she saw nothing wrong with anything I did and so I felt comfortable telling her everything. But as I was learning, she kept nothing to herself. Because she didn't judge, maybe it didn't occur to her that other people would.

Toni laughed. "Maybe I thought you had a problem, but now I realize it's part of your personality to keep things…uh…exciting. Or whatever."

I stood up. I wasn't even angry. "Let me clarify. So I'm a mess and I like it that way. Is that what you're saying?" I had already detached from Toni's friendship, so while a part of me wanted to cry and get all indignant, and well yeah—fall apart and get messy—I also knew it was about time that I keep what I'd found. I'd discovered some peace in my life, and reacting badly to being told I was a disaster was an irony I didn't feel like visiting.

Toni grabbed my hand and said, "No, I'm sorry, none of this came out right. I love you, Kelly. The way you are."

"I'm not quite sure I believe that, Toni."

We both turned as we heard a knock at the door. Toni said, "Who could that be?"

*I know who it is.*

Toni dropped my hand and walked toward the door, but the door opened before she could reach it and Jill stuck her head in.

"You busy, Toni?" Her eyes looked unfocused.

"Yeah, Jill. I mean, no, not busy."

Jill came in and closed the door behind her. Toni looked at me as if to say, "Is this okay?" I shrugged back at her. I wanted to watch the show and see what was going to happen next.

Jill's eyes focused on me. "What's she doin' here?"

"I came by to say hello to Toni."

"No, no. You don't come here to see Toni anymore. You guys aren't even friends anymore. I know why you're here..." Jill's bloodshot eyes got misty. "You're here because...because you saw...me."

Toni said, "Jill, are you all right? What's up with you?" Toni approached Jill, but Jill held her hands up, closed her eyes, and swayed. Toni stopped. "Jill, are you drunk?"

Jill opened her eyes slowly and smiled. "You could say that. I drink. Maybe I drank too much today. I guess I had what we would call a 'relapse' in the business. Yeah. You didn't know this about me. I was an alcoholic. I mean, is. I mean, am. I am an alcoholic. Is it okay if I sit down?"

Jill wobbled over to a chair and slumped into it. Toni brought her a glass of water, but Jill waved it away. Toni set the glass down and then hovered in between me and Jill. Toni and I looked at each other. I had no idea what to do or say, and I could tell Toni didn't know either. So we listened.

"I stopped going to my meetings. They told me if I stopped that this would happen. And you know, the power of belief is strong." Jill smiled. "I see it in my clients all the time. 'What you believe, you achieve,' I say to them. And I believed them. They said I was powerless. They said I had to go to meetings. And I believe that. I do now. I see that now. About me." Jill looked at me and said, "You should really go to a meeting. I believe I'm powerless and so this happened. But meetings help. They're the only thing. And the steps. Those too. You should do the steps."

I didn't react. I had heard enough, but I was now frozen on the spot. I didn't want to gossip about this. I didn't even want to witness it. I wanted to help Jill, but I had no idea how or what we were supposed to do. I looked at Toni again, but her face mirrored my confusion.

Jill was still looking up at me. "You know you're in denial, right? I mean, look at me. I look like I have it all together. But I've like, peed on myself. So I can't even imagine what you must do. You don't even look like you have it together. So you must be like...puking everywhere. All the time. Every day. You..." She laughed. "You must be the most epic drunk disaster ever. I'd like to party with you sometime. I mean, no. I mean we should go to a meeting together.

"Why don't you guys sit down? You're standing there, like, like, I dunno. Just standing there. I had a client like that once. She hated to sit down during our sessions. Used to pace. Made me nervous. The pacing. She would talk to herself and she would pace really fast. And then she'd come right up to me. It was scary. I hated that. You guys, it's so hard to be a therapist. The energy of my clients. The stuff they've been through. The trauma. It's hard. You guys, to listen to that every day. It's really hard. You don't know." Jill started to cry.

Toni said, "Jill, is there someone we can call? A sponsor? Or someone you can talk to?"

Jill's face changed and she said, "I'm talking to you! I'm talking right now! Listen! God. I have to listen to patients all fucking day, could you just listen to me for, like, ten minutes? Would it kill you? Fucking..." Jill sniffled. The tears were done. "Man. Some of my clients are, like, so fucking boring. They invent these stupid problems and sometimes the answers are so obvious, like, I dunno, dump that asshole and ninety-nine percent of your problems are solved, but they come in week after week...and if I have to hear about the same fucking problem for another week...

"But it's not all bad. I mean, it's fun to pretend I have all the answers. I get to feel superior to them, like I have it all together and they don't. And it's nice to feel needed, honestly. People come in looking at me like I have all the answers, like I hold the keys to their happiness. It feels powerful. And when people have a drinking problem, well. I know about drinking problems. Obviously. I mean, you guys figured that out. Or I told you. Or whatever. I mean, other people have problems. Of course I also have a problem. I don't want to feel alone about it. It's good to know other people have the same problem. I don't need to feel ashamed or embarrassed to have a weakness. I mean. Look at Kelly here! Toni, am I right? I mean, we've talked about this. Kelly is a fucking mess!"

Toni said, "Jill, I think it's time for you to go now. Do you have a colleague you can call? A sponsor?"

"No! You already asked me that." Jill got up from her chair and looked at me. "Well, there's always a meeting somewhere. I'm gonna go find a meeting."

Toni looked relieved as Jill walked to the door and opened it. Jill turned to look at me as she said, "You want to come?"

"No thanks. But thanks for inviting me."

"Okay, bye." Jill left and slammed the door behind her.

Toni and I stood there looking at each other. I raised an eyebrow and said, "You were saying?"

# CHAPTER THIRTY-TWO

Earnest was wearing all white. His triceps flexed as he clasped his hands behind his back and paced in front of the classroom. "Today I'm going to teach you about the Deprivation Trap. When we start out in the creation of our blissful lives, and we embark on creating new lifestyles, it's easy to fall into the"—he hooked his fingers in mock quotes—"'Deprivation Trap.'

"After all, we need to give something up in order to get something different. We're not actually deprived, but we're conditioned to think of unhelpful behaviors as treats or pleasures, and that's why giving them up can feel like deprivation.

"We whine about how we're going to feel so deprived when we can't stuff ourselves with unhealthy foods. We're afraid that if we live a bigger life, we'll have too many obligations. We're afraid we won't be able to relax or enjoy a lazy Sunday.

"We cling to our bad habits and our low expectations of ourselves because we're afraid of the negatives that change might bring. But you have a choice. You can either deprive yourself of a blissful life, or you can deprive yourself of doing crap or eating crap that makes you feel like crap.

"I'm not saying that you should never again in your life let a cookie pass your lips, or that you'll never again sleep in on the weekend, or spend the whole morning lingering over the newspaper with a cup of coffee, or that you will never again in your life go out with friends and stay out too late and feel rough the next day.

"The idea is to get out of the mindset that these things are everything, or that these are the only things worth living for, because they're absolutely not. Perhaps these indulgences add a little flavor to life at times, but when we create our lives around empty pleasures, then we're eating a jar of spices and leaving out the meat.

"Take out your journals, please. I want you to journal around any hesitancies or reluctance you might have when it comes to giving up your bad habits, your time wasters, or any other activities that might stand between you and your blissful vision. Rather than bemoaning what you're giving up, think back to the vision you have for a bigger, more fulfilling life: more love, more happiness, more excitement, more fulfillment, and more life satisfaction. Figure out what positive substitutes will help you get by while you're adjusting."

We all pulled out our journals and began writing as Earnest moved about the room, reading over our shoulders as he talked.

"When I was a young man, I used to enjoy Irish whiskey." My heart squeezed as Lydia's comment during the last class ricocheted through my head: *I bet it would involve Irish whiskey and lots of women.* I looked at her sitting next to me as she stared at Earnest. *How much time do Earnest and Lydia spend together?*

"When I realized that whiskey was one of the things standing between me and my dreams for my life, I gave it up. It wasn't easy at first, because I was caught in the Deprivation Trap. I felt deprived of my whiskey. Until I turned that thought around. I could either be deprived of whiskey, or deprived of happiness.

"But at first, I worried about the 'risk' of giving up whiskey—what would I miss out on? The answer is nothing. Yes, as I young man, when I was with friends who were drinking, I wished for small instances that I was drinking too, but I always felt thankful later as I went to sleep that I didn't imbibe. And to this day, I still remind myself that I sleep better and wake up fresher the next day for having avoided alcohol.

"Yet I missed having a comforting drink, so I used tea as a substitute. I still love tea. Sometimes during a special evening out, I will enjoy sparkling water with fresh-squeezed lime; it feels celebratory to me. On a day-to-day basis, I drink plain water, the healthiest option.

"For whatever habits and changes you're trying to make, don't go cold turkey; figure out a healthy replacement that will help ease you through the transition. In your journal, consider alternatives now. If you waste time surfing the Internet or mindlessly flipping through channels, see if you can't replace that time reading inspiring books.

"As many of you have already discovered, unhealthy pleasures repeated too often eventually lead to deep unhappiness. Resisting temptation, while uncomfortable in the short term, can lead to a lifetime of fulfillment. Rather than feeling deprived when giving up bad habits, celebrate the amazing new experiences and thoughts that are open to you when you take the steps to improve your life. In your journals, I want you to write down the effects of short-term gratification in your life, and how it's slowly killing long-term life satisfaction.

"Are you worried that making certain changes will lead to deprivation? How might you *not* feel deprived? What benefits will positive change bring? What are you getting in return for sacrificing old behaviors? Again, write down any substitute behaviors that might make the transition easier for you."

For the first time, I felt like I was slightly ahead of the lecture. Writing had taken precedence over drinking. My schedule included music, exercise, and socializing with Amy. Could my diet be healthier? Sure, but I was paying more attention to eating nourishing foods every day rather than obsessing about my weight.

Earnest clapped his hands and said, "Okay, close your journals. You can write more when you get home. I want to change gears now and talk about how to honestly evaluate your current relationships.

"As you pursue your blissful life, you will change in unexpected ways. One side effect of this is that you will find yourself incompatible with people you once felt close to. Friendships that nurtured you in the past may start to feel less fulfilling. Family or loved ones who we found simply grating can suddenly seem completely intolerable or offensive.

"When I was a young man, I had a friend who was a drinking buddy. We went out together frequently and enjoyed whiskey and the pursuit of women. As I began to change and my priorities shifted, this friendship began to feel like a downer.

"Drinking made me feel bad afterwards. As I changed, I grew tired of spending all my spare time at the bar. I began to distance myself from our friendship. Part of it was intentional, but it was also simply convenient timing in that I was absorbed in my schooling. Regardless of my feelings, I didn't have time left over to devote to the friendship. Sometimes we simply need to back-burner a relationship and let people know that we're busy moving in a new direction.

"My friend was hurt at the change in our friendship status, and that's normal. My only regret is that I didn't have more compassion for what he may have been feeling as I pulled away from the friendship. Eventually we talked about it, and I was kind, yet I resolved to make changes in my life.

"We need to remember that we're all connected. Sometimes remaining tight with someone who drags you down prevents you from making connections that can elevate you. Always remember kindness and compassion as you free others as much as yourself to pursue the right connections. While some might be disappointed in the changes you're making in the short term, remember that people adapt to fill the void. They make new friendships that meet them where they are in life.

"I had to jettison some other friendships in order to make room for the new connections that would eventually come into my life. I had two friends who, like me, are very interested in personal development. Getting Ducklings to Swans started was obviously very important to me, and since these two women were also very important to me and they share the common interest of personal growth and development, I thought they would be a natural fit to be part of my support system. I thought perhaps they could review the course materials I was creating and give me encouragement and insight.

"Only it didn't work out that way. One friend said she wanted to help but then never got back to me, and I don't think she ever read what I gave her. The other friend gave me feedback that was disconnected to what I'd written, like she missed the point. I was surprised that I had to look for new friendships and connections even sooner than expected.

"That's when I learned an important, yet strange, lesson. We need a support system when we're making big changes in pursuit of our blissful visions. And those closest to us don't always make the best support system. While we need some close friendships in order to feel happiest in this life, we need to choose carefully.

"As many of my Ducklings to Swans students have learned, there's nothing worse than confessing your plans to loved ones and having them take the wind out of your sails. If you tell people who are indifferent to your success—or worse, jealous at the prospect of it, or in any way discouraging—then sharing your goals and hopes with the wrong people is certainly worse than keeping them a secret.

"I know this sounds strange, but you must believe me when I tell you that those closest to us aren't always the most helpful. They have biased opinions about what we're like and what we're capable of. Be especially wary of sharing your dreams with friends who know the 'old' you, even your parents.

"When they've seen us in diapers or they've witnessed our old, immature behaviors, they don't always comprehend how to view us as full-fledged, accomplished grown-ups who are capable of amazing and miraculous feats. Some of your friends and family might catch up to reality, but others will always view us as we were in the past. They will assume that any success that befalls you is dumb luck. Or they will deny your success altogether and pretend it never happened. Be honest with yourself about what kind of support those closest to you are capable of providing.

"When I wanted to create Ducklings to Swans, I explained the concept to my mother. She was perplexed and discouraging. I couldn't make her see the value in what I was doing. At first, I desired my mother's support and approval more than anything, but I quickly realized that looking to her for encouragement was a fruitless endeavor.

"This was my mistake, not hers. She has a long history of wanting to keep my expectations low. It's not because she doesn't care. On the contrary. It's because she doesn't want me to be disappointed in case I don't get what I'm aiming for.

"But when I allow her cynical viewpoint to water down my enthusiasm, I get frustrated and exasperated that she didn't give me the encouragement I was seeking. This little sideshow of my feeling overly offended distracts me from taking dedicated, persistent action toward my goals.

"If I were to adopt my mother's viewpoint and set low expectations, then guess what I'd get? I'd be disappointed because I aimed too low. The irony is that disappointment is the very thing she's trying to save me from. We make a terrible team, and this is one of those lessons that I had to learn over and over again before absorbing the wisdom.

"If I'd been honest with myself about the kind of feedback I can expect from her, I wouldn't have asked her for something she can't give. She's not a cheerleader. She never claimed to be one, she's never been one, and she probably never will be. My mother is a pessimist. This isn't a value judgment; it's simply a statement of fact. If I had settled on her as a member of my support system rather than realizing my mistake, it's possible you wouldn't be sitting here with me in this classroom right now.

"You must adjust your expectations of others. An easy way to find yourself disappointed over and over again is to have expectations for friends and loved ones that don't match up with reality. When I was busy designing my business and creating concepts, I knew that my own mother was not someone I was going to look to for appreciation, credit, or approval. Not that we need those things from anyone, but it's in our nature to seek approval.

"There are occasions when we can act like getting the appreciation or approval of a particular person is important to us, even though this person is particularly stingy or incapable of delivering the support we're seeking.

"I would like to make an important point about judgment. While we're busy assessing who might serve as our support system, we can fall into the blunder of negatively judging other people. There's a difference between making an honest assessment of what we can expect of others and mentally condemning them for their flaws.

"It's important that we appreciate others for who they are, and recognize that they're exactly where they're supposed to be in life, and that they're deserving of love and respect even though they might be on a different page.

"We need to be mindful of remaining above the fray of emotionally criticizing and judging as we make these tough evaluations. Here's one reason why, and I want you to listen carefully. The more we judge others, the more we fear being judged. The more we fear being judged, the more we judge others.

"Living in fear of judgment is a terrible feeling. When we live in fear of judgment, we get caught up in a vicious cycle. Once we've judged someone, we will continue to point fingers at others in order to distract from the uncomfortable feelings caused by the fear of judgment.

"Here's an interesting thing that I've noticed. When I suspect that I'm being judged, my inner dialogue enters attack mode. As a means of self-defense, I mentally criticize and judge the person who I fear is judging me. Then my thoughts ping back to what I think I'm being judged about, whatever is 'wrong' with me, and then I turn back to judging the other person to distract myself from that uncomfortable feeling.

"I've also noticed that the most judgmental people I know are frequently the most insecure. When people feel insecure, they judge others to feel better.

"Now that I've noticed these two concepts, I'm able to wake up. When I catch myself judging, I ask myself, 'What do I think I'm being judged on?' Sometimes I think I'm being judged because I did something that needs to be cleaned up, or there's a flaw in my behavior that needs to be acknowledged, or maybe I need to issue an apology for something I did.

"Sometimes I'm being self-critical, and it's simply a wake-up call to be kinder to myself. Sometimes I'm judging because I'm putting an unreasonable expectation on another person.

"When we judge others, it's often a mental dance to avoid cleaning up our own messes. Or we're judging others because we're actually being self-critical, in a roundabout way. Or sometimes we judge because our expectations of the other person are out of whack.

"Remember that the next time someone else really is judging you—out loud—and letting you know that they think you're doing it wrong. Their judgment is frequently a reflection of their own crap and what they are leaving unaddressed in their own lives. Their judgment of you most often reflects bad feelings they have about themselves. Or perhaps their expectations of you are simply deranged."

I thought about Toni's diatribe about how I'm such a mess, and I wondered, *Was she judging me because her own life is screwed up? No. I really do think she has it all together. But her expectation that everyone else should be perfect is deranged. She wants everyone to fake how perfect their lives are. And that's sad.*

"Judging others is a problem you need to solve. While you're busy giving somebody the side eye, you're distracting yourself from your own issues. Learn to stop your mind when you feel a judgment rising up; then roll up your sleeves and do something to improve your own life.

"When you get home tonight, in your journal, I want you to make a list of the ways in which you judge other people. Who in your life do you find yourself judging most often? What kinds of things do you judge them for? If it's because they are unaccepting of you, do you find it ironic that you are unaccepting of them too?

"Choose to accept that person, warts and all. You aren't perfect either, but you are still worthy of unconditional love. By accepting and loving that other person along with her faults, you will find it easier to accept and love yourself with all of your faults. This doesn't mean you need to stay in a relationship or friendship that doesn't work. It means you drop the baggage and leave with good feelings.

"Sometimes when we're judging someone harshly, repeatedly, it's because we're trying to force them into a role in our lives that they aren't suited for. Do you need to change your expectations for the role you want this person to play?

"I want you to become comfortable making 'unreasonable' demands. Sometimes when we're making these tough decisions about people we love, and who we dismiss versus who we invite to support us, we feel like we're being unreasonable or demanding. But it's not unreasonable to seek the kind of support you need. It's imperative.

"Sometimes we underestimate the people around us. We're afraid to ask them for help and support because we assume they won't be helpful or reliable, or we're afraid of imposing on them. But there's also a chance that when we make our feelings known—and we get very specific in our request—our friends and loved ones will be perfectly happy to help out. But we can't find out until we have that conversation and we try to make their help work within the context of real life.

"Moods and ideas are contagious, and what you focus on persists and emerges. It's vital that you find people who have positive information and input, people who can elevate you to new heights. As you look for your own support system, when you evaluate the people you know, take an honest look at their personalities and how they might view you and how they might support and encourage you...or not.

"When I had the idea for Ducklings to Swans, it soon occurred to me that I had no one close to me who would understand. This isn't a poor reflection on them. I'm sure many of my loved ones want me to succeed. But I had the strong sense that I needed to find other people who were going through similar changes and who had firsthand experience of the journey on which I was about to embark.

"Once I realized that I needed to find a new tribe, it took me nine months of being on the lookout before I stumbled on a group of supportive people I could count on. What I found was better than what I could have imagined; I linked up with a group of entrepreneurs who were focused on helping other people.

"In order to succeed, you must ask for help. Now, I could tell you to start looking both near and far for your support system. I could tell you that if you don't want to enlist friends or family, then start looking. But that's ridiculous. You have all the support you need within Ducklings to Swans.

"This group is already available to you as a sounding board, for love, for friendship, for encouragement. Look no further. You are sitting amidst the perfect support system. You only need to make it known what you're trying to accomplish and what you need from us. Invite us onto your team."

I could sense the other women in the group looking around, seeking out eye contact with each other. I looked down at my hands. Earnest's speech made me bristle. I mean, I liked Lydia and all, but deep down I knew...I couldn't make myself form the words. But I knew.

*How can I trust them fully? What if there are...others...right here in this room? My heart might be on the line...I know what's going on here...and if I lean on the group, if I put all of me into their arms and let them support me while I try to reach my vision, the bottom will fall out of my life sooner or later. Ultimately, I will self-destruct.*

I absorbed Earnest's point about making unreasonable demands of people. *Is it so unreasonable to want love and friendship without worrying that you're involved in a love triangle? Or a love rhombus or a love octagon, or whatever the heck's happening here?*

Earnest went on with the lecture. "The company you keep will make you or break you. I want you think about the company you keep. Do you have friends or family that drag your focus downward? Do they gossip or complain? Are they wracked with pessimism or cynicism? Bad moods? Drama? Do they have low standards for how amazing and fulfilling life can be? Do they engage in habits such as drinking, drugs, unhealthy eating, or excessive TV watching that are counter to your goals?"

*Toni is really on my last nerve. In fact, I'm pretty sure I kicked her out of my tribe a long time ago. But what about Amy? I love Amy. I'm glad she's on board with the thirty days without alcohol. But what about after that? I don't want to go back to our old habits, but I'm worried she'll pull me right back down into it. Will I have to let Amy go too? Who would I be left with? I need to find new friends. More friends. I guess I have Sandy. But are Amy and Sandy enough? And are they the right people for me? Maybe I need to find other writers.*

Earnest looked right at me as he said, "You must align yourself with supportive people. You cannot make changes by simmering in your own soup. If you remain in your own personal closed-feedback loop, then you will always get what you always got. The process of change isn't spontaneous from inside a single person. A person needs to expand her mind by taking in the wisdom and skills shared by other people."

I got the sense that Earnest knew I wasn't buying his line about throwing myself headfirst into Ducklings to Swans. *I hear his message. I need to find my tribe. But it's not here. Not in this room.*

"We can make meaningful changes in our lives by gaining fresh internal wisdom from supportive people. In my journey, I've had to try many different strategies to get where I'm going. When I feel stuck, I read a new book or I take a new class. I keep reaching forward and learning new skills. I keep aligning myself with supportive people.

"The people I align myself with are growing and changing every day. New characters come in and out of the picture in order to keep me evolving to higher levels. I gather wisdom from other people, I let that wisdom percolate, and then from inside me, new wisdom bubbles up. By taking this course, you're taking in the information that I'm sharing with you, and new wisdom will bubble up inside you as you process it and add your own unique insights and experiences.

"You'll need to find out what works for you when it comes to seeking support. You might not hit on the exact right answer from the beginning. You might need to try a few different things before you find your support system. Supportive people can hold us accountable.

"When we doubt our ability to succeed, sometimes we keep our intentions a secret because we fear the embarrassment we might suffer if we fail publicly. There are times when we're afraid to ask for help because we fear wasting someone else's time helping us if we don't stick to their advice or their program. However, by not seeking support, the entire pressure of our endeavor rests solely on our shoulders. When we feel tired, when we feel weak, when we need encouragement, we have no one to turn to. There's no one there to help us carry the load, and that makes it too easy to give up.

"Successful people don't get that way by operating in a bubble. They announce their intentions. They enlist friends or coaches for support, encouragement, and advice. Think of pro athletes. They are the best in the world at what they do. Do they think they're too good for coaches? Of course not. No one is above the need for help and support. We all need help at some point. It's part of being human.

"I used to try to do everything alone. We know that doesn't work, yet I still insisted on operating under the totally false assumption that I could go through life in a bubble. The older I get, the more I realize in a very real sense that I absolutely need people; in fact, I love to need people. When we resolve to accomplish something, an extremely helpful tactic is to rely on others to help us reach our goals.

"I leave you with this thought tonight: Sometimes the best way to get support is to help others with the very things that you need help with. That's all for tonight. You may go. Except Kelly. Come up here, please. I'd like to see you for a moment." I caught Lydia's eye. She looked upset. I felt bad for her, but when Earnest called my name, there was no question I would stay to find out what he wanted.

# CHAPTER THIRTY-THREE

After the room emptied, Earnest and I stood facing each other in the quiet. He began, "Kelly, I get the sense that there's something wrong. That you aren't feeling connected to the program like the other women are. Is there something bothering you?"

"No, everything's great!" I lied. I knew he knew I was lying. He looked frustrated.

"Kelly, Bernadette has come to me with a rather bothersome issue. She was supposed to discuss payment with you months ago, but she neglected to do so. And this leaves me in an awkward position. I know you've had a period of unemployment recently, and your finances may be…well…depleted somewhat, and the cost of the class is ten thousand dollars."

I coughed and sputtered. "Ten thousand dollars?"

"Yes, you can see how this is extremely awkward, as we now approach the end of my lecture series, and you are just now coming to learn about my fees. I don't expect you to magically come up with the money immediately when you've essentially taken the course without knowing the cost. But at the same time…ahem. I expect payment for my services."

I stood there in stunned silence. *Ten thousand dollars? Is the course worth that?* I remembered how I felt before I met Earnest. *Constantly confused. Desperate. Tired of killing myself with food and alcohol and unsure of how to stop. Lately, I feel almost like a normal person with some level of inner peace. I no longer argue with myself constantly. I finally feel smart and creative and like I might have something to offer the world. Is feeling like this worth ten thousand dollars? Yes. It's priceless.*

I said, "Earnest, I'm sorry. You're right. I don't have the money. But…I do want to pay you. I'm just not sure how."

Earnest smiled. "Well, I think we can get creative with an arrangement, don't you think?" He put his arm around me, nuzzling into me. At first, I leaned into him, excited, nervous, but then my brain processed what he might have been implying and I pulled back.

"Wait, what? What kind of an arrangement?"

Earnest straightened up and said, "Oh, did you think I meant…prostitution?" He laughed a deep belly laugh, like this was the funniest thing he'd ever heard. "No, no, my sweet Kelly. No offense, but I've been getting plenty of milk for free. We don't need to trade sex for money. While I find that acceptable for some as a business model, it doesn't really make sense for us, now does it? Which one of us would be the prostitute in this arrangement? You see, it all falls apart for us as a financial model. What I mean is that you could work for me as a referral engine. You can help bring me more clients, and I will credit you one thousand dollars per person who signs up for Ducklings to Swans. That way you can work off your debt after ten successful referrals."

Judging by how easily it rolled off his tongue, I got the sense that this was far from the first time Earnest made this offer. I cringed. *I'm not a salesperson, and I don't know anyone I could refer to Earnest. Who would I talk into this mess? I'd be delivering people into a situation that could make them whole, but if they got involved in the wrong way, it could also break them wide open. I don't want to be responsible for that.*

"Let me think about it, Earnest. I appreciate the offer. It's generous of you."

On my way home, my head churned. *Ten thousand dollars. Where am I going to get that kind of money?* I'd ground my savings down to nothing, and now I was living hand to mouth. A little voice inside me said, "Maybe you could publish a book? And pay Earnest out of your book sales?"

I shook my head, and then hoped the people around me wouldn't notice. *What kind of author can quickly pull in ten grand on her first book without a book deal and no audience? No. Maybe? No. It sounds like a fun thing to try, but not a solid plan that will promise a payout.*

My head was in tatters. *Earnest is right. I need help. I need support. We can't figure everything out on our own. I don't need to operate inside a bubble. I need to talk to someone. But first I need sleep.*

★

When I woke up the next morning, it all came rushing back to me. *The incident with Jill. Toni's going on about how I'm such a wreck. And I need ten grand to pay off Earnest. Who am I going to talk to?* While I wanted desperately to vent about everything that had happened to Amy, I knew it would all get back to Toni, and I didn't want Toni to know I was talking about her and Jill. *And I really don't want Toni to know I'm ten thousand dollars in debt to my guru that I'm having sex with.*

*Having sex with? Had sex with? Where do we stand?* I was still obsessed with Earnest, even after he sprung the bill on me. I had changed so much with his help. He had an overwhelming effect on me. For all of the dysfunction I found myself in, I still wanted to crawl inside his head and make my home there, and I wanted him to get inside me and make his home here.

I thought again about publishing a book. *Maybe Earnest would support that idea as part of the payment plan. Maybe Earnest would like the idea of being a patron of the arts, like how the Medici family sponsored Michelangelo, except instead of funding me, it would be like a debt payment plan. I could write a book, and Earnest could collect the first ten thousand dollars off the book, no matter how long it took.*

Even though I doubted Earnest would accept such an arrangement over his idea of my making referrals to Ducklings to Swans, I wanted to ask him. *There have to be other ways we can figure this out.* I picked up my phone. I only had Bernadette's number, and since she helped us get into this mess, I'm sure she would know why I needed to speak to Earnest.

She answered, "Ducklings to Swans, this is Bernadette speaking."

"Hi, Bernadette, it's Kelly."

"Oh. Kelly, hi. I…"

"Is Earnest there? Can I talk to him?"

"No, I just take messages for him. I can tell him you called. What's this about?"

"Well, it's about payment."

"Right. Kelly, I'm sorry. I thought I'd talked to everybody about that. This has never happened before, I…"

"Okay. Well, have him call me."

"I will."

*This has never happened before? I doubt it.* I thought back to the first time I heard about the program from Sandy. *There was nothing online about it. I couldn't find it advertised anywhere. This must be how he gets clients: Word of mouth from people like Sandy who get a lot out of the class. And then they pick scrubs like me to work on getting enough referrals to keep the business humming. But no matter.* I reminded myself how far I came in the class. *It's still worth it.*

I remembered my first conversation with Lydia, about how her bakery wasn't doing so well. She had to let an employee go. *How did*

*Lydia come up with ten thousand dollars to pay for the course? It doesn't make sense. But Lydia is so resourceful. Maybe she can think of a solution.*

I called the bakery, and Lydia answered, "Creamy Cake Cups, how can I help you?"

"Hi, Lydia, it's me, Kelly."

"Oh hey, Kelly, what's up?"

"I was wondering if we could get together, have a cup of coffee. I'd love to pick your brain on something. Is now a good time?"

"Oh, I wish I could, Kelly, but my boyfriend is gonna be here in like forty minutes, and I'm not even close to being done frosting the cupcakes. I've gotta go!"

It was just me and my journal. I lay down on the bed with my notebook and turned to the pages where I recorded my vision. I closed my eyes and imagined myself sitting on a beach, cooking up my fictional stories and tapping them out on my laptop in the warm breeze. *Where am I? Key West? Aruba?*

I don't know how long I was daydreaming when the ringing of my phone brought me back to reality. I snapped to attention when I realized it was Earnest.

"Kelly, Bernadette said you called?"

"Yes! Yes. Earnest. I have an idea for how I can pay you back. Can we meet to talk about it?"

# CHAPTER THIRTY-FOUR

That evening, Earnest and I sat at a candlelit table at a French bistro in SoHo called Félix. Our very tall, very thin, and very French waiter took our order. Earnest ordered expertly in French, *"La salade d'endive, noix et Fourme d'Ambert, julienne de poire."*

I ordered a ham and cheese sandwich, in a stammering and clumsy fashion, in English.

Earnest smiled warmly and put his hand over mine. *Be still my beating heart.* "Kelly, please tell me, what brings us together tonight?"

"Earnest, I have an idea. You know my dream is to become a published author. And I thought of something that could help both of us…could help me get a book out, and could help me pay you the ten thousand."

"Go on, Kelly. I'm intrigued."

"Well, what if I wrote a book and I gave you the revenue? Up to the first ten thousand, I mean."

Earnest's eyes sparkled. "Yes, Kelly. Yes. I like this idea. I was thinking about writing a book myself, but this would be more impactful to have a client like you write the book. You could write a testimonial about what it's like to participate in the Ducklings to Swans program. You could write about your experiences and how you've changed."

I had a bad feeling in my gut. *No, that's obviously not what I planned on writing about. I want to write fiction. But I owe him ten grand, and there's no way I can work it off by getting that many referrals.*

Earnest went on, "I have an extensive network who can promote sales and distribution of the book. Every future Duckling will get a book. Your book will be like my business card. Yes, Kelly. Yes. Oh, I could kiss you. May I kiss you?"

I nodded mutely. *Oh yes, please, please, please kiss me.*

Earnest got up from his chair and sat next to me on the wooden banquet. He placed a finger under my chin, raising my lips to his. Then came the most sensual, panty-melting kiss I ever experienced.

We ate dinner in silence. I knew what would come next. He would say, "Kelly, I would like you to invite me to your apartment." I was right.

★

Earnest left me panting and naked on my bed. *So many orgasms. Too many to count. I don't care that it will get back to Toni, I have to tell Amy about this.* I thought I would explode with excitement as I dialed the phone.

"Come to the bar!" she said. "I'm working and bored."

I dressed quickly and jogged up the street. I noticed that my energy was higher than ever. I felt light, happy, free.

Amy poured me a glass of water while I told her everything. About Toni's twisted apology, about Jill's drunken performance, about owing Earnest a ton of money, about our book-writing arrangement to pay off my debt…and of course all about the sex.

When I finished, Amy stood there wiping the bar in silence. After a few long, drawn-out moments, I couldn't take it anymore. "Well? What do you think? Did you hear what I said? We had sex again! I'm going to write a book!"

"I'm a little worried."

"Worried? *Worried?* About what?"

"Ten thousand dollars? And now you're going to give away your first book, just like that? I think it stinks."

"As of right now, I don't have a book. And at least this will give me a deadline, accountability, a way to get a book out there. He said he has an extensive network. And they can help distribute the book, whatever that means."

"I dunno. Maybe it's all right. But ten thousand dollars? Yikes. I can't imagine Sandy paying that much money for anything. When do you start writing?"

"Like, right fucking now. He wants the first draft in a month."

"*A month?* Kelly, what the fuck did you get yourself into?"

I felt pissed. I wasn't a little kid, and I didn't need to be scolded. "Well, actually, a month is pretty reasonable. He said write one or two thousand words per day, and at the end of the month, I'll show him the draft. That's doable."

"Yeah, I guess it's doable."

"And then I'll have my first book written! And anyway, haven't you ever heard of NaNoWriMo?"

"What's that?"

"National Novel Writing Month. Thousands of people do it every year. They write a whole book in one month. So I'll do one on my own. No biggie."

"No biggie? If you say so."

I sighed. *So Amy doesn't approve. Fine. Whatever. Let's change the subject.* "So what's new with you? How's Tom? Did you go kayaking this morning?"

"Yes!" Amy grinned. "We've been going every single day! I love not drinking. Well, honestly I felt like shit for the first week. That was hard. But now I love it!"

"That's so cool. Sounds like things are going really well with Tom."

"Yeah. Kelly, I think I love him. And this morning he suggested I train as an instructor. He said I could help him run the kayaking school."

"That's awesome!"

"Yeah."

I could tell there was something bothering her. "Yeah, but what?"

"But my family. I don't think they'd like Tom. And they wouldn't want me to leave the bar business."

"What? Why?"

"When I was growing up in Boston, my dad owned a neighborhood pub. Our clientele were like family. He's proud that I'm a bartender. He wants me to open my own bar someday."

I had no idea that this was what Amy had aspired to. I thought working in a bar was just an irresponsible whim, an excuse to stay out late and party every night. I'd thought she was stuck there and not that she was working at a bar on purpose. I asked, "Is this your dream job? Working in a bar?"

"Not anymore. I love being out on the water. I love being with Tom. I've never felt so happy and clearheaded before. Getting up with the sun. Getting fresh air. Watching Tom teach people about the river and the currents and kayaking...and honestly, I love *not drinking.*" She laughed. "I never thought I would say that. I didn't realize how bad I felt all the time. I didn't know what a good night's sleep felt like without a drink in my system. Well, again, after that first week of feeling like garbage. And if I stay here, working in the bar, I mean, it's hard. Being up so late and then getting up so early. I'm tempted to leave the bar business. I really am. But my dad..."

I channeled Earnest and said, "Why do you care about your dad's disappointment more than you care about your own feelings of fulfilment and happiness?"

"I'm not sure…"

"It's because you think your dad's feelings about your life are more important than *your own* feelings about *your own* life. You're going to have to accept the fact that you alone are responsible for your happiness, and that to be happy, you need to start respecting your own feelings and making choices that honor your life and your happiness without worrying that your dad might prefer you sling drinks for a living."

Amy looked pissed. "Look, it's not that easy. My family disowned me when I worked a corporate job. They accused me of being a traitor. My dad said, 'You think you're better than us!' And yeah, I did think that. And I was ashamed to think that way. I was glad when I quit and they took me back in. I love my family. I need them to love me back. And so I went back into hospitality."

"But don't you want to know who you are? I mean, outside of ego and external pressure."

"What do you mean?"

"Your family is applying this external pressure. And that influences what you think will make you happy. Your ego thought you should take a corporate job. Your ego thought it would make you better than your upbringing. Don't you want to shed all of those expectations and do what would really make you happy?"

"You should talk."

"I don't understand what you mean. I left my old job behind. I'm writing. I'm doing what makes me happy. I've done a lot of work to get myself to this point."

"Yeah, but talk about ego and external pressure."

"External pressure from who?"

"Earnest!"

"Well, duh! I owe him everything."

"You say you want to write fiction, but this whole first book is going to be about your experience with Ducklings to Swans. That sounds like bowing to external pressure to me. And ego. God. Earnest's ego sounds enormous."

"No, he's not like that."

"Oh really?"

"Yeah really."

"Then why does he need to sleep with all of his students? So they can swoon over him and tell him how great he is?"

"That's enough, Amy."

"I'm sorry, Kelly, I see that Earnest has had a positive influence on you, but at some point you've got to cut the cord and get out from underneath that guy."

I shouted back at her, "Oh yeah? What if I *like* being underneath that guy?"

All the anger that was building between us left as we both started laughing.

Amy said, "All right. I'll admit it. You've given me a lot to think about. I might go work with Tom. Maybe. But if I do that, then I need to figure out the right way to handle my family."

Amy had given me a lot to think about too. She called me out, and she was right that I was absolutely bowing to external pressure. Just when I thought I was free for the first time in my life, Amy pointed out that I wasn't. But I couldn't admit it to myself. Not yet.

On my way home, Amy's words and my own doubts bounced around my head like a game of Pong. *I can't imagine Sandy paying that much money for anything. And Sandy took the class more than once. At ten thousand a pop? I need to talk to her. I have to find out what she paid.*

# CHAPTER THIRTY-FIVE

Early the next morning over a hot mug of tea in Sandy's apartment, I told her about the money I owed Earnest and our arrangement to pay it back. Then I said, "Sandy, can you please tell me what you paid? It wasn't ten thousand, was it?"

Sandy gripped her tea mug with both hands and looked sympathetic as she shook her head. "I'm so sorry, Kelly. I don't know what Earnest is up to with this. I only paid two thousand."

I sat back in my chair and absorbed the news. I tried to stay hopeful. "Maybe he raised his prices? And this is just what he's charging now."

Sandy tried to sound encouraging. "Yeah, maybe that's it. Maybe he raised his prices." We sat slumped in our seats, pondering the idea of such a massive price hike. "Can you find out what other students in your class paid? Is there anyone you feel comfortable asking?"

"I could ask Lydia. She's my buddy. Although she's kind of wrapped up with her boyfriend right now. But I guess I could try."

"Yeah, there's no sense jumping to conclusions yet. Definitely ask Lydia."

"Okay, but what if she paid way less than I did? Then what? I told Earnest I would write a book and he could take the profits. If it's two thousand, I mean, does it make sense to write a whole book and give Earnest the money? Especially if it turns out he's trying to cheat me. What do I do?"

"I don't know. I don't know why he would try to charge a student five times what he's charging others."

"Do you think it's just a way to get referrals?"

"I didn't think he would need to stoop to that. I mean, I gave you a referral, didn't I?"

"Yeah, but when you referred me, you kind of left out the part where he's a slut, and if someone needs to make ten grand in referrals, they're probably going to leave out that pesky detail."

"I told you!"

"Yeah, but not until later."

"Well, I wanted to make sure you'd go. I knew he could help you. And I waited a little too long to tell you about the whole sexual predator part. Sorry about that."

"It's okay, really. I've enjoyed that part. Possibly more than the class."

"I really do feel bad about that."

"Please! Don't. I mean it. I appreciate my body a lot more now."

Sandy held up her hand to stop any more detail from escaping my mouth. "Why don't you track down Lydia? And tell me what she says."

★

I got on the M15 bus heading south and gazed out the window. I couldn't deny the lump in my throat and the bad feeling in the pit of my stomach that was there now for a second day. *I have to talk to Lydia.*

When I saw the pink-neon sign for the Creamy Cake Cups storefront, I binged the stop indicator and moved to the front of the bus. My hands began to sweat and I felt anxious as I thumped down the high, uneven bus steps to the ground.

After the bus left me in a cloud of dust and exhaust, I looked across the street at the cupcake shop and noticed the closed sign hanging on the door. *Crap. Closed?* I looked at my watch. It was only eight thirty in the morning. *The only problem I'm finding with my thirty days away from booze is that when I wake up early and refreshed, the rest of the city is still asleep. Except for Sandy. And Tom and Kelly, out there on the Hudson in their kayaks. And probably Earnest, wherever he is right now. Probably meditating on top of a giant pile of money. And Lydia because she's a baker. Why is the shop closed? I thought she said they serve coffee.*

I sensed movement inside the shop, so I stood and watched the storefront from across the street. Someone inside the shop approached the front door, and I thought maybe they'd turn the sign around. *No dice.* I crossed the street toward the shop so I could read the hours printed on the window.

As I stared into the shop, I saw Lydia's blond head behind the counter. I decided to knock on the door. *I only need to ask her a quick question.* As I got closer to the door, I stopped. *Is that Earnest? Sitting at the counter of the bakery?*

*It is. Oh my God.* My heart dropped into my stomach. *Why is he here? Did he go to her after he left me last night? Did Earnest spend the night with Lydia right after he had sex with me?*

Earnest stood on the rung of his stool and leaned over the counter to kiss Lydia on the mouth. Then he sat back down and spun his stool around as Lydia came out from behind the counter. She stood in between his legs and put her arms around him. He honked her boobs with both hands. They threw their heads back in laughter. She fell into his arms, and they kissed deeply.

My mind stitched together the details. Their casual intimacy, and their easy way around each other. Lydia was not at all like the awkward, stilted muddle I was with Earnest. The contrast hit me in the face. When I was with Earnest, everything felt uncomfortable and mentally perplexing and serious and bewildering. Well, and thought provoking and inspiring too. *But that's all him. I have nothing to offer. No wonder he likes her. This looks playful, natural, fun.*

Lydia turned her face toward the front window of the shop, and I held my breath. *Can she see me?*

She shouted through the door, "We're closed!"

I didn't move. *Does she know it's me?* My feet stayed planted. I couldn't stop staring at them. Lydia broke free from Earnest's embrace and marched to the door. She looked impatient. Then she looked at me. Our eyes locked. Her mouth opened. She looked scared.

My insides crumbled. Then I ran.

★

As I cried on my bed, my mind split in two. Half of me was devastated and full of tears. The other half was the Witness: detached, curious, and full of questions for the sad part of me.

*Are you surprised?*

*Well, no, of course I'm not surprised.*

*If you already knew, then why are you so sad?*

*I guess I was holding out hope that he wanted to be with me. And I thought maybe I would impress him by writing a really good book. And while we were working on it together, we'd be like partners and we'd grow closer.*

*But that's ignoring the fact that you already knew he was sleeping with other people. And that you two weren't exactly an item.*

*Yeah, I was ignoring that fact. I knew it, but I was trying to hide it from myself.*

*Why did you hide it from yourself?*

*I wanted things to be different.*

*Earnest showed you who he was very early on. Why didn't you believe him?*

*I needed Earnest to be someone else, a romantic instead of a womanizer. I was wishing he loved me. I wanted to be the only one.*

*And you knew all along that he wasn't. Yet you still played this pretend game.*

*I did. Why did I do that?*

The Witness was silent.

*Why did I do that?* I might never know the answer to that question. But I did it. And now I could see I was at a crossroads. I could fall apart. In the midst of all this freaking out, I could try to get sympathy from Amy and Sandy, but I knew there was none coming.

They knew that I'd known all along what Earnest was like. How many times had Sandy warned me? *He's a manwhore. Don't fall for him.*

*Why did I do it?*

*Because he's hot. Because he's smart. Because I felt like the only woman in the world when he touched me. Because I felt the grace of God in his presence. Because he taught me that I deserve love. And I wanted that love to come from him. But I knew it wouldn't.*

*So again, why did I do it? And what will I do now that the charade is over?*

I could drink a bottle of wine and then cry endlessly and feel sad and then feel even sadder when I woke up with a hangover. Then I could get angry and crazy about the whole thing.

*But that won't change anything.*

And so I considered another choice. I could face reality with calm dignity. It was an easy choice, as long as I kept the Witness with me.

Still, I was caught off guard by a deep melancholy caused by the thought: *I can never sleep with Earnest again.* My heart ached. *I had worshiped him. He'd been inside me. And Lydia was calling him her boyfriend. Does she know that Earnest and I have been together? She has to. She knew that we had a date. She knew that I would see him after class. She has to know.*

I was jarred from contemplation by the ring of my phone. I didn't recognize the number, but the call was from a Manhattan 212 exchange.

"Kelly?" asked a strangled-sounding voice.

"Lydia?"

"Yes. Kelly, I…" I could hear muffled sobs coming from the other end. "Earnest admitted that…"

I waited patiently through fumbling noises.

"Kelly, are you still there?"

"Yes."

"Can we talk?"

"Sure. Do you want me to come back to the shop?"

"No. No, I need to get out of here. I need to go somewhere private. Can I come to you?"

I gave Lydia the walking directions to my apartment. Fifteen minutes later, I heard a soft knock on my door.

# CHAPTER THIRTY-SIX

When I opened the door, Lydia was standing there with a tear-streaked face and red eyes. "Kelly, I…I…" She caught her breath and then wailed, "I thought he was my boyfrieeeend!" She fell into my arms and sobbed.

I wasn't sure how to react. *At least she's not angry with me. Some women would paint me as "the other woman" and blame me for everything.* While I was relieved she wasn't taking it out on me, witnessing her grief was heart-wrenching. *My heart got off easy.* I invited her in.

As we settled into our chairs, I handed Lydia a tissue. She blew her nose loudly and said, "Thank you."

"So…," I said. I suddenly recalled my ten-thousand-dollar debt. It wasn't an appropriate time to raise the topic, clearly. *But I need to find out what Lydia paid.* I bookmarked the page in my brain and focused on Lydia.

"So," she said. "Earnest was cheating on me with you."

"I didn't know you guys were…" *An item? Committed? How do I put this?*

"Exclusive. Yes. Well, at least I thought we were." She laughed a sharp, bitter laugh. "But he cleared that up for me this morning. He said you guys were…were…*involved.*"

*Involved? What did Earnest say? We're involved? Does this mean we're still involved?*

Lydia dabbed at her tears and asked, "He said you're going to write a book for him. I had no idea you guys were that involved. How many times did you…?"

The Witness said, *No, you don't want to get caught up in this. Don't feed this line of questioning. She's trying to piece together all of the details. She wants to figure out how and when the betrayal happened. This isn't helpful.*

"Oh, well, that doesn't matter now."

"Do you love him?"

"Love him? No, I…" *I worshiped him. But do I love him?* "No."

"Then why? Why would you? How could you?"

"He's Earnest," I said simply.

She sat back, defeated. "He's Earnest." Her head dropped into her hands, and she began sobbing again. "Why? Why did this have to happen to me? I knew you went on that date with him. Before we went to Tao together, I wanted to ask you how things stood between you, but…I didn't want to know."

"He took you to Tao?" I felt sick.

"Yeah, it was amazing. I got the giant fortune cookie for dessert." Fresh tears sprung to her eyes, and her bottom lip crumpled. I handed her another tissue, and she blew her nose again.

In an effort to distract myself, I asked her, "Can I get you anything? Water? Tea?"

Lydia laughed that bitter laugh again. "Do you have any beer?"

"I might. Let me look." I walked slowly to the refrigerator. *Should I give her alcohol? Is that a good idea? She's an adult. She can make her own decisions. If she thinks it will help her…* "I have a Corona, but I don't know how long it's been in here. It's probably skunked."

"Gimme. Do you have any lime?"

"Nope."

"I don't care. I need a drink."

I popped the top off and walked the bottle over to her. She grabbed it from my hand and sucked down half the bottle, then she let out a noisy belch. "Ah, that's better. Can we get breakfast? What do you think is the best brunch around here?"

"Is Essex okay?"

"Yeah, I love that place. Good mimosas."

As we walked to the restaurant, Lydia's tears subsided. We were seated quickly, and Lydia ordered chocolate-banana pancakes and a mimosa.

*Damn, that sounds good. No. Amy and I are doing thirty days together. Be strong.* I ordered the veggie omelet and tea. *It's hard now, but you know you'll be glad later.*

Lydia folded her hands on the table, her eyes cast downward. I asked, "Are you going to be okay?"

She tried out a weak smile. "Yeah, probably. I mean, eventually. You know how these things go. It gets worse before it gets better."

*Not for me, not this time.* I asked, "What are you going to do now? Are you going to finish the class?"

"We have one more session left, don't we?"

"I think so."

"I don't know if I can make myself go. I don't know if I can see him again."

"But what about your vision? Don't you care about it at all anymore?"

She looked thoughtful for a long moment. "Actually. Yes. More now that I know what Earnest was doing behind my back. I think I was using the relationship as a distraction. It's easier to hang out with Earnest than getting my teaching certification." She sighed. "But still. I don't know. I might have to close the bakery and get student loans and go back to school, and finding the momentum to do all that seems impossible. Maybe the relationship was a way for me to avoid making the decision."

"Yeah, but like Earnest said, what if teaching is the right thing for you? If you don't do it, you'll wind up on your deathbed wondering why you never tried to become a teacher. And even if teaching turns out to be the wrong thing, you'll get closer to the right thing by getting out there and trying things."

"It's hard to think about disappointing my mom and my grandma and making the rest of my friends find new jobs. Like, who am I to upset all these people? I don't think the self-worth talk from Earnest ever reached me on a deep level. It's still really hard to invest in myself. The thought of standing in front of a room of students and shaping their minds...I don't know if someone like me should be allowed."

"It's shocking to hear you talk that way about yourself."

"Why?"

"The class completely changed the way I feel about myself. I feel strong, normal. Whole. Don't you know you're amazing? We're all amazing."

"I've been looking around at our classmates and seeing them all change. Seeing their confidence grow. They look more relaxed and happy every week. Why isn't it working for me?"

"Because you haven't started work on your vision. Once I started writing every day, that was a huge game changer for me in the confidence department. I sucked at first. I mean I was embarrassingly bad. But I'm improving. I can see it. So if you start teaching, maybe your confidence will grow. Maybe you'll start seeing you've got a gift to share with the world."

"When I think of teaching, I think, 'I can never command a room like Earnest. I can't teach.'"

"And I look at you and think, 'Of course you can teach.' You'd be a great teacher. Look at how you taught me to motivate myself with my work. Look at how you motivate your staff every day. You think you can't translate some of that to the classroom?"

"I never thought of it that way. Yeah, I'm pretty good at motivating people. And I teach people stuff all the time at work. I could definitely be a baking teacher if they had that class at school." Lydia giggled.

"Well, there are baking classes. Maybe not in every grammar school and high school. But there are after-school programs. Continuing education classes. Culinary classes. There are a million ways you could teach. If you teach baking, then you probably don't need to get your master's for that. You probably don't even need to close the bakery."

Lydia looked happy for the first time since she knocked on my door. "Why didn't I think of that? I always had teaching and baking separated out in my mind because I've wanted to teach ever since I was a little kid. Like teaching equals apple-on-the-desk typical school classroom. Yeah, I can just start slowly. Teach baking. Maybe that's what I should be doing. I could teach a class right in the bake shop! Oh my God! This is so simple! Kelly, thank you! I'm such an idiot!"

"You're not an idiot. I mean, most people think of teaching in the usual way."

"But if I want to teach, there are a million ways I could do it. Right now. I can start creating a class today! Kelly, I could kiss you."

I laughed. "I'll settle for a hug." Lydia stood up and gave me a squeeze. As she sat down, she looked like a new woman.

She said, "I have a little secret to tell you. I was kind of mad at you for being involved with Earnest. But now I'm not. Thank you for helping me."

"No problem."

"But there's one thing that's bugging me. Why didn't you fall for him? You looked upset when you saw us kissing, but now you don't seem the least bit bothered. How is that?"

"I was lucky that a friend of mine warned me about Earnest before our first date. Part of me fell for him, sure. I cried after I saw you two together. But I think I knew all along that this was happening. I started to see that getting involved with women was Earnest's personal willpower battle. He told me that I needed to go thirty days without alcohol before we'd have sex again, and he broke that rule. Maybe knowing Earnest was flawed like a regular human being from the get-go helped me get the message that it's okay to be flawed. Like he says, we're all perfect anyway, just the way we are."

"Wow, that makes me feel a little less like stabbing Earnest in the butt with a spork. He's flawed, like any other human being. He always seemed beyond human. Superhuman."

"Speaking of feeling like stabbing Earnest, I have to ask you something. How much did you pay for the class?"

"Two thousand dollars. Why? Isn't that what everybody pays?"

"Oh my God."

"What?"

"He told me I owe him ten thousand. And I could work it off by getting him ten referrals, so I offered to write him a book about Ducklings instead. I promised to give him the first ten grand in profits."

"What a dick!"

"I know!"

"What are you going to do? After all this, you can't write a book promoting him, can you?"

"Maybe I can. Maybe I can tell the truth. About all of it."

"Yeah, see how he likes that."

"Fuck him."

"Fuck 'im."

# CHAPTER THIRTY-SEVEN

When I got home, I wanted to start work on the book. But first, I had to apply for a new job. I was sick of struggling through the QA job. I had gotten on a steady schedule for the most part, but even with Lydia's suggestions of music and breaking up my day, I still hated it. Some days, I still didn't work at all. Rex had stopped bothering me about being so unreliable, which was almost worse. It's like he knew I was a hopeless case when it came to this work. And he was right.

I took an hour to surf job boards and collected some nice leads. Then I sent off a dozen résumés to various editorial jobs. Satisfied with my attempt to free myself from the QA job, I settled in to begin work on Earnest's book. *I'll write the truth. Nothing more, nothing less.*

As I wrote, I discovered that the truth was, Earnest's class did help me. And the truth was, Earnest liked to have sex with lots of women. Maybe there was nothing wrong with that. Did he intentionally deceive Lydia? *I don't know. He never promised me a rose garden. The story isn't for me to analyze, only to write.*

After several hours of typing, I needed something to eat. I was determined to make a healthy choice.

★

A day later, I found myself sitting in Sandy's living room, begging her to help me.

"What seems to be the problem?"

I buried my face in my hands. "I ate a pound of angel-hair pasta. I feel like I'm gonna die."

"It's okay. No shame, girl. We've all been there. But let's troubleshoot. Tell me what happened."

"I had a decent breakfast, a veggie omelet with tea out at brunch. Then I was writing and I got hungry. I wanted to make a healthy choice, so I went down to Essex Street Market to buy something simple to cook. I ended up walking out of there with pasta. No big deal, I just thought I would eat a serving. I honestly didn't think I was going to go crazy on it. And I didn't, at first. I blended up a sauce with avocados and basil and lemon juice and garlic."

"Mmm, that sounds awesome."

"Oh God, you have no idea. It was fucking delicious. So for lunch, I swear, I ate like a normal person. A regular portion. I wasn't stuffed, I felt good, and I went back to writing. I had a ton of leftovers, so I had the same thing for dinner. Again, a regular portion."

"So far, so good."

"Yeah. Then this morning I had it again."

"For breakfast?" Sandy raised an eyebrow slightly.

"Well, I was kind of obsessed with this stuff. It was so good. And I kept thinking about it when I wasn't eating it. I was excited to have it again when I woke up. I started out with a regular portion. And then I went apeshit bananas."

"What do you mean? You stuck your face in the bowl? What?"

"When I ran out of sauce, I still had a giant bucket of pasta left. So I poured olive oil and salt over the rest of it and I sat down in a chair with the container and my fork and went to town. I ate an enormous amount. I don't know why. It didn't even taste good without the sauce. My brain went on autopilot and I was numb, sitting there shoveling pasta into my face. It's like I snapped!"

"Did anything happen? I mean, is there anything going on with you emotionally? Are you upset about anything?"

The bloodhound in my brain sniffed and searched the corners. He ran back and presented me with a debt of ten thousand dollars and a book to write in a month. He sniffed some more and brought back Earnest's honking Lydia's boobies. "Okay, well, yeah. There's some stuff going on. The other day I left your place and went to Lydia's bake shop to ask her what she paid for Earnest's class. And, well, I don't even know how to say this, so I'll just say it. Earnest was there. In the shop. And they were making out."

"Ew. God. I'm so sorry, Kelly."

"No, no. It's fine. You warned me. I wasn't surprised. I mean I *was*, to be honest. I didn't think I'd have to see them playing tonsil hockey in the flesh. But after I got home, I was like, what did I expect? So I'm okay about it. Lydia's pretty upset, though. She saw me through the door, I ran away, long story, whatever. But I guess Earnest told her that we're *involved* and now she's brokenhearted. And he told her about the book. Oh yeah, about that. I asked Lydia what she paid."

"And?"

"Two thousand."

"Get *out*."

"I know."

"What are you going to do? You're still writing the book?"

"Yup. Now that I know the score, I'm going to write the book, but I'm going to be honest. About everything. And I mean ev…ry…thing, if you get my drift."

Sandy covered her smile with her hand. "You mean about…the manwhore stuff?"

"Oh yeah. The whole shebang. I'll give him a fair shake. I'll write about the class too. All sides. The truth."

"The truth. Awesome. That's a lot going on. Good to know. Now let's talk about this pasta binge."

"Yeah, but all things considered, I feel emotionally steady. I'm trying to get out of my crap job. I applied for new jobs. I'm honestly not freaking out too much about the Earnest-Lydia thing. I'm enjoying writing the book. The ten grand will work itself out somehow. I'm really not too worried about anything. The pasta binge was so weird. So weird. I can't believe I did that. I mean, after how far I've come and all the work I've done. I'm curious about how that could happen."

"Let's take a minute to give you some credit here. So you didn't fall right back into the habit of eating pasta. You're sitting here talking to me about it, not prowling the mean streets trying to score another pound of pasta."

"Yeah, it's progress, I guess. No, you're right. It is. Because I would have been beating myself up about it and feeling bad before, and then for dinner tonight I'd be eating lo mein to drown out the bad feelings about having eaten the angel hair. Oh—and wine. I probably would have had a bottle of wine to numb the guilt over the pasta. Ridiculous."

"It's not ridiculous. But it sounds like noodles are a trigger food for you."

"A what?"

"A trigger food. Almost like a drug. A lot of my clients have them. It's a food that, once it's in front of you, you have a hard time putting down. Some people use trigger foods to numb emotional pain. Some are emotionally steady, as you put it, but they go into an eating trance when they have this certain trigger food. And the foods people have as triggers aren't always what you'd expect. I've heard of cold cuts being a trigger for some."

"Ick. Cold cuts. Why?"

Sandy shivered with disgust. "I have no idea. The most common I've come across is wheat-based products. Like pasta. Bread. Cookies. Crackers. One or all of those set some people off. But then I have another client who eats a turkey sandwich on wheat bread for lunch every day, and having bread isn't a problem for her. It's different for everybody. I have one client who goes crazy with quinoa."

"Wow, I had no idea that quinoa could be a trigger. Do you have any triggers?"

"Mine used to be peanut butter. Oh yeah, and Nutella. I would stand in the pantry with a spoon and eat it straight out of the jar. I'd keep telling myself, 'One spoonful. Okay, just one more. All right, *one* more. Last one!' But I would keep eating it. And red wine too. I started drinking it because I heard it was heart healthy, but then I began using it to relax after a long day, to cope with emotions, that kind of thing, and well, you know how that goes."

"Yeah, I know how that goes. For me anyway."

"Yeah, it's different for everybody."

"So then how do you get over it? How did you? Like with your peanut butter thing?"

"I don't know if you get over it. I stopped buying peanut butter."

"So you can never have it again?"

Sandy shrugged. "It's not like my life is suffering for it. In fact, any food that makes you behave like that is more trouble than it's worth. My life is better without peanut butter in it."

"So you think I should give up on pasta? Never eat it again?"

"You can save it for special occasions. When you go out to a restaurant, you're not going to storm the kitchen and shove the cooks out of the way so you can eat pasta out of a giant vat."

"Excellent point. All right. Special occasions."

"As long as you're here, what else can I help you with? How are you doing with eating aside from the pasta binge?"

"Eh, I'm doing okay."

"What's your schedule like? Do you eat set meals?"

I talked Sandy through my routine between writing, work, exercise, and visiting with Amy.

She said, "It sounds like you're waiting until you're starving and then grabbing whatever's around."

"That's pretty much it. There's a bodega across the street that makes these awesome sausage, egg, and cheese sandwiches. They're pretty big, more food than I need, but I find myself only going there out of convenience when I've waited too long to eat, and then I scarf the whole thing."

"Okay, we need to lay the groundwork for equilibrium, emotionally and healthwise. Every day you need enough sleep, enough exercise. Don't get too hungry, and the only way I've found people can do that is to stick to a loose meal schedule and prep food ahead. Keep big, hearty, healthy meals on hand. Lots of vegetables and protein, plenty of fat. Don't be such a puritan about your diet. I mean, minus the pasta, obviously. Wait until you're hungry to eat, but not too hungry. Keep yourself well-fed using *real* food—I can't stress that enough, nothing processed—and you'll be fine."

"I can see now that since I got a lot of this emotional stuff worked out, I've been undereating and skipping meals. Even with all the current crap going on, I feel pretty excited because I'm writing a lot, and food takes a back seat. Until it climbs into the front seat and wrestles the wheel of the car away from me."

"Keep telling yourself: *Eat when I'm hungry, stop when I'm full.* Eat thoughtfully and regularly. Plan on shopping once or even twice per week. Think a few days ahead and make sure you have food for breakfast, lunch, a snack, and dinners on hand. You might want to prepare casseroles. Yesterday I made an egg frittata, and now I've got four days' worth of breakfasts on autopilot. I cut it into servings, wrap them in foil, and then each morning I heat up a portion in my toaster oven."

Sandy gave me lots of great tips that day. She keeps cooked chicken and salad makings on hand for lunch, but she said on days when she doesn't feel like shopping for chicken or cooking, she puts beans, nuts, and cheese on her salad. She told me to plan to cook dinners every night or to reheat leftovers. She also told me my snacks should be more hearty. Cheese and nuts, soup with a handful of beans and veggies.

Now that I was almost finished with Ducklings to Swans, I could finally hear what Sandy was saying and put it into practice. I remembered the first time Sandy tried to coach me at the farmers market, and how I couldn't even begin to take her advice. What a long, strange trip it's been to get to this point.

★

"I got a new job!" I said.

Amy looked happy for me. "Look at you, still a little job magnet. You were so worried when you got canned, and now here you are changing jobs like you change your underwear."

"I know, I know. Once again, you were right, I was wrong."

"Tell me about it. What are you going to be doing?"

"I'm going to write articles for a website. Freelance. I've decided to keep myself free of office politics."

"Good for you, putting your writing talent to work." Amy smiled big. "I have a new job too."

"No! Really? Are you going to work with Tom?"

"I am! This is my last night at the bar. I gave a lot of thought to what you said, about making my dad's opinion about my life more important than mine, and, well, you convinced me. And Tom convinced me. He says he can pay me more than what I'm earning at the bar."

"Lucky duck. I'm still going to be living hand to mouth. God, it sucks. I should never have pissed all my savings away."

"Move to Brooklyn! We could be neighbors. It's so much cheaper than Manhattan."

"Nah. I'm thinking about going somewhere warm and easy. No office means I can go anywhere."

"Tom talks about that all the time, about moving to Florida to teach kayaking. The season is too short in New York. He has to pick up odd jobs all winter long. I'm probably going to have to bartend over the winter when the kayaking business goes on hiatus, which will probably keep my dad happy. But anyway, yeah, Florida. Maybe someday we'll both be down there."

"Why not?"

"Yeah, why not? So, the end of our thirty days is coming up. Are you going back to drinking?"

I mulled over the question. "No, I doubt it. I finally feel free. Like I just escaped from a nightmare. I don't want to sink back into old habits. What about you?"

"Maybe socially, once in a while."

"Yeah. Maybe socially. Maybe once in a while, but then again, maybe not." I remembered Earnest's words: *If you return to old habits after thirty days, you'll get what you've always gotten.* "Never again like I did. Never to numb my emotions."

"I'll drink to that." Amy held up her water glass and chugged it.

# CHAPTER THIRTY-EIGHT

A s I sat and watched Earnest deliver our last lecture, I stole glances at Lydia. *I'm so glad she came. She looks sad, though. I hope she'll be okay.*

Earnest said, "People are nuts. Here's the funny thing. Even though meditation is such a treat and the benefits are incredibly far-reaching—meditation gives us the ability to transform our minds from chaos to peace, and our lives will follow suit—yet the human tendency is to resist the practice.

"You may hear people talk about meditating every day for twenty or thirty minutes at a time or even an hour. My dear friend Elizabeth, who happens to be a founder of the Omega Institute, admitted that she struggles mightily to force herself to keep up her sixty-minute-per-day meditation practice, and she fails more often than not.

"However, what I've found is that committing to these long meditation periods invites failure. First of all, who the heck has an hour to spare? Second, meditating for five minutes can, admittedly, feel uncomfortable, so imagine the mental hurdle to force an hour out of yourself. But the beauty is this."

A hush came over the room, and we all leaned in before Earnest shouted, "YOU CAN DO ANYTHING FOR FIVE MINUTES." Startled, we all shot an inch off the floor. He said quietly, "There's no excuse in the world that can keep you from meditation if you commit to five minutes every day.

"Then as you start to love it, you can lengthen your practice as you wish. But you don't have to. What's more important than length is that you're consistent. Meditating daily for five minutes is going to help you a lot more than meditating for long periods only once in a while.

"Like all of the lessons in this course, focus on practice, not perfection. When you commit to a short period of time, you avoid the 'not enough time' excuse. Plus it's easier to do it in bite-sized chunks, and I want you to feel motivated to do it.

"When you leave my classroom, I want you to have a selection of impactful tools that will keep you feeling strong and present to the beauty of your lives. Another such tool is journaling. When you write down your thoughts, you enter into a daily conversation with yourself. And you are the most important person you should check in with every day.

"Imagine that, instead of hiding or stuffing down your negative emotions, you are always going to be present to your inner dialogue. It doesn't mean that you need to take orders from the voices in your head or buy into overdramatic or destructive emotions, but you should definitely eavesdrop on yourself to see what you've been plotting in your absence. And then steer yourself in the right direction.

"Journaling helps us to tease out the swirl of emotions by parsing out the circumstances—what the heck is happening? Then there's the meaning we ascribe to what actually happened. We often have thoughts that aren't necessarily true, and this immediately catapults our emotions into negative territory.

"When we journal, our goal is to root around and find reality. It's to define our circumstances in real terms, to parse out our thoughts and to evaluate them rationally, to soothe our emotions and to recognize when negative emotions are generated due to inaccurate or imaginative thoughts about what circumstances mean.

"When we stay in touch with reality, we live authentic lives. We can live honestly and openly in our truth. And if we don't like our truth, we can fix it. We can choose to live differently, and in doing so, we can stay in touch with all parts of ourselves. This is how we come to feel whole and worthy.

"I believe in unconditional love. But it simply makes it harder to love yourself unconditionally when you continue to act in ways that you know are wrong. The first step is to look at your shortcomings with open eyes, without shame. Only then can we take steps to make lasting change.

"The acceptance of reality sounds pretty basic, but it's actually quite a challenge for most people. We all fool ourselves to some degree, because truly embracing reality often means that you need to abandon an emotional investment in a soothing fantasy or fairy tale.

"For many of us, when we consider some vice that we're giving up, we might think, 'I can't give it up,' as if we're somehow unable. When you consider, um, REALITY, saying 'I can't give it up' is completely absurd!

"Consider the possibility that you've been snowing yourself with fairy tales in order to hang on to your old habit or way of living. The fairy tales we tell ourselves usually involve some kind of half-truths or outright falsehoods that prevent us from committing ourselves one hundred percent to our goals.

"We all delude ourselves at times so we can feel better or to escape unpleasant consequences. Successful, happy people are keenly aware that it's much easier to face reality and the consequences rather than to keep ducking what's true. We all have unhelpful habits that we unintentionally go to great lengths to protect, simply because the status quo is easier and thus comforting.

"Don't be afraid to look at your reality and to challenge your views. Don't fear that you'll uncover something in life you can't deal with. At this stage in your Ducklings to Swans training, you can handle anything. Don't be afraid to find out you could be wrong or out of touch. Despite scary consequences, seek to know what's real. It's only by being in touch with reality that we can improve our stations in life.

"Look at your problems head on. Merely look at them. It's not going to hurt to see them so you can assess the damage. As you get into this process, you will notice more snippets of truth emerge over time. Take note rather than shoving them under the rug.

"More pieces of the puzzle will present themselves, but get started right now by noticing where you're trying to airbrush out unpleasant realities that might need to be dealt with.

"Some of you may be involved in unhealthy relationships. We all influence each other. When it comes to making healthy changes, you need to ask yourself: Are you going to be the influencer, or are you going to let others weaken your determination?

"Are you going to live longer and healthier with fewer medical expenses and without the burdens of ill health that can be prevented by a healthy diet? Or are you going to be influenced by your friends or your mate, who are kicking and screaming about change?

"If you want healthy change to happen, then you need to make a firm decision and go for it. Make healthy meals for yourself. If your mate insists on a stash of unhealthy food, kindly ask that these foods be kept on a high shelf that's inconvenient and out of sight.

"So many of you are still thinking like this: 'It would be so much easier if my boyfriend didn't order pizza every Friday night.' 'I can't resist buying chips when they're on sale.' 'She would be offended if I didn't eat it.' You are too swayed by outside influences.

"You think, 'It's not fair they get to enjoy themselves and I can't!' This is a common complaint among people who are trying to diet or give up alcohol; they think a lot about what their mates or their friends are doing. They fixate and feel bitter or jealous that they feel restricted while others skip merrily along, oblivious, continuing on with all the same old behaviors you're trying to leave in the dust.

"When you find yourself thinking like this, you must ask yourself: Is it really not fair? Along with that big plate of all your favorites, would you like a side of open-heart surgery at age fifty-five, or perhaps a stroke, or diabetes, or maybe another health problem that comes along with eating or drinking that way? Again, do you want to be influenced, or do you want to be the influencer?

"Many people have no problem pointing at their partner, their friends, or at the way they were raised for why their diets and their habits are less than optimal. What do we get out of doing that? We can pretend that the guilt and the culpability lie outside of ourselves. We can fool ourselves into thinking that our eating patterns or other bad habits are out of our control.

"When we blame others for our eating habits, we feel weak, like victims of our circumstances. People naturally like to blame people and circumstances for their own decisions and actions. Frankly, it feels good to give in, and it feels good to act like we can't help ourselves. When we blame other people, we get to pretend that we're not in charge.

"But the problem with this way of thinking is that the fastest way to get stuck in bad habits is to blame circumstances and people for that which you have control over. You are in charge.

"The reality is, whether we accept it or not, we are always in charge. It's hard for a lot of us to hear, but you alone are responsible for your actions, your habits, and your life.

"People with extraordinary willpower fully accept that they alone are in the driver's seat. If they can hold a fork, they are in charge of the kinds and amounts of food they bring to their lips. Instead of looking to blame, they divert their attention to how they can succeed and how they can make healthy decisions and actions.

"The good news is this: By holding fast to healthy values, you will influence your partner and possibly even your friends—or you will find new friends who share your interest in remaining alive and well. It might take a very long time, but when your mate witnesses positive changes and sees you enjoying the pleasures of healthy meals, there's no way to go but up. You can either be influenced or be the influencer. The choice is yours.

"Know that by accepting the truth—that you are responsible for your behavior and your circumstances—you gain leverage. You have buttons to push, knobs to twist, levers to press. You alone hold the power to affect change in your life. Every single aspect of your life is yours. Own it. Take control over it. Love it.

"And now go into the night with your journals. It was my pleasure having you all as students. And tonight I bid you *adieu. Ciao. Adios. Gute nacht.* Except Kelly. Come up here, please."

I shot a look at Lydia. Her eyes teared up, and I was afraid she'd start sobbing. She pointed at the door and mouthed at me, "I'll wait for you."

I nodded as I stood up. I was glad he invited me to speak with him because I was going to confront him about the ten grand. *I need to know why he's charging me so much more than Sandy and Lydia.*

When the room was quiet, he gestured me toward him and said, "Kelly, my beautiful Kelly. How are you?"

"Fine. I'm working on the book. I'm almost done."

"And are you enjoying the work?"

"Yes, actually. I love writing."

"Good. When will I see the draft?"

"In a few days. And about that, I need to ask you something." My heart started pounding and my mouth was dry. *Here I go. I want to know why you think you deserve ten grand from me, you fucker.*

I didn't get the words out before Earnest said, "I want to apologize to you. I'm sorry that you saw me kissing Lydia. I like you, Kelly. I want to be loved for who I am. I'm a human being. A flawed individual. I want to stop objectifying my students and looking at them like wads of cash with vaginas attached."

I narrowed my eyes. "I think you like this lifestyle. There's no real fallout for you."

"Yes. There is. I lost you. I knew when I saw you run away. You didn't come into the shop and fight for me. You left and you didn't even try to get in touch with me. I don't want Lydia. She's a cheap substitute."

The door burst open, and Lydia soared into the room, hair flying, her face twisted in rage. *"A cheap substitute?* You fucking bastard! You said the same exact thing to me about Kelly! You fucking dick! I'll kill you!"

Lydia ran at Earnest. Her hands were balled into fists and her arms were windmilling at a fearsome pace. Her fists grazed me as I grabbed her around the waist and held her back. I said into her ear, "He's not worth it, Lydia. He's not worth it."

I could feel the tension in her body dissipating. I held her as she slumped against me, weeping. I repeated, "Shh, Lydia, he's not worth it. He's not worth the fight. He's an asshole. He's not worth getting upset over." Still holding Lydia, I turned to Earnest and said, "I'm sure Lydia and I aren't the only ones. How many others?"

Earnest looked surprised that I would ask such a direct question. He stammered, "I...I don't know." He looked up toward the ceiling and moved his lips like he was counting names.

Lydia shrieked at him, "Oh my God, you fucking slut! Taking advantage of students is gross!" Lydia pushed me away and stormed out. When she was just outside the open door of the classroom, I heard her pound the wall and yell, "Motherfucker!"

I said, "Lydia's right. Taking advantage of students is gross—the serial fucking and the cheating, and playing on emotions when you never intended to commit, wooing all of these women to gain access to their private parts... Lydia wanted a boyfriend, and you took advantage of that."

Earnest stood there looking stupid. He flinched when Lydia stomped back into the room, looked at me, and yelled, "Are you coming?"

"Yes." I shot Earnest a dirty look and stomped after Lydia.

When we got down to the street, I said to Lydia, "Damn it. I forgot to ask him about the ten grand."

She said, "Fuck it. Put all this in the book, and there's his stinkin' ten grand. What a dick."

# CHAPTER THIRTY-NINE

A few days later, I gripped the full manuscript in my hands. I was impressed by the massive stack of pages I'd been able to accumulate in a month. It was time to show Earnest. When I picked up my phone to double-check the time I was supposed to meet him at the loft, I noticed I had a text from Toni. She wanted me to come over.

I sighed. *Do I want to see Toni again? Not really. Besides, why do I always have to go to her place?* I read her text again. It said, "Kelly, please come over when you get this. I need to apologize. For real this time. Forgive me? Please?"

I thought back over our long history. *We were tight. Toni was my best friend for years. Then Jill got in the middle and it was all over. Just like that. Fucking Jill. Maybe after Jill's performance, Toni realized she's wrong about me. Maybe she'll take back everything she said about my being a mess. Maybe we really can be friends again.*

I put the manuscript in my bag. *Toni first. Earnest can wait.*

★

I knocked on Toni's door and waited for her to answer. *Depending on how this goes, this might be the last time I'm in this apartment.*

Toni opened the door looking contrite. I stepped in, and she hustled me over to the couch saying, "I'm so glad you came, Kelly. I was afraid you were going to ignore my text."

I felt disinterested but also wary as I sunk into the couch. I wondered what zingers Toni would insult me with today as she sat down in a chair.

Toni looked nervous. She cleared her throat. I looked at my watch. After we basked in a few moments of awkward silence, I said, "Toni, I have an appointment, so…"

"I'm sorry, okay. This is hard for me. I realized that I'm a perfectionist."

"No shit, Toni."

"No, what I mean is…after Jill…that day…I see now that you and Jill are both only human and that I can't expect everyone to be perfect."

"Oooookaaaaay."

"What?" Toni looked confused.

"So you, as a perfectionist, can't expect all of us sloppy humans of Earth to meet your perfect standards. So you're perfect, Toni? And this is your apology? You're sorry the rest of us can't be perfect. That's great. That's just *perfect*."

"No, no. I'm sorry, Kelly. Jeez, I am really fucking this one up, aren't I?"

"I'm sorry. It's just…my patience is a little thin. I'm tired of feeling defensive around you. Like you just have it all together, and you think I'm one step away from crashing through your coffee table like Chris Farley."

"No, of course I don't think that way about you, Kelly. What I mean is, I keep trying to *look* perfect, but of course I'm not. I act like I'm little Miss Perfect because I feel insecure. I've always been afraid to try new things."

"Like what?"

"I want to take some art classes, but I don't because I know I'll suck at it and I'm afraid of looking stupid. I can't throw myself into sharing like you do. You just meet people and tell them what's on your mind. I keep my insides to myself."

"Why?"

"Because…because what if I let people know what I'm really like, and they don't like me? What if they criticize what I say?"

"Simple. If someone doesn't like you, then she's not your friend."

"You were my best friend. And I couldn't stop judging you and criticizing you, and who'd stick around for that? I'm so used to sitting on the sidelines and pointing out everyone else's flaws. It's easier that way. But it's also lonely. I don't blame you for ending our friendship. But it makes me sad. I thought you'd always be here." Toni started to cry.

*She's only just now trying to figure out how and why she hurt me? But it's nice to see her make an effort. I'll try to go easy on her.* "Do you think you can learn to love people unconditionally?"

Toni stopped crying as she smirked. "Love people unconditionally? What the heck does *that* mean?"

"I'm asking if you can stop being such a judgmental bitch."

Toni looked offended.

*Oh, please.* "Okay. Well, it's great that you realize you aren't perfect. But you certainly seem to think you're somehow superior. Admit it. You think you're better than other people."

I could tell by the look on her face that she agreed with that statement. She said slowly, "Well, not *better*, exactly, but…"

*I'm done with this. Let's wrap this up with a little small talk and I'll get out of here.* "So how's Jill?"

Toni looked relieved that she was off the hot seat. "She's in rehab."

"Good. Good for her."

"Yeah."

I could tell she was itching to gossip about Jill, so I stood up and said, "Good to see you, Toni. I need to run to my appointment."

★

As I stood in Earnest's loft, he felt the weight of the stack of papers in his hands and said, "This feels substantial, Kelly. Let's see what these pages hold." He carried the manuscript to his desk and set it down. As he read the first page, he smiled. He nodded. He chuckled. "Oh, ho, ho, what a beginning." He turned the page and said, "This is good. These words capture the essence of my customer, the Duckling."

As he leafed through the book, I basked in the glow of his compliments. But then I remembered his words from class. *When praise ebbs and flows like the tide, you remain unaffected. You write heedlessly. You write across the gaps. You don't fall in, hoping and praying for a book deal or to reach a certain number on some list that represents someone else's manufactured and branded notion of success. No. You write. And you keep writing to heed the call of your soul.*

*It doesn't matter what Earnest thinks about the book. I'm a writer. And I will keep writing.*

I watched his face as he picked his way through the pages, skimming, skipping pages, evaluating. I saw a frown take hold of his face. "I'll have to make a list of changes for you to make in the next draft."

I said, "There won't be a next draft. I never agreed to rewrites. This is the book. Right here. Exactly as it is."

Earnest took on a condescending tone. "The book is good. Your writing is good. But it would be too embarrassing for me if you published this. You've detailed some of my personal dalliances, and of course that's not what I wanted this book to be about."

"Oh, you didn't tell me you wanted the extracurricular activities of Ducklings to Swans edited out of the picture."

Earnest gritted his teeth. "I told you this book will be my business card. This is not an entirely flattering portrayal of me."

"I told the truth. You said yourself in the last class, 'Successful, happy people are keenly aware that it's much easier to face reality and the consequences rather than to keep ducking what's true.' Why don't you want to look at your behavior?"

He was getting more agitated. "You've reproduced entire sections of the Ducklings to Swans course. If we print the lectures in this book, it will eat into my course profits."

"But not everyone can afford your course. And most people can't travel to New York City for it. Don't you want to help people?"

"Yes, sure, if they want to pay the course fee. After all, why would a student pay two thousa...uh, I mean, ten thousand dollars for a class when she could just buy the book?"

"Yeah, about that. I know it's not ten thousand. I know that others only paid two."

"Yes. You caught me. All right. I will release you from our agreement, but only if you give me your word that this manuscript will never see the light of day. Do not publish it. Do not share it. I expect you to shred this and to destroy any other copies you have."

"It's a deal."

"Thank you, Kelly. You and Lydia have brought my issues to the forefront. You may take comfort in knowing this is something I will work to correct in my interactions with future students. Please accept my apology."

"Apology accepted."

"Thank you. I'm glad we're clear." Earnest took a deep breath, clasped his hands behind his back, and rocked on his heels. "Kelly, tell me. What's next for you? Are you going to write another book?"

"Yes. But first I'm going to move somewhere warm. All I need is a community of writers and a warm beach and I'm all set."

★

## NOTE TO EARNEST

*Hi, Earnest. It's Lydia. Kelly kept her word. She didn't publish the book. I did. Kelly revised the manuscript to finish the story. Then she left the pages in* a drawer, and she told me she intended to shred it, but I stole it from her and I published this book because I wanted you to know how it feels to be betrayed.

Besides, I owe it to future Ducklings to Swans students. They should know what they're getting into with you, in case you don't fix your issues.

—Lydia

P.S. Fuck you. You're a disgusting pig.

★

Dear Reader,

I hope this book entertained and inspired you. I would be honored if you wrote an honest review on Amazon, letting other readers know what you think. Or if you're a writer or a blogger, then go ahead and spread the word! And then please let me know by email at Katie@KatieMorton.com.

If you're interested in staying in touch and applying the concepts of this book to your own life, join my newsletter at KatieMorton.com.

After signing up at KatieMorton.com, you'll gain free access to an electronic copy of the Ducklings to Swans Workbook, which contains many of the exercises in this book, plus some new ones. This novel and the companion workbook are self-discovery tools to help you design a life you love.

Thanks for reading. May you live a blissful life, full of joy and laughter.

Katie Morton

Printed in Great Britain
by Amazon.co.uk, Ltd.,
Marston Gate.